THE
EXILED
QUEEN

Cinda Williams Chima began writing romance novels in middle school, but they were often confiscated by her English teacher. Her first published novel was *The Warrior Heir*, a modern young adult fantasy set in Ohio (Hyperion, 2006). A sequel, *The Wizard Heir*, was released in May, 2007, and her third novel, *The Dragon Heir*, in August, 2008. The Heir series is a New York Times Children's Series Bestseller.

D1352128

ALSO BY CINDA WILLIAMS CHIMA:

The Demon King
The Exiled Queen
The Gray Wolf Throne

CINDA WILLIAMS CHIMA

THE
EXILED
QUEEN

HARPER
Voyager

HarperVoyager
An imprint of HarperCollinsPublishers
77–85 Fulham Palace Road,
Hammersmith, London W6 8JB

www.harpercollins.co.uk

This paperback edition 2011
1

First published in Great Britain by
HarperCollins 2011

A catalogue record for this book is
available from the British Library

ISBN: 978-0-00-732199-5

Set in Bembo

Printed and bound in Great Britain by
Clays Ltd, St Ives plc

MIX
Paper from
responsible sources
FSC® C007454

For Linda and Mike—who shared a world
of make-believe and kick-butt Barbies.
Thanks for putting up with all the talking animals.

CHAPTER ONE
THE
WEST WALL

Lieutenant Mac Gillen of the Queen's Guard of the Fells hunched his shoulders against the witch wind that howled out of the frozen wastelands to the north and west. Looping his reins around the pommel of his saddle, he let his horse, Marauder, navigate the final half mile descent to the Westgate garrison house on his own.

Gillen deserved better than this miserable post in this miserable corner of the queendom of the Fells. Patroling the border was a job for the regular army—the foreign mercenaries, called stripers, or the Highlander home guard. Not for a member of the elite Queen's Guard.

He'd been away from the city only a month, but he missed the gritty neighborhood of Southbridge. In Southbridge there was plenty to distract him on his nightly rounds—taverns and gambling halls and fancy girls. In the capital he'd had high-up connections with deep pockets—meaning plenty of chances to do private work on the side.

Then it had all gone wrong. There'd been a prisoner riot at Southbridge Guardhouse, and a Ragger street rat named Rebecca had jammed a burning torch into his face, leaving one eye blind, his skin red and shiny and puckered with scar tissue.

In late summer he'd taken Magot and Sloat and some others to retrieve a stolen amulet over in Ragmarket. He'd done the job on the quiet under orders from Lord Bayar, High Wizard and counselor to the queen. They'd searched that tumbledown stable top to bottom, had even dug up the stable yard, but they didn't find the jinxpiece nor Cuffs Alister, the street thief who'd stolen it.

When they'd put the question to the rag-taggers who lived there, the woman and her brat had claimed they'd never heard of Cuffs Alister, and knew nothing about any amulet. In the end, Gillen had burned the place to the ground with the rag-taggers inside. A warning to thieves and liars everywhere.

Sensing Gillen's inattention, Marauder seized the bit in his teeth and broke into a shambling run. Gillen wrenched back on the reins, regaining control after a bit of showy crow hopping. Gillen glared at his men, sending the grins sliding from their faces.

That'd be all he needed—to take a tumble and break his neck in a downhill race to nowhere.

Some would call Gillen's posting to the West Wall a promotion. He'd been given a lieutenant's badge and was put in charge of a massive, gloomy keep and a hundred other exiles—all members of the regular army—plus his own squadron of bluejackets. It was a larger command than his former post at Southbridge Guardhouse.

Like he'd celebrate ruling over a dung heap.

The Westgate keep guarded the West Wall and the dismal, ramshackle village of Westgate. The wall divided the mountainous

Fells from the Shivering Fens. A drowned land of trackless swamps and marshes, the Fens were too thick to swim in and too thin to plow, impassable except on foot until the hard freezes after solstice.

All in all, control of Westgate keep added up to little opportunity for a man of enterprise like Mac Gillen. He recognized his new assignment for what it was: punishment for his failure to give Lord Bayar what he wanted.

He was lucky to have survived the High Wizard's disappointment.

Gillen and his triple splashed through the cobbled streets of the village and dismounted in the stable yard of the keep.

When Gillen led Marauder into the stable, his duty officer, Robbie Sloat, swiped at his forehead, his pass at a salute. "We got three visitors to see you from Fellsmarch, sir," Sloat said. "They're waiting for you in the keep."

Hope kindled in Gillen. This might mean new orders from the capital, at last. And maybe an end to his undeserved exile.

"Did they give a name?" Gillen tossed his gloves and sopping cloak to Sloat and ran his fingers through his hair to tidy it.

"They said as they'd speak only to you, sir," Sloat said. He hesitated. "They're baby bluebloods. Not much more'n boys."

The spark of hope flickered out. Probably arrogant sons of the nobility on their way to the academies at Oden's Ford. Just what he didn't need.

"They demanded lodging in the officers' wing," Sloat went on, confirming Gillen's fears.

"Some in the nobility seem to think we're running a hostel for blueblood brats," Gillen growled. "Where are they?"

Sloat shrugged his shoulders. "They're in the officers' hall, sir."

Shaking off rainwater, Gillen strode into the keep. Before he'd fairly crossed the inner courtyard, he heard music—a basilka and a recorder.

Gillen shouldered open the doors to the officers' hall to find three boys, not much older than naming age, ranged around the fire. The keg of ale on the sideboard had been breached, and empty tankards sat before them. The boys wore the dazed, sated expressions of those who'd feasted heavily. The remnants of what had been a sumptuous meal were spread over the table, including the picked-over cadaver of a large ham Gillen had been saving for himself.

In one corner stood the musicians, a pretty young girl on the recorder, and a man—probably her father—on the basilka. Gillen recalled seeing them in the village before, playing for coppers on street corners.

As Gillen entered, the tune died away and the musicians stood, pale-faced and wide-eyed, like trapped animals before the kill. The father drew his trembling daughter in under his arm, smoothed her blond head, and spoke a few quiet words to her.

Ignoring Gillen's entrance, the boys around the fire clapped lazily. "Not great, but better than nothing," one of them said with a smirk. "Just like the accommodations."

"I'm Gillen," Gillen said loudly, by now convinced there could be no profit in this meeting.

The tallest of the three came gracefully to his feet, shaking back a mane of black hair. When he fixed on Gillen's scarred face, he flinched, his blueblood face twisting in disgust.

Gillen clenched his teeth. "Corporal Sloat said you wanted to see me," he said.

"Yes, Lieutenant Gillen. I am Micah Bayar, and these are my cousins, Arkeda and Miphis Mander." He gestured toward the other two, who were red-haired—one slender, one of stocky build. "We are traveling to the academy at Oden's Ford, but since we were coming this way, I was asked to carry a message to you from Fellsmarch." He cut his eyes toward the empty duty room. "Perhaps we can talk in there."

His heart accelerating, Gillen fixed on the stoles draped over the boy's shoulders, embroidered with stooping falcons. The signia of the Bayar family.

Yes. Now he saw the resemblance—something about the shape of the boy's eyes and the exaggerated bone structure of the face. Young Bayar's black hair was streaked with wizard red.

The other two wore stoles also, though with a different signia. Fellscats. They were all three wizardlings, then, and one the High Wizard's son.

Gillen cleared his throat, nerves warring with excitement. "Certainly, certainly, your lordship. I hope you found the food and drink to your liking."

"It was . . . *filling*, Lieutenant," Young Bayar replied. "But now it sits poorly, I'm afraid." He tapped his midsection with two fingers, and the other two boys snorted.

Change the subject, Gillen thought. "You favor your father, you know. I could tell right away you was his son."

Young Bayar frowned, glanced at the musicians, then back at Gillen. He opened his mouth to speak, but Gillen rushed on, meaning to have his say. "It wasn't my fault, you know, about

5

the amulet. That Cuffs Alister is savage and street-smart. But your da picked the right man for the job. If anyone can find him, I can, and I'll get the jinxpiece back, too. I just need to get back to the city is all."

The boy went perfectly still, staring at Gillen through narrowed eyes, his mouth in a tight, disapproving line. Then, shaking his head, he turned to his cousins. "Miphis. Arkeda. Stay here," Bayar said. "Have some more ale, if you can stomach it." He flicked his hand toward the two musicians. "Keep these two close. Don't let them leave."

Young Bayar crooked his finger at Gillen. "You. Come with me." Without looking back to see if Gillen was following, he stalked into the duty room.

Confused, Gillen followed him in. Young Bayar stood staring out the window overlooking the stable yard, resting his hands on the stone sill. He waited until the door had closed behind him before he turned on Gillen. "You . . . cretin," the boy said, his face pale, eyes hard and glittering like Delphi coal. "I cannot believe that my father would ever engage someone so stupid. No one must know that you are in my father's employ, understand? If word of this gets back to Captain Byrne, it could have grievous consequences. My father could be accused of treason."

Gillen's mouth went dead dry. "Right. A course," he stuttered. "I . . . ah . . . assumed the other wizardlings was with you, and . . ."

"You are not being paid to make assumptions, Lieutenant Gillen," Bayar said. He walked toward Gillen, back very straight, stoles swaying in the breeze from the window. As he came forward, Gillen backed away until he came up against the duty table.

"When I say no one, I mean no one," Bayar said, fingering an evil-looking pendant at his neck. It was a falcon carved from a glittering red gemstone—a jinxpiece, like the one Gillen had failed to find in Ragmarket. "Who else have you told about this?"

"No one, I swear on the blood of the demon, I an't told no one else," Gillen whispered, fear a knife in his gut. He stood balanced, feet slightly apart, ready to leap aside if the wizardling shot flame at him. "I just wanted to make sure his lordship knew that I did my best to fetch that carving, but it wasn't nowhere to be found."

Distaste flickered across the boy's face, as if this were a topic he'd rather not dwell on. "Did you know that while you were searching Ragmarket for the amulet, Alister attacked my father and nearly killed him?"

Blood and bones, Gillen thought, shuddering. As the long-time streetlord of the Raggers gang, Alister was known to be fearless, violent, and ruthless. Now it seemed the boy had a death wish, too. "Is . . . is Lord Bayar all right?" *Is Alister dead?*

Young Bayar answered the spoken and unspoken questions. "My father has recovered. Alister, unfortunately, escaped. My father finds incompetence difficult to forgive," he said. "In *any-one*." The bitter edge to the boy's voice caught Gillen off guard.

"Er, right," Gillen said. He plunged on, compelled to make his case. "I'm wasted here, my lord. Send me back to the city, and I'll find the boy, I swear. I know the streets, and I know the gangs that run 'em. Alister's bound to turn up in Ragmarket sooner or later, even though his mam and sister claimed he hadn't been around there for weeks."

Young Bayar's eyes narrowed and he leaned forward, fists clenched. "His mother and sister? Alister has a mother and sister? Are they still in Fellsmarch?"

Gillen grinned. "They're burnt up, I reckon. We torched their place with them shut up inside."

"You killed them?" Young Bayar stared at him. "They're *dead*?"

Gillen licked his lips, unsure where he'd gone wrong. "Well, I figured that'd show ever'body else they'd better tell the truth when Mac Gillen asks questions."

"You *are* an idiot!" Bayar shook his head slowly, his eyes fixed on Gillen's face. "We could have used Alister's mother and sister to lure him out of hiding. We could have offered a trade for the amulet." He closed his fist on thin air. "We could have *had* him."

Bones, Gillen thought. He never could say the right thing to a wizard. "You *might* think so, but believe me, streetlord like Alister, his heart's cold as the Dyrnnewater. Think he cares what happens to his mam and sis? Nope. He cares about nobody but hisself."

Young Bayar dismissed this with a wave of his hand. "We'll never know now, will we? In any event, my father has no need of your services in hunting Alister. He has assigned others to that task. They've succeeded in cleaning the street gangs out of the city, but they've had no luck finding Alister. We have reason to think he's left Fellsmarch."

The boy rubbed his forehead with the heel of his hand, as though he had a headache. "However. Should you *ever* cross paths with Alister, by accident or otherwise, my father desires that he be brought to him alive and intact, with the amulet. If you could manage that, you would, of course, be richly rewarded." Young Bayar tried to look indifferent, but the tightness around his eyes told a different story.

The boy hates Alister, Gillen thought. Was it because Alister tried to kill his father? Anyway, Gillen could tell that there was no use pressing the matter of his return to Fellsmarch. "A'right, then," he said, struggling to hide his disappointment. "So. What brings you to Westgate? You said you had a message for me."

"A delicate matter, Lieutenant. One that will require discretion." The boy made it clear he doubted Gillen had any discretion. Whatever that was.

"Absolutely, my lord, you can count on me," Gillen said eagerly.

"Had you heard that the Princess Raisa is missing?" Bayar said abruptly.

Gillen tried to keep his face blank. Competent. Full of discretion. "Missing? No, my lord, I hadn't heard that. We get little news up here. Do they have any idea . . ."

"We think there's a chance she may try to leave the country."

Oh, ho, Gillen thought. She's run off, then. Was it a mother-daughter spat? A romance with the wrong sort? A commoner, even? The Gray Wolf princesses were known to be headstrong and adventuresome.

He'd seen the Princess Raisa up close, once. She was small but shapely enough, with a waist a man could put his two hands around. She'd given him the once-over with those witchy green eyes, then whispered something to the lady beside her.

That was before. Now women turned their faces away when he offered to buy them a drink.

Before, the princess might have been swept off by someone like himself—a worldly, military man. He'd even had thoughts, himself, of what it would be like to—

Bayar's voice broke in. "Are you listening, Lieutenant?"

Gillen forced his mind back to the matter at hand. "Yes, my lord. A'course. Uh. What was that last bit?"

"I *said* we think it's also possible she might have taken refuge with her father's copperhead relatives at Demonai or Marisa Pines camps." Bayar shrugged. "They *claim* she's not with them, that she must have gone south, out of the queendom. But the southern border is well guarded. So she might try to leave through Westgate."

"But . . . where would she go? There's war everywhere."

"She may not be thinking clearly," Bayar said, color staining his pale face. "That is why it is critical that we intercept her. The princess heir may put herself into danger. She may go somewhere we can't reach her. That would be . . . disastrous." The boy closed his eyes, fussing with his sleeves. When he opened them to find Gillen staring at him, he swiveled away and gazed out the window again.

Huh, Gillen thought. Either the boy's quite the actor, or he really is worried.

"So we need to be on the watch for her here at Westgate," Gillen said. "Is that what you're saying?"

Bayar nodded without turning around. "We've tried to keep the matter quiet, but word is out that she's on the run. If the queen's enemies find her before we do, well . . . you understand."

"Of course," Gillen said. "Ah, do they think she's . . . traveling with anyone?" There. That was a clever way to put it, to find out if she'd run off with somebody.

"We don't know. She may be on her own, or she may be riding with the copperheads."

"What exactly would Lord Bayar like me to do?" Gillen asked, puffing up a little.

Now the boy turned to face him. "Two things. We want you to set a watch for Princess Raisa at the border and intercept her if she tries to cross at Westgate. And we need a party of trusted guards to ride to Demonai Camp to verify that she's not there."

"Demonai!" Gillen said, less cheerfully. "But . . . you can't be—you're not thinking we'd be taking on the Demonai warriors, are you?"

"Of course not," Bayar said, as if Gillen were a half-wit. "The queen has notified the Demonai that her guard will be visiting the upland camps to interview the savages. They can hardly refuse. Of course, they'll know you're coming, so you'll have to dig deeper to find out whether the princess is there, or has been there."

"You're sure they're expecting us?" Gillen said. The Waterwalkers were one thing—they didn't even use metal weapons. But the Demonai—he was in no rush to go up against them. "I don't want to end up full of copperhead arrows. The Demonai, they got poisants that will blacken a man's—"

"Don't worry, Lieutenant Gillen," Bayar said sharply. "You'll be perfectly safe, unless, of course, you are caught snooping around."

He'd send Magot and Sloat, Gillen decided. They were better suited for that task. It was best if he stayed behind and kept an eye out for the princess. That would need careful handling and a clear head. And discretion.

"I expect you'll need at least a salvo of soldiers to make a thorough search."

"A salvo! I only got a hundred or so soldiers total, plus a squadron of guards," Gillen said. "I don't trust the sell-sword stripers and Highlanders. It'll have to be a squadron, that's all I can spare."

Bayar shrugged; it wasn't up to him to solve Gillen's problems. "A squadron, then. I would go myself, but as a wizard I am, of course, forbidden to venture into the Spirits." Bayar again fondled the gaudy jewel that hung at his neck. "And my involvement couldn't fail to raise difficult questions."

'Course it would raise questions, Gillen thought. Why would a wizardling involve himself in military matters anyway? Protecting the Gray Wolf queens was the job of the Queen's Guard and the army.

"We would like you to proceed without delay," Bayar said. "Have your squadron ready to leave by tomorrow." Gillen opened his mouth to tell him all the reasons why it couldn't be, but young Bayar raised his hand, palm out. "Good. My companions and I will remain here until you return."

"You're staying here?" Gillen stuttered. That, he did not need. "Listen, if the queen wants us to go into the Spirits after the princess, she ought to send reinforcements. I can't leave the West Wall unprotected while we—"

"Should you locate the princess, you will discharge her into our custody," Bayar went on, ignoring Gillen's protest. "My cousins and I will escort her back to the queen."

12

Gillen studied the boy suspiciously. Was he being set up somehow? Why would he give the princess over to these wizardlings? Why wouldn't he take her back to Fellsmarch and collect the glory (and possible reward money) himself?

Sometimes when he did work for the High Wizard he wasn't sure who he was working for—the wizard or the queen. But this was big. He meant to get more out of this venture than the Bayars' undying gratitude.

As if reading Gillen's thoughts, the boy spoke. "Should you find the princess and deliver her to us, we will pay a bounty of five thousand crowns and arrange your return to a post in Fellsmarch."

Gillen struggled to keep his mouth from falling open. Five thousand girlies? That was a fortune. More than he'd expect the Bayars to pay to take credit for returning the princess to court. Something else was going on. Something he didn't need to know about, in case he was ever questioned.

It made risking Sloat and Magot in the Spirits a lot more appealing. And all the more reason for Gillen to keep a close watch at the border.

"I'd be proud to do whatever I can to help return the princess to her mother the queen," Gillen said. "You can count on me."

"No doubt," Bayar said dryly. "Employ people who know how to keep their mouths shut, and tell them no more than necessary to get the job done. There is no need for any of them to know about our private arrangement." Fishing in a pouch at his waist, he produced a small, framed portrait and extended it toward Gillen.

It was the Princess Raisa, head and shoulders only, wearing a low-cut dress that exposed plenty of honey-colored skin. Her dark hair billowed around her face, and she wore a small crown, glittering with jewels. Her head was tilted, and she had a half smile on her face, lips parted, as though she were just about to say something he wanted to hear. She'd even written something on it. *To Micah, All my love, R.*

There was something about her, though, something familiar, that he . . .

Bayar's hand fastened around Gillen's arm, stinging him through the wool of his officer's tunic, and he nearly dropped the painting.

"Don't *drool* on it, Lieutenant Gillen," Bayar said, as if he had a bad taste in his mouth. "Please make sure your men are familiar with the princess's appearance. Bear in mind, she will likely be in disguise."

"I'll get right on it, my lord," Gillen said. He backed away, bowing himself out before young Bayar could change his mind. Or take hold of his arm again. "You and your friends make yourselves to home," he said. Five thousand girlies would buy a lot of hospitality from Mac Gillen. "I'll tell Cook to prepare whatever you like."

"What are you going to do about the musicians?" Bayar asked abruptly.

Gillen blinked at him. "What about them?" he asked. "Do you want them to stay on here? They might help pass the time, and the girl's a pretty one."

Young Bayar shook his head. "They've heard too much. As I said, no one must connect you with my father or know that you are working for him." When Gillen frowned, still confused,

Bayar added, "This is your fault, Lieutenant, not mine. I'll handle my cousins, but you are the one who will have to deal with the players."

"So," Gillen said, "are you saying I should send them away?"

"No," Bayar said, straightening his wizard stoles, not meeting Gillen's eyes. "I'm saying you should kill them."

CHAPTER TWO

IN THE BORDERLANDS

Han Alister reined in his pony at the highest point in Marisa Pines Pass. He looked out over the jagged southernmost Queens toward the hidden flatlands of Arden beyond. These were unfamiliar mountains, homes to long-dead queens with names he'd never heard. The highest peaks poked into the clouds, cold stone unclothed by vegetation. The lower slopes glittered with aspens haloed by autumn foliage.

The temperature had dropped as they climbed, and Han had added layers of clothing as necessary. Now his upland wool hat was pulled low over his ears, and his nose stung in the chilly air.

Hayden Fire Dancer nudged his pony up beside Han to share the view.

They'd left Marisa Pines Camp two days before. The clan camp sat strategically at the northern end of the pass, the major passage through the southern Spirit Mountains to the city of Delphi and the flatlands of Arden beyond. The road that began as the Way of the Queens in the capital city of Fellsmarch dwindled into little more than a wide game trail in the highest part of the pass.

Though it was prime traveling season, they'd met little trade traffic along the trail—only a few hollow-eyed refugees from Arden's civil war.

Dancer pointed ahead, toward the southern slope. "Lord Demonai says that before the war, the wagon lines ran from morning to night in season, carrying trade goods up from the flatlands. Food, mostly—grain, livestock, fruits, and vegetables."

Dancer had traveled through Marisa Pines Pass before, on trading expeditions with Averill Lightfoot, trademaster and patriarch of Demonai Camp.

"Now the armies swallow it up," Dancer went on. "Plus, a lot of the cropland has been burned and spoiled, so it's out of production."

It will be another hungry winter in the Fells, Han thought. The civil war in Arden had been going on for as long as Han could remember. His father had died there, serving as sell-sword to one of the five bloody Montaigne princes—all brothers, and all laying claim to the throne of Arden.

Han's pony wheezed and blew, after the long climb from Marisa Pines Camp. The air was thin at this altitude. Han combed his fingers through the shaggy pony's tangled mane, and scratched behind his ears. "Hey, now, Ragger," he murmured. "Take your time." Ragger bared his teeth in answer, and Han laughed.

Han took a proprietary pride in his ill-tempered pony—the first he'd ever owned. He was a skilled rider of borrowed horses.

He'd spent every summer fostered in the upland lodges—sent there from the city by a mother convinced he carried a curse.

Now everything was different. The clans had staked him his horse, clothing, supplies, food for the journey, and paid his tuition for the academy at Oden's Ford. Not out of charity, but because they hoped the demon-cursed Han Alister would prove to be a potent weapon against the growing power of the Wizard Council.

Han had accepted their offer. Accused of murder, orphaned by his enemies, hunted by the Queen's Guard and the powerful High Wizard, Gavan Bayar, he'd had no choice. The pressure of past tragedies drove him forward—the need to escape reminders of his losses, and the desire to be somewhere other than where he'd been.

That, and a smoldering desire for revenge.

Han slid his fingers inside his shirt and absently touched the serpent amulet that sizzled against the skin of his chest. Power flowed out of him and into the jinxpiece, relieving the magical pressure that had been building all day.

It had become a habit, this drawing off of power that might otherwise pinwheel out of control. He needed to constantly reassure himself the amulet was still there. Han had become strangely attached to it since he'd stolen it from Micah Bayar.

The flashpiece had once belonged to his ancestor, Alger Waterlow, known by most people as the Demon King. Meanwhile, the Lone Hunter amulet made for him by the clan matriarch, Elena Demonai, languished unused in his saddlebag.

He should hate the Waterlow flashpiece. He'd paid for it with Mam's and Mari's lives. Some said the amulet was a black magic piece—capable of naught but evil. But it was all he had to show for his nearly seventeen years, save Mari's charred storybook and Mam's gold locket. They were all that remained of a season of disaster.

Now he and his friend Dancer were to travel to Mystwerk House, the charmcaster academy at Oden's Ford, and enter training as wizards under sponsorship of the clans.

"Are you all right?" Dancer leaned toward him, his copper face etched with concern, his hair twisting in the wind like beaded snakes. "You look witch-fixed."

"I'm all right," Han said. "But I'd like to get out of this wind." Even in fair weather the wind roared constantly through the pass. And now, at summer's end, it carried the bite of winter.

"The border can't be far," Dancer said, his words snatched away as he spoke them. "Once we cross, we'll be close to Delphi. Maybe we can sleep under a roof tonight."

Han and Dancer traveled under the guise of clan traders, leading pack ponies loaded with goods. Their clan garb offered some protection. That and the longbows slung across their backs. Most thieves knew better than to confront members of the Spirit clans on their home ground. Travel would be riskier once they crossed into Arden.

As they descended toward the border, the season rolled back, from early winter to autumn again. Past the tree line, first scrubby pines and then the aspen forest closed in around them, providing some relief from the wind. The slope gentled and the skin of soil deepened. They began to see scattered crofts centered by snug cottages, and meadows studded by sturdy mountain sheep with long, curling horns.

A little farther, and here was evidence of the festering war to the south. Half hidden among the weeds to either side of the road were discards—empty saddlebags and parts of uniforms from fleeing soldiers, household treasures that had become too much of a burden on the uphill trail.

Han spotted a child's homespun dolly in the ditch, pressed into the mud. He reined in, meaning to climb down and fetch it so he could clean it up for his little sister. Then he remembered that Mari was dead and had no need of dollies anymore.

Grief was like that. It gradually faded into a dull ache, until some simple sight or sound or scent hit him like a hammer blow.

They passed several torched homesteads, stone chimneys poking up like headstones on despoiled graves. And then an entire burnt village, complete with the skeletal remains of a temple and council house.

Han looked at Dancer. "Flatlanders did this?"

Dancer nodded. "Or stray mercenaries. There's a keep at the border, but they don't do a very good job patrolling this road. The Demonai warriors can't be everywhere. The Wizard Council claims wizards *could* take up the slack, but they're not allowed and they don't have the proper tools, and that's the fault of the clans." He rolled his eyes. "As if you'd find wizards out here in the rough even if they were allowed to be."

"Hey, now," Han said. "Watch yourself. We're wizards in the rough."

They both laughed at the double joke. They'd come to share a kind of graveyard humor about their predicament. It was hard to let go of the habit of making fun of the arrogance of wizards— the kinds of jokes the powerless make about the powerful.

They reached a joining of trails from the east and west, all funneling into the pass. Traffic thickened and slowed like clotted cream. Travelers trickled past, heading the other way, toward Marisa Pines and likely on to Fellsmarch. Men, women, children, families, and single travelers, groups thrown together by chance, or joined together for protection.

Loaded down with bundles and bags, the refugees were silent, hollow-eyed, even the children, as if it took everything they had to keep putting one foot in front of the other. Adults and younglings alike carried clubs, sticks, and other makeshift weapons. Some were wounded, with bloodstained rags tied around their heads or arms or legs. Many wore lightweight flat-lander clothing, and some had no shoes.

They must have left Delphi at daybreak. If it had taken them this long to get this distance, they were never going to make it through the pass by nightfall. Then it was two more days to Marisa Pines.

"They're going to freeze up there," Han said. "Their feet will be cut to ribbons on the rocks. How are the *lytlings* going to manage the climb? What are they thinking?"

One little boy, maybe four years old, stood crying in the middle of the trail, fists clenched, face squinched up in misery. "Mama!" he cried in the flatlander tongue. "Mama! I'm hungry!" There was no mama in sight.

Pricked by guilt, Han dug into his carry bag and pulled out an apple. He leaned down from his saddle, extending it toward the boy. "Here," he said, smiling. "Try this."

The boy stumbled backward, raising his arms in defense. "No!" he screamed in a panic. "Get away!" He fell down on his backside, still screaming bloody murder.

A thin-faced girl of indeterminate age snatched the apple out of Han's hand and raced away as if chased by demons. Han stared helplessly after her.

"Let it go, Hunts Alone," Dancer said, using Han's clan name. "Guess they've had a bad experience with horsemen. You can't save everyone, you know."

I can't save *anyone*, Han thought.

They rounded a turn, and the border fortifications came into view below—a tumbledown keep and a ragged stone wall, the gaps quilled with iron spikes and razor wire in lieu of better repair. The wall stretched across the pass, smashing up against the peaks on either side, centered on a massive stone gatehouse that arched over the road. A short line of southbound trader's wagons, pack lines, and walkers inched through the gate, while the northbound traffic passed unimpeded.

A village of sorts had sprouted around the keep like mushrooms after a summer rain, consisting of rough lean-tos, scruffy huts, tents, and canvas-topped wagons. A rudimentary corral enclosed a few spavined horses and knobble-ribbed cows.

Spots of brilliant blue clustered around the gate like a fistful of autumn asters. Bluejackets. The Queen's Guard. Apprehension slid down Han's spine like an icy finger.

Why would they be on duty at the border?

"Checking the refugees coming in, I can understand," he said, scowling. "They'd want to keep out spies and renegades. But why should they care who's *leaving* the queendom?"

Dancer looked Han up and down, biting his lower lip. "Well, obviously they're looking for someone." He paused. "Would the

Queen's Guard be going to all this trouble to catch *you*?"

Han shrugged, wanting to deny the possibility. If he was so dangerous, wouldn't they prefer he was out of the queendom rather than in?

"Seems unlikely Her Powerfulness the queen would get this worked up over a few dead Southies," he said. "Especially since the killings have stopped."

"You *did* stick a knife in her High Wizard," Dancer pointed out. "Maybe he's dead."

Right. There was that. Though Han couldn't really believe that Lord Bayar was dead. In his experience, the evil lived on while the innocent died. Still, the Bayars might have convinced the queen it was worth the extra sweat to put him in darbies.

But the Bayars want their amulet back, Han thought. Would they risk his taking by the Queen's Guard? Under torture, the history of the piece might just slip out.

Anyway, wasn't he supposed to be on the queen's side? He recalled Elena *Cennestre*'s words the day she'd dumped the truth on him.

When you complete your training, you will come back here and use your skills on behalf of the clans and the true line of blooded queens.

Likely nobody'd told Queen Marianna. They'd be trying to keep it on the hush.

"We know they're not looking for *you*," Han said, shifting his eyes away from Dancer. "Let's split up, just to be on the safe side. You go ahead. I'll follow." That would prevent any heroics on Dancer's part if Han got taken.

Dancer greeted this suggestion with a derisive snort. "Right. Even with your hair covered, there is no way you could pass for clan once you open your mouth. Let me do the talking. Lots of traders pass through here. We'll be all right." Still, Han noticed that Dancer tightened the string on his bow and slid his belt-dagger into easy reach.

Han readied his own weapons, then tucked stray bits of fair hair under his hat. He should have taken the time to color it dark again, so he'd be less recognizable. Survival hadn't seemed especially important until now. Han slid his hand inside his shirt, touching his amulet. He wished for the thousandth time he knew more about how to use it. A little charmcasting might do them some good in a tight spot.

No, maybe not. Better if nobody knew that Cuffs Alister, street thief and accused murderer, was suddenly a wizard.

Excruciatingly slowly, they worked their way toward the border. It seemed the guard was doing a thorough job.

When they reached the front of the line, two guards stepped out and gripped the bridles of their horses, halting them. A mounted guard with a sergeant's scarf angled his mount in front of them. He studied their faces, scowling. "Names?"

"Fire Dancer and Hunts Alone," Dancer said in Common. "We're clan traders from Marisa Pines, traveling to Ardenscourt."

"Traders? Or *spies*?" the guardsman spat.

"Not spies," Dancer said. He steadied his pony, who tossed its head and rolled its eyes at the guardsman's tone. "Traders don't get into politics. It's bad for business."

"You've been profiting from the war, an' everybody knows it," the bluejacket growled, displaying the usual Vale attitude toward the clan. "What're you carrying?"

"Soap, scents, silks, leatherwork, and medicines," Dancer

said, resting a proprietary hand on his saddlebags.

That much was true. They planned to deliver those goods to a buyer in Ardenscourt to help pay for their schooling and keep.

"Lessee." The guardsman unstrapped the panniers on the first pony and pawed through the goods inside. The scent of sandal-wood and pine wafted up.

"What about weapons or amulets?" he demanded. "Any magical pieces?"

Dancer lifted an eyebrow. "There's no market for magical goods in Arden," he said. "The Church of Malthus forbids it. And we don't deal in weapons. Too risky."

The sergeant gazed at their faces, his brow puckered with puzzlement. Han kept his eyes fixed on the ground. "I dunno," the guardsman said. "You both got blue eyes. You don't look much like clan to me."

"We're of mixed blood," Dancer said. "Adopted into the camps as babies."

"You was stole, more like," the sergeant said. "Just like the princess heir. The Maker have mercy on her."

"What about the princess heir?" Dancer said. "We haven't heard."

"She's disappeared," the sergeant said. He seemed to be one of those people who loved sharing bad news. "Some say she run off. Me, I say there's no way she would've left on her own."

So that's it, Han thought, happying up a little. This extra care at the border had nothing at all to do with them.

But the bluejacket wasn't done with them. He looked around as if to make sure he had backup, then said, "Some say she was took by your people. By the copperheads."

"That doesn't make any sense," Dancer said. "The Princess Raisa's of clan blood herself by her father, and she fostered at Demonai Camp for three years."

The bluejacket snorted. "Well, she's not in the capital, they know that," he said. "She might come this way; that's why we're checking everybody who comes through. The queen is offering a big reward for anyone that finds her."

"What does she look like?" Dancer asked, like he was sniffing at that big reward.

"She's a mix-blood too," the bluejacket said, "but I hear she's pretty, just the same. She's small, with long dark hair and green eyes."

Han was ambushed by a memory of green-eyed Rebecca Morley, who'd walked into Southbridge Guardhouse and wrested three members of the Ragger street gang from Mac Gillen's hands. That description would fit Rebecca. And a thousand other girlies.

Since his life had fallen apart, Han hadn't thought of Rebecca. Much.

The sergeant finally decided he'd held them up long enough. "All right, then, go on. Better watch yourselves south of Delphi. The fighting's fierce down there."

"Thank you, Sergeant," Dancer was saying, when a new voice cut into the conversation, sharp and cold as a knife blade.

"What's this all about, Sergeant? What's the delay?"

Han looked up to see a girlie about his own age, bulling her horse through the crowd of foot travelers around the gate like she didn't care if she trampled a few.

He couldn't help staring. She looked like no girlie he'd ever seen before. Her mane of platinum hair was caught into a single long braid that extended to her waist, accented by a streak of red that ran the entire length. Her eyebrows and eyelashes were the color of cottonwood fluff, and her eyes a pale, porcelain blue, like a rain-washed sky. She was surrounded by a nimbus of light—evidence of unchanneled power.

She rode a gray flatlander stallion as blueblooded as she was, sitting tall in the saddle as if to extend her already considerable height. Her angular features looked familiar. It wasn't a beautiful face, but you wouldn't soon forget it. Especially when she had a scowl planted on it. Like now.

Her short jacket and divided riding skirts were made of fine goods, trimmed in leather. The wizard stoles draped over her shoulders bore the stooping falcon insignia, a falcon with a songbird in its talons, and a glowing amulet hung from a heavy gold chain around her neck.

Han shuddered, his body reacting before his slow-cranking mind. The stooping falcon. But that signia belonged to . . .

"I—I'm sorry, Lady Bayar," the sergeant stuttered, his forehead pebbled with sweat despite the cool air. "I was just questioning these traders. Making sure, my lady."

Bayar. That's who the girl reminded Han of—Micah Bayar. He'd only seen the High Wizard's son once, the day Han had taken the amulet that had changed his life forever. Who was she to Micah? She looked about the same age. Sister? Cousin?

"Take hold of your amulet," Dancer murmured to Han, sliding his hand under his deerskin jacket. "It'll draw off the power so maybe they won't notice your aura."

27

Han nodded, gripping the serpent flashpiece under his jacket.

"We're looking for a *girl*, you idiot," Lady Bayar was saying, her pale eyes flicking over Han and Dancer. "A dark, dwarfish sort of girl. Why are you wasting time on these two copperheads?" she added, using the Vale name for clanfolk.

The two guards gripping Han's and Dancer's horses hastily let go.

"Fiona. Mind what you say." Another wizard reined in behind Lady Bayar, an older boy with straw-colored hair and a body already fleshy with excess. His twin wizard stoles carried a thistle signia.

"What?" Fiona glared at him, and he squirmed like a puppy under her gaze.

He's either sweet on her or afraid of her, Han thought. Maybe both.

"Fiona, please." The young wizard cleared his throat. "I wouldn't describe the Princess Raisa as dwarfish. In fact, the princess is rather—"

"If not dwarfish, then what?" Fiona broke in. "Stumpy? Stunted? Scrubby?"

"Well, I—"

"And she is dark, is she not? Rather swarthy, in fact, due to her mixed blood. Admit it, Wil, she is." Fiona did not seem to take well to being corrected.

Han fought to keep the surprise off his face. He was no fan of the queen and her line, either, but he'd never expect to hear such talk from one of the Bayars.

Fiona rolled her eyes. "I don't know what my brother sees in her. Surely you're a more discerning judge of women." She smiled at Wil, turning on the charm, and Han could see why the wizardling was taken with her.

Wil flushed deep pink. "I just think we should show some respect," he whispered, leaning close so the sergeant couldn't hear. "She is the heir to the Gray Wolf throne."

Dancer edged his pony forward, hoping to pass on by while the jinxflingers were embroiled in their debate. Han pressed his knees against Ragger's sides and followed after, keeping his head down, his face turned away. They were past the wizards, entering the gate, almost clean away, when . . .

"You there! Hold on."

It was Fiona Bayar. Han swore silently, then put on his street face and turned in his saddle to find her staring at him.

"Look at me, boy!" she commanded.

Han looked up, directly into her porcelain blue eyes. The amulet sizzled in his fingers, and some devil spirit made him lift his chin and say, "I'm not a boy, Lady Bayar. Not anymore."

Fiona sat frozen, staring at him, her reins clutched in one hand. The long column of her throat jumped as she swallowed. "No," she said, running her tongue over her lips. "You're not a boy. And you don't sound like a copperhead, either."

Wil reached over and touched her arm, as if trying to regain her attention. "Do you know this . . . *trader*, Fiona?" he asked, contempt trickling through his voice.

But she kept staring at Han. "You're dressed like a trader," she whispered, almost to herself. "You're in copperhead garb, yet you have an aura." She looked down at her own glowing hands, then up at him. "Blood and bones, you have an *aura*."

Han glanced down at himself, and saw, to his horror, that the magic blazing through him was excruciatingly apparent, even in the afternoon light. If anything, he was brighter than usual, power glittering under his skin like sunlight on water.

But the amulet was supposed to quench it, to take it up. Maybe, in times of trouble, he spouted more magic than the piece could manage.

"It's nothing," Dancer said quickly. "Comes of handling magical objects at the clan markets. Sort of rubs off sometimes. It doesn't last."

Han blinked at his friend, impressed. Dancer had developed a talent for "amusing the law," as they'd say in Ragmarket.

Dancer gripped Ragger's bridle, trying to tug the horse forward. "Now, much as we'd love to stay and answer jinxflinger questions, we need to move along if we don't want to sleep in the woods."

Fiona ignored Dancer. She continued to stare at Han, eyes narrowed, head tilted. She sucked in a breath and sat up even straighter. "Take off your hat," she commanded.

"We answer to the queen, jinxflinger. Not to you," Dancer said. "Come *on*, Hunts Alone," he growled.

Han kept his eyes fixed on Fiona, his hand on his amulet. His skin prickled as magic and defiance buzzed through him like brandy. Slowly, deliberately, he grasped his cap with his free hand and ripped it off, shaking his hair free. The wind pouring down through Marisa Pines Pass ruffled it, lifting it off his forehead.

"Take a message to Lord Bayar," Han said. "Stay out of my way, or your whole family goes down."

Fiona stared. For a moment she couldn't seem to get any words out. Finally she croaked, "Alister. You're Cuffs Alister.

But . . . you're a wizard. That can't be."

"Surprise," Han said. Standing tall in his stirrups, he gripped his amulet with one hand and extended the other. His fingers twisted into a jinx as if they had a mind of their own, and magical words poured unbidden from his mouth.

The road bulged and buckled as a hedge of thorns erupted from the dirt, forming a prickled wall between Han and Dancer and the other wizards. It was chest-high on the horses in a matter of seconds.

Startled, Han ripped his hand free of the flashpiece, wiping his hand on his leggings as if he could rid it of traces of magic. His head swam, then cleared. He looked over at Dancer, who was glaring at him like he couldn't believe his eyes and ears.

Fiona's tongue finally freed itself. She screamed, "It's him! It's Cuffs Alister! He tried to murder the High Wizard! Seize him!"

Nobody moved. The wall of thorns continued to grow, stretching spined branches into the sky. The bluejackets gawked at the trader who'd turned into a would-be murderer that pulled thorn hedges out of the air.

Dancer swung his arm in a broad arc, sending flame spiraling in all directions. The hedge smoked, then caught fire. Ragger reared, trying to shake Han off. The guardsmen flung themselves to the dirt, covering their heads, moaning in fear.

Han slammed his heels into Ragger's sides, and the startled pony charged forward through the gate, followed closely by Dancer, flat against his pony's back, hair flying. Ahead of them, travelers pitched themselves out of the way, diving into ditches on either side of the road. Behind them, Han could hear shouted orders and trumpets blaring.

Crossbows sounded, the guardsmen firing blindly over the gatehouse. Han pressed his head against Ragger's neck to make a smaller target.

Fiona shouted, "Take him *alive*, you idiots! My father wants him alive!" After that there were no more crossbows, which was a blessing because the road between the border and Delphi was broad and gently sloping. Once their pursuers made it over or around Han's barrier, he and Dancer would make pretty targets.

Han looked back in time to see Fiona blast a ragged hole through the blazing hedge. The two wizards burst through, followed by a triple of unenthusiastic mounted guardsmen. The bluejackets likely had no desire to come up against anyone who could fling flame and thorns.

"Here they come," Han shouted, urging Ragger to greater speed.

"Guess they've decided to get in your way," Dancer called back.

Han knew Dancer would have plenty to say later. If there was a later.

The wizards were already gaining on them, eating up their lead. They'd eventually catch up, with a broad road before them and their long-legged flatland horses giving them the advantage of speed. There was no way he and Dancer could win against two better-trained wizards. Not to mention a whole triple of bluejackets.

What came over you, Alister? Han said to himself. Whatever faults he had, stupidity wasn't one of them. It might be tempting to confront Fiona Bayar, but he'd never entangle Dancer in a grudge match he was likely to lose.

Han remembered how the magic had felt coursing through him like strong drink. And like strong drink, it had made him lose his head. Likely it was because he didn't know what he was doing. Tightening his grip on his reins, he resisted taking hold of the amulet again.

"We've got to get off this road," he shouted, spitting out dust. "Is there someplace we can turn off?"

"How should I know?" Dancer shouted back. He looked ahead, squinting against the declining sun. "It's been a while." They thundered on another half mile, and then Dancer called, "You know, there *is* a place up ahead where we might lose them."

Delphi Road followed a clear trout stream, sharing the valley it had carved through the declining Spirits to the south. Dancer looked off to the left, seeking a landmark. Han rode up beside him, trying to maintain their breakneck pace.

"Along here Kanwa Creek turns west, and the road runs due south," Dancer said. "We can turn off and follow the creek and maybe lose them. It's a narrow canyon, rocky and steep. Made for ponies, not for flatlander horses. Look for a rock shaped like a sleeping bear."

The turnoff couldn't come too soon. As the sound of pursuit grew louder, Han turned his head and saw that the two wizards were now only three or four pony lengths behind them. When Fiona saw Han looking, she stood in her stirrups and dropped her reins. Fumbling at her neck, she extended her other hand.

Flame rocketed toward Dancer. Had Fiona not been on horseback, it might have struck true. At it was, it seared Wicked's shoulder. The pony screamed and veered to the left, crashing into Ragger and nearly launching all of them from the road.

Han struggled to keep his pony from going down, while Dancer wrenched Wicked's head back into the straight.

The message was clear: Fiona Bayar wanted Han alive, but Dancer was fair game.

Han yanked his blade free, expecting to find their pursuers right on top of them. When he looked back, he was surprised to see Fiona and Wil falling behind, fighting to regain control of their rearing and plunging horses. The bluejackets bunched up behind them, trying to avoid colliding with the two wizards. It seemed the wizards' blueblood mounts weren't trained to carry riders launching flaming attacks.

"There it is!" Dancer pointed ahead to where a massive granite boulder bulked into the road, squeezing it from the left. It did, indeed, resemble a sleeping bear, its head resting on two massive paws. As if recognizing it as a sanctuary, Wicked surged forward, Han and Ragger following close behind.

The bluejackets and charmcasters must have got themselves sorted out, because once again Han could hear horses pounding after them.

Han and Dancer swerved around the promontory of rock, temporarily out of sight of their pursuers. Just on the other side, the ground fell away into dizzyingly steep rock terraces. Kanwa Creek plunged over a series of cascades between sheer stone walls and out of sight. The roar of falling water echoed up through the canyon.

"You mean to go down *there*?" Han looked around for other options. Ragger being his first horse, he didn't want to see him lamed his first week out. Not to mention stumbling and sending the two of them head over heels into the chasm.

Dancer urged Wicked down the first rock-strewn slope. "I've been this way before. I'd rather risk Kanwa Canyon than Lady Bayar."

"All right," Han said. "Ride ahead, since you can move faster. I'll catch up." Han reasoned that Fiona was less likely to fire if he brought up the rear.

The good thing was, nobody would come this way if they had any other choice. Especially on flatlander horses.

Dancer and Wicked disappeared around a curve in the canyon downslope, descending recklessly fast. Dancer and his pony had been together for two years. Han gave Ragger his head and let him follow after Wicked at his own pace, fighting the temptation to rush him forward. Han was keen to be out of sight before the wizards rounded Sleeping Bear Rock and began launching flame at them from above.

Ragger picked his way sure-footedly down the steep canyon, sending small stones sailing into the abyss below. The pony pressed so close against the stone wall that Han's right leg scraped against rock, ripping his leggings and taking off the top layer of skin.

When they reached creek level, the pony navigated a series of waterfalls, then splashed aggressively through the shallows after Dancer, eager to overtake his rival.

Han looked back and upslope. High above, he saw two riders at the top of the canyon, their wizard auras framing them against the brighter sky. They were arguing; their loud voices funneled down the canyon.

Han guessed that Fiona was insisting they pursue Han and Dancer into the canyon, and Wil was arguing against it.

Good luck, Wil, Han thought, and heeled Ragger forward.

They descended through several more steep gorges, navigating ledges so narrow that Han felt like he was treading air. Don't look down, he thought, keeping his eyes fixed on the path ahead. They made frustratingly slow progress compared to what they could have done on the road.

Han looked back often, but heard and saw nothing of pursuit. After several hours they stopped in a grassy meadow to water the exhausted horses. The sun had disappeared behind the tall peaks, the gloom under the trees thickened, and it grew cooler again, despite the lower altitude. Han didn't look forward to navigating this trail in the dark.

It didn't matter. They'd crossed the border, and for now, at least, it seemed they'd lost their pursuers.

Han flopped down on his belly and cupped his hands, scooping water out of the creek to drink. The water was clear and stunningly cold.

"What came over you back there?" Dancer demanded, squatting next to him and dipping his canteen to fill it. "We were nearly clear, and then you had to ruin it. Slipping across a border unrecognized isn't exciting enough for you?"

Han wiped his mouth on his sleeve and settled back on his heels. "I don't know why I did that. I can't explain it."

"You couldn't keep your hat on?" Dancer recorked his canteen and splashed water into his face, rinsing away the road dust.

"It was like there was this backwash of power from the flash-piece," Han said. "I don't know if there's something wrong with the magic I put into it, or if it's because I don't know what I'm doing."

Demon-cursed, his mother had said. Maybe it was true.

The normally easygoing Dancer wasn't done yet. In fact, he was just getting started. "You couldn't keep your mouth shut? I'm calling you Glitterhair from now on. Or Talksalot."

"I'm sorry," Han said. He had nothing else to say. He couldn't blame Dancer for being angry. It had been an unnecessary, foolhardy stunt. Dancer had never seen this side of him. It was like he'd gone back to his death-wish days as streetlord of the Raggers.

"Where did you learn to fling jinxes?" Dancer persisted. "You said you didn't know anything about magic. You didn't even know you were a wizard until a couple of weeks ago. Here I've been trying to teach you what little I know, and then you go and conjure up a thorn hedge. Maybe you should be teaching me."

"I don't know how I did that," Han said. "It just kind of happened." Dancer must think he'd been holding out on him, that he didn't want to share what he knew. When Dancer said nothing, Han added, "I didn't know *you* knew how to throw flame."

"I don't," Dancer said, his voice tight with betrayal. "It just spurts out like that when I'm scared to death." He stood, smacking the dust off his leggings, and left to see to the horses.

Han pulled his amulet out of his neckline and turned it in his hands, examining it for clues. He had to learn how to control the thing. Otherwise, there was no guarantee this wouldn't happen again.

Now the Bayars knew he was a wizard, and that he was heading south. At least they wouldn't know what he was up to or where he was going. Han rather liked the notion of the Bayars wondering and worrying about where he'd surface next, and what he'd do when he did.

CHAPTER THREE

IN THE AUTUMN DAMPS

Raisa shivered and pulled her wool cloak more closely around her shoulders. Soggy with rain and glazed with ice, it probably weighed more than she did. She scooted closer to the fire, extending her frozen hands. Steam rose from the sodden fabric.

Maybe if she actually sat *in* the flames, she'd be warm again. She already smelled like a wet sheep toasted over a wood fire.

It had taken a week to cross the high country between Demonai Camp and the West Wall. A week of freezing weather and early autumn snows, of huddling together in tents while the wind howled outside. Raisa had foolishly assumed that the weather would improve as they descended toward Leewater, the ocean to the west she'd never seen.

In that she'd been mistaken. The early high country snows turned to sleet and icy rains—relentless storms that rendered the trails treacherous. They'd been camped for a week in this miserable between-place. They'd pitched their tents in a small box canyon that blocked the worst of the winds, and waited for the weather to clear.

It would have been easier traveling by way of the Dyrnne-water Valley, which ran through a break in the Spirits from Fellsmarch to the West Wall. But there was too great a chance they'd be intercepted on the easy road.

"Lady Rebecca?"

It took Raisa a moment to realize she was being addressed. When she looked up, the cadet Hallie Talbot loomed over her, extending a mug of hot tea.

"Call me Morley," Raisa said automatically, accepting the tea and sipping the hot liquid. She shouldn't allow Hallie to wait on her, but it took more strength than she possessed to say no.

Rebecca Morley was her alias, meant to hide her from those hunting the runaway princess heir of the Fells. The other Gray Wolves believed she was a daughter of the minor nobility whose parents had bribed her way into the military academy at Oden's Ford. Nobody knew who she really was but her friend Amon Byrne.

Early on, Raisa had asked Hallie to cut her hair, to alter her looks. The cadet had obliged using her belt knife. Hallie's skills as a barber were dubious. The result was a ragged cap that reached to Raisa's earlobe on one side and her chin on the other.

Raisa's hair had always been a point of vanity for her—long and thick, a wavy mass falling nearly to her waist. It was her best physical feature. She closed her eyes and extended her neck, remembering how Magret used to brush it with a boar-bristle hairbrush. . . .

"You'd be warmer and dryer in your tent, my—Morley," Hallie said, breaking in on her thoughts once again. "You'll catch your death out here."

Raisa bit back a sharp retort. In camp, it seemed they were constantly on top of one another. Everything was difficult—from starting a fire to using the privy. Boredom and the constant close contact made them all snappish.

Well, it made Raisa snappish, at least. The others took it in stride.

"If I spend any more time staring at four canvas walls, I'll go mad," Raisa grumbled.

At first she'd shared a tent with Amon, Mick Bricker, and Talia Abbott. It was three per tent, with Raisa making the fourth since she was extra. That was fair in a triple of nine plus one. It had been cramped but cozy.

Then she'd awakened in the middle of the night to find herself snuggled up against Amon, one arm flung across his chest, nose buried in his wool undershirt. As children, they'd slept that way a hundred times.

This time it was different. Raisa crashed into consciousness, suddenly aware of his familiar scent, the thump of his heart under her arm, his rigid body. Amon lay on his back, still as stone, as though she were a viper who might strike if he twitched. He was jammed against the wall of the tent, eyes wide open, hands fisted, sweat beading on his forehead. He took quick, shallow breaths like he was in pain.

When he saw she was awake, he disentangled himself and stalked out of the tent.

After that, he'd swapped Mick with Hallie and moved into

one of the other tents, leaving the three female guards together.

It wasn't like she'd rolled onto him on purpose. It wasn't like she'd *attacked* him.

He was inconsistent. Half the time he insisted she act like any soldier, the other half he was making special rules that applied only to her. She never went on patrol, and she never stood watch alone. He told the others it was because she was a first-year cadet and the others more experienced. He'd turned into the worst kind of bully.

They had plenty of food, but it was nasty stuff—hard biscuits and dried meat of undetermined origin, cheese going moldy in the damp. The nuts and dried fruit weren't bad, but there was only so much of that Raisa could stomach. At the middays, if she didn't finish her portion, Amon would nag her until she did.

"You're losing weight, Morley. Up here, you need insulation. Once we start moving, you'll need to keep up. I don't want you fainting away from hunger. No one's going to carry you, skin and bones or not." And so on.

So what if she lost weight? Anyone would, under the circumstances.

They drilled every morning. Walked for miles in a large circle around the camp, in all kinds of weather. Every day, Amon assigned someone to match swords with Raisa, to work on her stance, her stamina, her form. Everyone took a turn but Amon Byrne. He probably knew what a mismatch that would be.

Still, the bouts were always humiliating. And exhausting. Everyone in the Wolfpack had a longer reach than she did. They could stand back in total safety and clip her at their leisure, smack her with the flat of their blades while she was kept constantly moving. It was like having eight big brothers and sisters to pick on her.

"If you're going to be a cadet," Amon would say, "you'll be competing with people who've been fencing since they could hold a stick." People such as Amon, who'd always known he would be a soldier like his father.

Maybe he wanted to work her hard enough to wear her down, to make her give up the idea of hiding among the warrior cadets at Wien House. *His* idea was that she'd stay in the temple close, cloistered with the dedicates, gardening and reading and studying healing and doing needlework with the speakers.

There, she'd be less likely to be recognized by students from home. Few Fellsians attended the Temple School at Oden's Ford. There were fine ones closer to home.

Raisa *knew* mingling with the other students was risky, but she'd accept the risk. She'd spent enough time in a cloister. She wanted to learn about the real world.

Raisa set her mug down on a rock, wrapped her arms around her trousered legs, and rested her chin on her knees. Sweet Hanalea in chains, she was tired of this.

Hallie was on watch in camp. Talia Abbott was on patrol, looking for trouble over a three-mile radius. Everyone else huddled in the other two tents. Except for Amon, who was missing, as usual.

Amon used the name Morley like a stick to keep her at bay. To bury the memory of the childhood they'd spent together, finishing each other's sentences, using their assets and talents to support and defend each other.

That younger Amon had taught her to hold her own in the

physical, rough-and-tumble world outside of court. He'd taught her the skills her mother had neglected—riding bareback, longbow archery, and a dangerous form of soccer played from horseback. He'd taught her tavern games—nicks and bones, darts, battle cards, and dicing.

Amon had been the conduit through which the skills he learned from his father and older cousins and on the streets of Fellsmarch were passed to Raisa. They'd sparred with wooden training swords. He showed her how to throw a knife and hone a real blade. When Raisa was twelve, he'd taught her how to disable an opponent in a street fight as soon as he learned it himself.

Raisa had her own talents to contribute to their childhood enterprises. People naturally deferred to her lineage, granting her an authority she didn't necessarily have. With Raisa to front them, they could get away with anything.

Of course we're allowed to ride out alone, she'd tell the stableman with breezy confidence. *Saddle up Devilspawn and Thunderheart. Yes, those two. Yes, the queen approves. Do you really want to bother her?*

Of course Amon is invited to the party/allowed to help himself in the pantry/allowed to choose weapons from the royal armory/can ride any horse he wants.

They were lucky they'd survived to their naming. But they'd had fun.

Then Amon had turned thirteen, the age when warrior cadets were named and sent to Wien House, the military academy at Oden's Ford. Raisa had gone to Demonai Camp, to be fostered with her father's family. They'd been apart more than three years.

Amon had returned to Fellsmarch at seventeen, tall, lean, and handsome, an intriguing combination of worldly soldier and familiar friend. Now Raisa wanted him to teach her different things, or to learn them along with her, but he was being uncooperative. A few tantalizing kisses—that was all they'd had. At first he'd seemed interested, but now . . .

There was no chance of a marriage between them. Her mother had made it clear that she disapproved of a dalliance with an officer of the Guard. Was that why Raisa was so fixed on him? Or was it because she was used to getting what she wanted?

That couldn't be it. The threat of a forced marriage to a wizard had sent her into exile. A marriage that violated the Næming—the agreement that had ended the wars between wizards and clans. Some days it seemed that no one got less of what they wanted than the princess heir of the Fells.

Still, Raisa's heart beat faster whenever she got close to Amon Byrne. She noticed everything about him—the way he moved, the way he sat on a horse, the way he tilted his head and chewed on his lower lip when working a problem, the way he rubbed his stubbled chin at the end of the day.

Whenever he turned those gray eyes on her, the blood rushed madly around her body, heating every part of her . . . when she wasn't fighting with him. They did a lot of that, lately. Sometimes it seemed he provoked her on purpose.

And now he was avoiding her. She was convinced of it. He left camp nearly every day for several hours. She had no idea where he went, but she couldn't help thinking it was because of her. She felt restless and tired of sitting around, freezing to death.

At court, it seemed like she never even had time to think. Out here, she thought too much. Chewed on things like a dog with a rawhide.

Maybe he thinks of you as a friend, she thought. He doesn't want to ruin that friendship by pushing it further.

Well, you *are* friends, but lately he scarcely talks to you.

Or maybe he's interested, but views you as unattainable. He's afraid if he makes a move he'll be refused or humiliated.

Or maybe it's the blasted Byrne honor getting in the way. He finds you attractive, but he knows there's no future in it, so he's not going to get entangled.

He just doesn't know how to say any of that. He's never been good with words.

Raisa was used to speaking her mind. She wasn't flighty Missy Hakkam, mooning over every officer in a uniform, dreaming of marriages to foppish nobles with big palaces and tiny brains.

I'll go and find him, she thought. We'll have a frank discussion, no tears or drama, and get this settled. But she needed to find a way to slip off on her own.

"I guess I *will* rest in my tent for a while," she told Talbot.

Hallie grunted approval and laid another log on the fire.

Leaving her empty mug where it was, Raisa crawled into her tent, which was only fractionally warmer than outside. She found her baldric and strapped it on. Crouching at the rear of the tent, she thrust her sword under the tent wall. Then she flopped down on her back and slid underneath the rear wall and back out into the rain.

Once on her feet, she shoved her sword into the baldric. Keeping at the back of the tents, she walked toward the entrance of the canyon until she reached the privy tent, the one farthest away from the others. She waited until Hallie was occupied stacking firewood, then slipped through the border of trees and out of the canyon.

Raisa had studied tracking with the Demonai warriors. She scanned the ground until she spotted boot prints amid the ruck of leaves. And there, another, where water collected and froze at a low place. She picked out a path beaten into the slushy ground from Amon's daily trips to wherever he went.

Raisa followed his trail for a mile or so, wiping rain from her face and blinking ice from her lashes. The path followed a clear, half-frozen stream for a while, then veered sharply off to the west, climbing into an aspen forest, ending in an upland meadow. Raisa stopped amid the trees edging the meadow and peered out.

Amon stood centered in the meadow, stripped to breeches and undershirt. His sword belt and other gear were arranged in a neat pile at the periphery of the field.

He held a long staff in his two hands, and he was in constant motion, bending, twisting, circling around, the staff a whistling blur as he swung it over his head, swept it forward, lifted it high, and skimmed the ground. It was an elaborate dance, and he'd clearly been at it for some time. His dark hair lay in wet strands on his forehead, and his skin steamed in the chilly air.

Raisa stared at him—at the muscles rippling across his chest and his corded arms—and all her good intentions flew out of her head. He was beautiful and deadly, totally unself-conscious. He went at it as if determined to work himself to exhaustion. He didn't look like he was enjoying himself. More like it was punishment. She could hear the rasp of his breathing from where she stood.

How in the name of the Lady could he be coatless? It was freezing out. Raisa shivered, the cold penetrating deeper now that she'd stopped moving.

She stood (almost literally) frozen for another long moment while her courage drained away. This was wrong, her spying on him. Whatever was going on, he meant it to be private. She'd find another time to speak her mind. She'd go back to camp, sneak into her tent, and stay there until he returned.

You're just a coward, she thought.

But before she could move, Amon paused in the midst of a sequence, the staff horizontal in front of him, his head cocked. He flipped the quarterstaff to a vertical position, turned, and looked directly at where Raisa was hiding.

"Rai?" he whispered.

Bones. How did he know? Timidly, she stepped out of the woods. They stood staring at each other across an expanse of frozen grass and stumpy shrubs.

"I came looking for you," she said finally. "I wondered what you were doing."

"You came by yourself? Where's Hallie?" he demanded, looking around as if the other cadet might be hiding in the brush, too.

Hallie's supposed to be watching me, Raisa thought. So much for being just another soldier. "I slipped away. She thought I was in my tent."

"You shouldn't have come. It's not safe for you to be out here on your own."

"If it's not safe for me, it's not safe for you," Raisa said. "Aren't you cold?"

"No. I'm not," Amon said, as if it hadn't occurred to him till then.

The silence coalesced around them once more.

"That's impressive. What you were doing," she said. "What is that called?"

He studied the weapon in his hands as if he'd forgotten it was there. He seemed absent, distracted. "I learned it from the Waterwalkers. They call it *sticking*. Their staffs are made of ironwood—it grows in the marshes. They don't use metal weapons, but a weighted staff is deadly in the hands of a stickmaster." He shut his mouth, as if to cut off the flood of words—a whole month's worth for him.

"Were there Waterwalkers at the academy?" Raisa asked, surprised. "Was that where you learned it?"

Amon shook his head. "No. I fostered in the Fens for six months during one of my terms at Wien House. I was sponsored by the marshlord, name of Cadri."

"Is this what you do every day? When you leave?"

He hesitated, then nodded. "Pretty much. I . . . ah . . . train in different ways. It helps relieve the tension."

Tension? Raisa squinted at him. It was miserable, true, what with the rain and ice and wind and bad food and all. But it was more tedious than tense, in Raisa's opinion. She almost wished something exciting would happen, to break the boredom.

Was he really worried about an attack? That seemed unlikely, despite his warnings. They were still in the Fells, and Demonai Camp kept this area well patrolled. Besides, who would venture out in this weather if they didn't have to?

Perhaps it was just the stress of knowing his father was counting on him to keep the princess heir safe; of not knowing what would happen when they reached Oden's Ford.

It had been too long since they'd had any fun. Raisa yanked off her gloves and stuffed them inside her coat, then strode toward him.

Amon flipped the staff horizontal, making a barrier between them. "We'd better get back to camp," he said, jerking his head in that direction.

Raisa stopped a foot away and looked up at him. "Amon. Could you teach me?"

"Teach you what?" he asked, his eyes narrowing.

"That battle dance. How to fight with a staff." She took hold of the staff, slippery with ice. She couldn't compete with his swordplay, but she could learn this.

It would be like the old days. Amon had been her first weapons master.

He shook his head. "It's too heavy for you."

"You can take most of the weight. Just show me the moves. If it works out, I can always get something lighter." She could see how it could work, using the staff. Being small wouldn't matter so much when she had a long staff to leverage her reach and the strength of her blows. Once she had the moves down, any kind of staff would serve. With a reinforced staff, she could fight off a swordsman. And the weight of it would build up her shoulders and arms.

"You might get hurt." Amon seemed to be looking everywhere but at her.

"I'm not breakable," Raisa snapped. "I'll try not to hurt *you*, either."

He cleared his throat. "I'm just . . . it's not a good idea for us to have a go at each other."

"Oh, really? Why not?"

"Just trust me, all right?"

Amon had never been one to be threatened by capable girls. And he'd never taken it easy on her in physical competitions because she was female. Any more than she gave him quarter in those areas in which she excelled. Was he angry that she wanted to be part of his military life? Maybe it had been a relief for him to be away from her, to go down to Oden's Ford and live with less demanding people.

"I'm stronger than you think," Raisa insisted. She should be, after all that drilling. "Here. We don't have to fight against each other. Let's try this." She ducked under the horizontal staff so she was inside the circle of his arms, between him and the staff. She turned her back to him, gripped the staff with her two hands, positioning them beside Amon's. "Now, give me some of the weight and let's try some moves."

Amon released a long breath of frustration. And resignation. Another moment, and she felt the weight of the staff in her hands. Amon spoke in her ear, and she could feel his warm breath on her neck. "Turn to the right, swing it up high, down to the ground, thrust forward. Turn again, fast to the left, now bend at the waist."

It was like an odd sort of front-to-back dance where you couldn't see your partner's face, only hear his voice. It was surprisingly graceful, anchored as they were, connected by the weight of the staff. Amon seemed to be taking special pains not to slam into her. His arms pressed against her shoulders, though, and she felt the heat of his body against her back, driving away the cold.

She heard only the whistle of the staff, the crunch of icy grass beneath their feet, the sound of their breathing. Her skin tingled, anticipating each contact between them.

Little by little, Amon gave her more of the weight. Raisa struggled to keep the staff moving, dragging in cold air in ragged gasps, sweating inside her heavy clothing.

Then it happened. She slipped on a patch of ice, Amon tried to adjust, their legs became tangled together, and they fell. He came down on top of her, but managed to brace himself and so avoid flattening her. She heard a *smack* as the quarterstaff landed some distance away. So they didn't get a self-administered clubbing, at least.

Raisa giggled, and then she was laughing, snorting with mirth, helpless to free herself. "W . . . we are a dangerous pair, Amon Byrne." She pressed her hands against his chest, and then noticed that he wasn't laughing. His gray eyes were roiled with frustration. Sliding his hands under her head, he kissed her, pressing her hard against the frozen ground. She wound her arms around his neck and kissed him back.

By the Lady, she thought. I do love kissing Amon Byrne.

He ripped himself free and sat up. "Blood of the demon," he said, his face ashen. He bent double, looking almost ill. "I'm sorry, Your Highness. We can't do this."

Your Highness? Raisa blinked at him, thinking it was the best thing that had happened in a very long time. But just then a strange voice broke in on them.

"Step away from the princess heir." This coincided with the metallic whisper of swords sliding free of their scabbards.

Raisa whipped around, yanking her own sword free, ending in a low crouch. A dozen horsemen had emerged from the trees, all wearing the camouflage scout uniform of the Queen's Guard. One wore a corporal's scarf tied around his neck. He looked familiar.

Amon sprinted for the edge of the woods, where his sword and clothing lay, but one of the horsemen wheeled his horse and charged toward him, swinging a large club with a spike at the end.

"Amon!" Raisa shouted.

Amon launched himself sideways. The club missed his head but slammed into his shoulder, sending him flying to the ground.

The other guards dismounted. Two of them grabbed Amon's arms and hauled him upright. Blood dripped from the wound in his shoulder and spattered the frozen ground.

The corporal dug in his carry bag and made a great show of pulling out a small, framed portrait. He looked from the portrait to Raisa and nodded with satisfaction, then tucked it back away. "Your hair's different, but it's you all right," he said.

"What is the meaning of this?" Raisa demanded.

"Calm down, Your Highness," the corporal said. "You're safe now."

"I was safe before, Corporal," Raisa said, advancing on Amon and his captors, her sword extended in front of her. It was foolish to confront a dozen armed men with one sword, but she was seized by the desire to cut someone. "It's only now I feel in danger. Release Corporal Byrne immediately and explain yourselves."

"We saw Corporal Byrne attacking you, Your Highness," the officer said, sliding a warning look at his comrades. "Who would have thought it, and him the son of the captain of the Queen's Guard."

"He was not attacking me," Raisa said. "We were practicing self-defense."

"Never you mind, Your Highness," the corporal said. "It must have been a scary thing, to be carried off by a member of your own guard. But he won't harm you no more. We'll make sure of that." He smiled chillingly, and Raisa suddenly remembered where she had seen the corporal before. He was Robbie Sloat, who'd been one of the guardsmen at Southbridge Guardhouse the day she and Amon had rescued the Raggers.

"We was on our way to Demonai Camp, to look for you, Princess," Sloat said. "Now we don't have to go there at all."

Sloat barked out orders, and the other guards collected Amon's sword and his belt dagger and tied his hands behind his back. They took Raisa's sword, but didn't bother to search her or bind her hands.

How had Sloat ended up out here in the rough, close to the West Wall?

Whatever he was doing here, she knew it meant they were in terrible trouble.

Sloat faced Amon, ignoring Raisa. "So, Corporal Byrne, I know you're not out here on foot. Where'd you come from? Where are your horses and who else is with you?"

Amon said nothing, his face hard and set, and an awful, blank look in his eyes.

Sloat slammed his fist into Amon's midsection, and Amon

doubled over, the air whooshing out of him. After a long moment, he straightened, but still said nothing.

"Corporal Sloat," Raisa said, and enjoyed seeing him flinch when she spoke his name. "Just stop it. I can tell you what you want to know."

"No, Your Highness," Amon said, shaking his head. "Don't tell him anything."

"We brought three salvos with us, Highlanders loyal to the line," Raisa said, looking Sloat in the eyes. "I expect they'll be here any minute."

Sloat laughed for show, but Raisa noticed he glanced around just the same.

Raisa pressed her point. "When my mother hears what you've done, you will find out what vengeance means to a Gray Wolf queen."

Startled into honest speech, Sloat blurted, "Oh, yeah? Well, we an't taking you back to the queen. Least not right away."

"What?" It was Raisa's turn to be startled. "Why not? What's this all about?"

Sloat smiled. "Never you mind, Your Highness. We're taking you back to Lieutenant Gillen, and he says the queen'll be no problem."

"Gillen? *Mac* Gillen?" That was the greasy-haired, snaggle-toothed sergeant of the Queen's Guard who had tortured prisoners at Southbridge Guardhouse and threatened to put her on the rack. And for that he was made *lieutenant*?

Raisa's mind raced. Gillen was in Southbridge, wasn't he? What could he possibly have to do with . . . Never mind. Gillen was nasty, but he was just the muscle. Somebody else was yanking his strings. Sloat must be convinced he'd never hang for it, or he wouldn't be telling her this much.

She glanced at Amon, bloody and bound tightly, his arms still pinioned by two of the renegade guardsmen, who no doubt knew his reputation as a fighter. Raisa could tell from his intent and focused expression that he was trying to think of something, any way, to change these impossible odds.

Sloat yanked on his gloves. "All right, let's get out of here," he said. "You'll ride double with me, Your Highness." Seizing Raisa's arm, he dragged her toward his horse.

"What about him?" one of the guards gripping Amon asked.

"Take him into the woods and kill him," Sloat said. "We'll ride on ahead."

"You—wouldn't—dare!" Raisa said, struggling to rip free.

"Well, yes, I would, Your Highness," Sloat said, grinning, keeping tight hold on one wrist while he swung up onto his horse. "You see, Corporal Byrne went mad with desire and kidnapped the princess he was supposed to protect. When we tried to rescue you, he resisted and was killed. And you're going to keep your mouth shut because you don't want word to get out that you was out here carrying on with a soldier." Looking pleased with the story he'd made up, Sloat leaned down and reached out his other hand, meaning to haul Raisa into the saddle in front of him.

When Sloat's smug face appeared at eye level, Raisa stiffened her fingers and stabbed them into his eyes, a technique Amon had shown her all those many years ago. Sloat howled, back-handing her across the face with such force that she landed on the ground, the breath exploding from her lungs.

Raisa spat out blood from a split lip. The mounted corporal

loomed high over her, rubbing his streaming eyes, his face purple with rage. Then he stiffened, eyes bulging, rage dissolving into surprise. He groped behind his back, flinched again, then toppled off his horse, narrowly missing Raisa. He ended with his head and shoulders on the ground, one foot caught in his stirrup. Two black-fletched arrows bristled his back.

Demonai arrows.

Bedlam ensued. Guards dove for cover, including Amon's captors, who abandoned him at the center of the field. Horses ripped free of their tethers and plunged into the woods. Spooked by the body dragging at its stirrup, Sloat's horse screamed and kicked, and Raisa had to roll one way, and then another, to avoid its flying hooves.

Running a zigzag course, Amon charged across the field and shouldered Sloat's horse so it wouldn't trample Raisa. "Go!" he shouted, jerking his head toward the trees. "Get under cover!"

He made too good a target standing there holding back the horse with his body. Raisa rolled to her feet and ran in a half-crouch to Amon. Pulling free her belt knife, she cut the cords binding Amon's hands.

"They're Demonai," Raisa gasped into Amon's ear. "The archers. On our side."

More Demonai arrows arced over the meadow, and two more guards fell, one with an arrow sticking out of his throat. The attack was all the more frightening because the archers were silent, apparently invisible.

Amon pulled Raisa into the edge of the forest, shoving her up against a tree.

"Stay here," he growled. Snatching up his quarterstaff, he

waded into the meadow, swinging it at the renegades fleeing in all directions.

"Amon!" Raisa called. "Be careful." She wasn't at all sure the Demonai would distinguish between Amon and the rest of the guards.

It was all over in a matter of minutes. Amon stood alone in the clearing, breathing hard. All of the guards were down, four felled by Amon and his wicked staff.

Raisa quieted Sloat's panicked horse and yanked the dead guardsman's boot free of the stirrup. Shadows in the fringes of the woods coalesced and came forward, some dragging the bodies of the guards who'd fled into the trees. All at once there were a half dozen Demonai in the meadow, clad in their nearly invisible traveling cloaks.

Two of them walked toward Raisa. One, tall and raptor-eyed, she recognized as the warrior Reid Demonai, called Nightwalker. His shoulder-length hair was sectioned off into multiple plaits wrapped in colorful thread. Raisa had met him at Demonai, though he wasn't in camp much. Only two years older than Raisa, he was already a legend, hotheaded and deadly, the object of much speculation by the girls in the camps.

In fact, he and Raisa had shared a brief romance during her time at Demonai Camp. But she'd found that a romance with Reid was like fighting a series of daily skirmishes in an ongoing war of egos.

The girl beside him looked to be about Raisa's age, and she moved with an easy, long-legged grace that Raisa envied. Her head of dark curls hung free from thread wrappings. Though dressed in Demonai colors and fully armed, she did not wear the

Demonai warrior amulet around her neck.

"Find out if any of them still live," Reid said to the girl, who broke away to kneel beside the nearest fallen guardsman.

"Princess Raisa, how goes it with you?" Reid asked calmly, as if they were meeting at a harvest feast.

But his eyes gave him away. They glittered with excitement and feral joy. His face and clothing splattered with bluejacket blood, the Demonai warrior looked elated, exhilarated by the recent battle. Nightwalker was much too fond of bloodshed.

"Did the Vale-dwellers harm you?" he asked, looking her up and down, taking in her cadet uniform. "I saw the guardsman strike you." He reached out and ran his thumb along the corner of Raisa's mouth, then wiped her blood on his leggings.

"I am well, Nightwalker," Raisa said, licking her finger and rubbing her face. "Please accept my thanks for your service to the line."

Reid inclined his head, accepting his due, his dark eyes riveted on her in a way that most girls found irresistible.

Raisa felt Amon's presence beside her, and turned. He'd found his shirt and sword belt, and slid them on. Blood already soaked through from his wounded shoulder.

"Corporal Byrne, this is Reid Demonai, called Nightwalker," Raisa said. "Corporal Byrne is a member of my personal guard," she said to Reid.

"Son of Edon Byrne?" Reid asked. When Amon nodded, Reid said, "I know your father. An honest Valesman," he said, as if that were a rare find.

"Do you have a healer with you?" Raisa asked. "Corporal Byrne is wounded."

"There's no need, Your Highness," Amon said, expressionless. "It's not serious."

Reid's gaze flickered from Raisa to Amon. "You fought well, Corporal," Reid conceded. "Once you were—ah—free."

The young warrior returned, having finished her survey. "All dead," she said.

"Too bad," Reid said. "I would have liked to have saved at least one for questioning." He tilted his head toward the girl next to him. "This is Digging Bird of Marisa Pines Camp, a warrior apprentice. Her arrows took three of the enemy today."

The girl bowed her head, her cheeks coloring.

Digging Bird has a bad case of Reid Demonitis, Raisa thought. "You fought very well," she said, smiling at the warrior. "I'm sure it won't be long before you carry the Demonai name and amulet."

"Thank you for coming to our aid," Amon said, the words propelled by his relentless honesty. "If not for you, I would be dead, and the princess heir a captive."

Reid shrugged as if to say, it was nothing.

"Which raises a question," Amon went on. "How did you happen to be here?"

"We often patrol this area," Reid said. "Watching for jinxflingers and trespassers. The Guard presence in these parts has been rather thin."

"Then you weren't following us?" Amon asked.

Reid's eyes narrowed. He glanced at Digging Bird, then back at Amon. "Well, yes. We were." Raisa suspected he might have lied had the girl not been there as witness.

"We would have welcomed you to our fire," Amon went on.

"We were watching over the princess heir," Reid admitted without apology.

"Well then," Amon said. "Good you were here." He did not smile. "We should get back to camp," he said, looking at Raisa. "Hallie may have missed you by now, and we'd better move on. Lieutenant Gillen may be nearby."

"You would be welcome to be our guest at Demonai Camp, Briar Rose," Reid said, using Raisa's clan name. "We would be glad to offer escort."

"We just came from there," Raisa said. "We're heading for Westgate. I'm leaving the Fells for now, until I can get things . . . sorted out with the queen."

"Are you sure that's wise? To leave the Spirits?" Reid raised an eyebrow.

Raisa felt a prickle of unease, the return of her earlier forebodings. "It's not that I want to leave," she said. "It's just that right now it doesn't seem wise to stay."

"We can protect you, Your Highness. No one will touch you at Demonai." He smiled and touched the longbow that slanted across his back. "No one should force you from your birthright. I urge you to seek the protection of the clans."

Raisa bit back a harsh response. After all, Nightwalker had just saved her from . . . Gillen, for a start. But she didn't like the suggestion that she was running away.

Wasn't that just what she was doing? Shouldn't she stay and hold her ground? When she was queen, she wouldn't be able to run from conflict.

When she said nothing, Reid pressed on, encouraged by her silence. "Given the dangers here, it may seem safer in the flatlands, but that is an illusion. Away from the protection of the camps, you will be vulnerable to flatlander assassins."

"It is not my own safety I'm worried about," Raisa snapped. "I do not intend to start a war. We can't afford it right now. It would tear the country apart."

"It's time to teach the jinxflingers a lesson," Reid said. "We cannot continue to appease them while they trample over—"

"If I meant to appease wizards, I would be married by now," Raisa interrupted. "I will protect the Gray Wolf line. But I will not choose between my parents. I will allow time for cooler heads and good sense to prevail."

"It seems to me the Princess Raisa has made her intentions clear," Amon said. "If there's nothing else, we need to get back and break camp before nightfall."

Reid stared at Amon for a long moment. Then turned to Raisa and inclined his head. "Of course, Your Highness. I just wanted you to know that you have options. Naturally, we would be honored to escort you back to your camp."

He swung around to Digging Bird, who was watching this exchange with intense interest and not a little surprise.

She's probably never seen anyone say no to Nightwalker before, Raisa thought.

"Round up the loose horses," Reid ordered Digging Bird. "Find suitable mounts for Princess Raisa and Corporal Byrne."

Reid Demonai would be happy to see a war, Raisa realized. It's what he lives for.

CHAPTER FOUR
DELPHI

Mountain towns are all different, Han thought.

Mountain towns are all the same.

Geography drives architecture in a mountain town. In Delphi, the houses and other buildings were jammed together, like they'd slid down the slopes and jumbled into the available space along the river.

Houses built onto a hillside are deceiving: short one-stories at the back, and tall four-stories at the front. They reminded Han of brightly painted fancy girls that had seen better days. They backed into the mountainside and spread their long skirts down to the valley floor, their dirty petticoats in the gutters. The streets were narrow and tangled and cobbled with stone—a material plentiful and cheap in the mountains.

Forced into the rocky Kanwa canyon, the streets veered drunkenly around the smallest obstacles—sometimes losing their way entirely.

It was fully dark when they finally descended into the town. A choking pall of smoke thickened the air, requiring extra effort to breathe.

"It stinks worse than Southbridge," Han said, wrinkling his nose. A different, unfamiliar stink, at least.

"They burn coal for heat and cooking here," Dancer explained. "The smoke gets trapped in the valley. It's worse in winter—the fires burn night and day."

There was money in town. Intermingled with stores and businesses and more modest dwellings were street-front palaces and rich-looking row houses. Some of the houses occupied entire city blocks, faced with kilned brick and carved stone.

"Mine owners," Dancer explained. "But even the miners make good money. The war in Arden has stoked the market for iron and coal, and prices are high. Lightfoot says the Delphians don't mind the stinking air. They say they're breathing money. It's allowed them to keep their own army and stay independent of both Arden and the Fells."

As they neared the center of town, the streets clogged up with people, reminding Han of Fellsmarch on market day.

It was a diverse crowd—black-skinned men and women from Bruinswallow, clad in the loose, striped clothing of the southerners. Southern Islanders with their dark skin, elaborate jewelry, and tangles of black hair. Leggy Northern Islanders with fair hair and blue eyes, some haloed with auras. Multiple languages collided in the streets, and exotic music poured from inns and taverns.

There was more evidence of wartime prosperity—elegant shops with all manner of trade goods; jewelry stores with glittering displays, take-away food stores with exotic offerings and intriguing, spicy smells. Han's stomach rumbled and his mouth watered.

"Let's find something to eat," he said, resisting the temptation to nick a twist of salt bread from a street vendor. Hunger always seemed to bring out his old habits, but he knew better than to do slide-hand in unfamiliar territory, with no escape route laid out.

You don't need to steal to eat, he reminded himself, touching the money pouch tucked inside his leggings as if it were a talisman.

Farther south, the city seemed darker than Fellsmarch. Everything was layered with a veneer of soot that soaked up light.

"Don't they have lamplighters here?" Han asked, as their tired ponies plodded through a splash of light spilling from a narrow storefront church skirted on three sides with tall steps. A black-robed cleric with a golden rising sun emblazoned on his robes swept leaves and dirt out of the doorway, sending debris raining down on their heads.

Dancer shook his head. "No lamps, nor lamplighters," he said. He fingered his amulet, conjuring a blossom of light on the tips of his fingers while Han looked on enviously. Han touched his own flashpiece, and power sizzled down his arm, exploding in flames that rocketed halfway across the street, startling passersby.

Embarrassed, Han tucked his offending hand under his other arm.

"Demons!" someone shouted in the Common speech. "Sorcerors! Blasphemers!" Han looked up in surprise to see the black–robed priest charging down the steps, swinging the broom over his head like a weapon, his face contorted with rage.

Ragger skittered sideways, rolling his eyes and showing his teeth to the irate priest. Han dug in his heels, and the pony lunged forward, carrying him out of danger. Dancer ducked his head and wrenched Wicked to one side as the broom whistled past.

The priest screamed after them, "Abominations! Harlots of evil! Begone, you wicked tools of the Breaker!" He shook the broom at them, seeming to think he'd driven them off.

"Shaddap, ya nasty crow of Malthus, or I'll break *you*!" a bulky, bearded miner shouted at the priest, to general laughter. The priest retreated back inside, driven by a chorus of catcalls and threats.

"What was *that* all about?" Han said, when they were a safe distance away. "I've been called a lot of names, but never a harlot of evil before."

"Meet the Church of Malthus," Dancer said, grinning. "The state church of Arden. They have a foothold in Delphi, but I guess they're not especially popular up here."

Speaker Jemson had talked about the Church of Malthus at the Southbridge Temple School. After the disaster of the Breaking, the ancient empire of the Seven Realms had fractured. In the Fells, the old faith had continued, anchored by the temples where speakers taught about the duality of the Maker and the Breaker, and the Spirit Mountains, where dwelt the dead and sainted queens.

In Arden, after the Breaking, there arose an influential speaker who had pruned and shaped the ancient faith in a new direction.

Saint Malthus attributed the Breaking to the Maker's displeasure with the charmcasters that had caused it. Magic, he'd taught, was not a gift but the tool of the Breaker, and wizards were demons in his employ. Seduced by wizards, the queens of the Fells were equally to blame. Queen Hanalea in particular was seen as a kind of beautiful witch—a wanton totally without scruples.

Ever since, Church of Malthus had thrived as the state church in Arden.

"Do you think this is the kind of welcome we'll get in Arden?" Han mused.

Dancer grinned wryly. "I think the less jinxflinging we do in Arden, the better."

This was new to Han—the notion that magic was somehow sinful. The clans despised wizards, but it was more an issue of history and abuse of power. The clans, after all, had their own magic.

It was only the Demon King—Alger Waterlow, Han's ancestor—who was thought to be unequivocally evil.

"This place looks good," Han said, pointing out a two-story building with a broad front porch crowded with locals and soldiers. The tavern was called The Mug and Mutton, and the wooden sign out front bore a grinning sheep hoisting a mug of ale.

Han had an eye for taverns and inns. They'd been a second home for him since he was small—where food, drink, and easy pickings came together. He could tell which places were worth a visit by the smells spilling from them and the custom on hand.

He and Dancer dismounted. Dancer stayed with the horses while Han fought his way through the crowd onto the porch and into the noisy interior.

The clientele inside mirrored those on the porch, except for several families seated around tables. Some had come straight from the mines, their clothes black with soot, and their eyes shining against their grimy faces. Soldiers leaned against the walls, clad in a motley of uniforms—the sober dun colors of Delphi, the scarlet of Arden, unemployed mercenaries who showed no colors, and a few Highlanders and stripers.

Otherwise there were students, tradespeople, and fancies.

Han parted with a few of his precious girlies, booking a room and spending a couple of extra coppers on a chance at a bath. Delphi was pricy, all right.

Han and Dancer led their horses down a narrow alley to the stable behind the inn, ordered extra grain rations for the ponies, and entered the tavern by the back door.

Dinner came with the room and consisted of pork stew (not mutton), a hunk of brown bread, and a tankard of ale.

Han claimed a table in the corner with his back to the wall but close to the back door. That way he could see all the comings and goings without being obvious about it.

The serving girl hovered, flirting. At first Han put it down to personal charm until he realized with some surprise that, despite their days on the road, he and Dancer were as prosperous-looking as anyone in the room.

Han had been booted from plenty of taverns in Ragmarket and Southbridge on suspicion of slide-hand and cheating at cards. That and his chronic inability to pay. He found he rather liked sitting at a table to eat until his stomach was full, chatting up pretty girls without fear of being chased off.

"What's the news of the war in the south?" Han asked the

plush, apple-cheeked server. He touched her arm. "Who's winning?"

She leaned close to Han. "There was a big battle outside the capital last month, sir. Prince Geoff's armies won, so he holds Ardenscourt. He's declared himself king."

"What about the other brothers? Have they given up?" Han asked, wondering if the war would soon be over, and what that would mean for his future.

The girlie shrugged. "All I know is what I hear in the taproom. I believe Prince Gerard and Prince Godfrey are also still alive, and as far as I know, they've not given up."

"There aren't any princesses?" Han asked.

She squinted at him. "Aye, there's one princess. Lisette. But princesses in Arden are just for show. And marrying off."

Han glanced at Dancer, who shrugged. How would you even tell if a king's blooded heirs were really his? Flatlanders were peculiar, for sure.

Han watched as the server walked away, wondering when she'd be off work.

He continued his study of the other patrons. It didn't take long to figure out who was armed and who wasn't, what weapons they carried, and who toted a heavy purse. A while longer, and he knew who was skilled at cards, who at nicks and bones, and who was cheating at both.

This was courtesy of Han's brief stint as a card hustler. That kind of thievery was harder to prove, if you were any good at it. The bluejackets weren't so likely to toss you in gaol for picking pockets at cards.

But he'd learned it was easy to get cornered in a taproom full of sore losers. Also that angry gamblers aren't above smashing your head in, whether they know how you're cheating or not. Especially when you're only thirteen, and haven't got your growth.

Dancer was edgy and restless all through the meal, flinching at sudden noises—the clatter of pots and pans on the hearth or two drunks shouting at each other. Despite his knowledge of Delphi and Delphian ways, he didn't care for cities in general and crowds in particular. As soon as he finished eating, he stood. "I'm going up," he said.

"I booked a bath," Han said generously. "You go first."

Dancer eyed him suspiciously. "Stay out of trouble, will you?" he said.

"Yes, Dancer *Cennestre*." *Yes, Mother*. Han grinned at Dancer's back when he turned away. Han motioned to the server and ordered cider. He meant to keep his wits sharp and his hand off his amulet.

Han idly surveyed the next table, where a foursome played royals and commons, a Fellsian card game Han knew well. The man facing Han was cheating—a needle point for sure. An over-plush man in Ardenine flatlander garb, his round face was cratered from some ancient bout with the pox. Though it was cool in the common room, he mopped at his sweating face with a large handkerchief. Coppers and girlies and notes of promise were stacked in front of him, evidence of his success.

It didn't take long for Han to figure out his system. The sharp was a busy man for someone so large, always flailing his hands around in a distracting way. He used the distraction to second deal, bottom deal, and palm cards. He won nearly every hand he dealt, and a good number of those he didn't—losing just often enough to kill suspicion.

Han wasn't impressed. The sharp was just your standard hand mucker with a rowdy, aggressive style of play. The smart players came and went, soon perceiving that they were at a disadvantage. But one player stayed throughout, stubbornly trying to win back her losses.

She sat with her back to Han, a brimmed hat pulled low over her head, collar turned up, shoulders hunched. Han guessed she was a girlie close to naming age, a Southern Islander from her dark skin and curls. Under her overlarge coat, she wore the brilliant colors Southern Islanders favored, but her clothes were ill-fitting, as though they had been borrowed, begged, or stolen.

Something about her seemed familiar—the way she tilted her head and danced in her chair, jiggling her leg as if she couldn't quite sit still. Han craned his neck, but couldn't get a good look at her face under the hat.

Han drank his cider and tried to ignore the drama playing out in front of him, but his eyes kept straying back to the girl and her increasingly desperate wagers. She ran out of money and continued with scrips for payment.

She should know better, Han thought. Anyone who wins that much is cheating.

Finally, the flatlander drained his mug of ale and slammed it down on the table. "Well, I'm cashing in," he said loudly. "Mace Boudreaux knows enough to quit while Lady Luck's still smiling."

Two of the players scowled, collected their depleted stakes, and left.

The island girl did not rise. She sat frozen for a moment, then leaned forward. "Nuh-uh. Let's keep playing. You got to give me a chance to win it back," she said. Her voice was soft and musical, carrying the familiar cadence of the Southern Islands.

Han's skin prickled in recognition.

"Sorry, girlie, I'm done," Mace Boudreaux said. "Guess luck's running against you. Time to pay up." He raked in the money in front of him and secreted it in several hidey places on his person. Then pushed the payment notes across the table to the girlie.

She stared down at the scraps of paper on the table in front of her.

She doesn't have it, Han thought. She's done.

"I'll be right back with the rest of it," she said, jackknifing to her feet and turning toward the door.

The sharp's hand snaked out and grabbed the girlie around the wrist, jerking her toward him. "Oh no you don't," he growled. "I'm not letting you out of my sight until you pay up."

The girl tried to yank her hand free. "I don't carry that kind of money around. I got to get it from my room."

Boudreaux stuck his face in close to the girl's. "I'll just come with you, then," he said, licking his lips and looking her up and down with a greasy smile. "If you don't have the money, there may be a way you can earn it out."

The girlie spat in his face. "In your dreams, you scummer-sucking, limp-nippled, gutter-spawned—"

"Do you want to go to gaol?" Boudreaux growled, brushing away the spit and giving her a bone-rattling shake.

The girl stiffened. Han could tell from the ropy scars on her wrists and ankles that she'd been in gaol. He guessed she didn't want to go back.

"I'll call the guard," Boudreaux threatened, his voice rising. "I got rights."

Before Han could put two thoughts together, he was standing next to their table. "Hey, now. Just a friendly game, right? No need to get the guard involved, is there?" He slapped the sharp on the back and punched him in the shoulder, grinning like a country boy deep in his cups.

Boudreaux glared at Han, unhappy with the unexpected intrusion. "It'll be friendly as long as the girlie pays up. I got rights."

"You can work something out." Han swung around to face the girl, and nearly fell over from surprise.

It was Cat Tyburn, who'd replaced Han as streetlord of the Raggers. She stared back at him, frozen. Han blinked, looked again, and she was still Cat. She'd changed, and not for the better. No wonder he hadn't recognized her at first.

She'd always been thin, but now she was skin and bones, like a razorleaf user. Her eyes seemed to take up half her face, and they were cloudy and dull—likely from drink and leaf. She'd always been proud, but now she looked beaten down. There were holes in her ears and nose where her silver had been, and her silver bracelets and bangles were gone also. All of it lay in front of the sharp.

Her face said that the last person she expected to see in the world was Han Alister.

Han grabbed Boudreaux's arm to steady himself and cover his amazement. As he did so, he slid a spare deck off the table and into his pocket, his mind working furiously.

What was she doing there? Cat had been born in the islands, but as long as he'd known her, she'd never strayed far beyond the few blocks that made up Ragmarket. Why would she leave when she had a good gang, good turf, and a good living?

More important, how could he help her out of the mess she was in? It sure wouldn't do her any good to land in a Delphian jail.

He could accuse Boudreaux of cheating, but he'd long ago learned to keep his mouth shut in a tavern unless he knew the clientele. For all he knew, he was surrounded by Boudreaux's best mates.

Cat still stared at Han like he'd crawled out of the grave and given her a cold cadaver kiss.

"C'm over here, girlie," Han slurred, taking her elbow. "Le's you and me talk." Her body went rigid under his hand, but she allowed him to tow her out of earshot of the pock-faced sharp.

When they were at a safe distance, Han suddenly sobered up.

"What are you doing here?" he hissed.

"I could ask you the same question," she retorted.

"I asked first."

Cat's face shuttered tight. "I had to leave Ragmarket."

"Who's streetlord, then?" Han asked, stumbling into speech. "What about Velvet?"

"Velvet's dead," Cat said. "They all are—or disappeared. No need for a streetlord in Ragmarket now." She shivered, her ragged nails picking at her coat. "They came right after you left. Killed everyone. I'm alive because I wasn't there."

"Who came?" Han asked, because it seemed expected, though he already knew.

"Demons. Like the ones that did the Southies." She wouldn't meet his eyes.

Han's mouth was dry as dust. "Did they . . . were they looking for me?"

"Like I *said*, I wasn't there." Not an answer. "I didn't know where you'd gone. I thought they'd hushed you too."

Bones. He left death behind him even when he went away. No wonder Cat was jittery.

"I'm real sorry about Velvet," Han said. "And . . . everything."

She just looked at him, eyes wide, shaking her head no.

"Come on, girlie!" Boudreaux roared. "You two gonna talk all night or what? I want my money."

Han waggled his hand at the sharp to quiet him and leaned in close to Cat. "How much do you owe your friend over there?" he whispered.

"Why?" Cat demanded with her usual charm. "What business is it of yours?"

"I don't got all night," Han said. "How much?"

She looked around the room, as if seeking escape from the question. "Twenty-seven girlies and some change," she said.

Hanalea's blood and bones. Han had money, but not enough to pay off her debt and still get to Oden's Ford. And he didn't mean to beggar himself paying off a cheating needle point.

Han tilted his head toward Boudreaux. "He's cheating, you know."

"He is not!" Cat hissed, looking over her shoulder. "I'm cheating him."

Han knew not to smile. "Well." He rubbed his chin. "He's doing a better job."

Cat's hand crept to the blade at her waist. "The thieving dung-eater. I should've known. Well, we'll see how he looks without his—"

"No." Han put his hand on her arm to stay her. "I'll play for you and win it back."

Cat jerked away from him. "Leave off, Cuffs. I don't want your help. I got into this myself, and I'll get out of it my own way."

"By cutting his throat?" Han shook his head. "In Ragmarket, maybe. You don't want to get into trouble so far from home."

She shook her head. "I don't want to owe you," she said.

Well, that he could understand. "You won't owe me. I'm the one owes you a blood debt."

Again, she shook her head wordlessly, swallowing hard several times.

"Let me do this," Han said. "Please."

"Anyway, the needle point's done," Cat said. "He won't play. He said so."

"He'll play me," Han said, pulling out a bulging purse and waving it under her nose.

Cat's eyes went wide again. She swept back her hair, trying to act offhand, like she saw that kind of plate every day. "What if you lose?"

"Trust me. I won't. I'm better than him," Han said, looking into her eyes and willing her to believe him, though he had no idea why she would. "Just play along with me, all right?" he said. Facing away from the gambler, he prepped for the game, moved money around, stacked and stowed his cards while Cat watched, all squint-eyed.

"All set. Come on," he said, possessing her arm and strutting back to Boudreaux's table like he was the cock of the yard. "I'll cover the girlie's debt," he said to the sharp. "If you play me."

"Play *you*?" Boudreaux said disdainfully. "Nuh-uh. I told you I was done. If you want to pay what the girlie owes, go ahead, boy. If you even got the money."

"My da's a trader," Han said, conjuring an aggrieved expression. "I got plenty of money. See?" He plunked his full purse on the table, in the process knocking over the sharp's glass of ale, spilling the remains. "Oh, sorry," he said. "Don't know m'own strength." He plucked Boudreaux's handkerchief out of the sharp's pocket and mopped clumsily at the spillage.

Boudreaux's greedy eyes fastened on the purse. It was much more than Cat owed. "Well," he said, wedging himself back in his chair, "mayhap I can stay a little longer." He snapped his fingers at the server. "Bring me another ale," he said with a toothy smile.

Han handed the sopping handkerchief back to Boudreaux and settled into the chair opposite the sharp. It figured. He had no trouble swaying a mark these days, now that he was out of the game. It was easier to believe in a sixteen-year-old with a wad of cash than a twelve-year. It was that lack of respect as a *lytling* that had forced him out of sharping into slide-hand and rushing on the streets.

Now he was better suited to the con. He could play the role of the son of a trader, out on his own for the first time. A warm and loaded mark for sure.

"You sit here, girlie," Han said, patting the seat of the chair next to him and leering at Cat. "Bring me luck."

Cat perched on the edge of the chair, angled away from Han

like she might catch the itches. Her hands twisted together in her lap, her face hard and inscrutable.

"You deal first, boy," Boudreaux said blandly. Typical sharp. Let the mark win first, to encourage him to bet bigger on the next round.

Han shuffled the cards, at one point losing hold of them, spilling them onto the table. Careful, he thought. Don't overdo it. He scooped them up and reshuffled them with the bleary, intense attention typical of the very drunk.

It was easy enough to win the first round. Boudreaux folded, shaking his head mournfully, before there was much money on the table.

"Ha!" Han crowed, closing his hand over Cat's. She flinched as if stung, and he let go. "You've brought me luck already." She just looked back at him, unsmiling.

Why, Alister, *why* do you get yourself tangled up in these things? Han thought.

Now Boudreaux dealt the cards, and won, though Han didn't allow much money to go out before he called for display. After that, it was back and forth a few times, and at the end of it, Han was ahead by ten girlies. He continued to play the drunken fool, loudly celebrating his good fortune and boo-hooing when he lost.

Han hadn't even mucked the deck so far. The handkerchief was out of play, and Han ruined Boudreaux's sleight of hand by insisting on cutting the cards before the deal. Plus he was naturally lucky at cards.

As Mam had always said, *Lucky at cards, or lucky at life. One or the other. Not both.*

Boudreaux's enthusiasm waned along with his winnings. Cat

just sat there scowling, as though Han were playing with her money.

Time to finish this, Han thought. I'll teach the sharp a lesson, send Cat away with her money, and go to bed. The deck came back to him, and this time he seized it in a sharp's grip and mucked it good during the shuffle. Boudreaux made the cut, and Han remade the deck during the deal. He watched Boudreaux's face as he scanned his cards. The sharp cradled his hand close to his chest like a baby, and Han knew he had him.

They bet and raised and bet and raised, and soon there were stacks of girlies in the center of the table. The sharp asked for one card, and Han handed him the demon card that would seal the deal. Han fanned his cards within the shelter of his hands, peered at them, licked his lips nervously, and matched the sharp's bets every time.

Cat kept looking from Han to the stacks of money at the center of the table, twitching the way she did when she was nervous. If he lost, he'd be in the hole big time.

But he wouldn't lose.

By now several patrons had wandered over from the bar to watch the action.

"What about her silver?" Han asked, waving his hand at the pot as the wagers mounted. "Put that in and I'll match it in girlies." He grinned over at Cat.

Boudreaux pushed Cat's studs, bangles, and earrings into the center of the table. "Display," he said, spreading his cards on the table. "A demon triple, red dominant." He looked up at Han and grinned a wolfish grin.

It *was* a fine hand. A very fine hand. That hand would beat just about anything. Except: "Four queens, Hanalea leads the line." Han displayed *his* cards on the table and sat back, watching the sharp.

For a long, charged moment, Boudreaux said nothing. He stared down at the table like he couldn't believe what he was seeing. Reaching out his thick forefinger, he stirred the cards in front of him as if they might reveal something else.

The flatland sharp opened and closed his mouth like a beached fish, and it took several tries before any sound came out. "That—that ain't right!" he bellowed, slamming his hand down on the table, putting his replacement ale at risk.

Han briskly raked his winnings into his carry bag and tossed it over his shoulder, leaving enough girlies on the table to pay Cat's debt. The key in such situations was a quick getaway.

Boudreaux's piggy eyes narrowed with rage. He slung out an arm and took hold of Han's shirtfront. "Not so fast," he hissed.

"Let go!" Han said, trying to pull free.

"You're a cheat!" Boudreaux shouted, producing a large curved knife from under his coat and pressing it against Han's throat. "A cheat and a thief and a fraud."

The onlookers surrounding the table stepped back a pace.

The blade was a nasty surprise. Most sharps and card muckers were cowards at heart, which was why they chose that mode of thievery. But Boudreaux outweighed Han twice over, and Han knew from experience that there was nobody more furious than a cheat cheated.

Han thought of the flash under his shirt, the knives at his waist, wondering if he could reach either or any without getting his throat cut.

"Now," the sharp said, his florid face inches from Han's, his beery breath pouring over him, "give over the bag, boy, and I might not cut off your ears."

Focused on the blade under his chin, Han didn't quite follow what happened next. Boudreaux yelped and disappeared, hitting the floor hard enough to dent it. His knife spun across the room, nearly beheading a miner snoring softly at the next table.

Han threw himself back, out of danger. Boudreaux flailed about on the floor like he had the spasms. And behind him, deftly avoiding his flying limbs, was Cat, a garrotte twisted around Boudreaux's throat.

Oh, right, Han thought. Cat was a deft flimper, as well as a demon with a blade.

The sharp's face turned red, then blue, and his eyes bulged out alarmingly. Cat bent low over Boudreaux, crooning to him, some lesson she wanted him to learn.

Boudreaux's flailing diminished, became less organized.

"Cat!" Han shook off his astonishment and put his hand on her shoulder. "Leave him go. You don't want to swing for him."

Cat looked up at him, blinking as if surfacing from a trance. She let go of Boudreaux and sat back on her heels, stuffing the garrote into her pocket.

A commotion at the front drew Han's attention. A clot of brown uniforms filled the doorway, colors of the Delphian Guard. Han swore, knowing he'd stayed too long. He stood slowly and pulled Cat to her feet. Keeping hold of her hand, Han began backing toward the rear door, but a bristle-bearded miner the size of a small mountain stepped into their path.

"You'd best stay, boy, and take what's coming to you for what you done," he growled, grinning as though he personally were looking forward to the show.

"I didn't do anything," Han complained, the refrain of his entire life. It was just his luck to get mixed up in a barroom brawl in a strange country and get tossed in gaol. It would mean a quick end to his career as a wizard sell-sword for the clans. He'd let down Dancer, who'd have to travel on alone. What was the last thing Dancer had said to him before he went up to bed? *Stay out of trouble.*

Han closed his hand around the hilt of his knife, looking for the clearest path to the door. Then slowly he released his grip. He might get through the door, but he wouldn't get away clean with Dancer upstairs and his horse in the stable.

Cat pulled her hand free and drew her own blades, keeping them hidden flat against her forearms.

"What's going on?" one of the brownjackets demanded. He wore an officer's scarf knotted around his neck, in unfamiliar flatland colors. He pointed at Boudreaux, still on the floor. The sharp rubbed his bruised throat and sucked air in great gasps. "What happened to him?" the officer asked.

Han opened his mouth, but the miner beat him to it. "That cheating thiever Mace Boudreaux got beat at cards for oncet. Turns out he's a sore loser. He jumped the boy what beat him, and we had to settle him."

To Han's astonishment, heads nodded all around.

"Who settled him?" the officer persisted.

"We all did," the miner said, glaring around the room as if daring someone to contradict him. "We all joined in."

It seemed that Cat was not the only one who'd lost money to

Mace Boudreaux. He wasn't getting much sympathy from this crowd.

"Where's the boy what beat him?" the guardsman demanded.

For a moment, nobody spoke, but then Han's miner gave him a shove forward. "This is the one," he said. "He done it."

The brownjacket looked Han up and down as if he couldn't believe it. "Good at cards, are you, boy?" He raised an eyebrow.

Han shrugged. "I get by." He felt rather than saw Cat moving up beside him. Just like the old days, when Cat had his back.

The brownjacket grinned and stuck out his hand. "I'd like to buy you a drink, then," he said, and the rest of the patrons whistled and clapped and stamped their feet.

It just goes to show you, Han thought. You never know who's in the room when you get into a fight.

It was a struggle to get out of there after that. Boudreaux recovered and slunk away unnoticed. Han had to turn down a dozen offers of drinks or he'd have ended up under the table. Cat retreated to a corner, seeming to disappear into the shadows, but every time he turned to look, her eyes were fixed on him.

Probably wants her money, he thought.

It was near closing time when he finally extricated himself from the crowd of well-wishers and joined Cat at her table. Fishing into his carry bag, he withdrew a handful of girlies and counted them out.

She watched, saying nothing. Han didn't expect effusive thanks, but still. Cat usually had plenty to say.

He pushed the stacks of coins across the table toward her. "There you are; you've made up your losses and more."

She looked down at the money but made no move to touch

it. "What is it about you?" she demanded. "Wherever you go, people make way for you. You walk in a stranger and end up the toast of the taproom."

"What are you talking about?" Han growled. "I got nothing—no family, no place to live, no way to make a living."

She reached out and fingered the sleeve of his jacket hesitantly, as if he still might turn to vapor and smoke. "You got fine new clothes and you got a full purse. You sell off a big taking or what?"

Han instantly felt even guiltier. He pressed his lips together and shook his head.

"Why would you risk your stash for me?" she persisted.

"Wasn't my stash," Han said. "I took it off Boudreaux before we played."

Like he was some robber out of the stories that took from the rich and gave to the poor. Ha. He *was* the poor, usually.

"If you already had his money, why'd you play him, then?" Cat asked.

Han shrugged. "He needed beating and I thought I could do it. Never thought he'd pull a knife." He didn't say aloud what else he was thinking. If you beat somebody at the thing they're best at, they're more likely to give way.

Cat eyed him like she didn't much believe him. "You still never said. What are you doing here? Where are you going?"

Han shrugged. "I had to leave Fellsmarch, too. We thought we'd try our luck in Ardenscourt," he lied. The fewer people who knew where they were going, the better.

She lifted an eyebrow. *"We?"*

"I'm traveling with a friend," Han said, leaving Cat to make whatever assumption she chose. "How about you? I didn't know you played nickum sharp."

"I'm still learning, as any fool can see," she said, scowling.

"Well, you can't earn reliable money sharping unless you get more practice at card mucking. Better find another line of work meantime."

"I've looked," Cat said glumly. "I been here for a couple weeks. I tried to get on at the mines, but they won't hire if you're marked as a thief." She held up her right hand, branded by the queen's law. Least they hadn't chopped it off.

"How'd you end up here, anyway?" Han asked.

"I was on my way to a place called Oden's Ford."

Han was taking a gulp of cider, and nearly inhaled it. Coughing, he set the mug down. "Oden's Ford! Why are you going there?"

"It was Speaker Jemson's idea," Cat said, poking at the stacks of coins. "They got schools there, he says. He wanted me to go to the Temple School."

"Why not go to Southbridge Temple School?" Han said, trying to sort out what this might mean to him. "Why would Jemson send you all the way to Oden's Ford?"

"If I was still in Southbridge, I'd be dead. Just like Velvet." Cat yanked off her hat and slapped it down on the table. "They was hunting me, the demons that killed the others. It was just a matter of time before they caught me. So Jemson, he says, go to Oden's Ford. He's always dogging me to go and study music, and he's tight with the master of the Temple School there. He told her all these stories about how I can play the basilka like some kind of angel choir, and got me enrolled. He paid my fees—said the Princess Raisa gives money to Southbridge Temple students. He give me an old horse and some money, and put me on the road." Cat scrubbed her hand through her curls.

Cat was a rum player on the basilka. Back in Ragmarket, she used to play to pass the time until darkman's hour, when the Raggers went to work. Some days Han would just lie there, halfway between waking and sleeping, letting the music carry him someplace else.

"Jemson says if I study music and art and reading and writing and pretty talk, I might get on as a lady's maid or teacher or something." Cat snorted. "Like they'd hire a marked thief."

Han tried to get his mind around the notion of Cat as a lady's maid.

Cat looked up and read his expression. "Forget it. I got this far, then I decided I an't going. Jemson, he thinks he got me backed into a corner, but I an't taking vows."

"You don't have to take vows to go to the Temple School," Han said. "Some do, but you—"

"I don't care. I don't belong there, in a covey of bluebloods. They be sweet as flatland cider to your face while they're gibing behind your back."

She's afraid, Han thought. She's afraid she'll be made fun of. Afraid she won't be good enough. Maybe with good reason. What did he know about Oden's Ford? Nothing.

Cat pushed the money toward Han and stood. "I'm glad for what you did, but I can't take this."

Han made no move to pick it up. "It's your money. Not mine. I just took it back from a thief. If you don't take it, you'll be leaving it for the help."

She shook her head stubbornly, biting her lip.

"Look," Han said. "Here's how I see it. I got a lot to answer for. I owe you. Just let me do this thing, will you?"

It was true. He desperately wanted to ease the load of guilt he carried around.

"If you want to do something for me, here's what I want," Cat said abruptly. "Let me come with you."

"What?" Han gaped at her. It had been a whole evening of surprises. "You don't even know what we're doing!"

"It don't matter," Cat said. "I an't cut out for temple life, no matter what Jemson says. I'll swear to you. Like before."

Like when Han was streetlord of the Raggers, and Cat was his right hand. And more.

Han eyed Cat warily. With Velvet gone, was Cat looking to rekindle what had once been between them? That seemed like a bad idea. When they were together, they'd fought like two cats stuffed into a bag. He had enough drama in his life as it was.

As if she'd read his thoughts, she said, "If you're walking out with a girlie, I won't be inching in," she said. "This is strictly shares. Strictly business."

Thoughts pinged around Han's head like coppers in a jar. Cat thought joining up with her old streetlord was a way to avoid going to school. But he was heading for school himself. He had no need of a crew and no way to support one. He'd be spending money, not earning money, so there'd be no shares.

He looked at Cat. She glared at him, tapping her foot because he was taking too long to answer. He couldn't help recalling that when he'd wanted to go to Demonai Camp with Bird and she'd refused him, she'd had some good reasons, too.

If he refused her, she'd go back to the life for sure. If she went back to the gangs, she'd be dead before she turned twenty, demons or not. Streetlords never got old.

Maybe Jemson was right—maybe school *was* what she needed. Han wouldn't get any thanks for trying to save her. But there might be a way.

"You can come," Han said finally. "But we're going to Oden's Ford ourselves. You come with me, you got to go to school."

"What?" She sat frozen, hands pressed against the table so hard her knuckles were white. "That's a ripe clanker if I ever heard one."

"It's true," Han said. "Why else do you think we—"

"Liar!" Cat shook her head, eyes glittering. "You're a glavering, gutter-swiving, muck-sucking liar, Cuffs Alister, that's what you are. You an't going to Oden's Ford, no bloody way." Cat scraped back her chair and stood, fists clenched, vibrating with rage.

"I swear it," Han said, sliding to his feet and keeping the table between them in case she drew a blade on him. "I'm sorry. I should have told you, but I thought you—"

"Shut it, Cuffs. If you didn't want me to come with, you should've just said so." She scooped up her money and stuffed it into her carry bag. "You think because you're pretty that every girlie wants to walk out with you. Well, you an't so pretty that I can't find somebody else."

She stalked out of the tavern, letting the door slam behind her.

Well, Han thought. Least she's more like her old self, anyway.

CHAPTER FIVE
INTO THE
FENS

After the encounter with the renegade guards on the western slope, Raisa worried they'd have more trouble at Westgate. But when they arrived at the West Wall in the early morning, Mac Gillen was nowhere to be seen. The guards at the gate were mostly regular army, a mixture of gray-jacketed Highlanders and mercenaries with striped trim.

The sergeant in charge was a Queen's Guardsman, though, named Barlow. When Amon told Barlow that they were cadets traveling to Oden's Ford via Westgate, the sergeant greeted him with derision.

"So you don't want to go through Arden, eh? You cadets wouldn't want to get your uniforms dirty, would you?" he said, rolling his eyes. "Wouldn't want to have to blood your shiny new weapons before you show 'em off at school."

It was the typical disdain of the line soldier for the academy-bred. The members of the Wolfpack seethed, but Amon ignored it. He'd seemed preoccupied, having even less to say than usual since the incident with Sloat and the rescue by the Demonai warriors.

Disappointed that Amon didn't rise to the bait, Barlow added, "Well, Corporal, if you think this way's safer than travelin' through Arden, you'll soon find out different."

"What do you mean?" Amon asked, finally granting Barlow his full attention.

The sergeant spat on the ground. "The new road is gone. The Waterwalkers done wrecked it. They heaved a mess of boulders into there."

Amon stared at him. "What? I helped build that road. Why would they do that?"

"The Waterwalkers been raiding over the border, stealing livestock and food," Barlow said. "We put a stop to it, so they busted up the road. Nowdays, if you want to get down to the Fens, you have to take the old road. An' that means climbin' down over the cliff and clinging to the icy rocks by your toenails. Them horses'll never make it."

"I still don't see why they'd destroy the road," Amon persisted. "It was built just a year and a half ago. It seems like they'd be hurting themselves."

The sergeant shrugged, not meeting Amon's eyes. "Guess we an't welcome there no more. Anyways, if you do manage to climb down without breaking your necks, you'll find out why they call it the Shiverin' Fens. You'll be shivering all right. You'll wish you'd gone the other way. Them Waterwalkers'll have you crying for your mommies."

"I assume you're speaking from experience, sir?" Raisa asked.

This drew grins from the other Wolves and a warning look from Amon.

"I was there just a little more than a year ago," Amon said to Barlow, "and had no trouble. I stayed at Rivertown and Hallowmere."

"You did, did you?" The sergeant wet his lips and swallowed. "Well, there's trouble now. Skirmishes all along the border. Bad blood all around."

"Is it really as bad as that?" Raisa asked. "We've not heard anything about this in the capital."

"You listen to me, cadet," Barlow said, his jowly face pinking up with anger. "The Waterwalkers, they got special plans for such morsels as you. They'll feed you to the watergators. That's how they sacrifice to their gods."

"There are no such things as watergators, sir," Raisa said, rolling her eyes.

The sergeant snorted. "Aye, you say that now. We'll see what you say later. If you're alive to make the report. Them watergators grow to be a hunnert feet long with teeth the size of broadswords and just as sharp. I spoke to a man saw one swallow a pole boat whole, with everybody on board."

"We'll be careful, sir," Amon said. "Thank you for the warning. Now move along, Morley," he said to Raisa. "Or you'll be the one raising tents in the dark."

Now what? Raisa wondered. Are we going to walk all the way to Oden's Ford? If we can't take the horses along, we won't have a choice.

The sergeant raised his hand. "Just a minute," he said. "You there. Lady cadets. What's your names?"

"Why do you ask, sir?" Amon asked, edging his horse between the Wolves and the sergeant.

"Well . . ." The sergeant looked up at the garrison house, scowling. "There's some wizardlings in there want to see every young lady what passes through here."

"Why is that, sir?" Hallie drawled. "If you're playing match-maker, I don't go in for jinxflingers, just so you know."

The Gray Wolves snickered, and Barlow's color deepened. "Seems the princess heir has run off or been carried off or some such," he said. "So they're on the lookout for her to cross the border here. Even though, as I said, she'd be a fool to come this way."

"Why are wizards out hunting for the princess?" Amon asked, trying to sound casual. "Isn't that our job?"

"Well, that's what I thought," Barlow said. "You never know, these days. Wizards are sticking their noses where they don't belong."

"Sir, I'm surprised wizards would come to a place as remote as this," Raisa said, trying to keep her voice steady. "Being so used to servants and rich food and all that."

"You got that right," Sergeant Barlow said, eyeing Raisa with a little more approval. "There's three of 'em, and they an't any older 'n you. I hear one of 'em's the son of the High Wizard himself."

Micah! Raisa's mouth went metallic, and a shiver ran through her. She glanced over at Amon, who was expressionless as any statue in the temple.

"Lieutenant Gillen said to give them whatever they want," Barlow went on, "but they been eating and drinking up all the best we got, stayin' up to all hours, then sleeping in, demanding this and that, and never happy with what we give 'em.

"At first they stayed down here at the gate, but there's so little traffic I guess they didn't think it was worth their time. So now they can't be bothered to come down here theirselfs, but they want us to detain any ladies that come through and fetch 'em down here to look 'em over." He hawked and spat on the ground. "We're shorthanded as it is. Sent half a squadron up to Demonai Camp and they an't returned."

Raisa looked up at the garrison house, a huge stone structure with slitted windows that frowned over the road. She turned away quickly, resisting the urge to hide her face. The back of her neck prickled and her heart tremored. At that very moment, Micah Bayar might be gazing down on her.

The memory of his treachery still stung. Micah had bewitched her with his wizard kisses and the help of an illegal seduction amulet. *I think we could be good together*, he'd said. *Once we get through this. This* being a forced wedding between them.

"Well, sir, it seems to me that Talbot, Abbott, and Morley are *soldiers*, not ladies," Amon said calmly, though he clenched his reins so tight his knuckles whitened. "It's bad enough that wizards are poking into places where they have no business. D'you think Lieutenant Gillen would want them interfering with cadets in the Queen's Guard?"

Sergeant Barlow pondered that a moment. "You know, I don't think he would." He took in Hallie's straw-colored braid, Talia's lanky build, and Raisa's ragged cap of hair. "None of you favor the princess anyways."

He looked over his shoulder at the garrison house. "But

mayhap you'd better move along before them wizardlings haul theirselfs out of bed."

Wasting no time in taking the sergeant's advice, they clattered over the stone pavers surrounding the garrison house and between two great statues of carved stone: Queen Hanalea and her daughter, Alyssa, founders of the new line of queens. The ancient queens faced each other across the road, their long shadows pointing the way. Raisa resisted the temptation to look back over her shoulder. They kept moving until they had rounded the shoulder of the mountain and were well out of sight.

"That was close," Raisa said, reining in and speaking low in Amon's ear. "If Micah had been down at the gate . . ." She didn't finish.

Amon nodded. "Thank the Maker that Barlow has no love of wizards."

"What about the Waterwalkers?" Raisa asked. "Was he just trying to scare us?"

Amon shook his head. "I don't know. It doesn't make sense, what he said." He turned away from Raisa and called, "Hey, Garret, ride ahead and check out the road, see if what Sergeant Barlow says is true."

"Aye, Corporal Byrne," Garret said, touching his heels to his pony's sides.

"When can a soldier disobey an order?" Raisa asked.

Amon drew his dark brows together and tilted his head back, looking down his nose at her. "Why do you want to know?"

"I want to know what to expect from my guard in the future."

"Well, soldiers are taught two important rules. One is that

you obey orders, even those you don't like, even those you disagree with. If you don't, it's insubordination. The other is that following orders is no excuse for doing wrong or wasting soldiers' lives needlessly. A good soldier is a thinking person."

Raisa blinked at him. "But . . . isn't that contradictory?"

Amon nodded. "It's the soldier's dilemma. Most of the time it's simple enough. If your commander tells you to clean the latrine, you do it, even though you don't want to. If your commander tells you and your salvo to lead the charge, you do it, even though you're afraid. If she tells you to retreat, you leave the field, even if your blood's up."

Raisa nodded, nudging Switcher in close. "When can you say no?"

"If you disobey an order, you'd better have a good reason. Lots of times you have to make that decision in a heartbeat. That's the problem with the guard these days. Too many soldiers don't know the difference between right and wrong."

Raisa put her hand on Amon's knee. His leg was all muscle and bone under the camouflage twill, and she felt the usual current of energy between them. "Do you feel that you know right from wrong?" she asked.

"I do," Amon said, looking down at her hand. "My da made sure of it." He said this with such intensity that it stopped Raisa's mouth and she waited. After a pause, he went on. "But it's not enough to know right from wrong. You need the strength to do what's right, even when what you want most in the world is the wrong thing."

With that, he urged his horse forward, breaking contact with Raisa's hand.

A mile or so farther on, Raisa became aware of a sound: a dull, sullen roar that grew louder as they traveled forward.

While they'd been talking, the others had gotten ahead of them. Mick rode back toward them. "It's the Dyrnnewater Cascades, sir. Careful. We're nearly on top of them."

It wasn't like you could come up on them unwarned. Ahead, a freezing white mist obscured the trail. As they rode into it, Raisa's skin pebbled and her hair clumped down in wet strings. Water dripped from the end of her nose. Amon turned up the collar of his uniform jacket and raked wet black hair off his forehead.

Now that they were crowded in close to the river, Raisa could smell the faint but familiar stench of the city of her birth. She wrinkled her nose.

A low wall enclosed the road to either side. Ahead, the river split around several large rocky islands and foamed through a series of violent rapids as they neared the escarpment. Switcher became skittish, dancing nervously and tossing her head.

At that point, the new road veered off to the east, descending in a series of switchbacks toward the valley floor. The old road continued straight on, following the river. It was hardly more than a rocky path.

Garret waited at the split. "It's true, sir. The new road's impassable. Road's smashed up less than a mile ahead."

Now what? Raisa thought. Would they have to go back by way of Westgate, past Micah Bayar again? Maybe this time they wouldn't be so lucky.

"Guess we'll have to take the old road," Amon said.

You mean the one where we have to hang on by our toenails? Raisa thought.

"Dismount!" Amon called, then said to Raisa, "Careful. The rocks are slippery, even for the ponies. And if they spook, they'll go right over the edge."

The Gray Wolves swung out of their saddles, clutching nervously at their horses' reins. They walked forward, boots crunching in the strange gray gravel of the path.

And suddenly they were at the edge of the world Raisa knew, overlooking a sea of mist. Hawks wheeled and pivoted over the cliff's edge, borne skyward by the updrafts.

"Lady of light," she breathed. She took a step back, feeling dizzy, as if she might be swept away by the relentless movement of water. Amon gripped her arm to steady her.

The Dyrnnewater poured over the lip of a wide overhang and thundered into the valley below. The river was deep green as it furled over the edge, then exploded in foamy spray as it struck rock on the way down. Mist collected on their hair and clothing, then froze so that within minutes they resembled a collection of silver-headed elders.

This was a sacred place, full of history. During the War of the Wizard Conquest, Queen Regina, the last free queen of the old line, had been trapped with a small army of loyalists at the edge of the escarpment. She had thrown her daughters over the edge, then leaped after them to prevent their being captured. But the river had refused to swallow the queen and the princesses, had cushioned their landing and spat them out alive on the banks below. A miracle by the Maker's hand.

After that, Regina had bowed her proud head, knowing that the line was meant to survive and that its redemption lay somewhere in the future. The queens had passed three hundred years in captivity before the Breaking freed them.

Creeping forward, Raisa peered over the edge. It was like looking down into a milky sea, its features hidden under a mantle of mist. The Shivering Fens were an ocean of grass and stubby trees, nothing tall enough to poke through the grounded clouds.

Raisa shuddered, chilled by the damp and the prospect of climbing down into that mist. The Fells claimed to rule the Shivering Fens, but Raisa had never been there, and as far as she knew, Queen Marianna had not, either. How could they claim allegiance to a place they knew so little about?

Etched into the side of the bluff, alongside the river, she saw the faint tracings of a rocky path, obviously little used. At the top of the cliff stood an abandoned garrison house, the walls in disrepair, heaved and tumbled by repeated freezes and thaws, and next to it, a small shrine to Queen Regina. A marble statue centered the shrine, stained and worn by weather—the fearless queen cradling two babies. Raisa made the sign of the Maker and knelt in the weeds before the queen's altar.

We need to better honor the old ways, she thought. This is my blood, my inheritance, overgrown and neglected. We once ruled the Seven Realms, and now we can barely manage one.

Her prayer finished, she turned to find that Amon had come up beside her. He stood, hands tucked under his arms to warm them, the wind stirring his hair, studying the cliff face, as if he really meant to climb down there.

"That's a road?" she asked, pushing up to her feet. Surely not.

"That was the only road before we built the new one. The Waterwalkers don't use horses, so they had no need of a road that horses and wagons could use."

"And you helped build the new road?"

"Aye. My da offered up the sweat of my brow in trade for learning Waterwalker ways." He paused, chewing his lower lip. "They have a debt and payment system they call *gylden*. They're proud—they'd rather you were in debt to them than they to you.

"Lord Cadri is ruler of the Waterwalkers. Years ago, my father saved his life when he would have bled to death after a hunting accident. Ever since, he's been trying to find a way to pay off the *gylden*, and my da's trying to keep him beholden. Not because he expects repayment, but because it's an advantage to the Fells. My da asked Lord Cadri to foster me for a summer. That should've offset some of the debt. But I helped design and build the road—so he still owes *gylden* to my father."

"Does Queen Marianna know this is going on?" Raisa asked.

Amon shrugged. "I don't know. I don't think so. She's never paid much attention to the Fens, given the war in Arden and troubles at home. Da tries to make sure she doesn't need to. I don't like hearing that there's trouble along the border."

Raisa couldn't help remembering her mother warning her away from any dreams of a match with Amon. *They're soldiers,* the queen had said, *and that's all they'll ever be.*

You have no idea what a treasure you have in the Byrnes, Mother, Raisa thought.

"How do we get down?" she asked, mopping freezing slush from her face.

Amon knelt at the edge of the precipice, examining a rusted metal apparatus bolted to the rock. "We use ropes as a fail-safe," he said. "It's too risky to go down unroped." He turned and shouted orders to the other Wolves, who produced coils of rope from their saddlebags.

"What about the horses?" Raisa asked.

"They go down roped, too." Amon shouldered open the rotting door to the garrison house. Raisa heard him rummaging around inside. He emerged several minutes later, smeared with dirt, cobwebs powdering his hair, but looking pleased with himself. He carried an armload of leather straps, iron fittings, and swivels.

Raisa eyed them distrustfully. How long had they been there? How badly were they damaged by rot and rodents? Switcher tossed her head and snorted, as if sensing Raisa's dismay. Raisa stroked the mare's nose to soothe her.

Amon deftly looped a rope around the large pulley attached to the rocky outcropping, secured it with an iron catch, and attached a swivel. Then he strapped a broad leather harness around his body and between his legs, clipping it to the rope.

"How do you know this will work?" Raisa asked, imagining flailing horses slamming against the cliff face, breaking their legs.

"I've done it before." Amon turned to Mick and Hallie. "I'll go down first, secure the other end, and scout the situation at the bottom. I'll pull on the rope three times to let you know when to pull me up."

Amon tugged on a pair of deerskin gloves. He grasped hold of the rope with both hands, backed to the edge of the cliff, pushed off, and dropped out of sight.

Stifling a cry of dismay, Raisa leaned over the cliff and looked down. The cliff jutted into a severe overhang, nothing but yawning space below. Amon was a hundred feet down already, running rope through the pulley, using his legs to kick off from the cliff face. A moment later, he was swallowed by the mist.

He's done this before, Raisa told herself. How many other secrets was he hiding?

It took the better part of the day to lower the horses, soldiers, and all their supplies down the cliff face to the bottom. The Gray Wolves cut down several thick lodgepole pines and used them to build a hoist for the horses. Amon blindfolded the horses before they lowered them in great leather harnesses fashioned for the purpose. This arrangement kept the horses far from the rocky escarpment, so they couldn't injure themselves, and kept pony panic and mayhem to a minimum. To Raisa's relief, the leather strapping held.

Raisa descended halfway through, when there were equal numbers of guards on top and bottom. Aside from a nasty bruise on her elbow where she struck the cliff face once, some rope burns on her hands, and a raw place on her thigh where the strap chafed her, she arrived uninjured. She found the bounding descent exhilarating—like flying. It helped that she couldn't see all the way to the bottom because of the fog.

Amon seemed vastly relieved when she made it down in one piece. "Just don't ever mention this to the queen, all right?" he said, as if there weren't already a whole list of things not to mention to Marianna. "And don't tell my da you went down on your own."

By the time everyone was settled at the bottom, the daylight was fading. They pitched their tents in the shadow of the rock wall and struggled to kindle fires in the misty damp. After feeding and watering the horses, they stuffed down a quick cold meal. Nobody said much. The freezing fog seemed to press in on them from all sides.

"I'm surprised nobody is here to greet us," Amon said. "The Waterwalkers usually keep a close watch on the Cascades. I'd think they'd come meet anyone crazy enough to use the old road. Rivertown's just a little ways south, right on the river. Tomorrow we'll stop there and pay our respects and ask permission to pass through."

The wind picked up as dusk fell, and the mist stirred and eddied like restless spirits. Several times, Raisa thought she saw pale faces gazing at them through the trees, their eyes like dark holes torn in linen corpse wrappers. It was a relief to crawl inside her tent with Talia and Hallie and close the flap, shutting out the weird landscape.

What would it be like to live here full-time, walled in by mist?

The Gray Wolves rose early the next morning and struck camp without prompting. Everyone seemed eager to mount up and ride on.

The Dyrnnewater was like a river transformed. Rough and rowdy above the falls, it became a sluggish, placid, wide river that leaked listlessly into tributaries on all sides.

It was an alien landscape—tall grasses quilted with waterways and no way to tell where the solid ground was. Fallen trees lay everywhere, like a giant's game of pitch sticks, rotting and covered in a white, leathery fungus. The mist had frozen overnight, and the ground crackled under their boots. Ice glazed the still pools and every blade of grass, twig, and branch, transforming the marsh into a surreal, colorless world.

"It used to be drier here," Amon said. "They've dammed the Tamron River downstream, and water's backed up into these wetlands. That's what killed the trees."

The murk closing around them was oppressive. An enemy could be lurking a few feet away and there'd be no way to know. Plus, the moisture seemed to dampen and distort sound, so Raisa couldn't tell what direction it came from or how close the source.

Raisa's teeth chattered, and not just from the cold. It was like walking through a nightmare when at any moment a demon might reach out with cold fingers and grab you, claiming you for the Breaker. The cadets peered about, straining their eyes; their hands never far from their swords. Their usual cheer dissolved in the frigid damp.

After a half hour of walking, they rounded a curve in the river, and Rivertown loomed out of the mist. What was left of it, anyway.

"Blood of the Demon," Amon whispered. "Who could've done this?"

There hadn't been much to begin with—just a collection of frail stick-built dwellings centered around a small temple at the river's edge. Now it lay in ruins—most structures knocked down or burnt to the ground. A few boats lay foundered at the edge of the river like empty crab shells, their hulls pierced through or crushed. A series of pilings marched out from the shoreline, the remains of what had been several small docks.

The Gray Wolves dismounted to search the site, looking for traces of those who had once dwelt there. They found no corpses, at least, but perhaps they'd been dumped in the river or the survivors had carried them off.

Amon bent and picked up a rotting fish basket woven of twine and reeds. He turned it in his hands and poked at it gently with his forefinger. "Well, this *was* Rivertown," he said grimly. "Looks like nobody's been here for a couple of months at least."

"Do you think they were attacked, or did they destroy it themselves before abandoning it?" Raisa asked.

Amon shrugged. "I don't know, but I'd guess they were attacked or driven off. These people didn't have much to start with. They'd have taken everything with them, if they could." Blinking away raindrops, he looked downriver. "Could've been freelancers, come up from the south. But it'd be bloody hard to get to for what they got."

"I wonder where they went," Raisa said. "The Waterwalkers, I mean."

"Who knows?" Amon whistled to recall the other Wolves, who had spread out over the village. "Guess all we can do is go on," he said, when they had regathered. "Have your weapons to hand and stick close together. Morley, you're with me."

They rode on—for miles, it seemed—following the river until, as Amon had predicted, it fragmented into a web of streams in a trackless maze. Raisa had hoped the murk would clear, but it seemed only to thicken. It was impossible to get her bearings by looking at the sky. Up, down, all around— everything was a milky white blank.

The damp cold began at Raisa's fingers and toes, gradually penetrating her very core until shivers rolled through her. It was possible she would never be warm again.

Amon pulled out his compass and pointed them south. Now that they weren't following the river, the going got even rougher. They splashed through freezing pools and thickets of sharp-bladed grass that tore at the horses' legs and the cadets' heavy canvas trousers. They dismounted and led their horses, worried their mounts would step into hidden holes and end up lamed. The light changed as the sun went down, but there was no other evidence of time passing, save Raisa's growing weariness and the cavity in her middle that said she hadn't eaten for hours.

She soldiered on grimly, taking three steps for every one of Amon's. Several times he caught her when she stumbled, as if he knew she was about to falter.

Finally, the ground rose a bit. The footing became more solid as they passed through a grove of scrubby bushes with thick, leathery leaves lacquered in ice.

Amon grunted in satisfaction. "This is what I was aiming for. This is the highest ground for miles around. It should be as dry as anywhere in the Fens, and if the mist clears, we can take a look around. A little ways on, we can stop for the night."

Mick groaned. "We have to stay here in this . . . *muck* another night, sir?"

"Can't we just keep going?" Garret flexed his gloved hands and slapped them against his thighs, trying to thaw them out. "I'd rather walk than sit and freeze."

"The headwaters of the river are still a long ways off," Amon said. "We won't get clear of this for a few days, not this time of year. Besides, we can't walk in the dark. We'll break our necks or end up waist-deep in a bog."

"Buck up, Garret," Hallie said, cheerful as usual. "You'll feel better once we've a fire going and you got something in your belly."

"If we can even build a fire in this wet," Mick grumbled.

Raisa didn't like the idea of passing the night in this freezing swamp any more than the rest of them, but she did look forward to a fire. She increased her pace a bit.

They walked single file, leading their horses, the mist so thick they could scarcely see the person in front of them, when a shout from the rear brought the column to a halt.

"Hallie! Where are you?" Long pause. "Don't you fool around now. *Hallie!*"

Nothing.

"What is it, Mick?" Amon called from his position in the lead.

"It . . . it's Hallie, sir. She's gone." Hallie had been bringing up the rear.

"Gone? Since when?" Amon asked.

"Within five minutes, I'd guess, sir. I just looked back and she wasn't there."

Amon swore. "I told you to stick together."

"We did," Mick insisted. "She was right behind me, I swear it."

"Form up!" Amon shouted, and the Gray Wolves bunched in close, clutching their horses' reins, faces pale and anxious. "All right. We'll find her. She can't be far away.

"Garret, Talia, Morley, and I will build a fire and set up camp. The rest of you, form two teams of three and scout the back trail. Check back here in fifteen minutes. And be careful. Rope yourselves together if you need to. I don't want to have to explain to my da how I lost my triple in the Fens."

Ordinarily, there would have been some jibes and catcalls in response to this, but no one seemed to be in a joking mood. The other six cadets disappeared into the mist, walking back the way they'd come.

Raisa methodically laid a fire, pulling dry tinder out of the weatherized pouch at her belt and digging the clan-made fire kindler out of her saddlebags. Amon and Garret raised the tents while Talia stood guard. They set their weapons in easy reach.

Fifteen minutes passed, then twenty, then twenty-five, and none of the other Wolves returned. Raisa soon had a fire going, shielded from prying eyes by a wall of icy reeds and mud. She strung cording up to dry their wet clothing. Digging out the travel bread and smoked meat and dried fruit that would be their supper, she put water on to boil for tea. She forced herself to pretend that everything would be all right.

As the deadline came and went, Amon transitioned from impatient and irritated to tense and uncommunicative. He jumped at every sound, and there were lots of sounds in the surrounding marsh—frozen twigs creaking, and icy marsh grasses hissing as if stroked by unseen hands. The mist eddied and swirled about them, forming monstrous shapes in the firelight.

Amon stood staring down into the flames. The firelight glazed the hard planes of his face. He's only seventeen, Raisa thought. He's only a year older than me, yet he's been given this huge responsibility. If anything happens to the rest of us, he'll blame himself, since he's in charge. How is that fair?

Off in the mist, a horse whickered a greeting. Amon sprinted to where the ponies were tethered, his sword in hand. He disappeared into the fog, leading with his blade. "Hallie!" His shout came back to Raisa, muffled by the thick air.

Moments later, he reappeared, leading a riderless pony. "Hallie's," he said shortly, tethering it alongside the others.

Talia and Garret scouted the area around the camp, gathering any burnables they could find while being careful to remain within sight. Amon saw to the horses, but did not remove all of their tack, as if anticipating that they might need to leave in a hurry.

Where would we go? Raisa thought. There was nothing to recommend one spot in this trackless maze over another. Nothing to say that one place was safer than another. They might as well stay here, where there was a chance the others might find their way back. She crawled into the tents and began laying out the bedrolls, telling herself that the others would be exhausted and ready to make an early night of it when they returned.

She was finishing up in the third tent when she heard a shout, suddenly cut off. Then running feet and someone crashing through the underbrush, and Amon shouting, "Garret! Talia?"

Raisa froze in place, holding her breath. A moment later she jumped as Amon shoved aside the tent flap and crouched next to her, speaking into her ear. "They're gone," he said. "It's the Waterwalkers, it has to be. I don't know how many there are, but I think we have to assume we're outnumbered."

"Should we make a run for it?" Raisa whispered.

"If we run, we'll be taken, too. I'm going to try to get them to come to me so we can find out what's going on. It's not like them to attack unprovoked."

"Maybe things have changed since you were here," Raisa

said, then instantly regretted it when she saw the pain and guilt on Amon's face.

He thrust a saddlebag into her arms. "There's some food and supplies in here. I'll go out and ask for a meeting. You stay in here and listen. If things go wrong, slide out the back and run for it. Maybe you'll be able to avoid them, one person alone."

What would it be like, to hear Amon murdered, and then go fleeing through this awful swamp on her own with his killers on her heels?

"No. I will not," Raisa said. "We'll stay together, no matter what. We'll die together, if need be."

"Please, Raisa," he said, gripping her hands painfully hard. "This is my fault. We shouldn't have come this way. I thought I knew what we were getting into, but I should have listened to Barlow. Give me a chance to save you, even if I've lost the others."

"We all thought this was our best chance to cross the border," Raisa said. "Your father included. I'm not going to second-guess it now. No matter what happens, I think we're safer together." Raisa crawled to the front of the tent. "Now, let's go out. I think it's better to go out to them than to have them come in after us."

"All right." Sliding forward, Amon put his hand on her shoulder. "But stay back, will you? I don't want them to know who you really are. I'm going to call for a parley."

They emerged into the eerie vacancy of the campsite. Amon fetched his fighting staff from his horse. Resting it on his up-turned palms, he lifted it horizontally in front of him, then laid it down on the grass in the middle of the clearing. He stepped back from it, three long paces, then called out something in what Raisa assumed must be the Waterwalker language.

One more language she didn't know. Why had she never studied it?

The answer was this: her tutors and advisers in Fellsmarch considered the Waterwalkers scarcely more than savages. They did not use metal weapons or tools, they did not ride horses, and they lived simply, in dwellings they moved from place to place.

Amon waited for a response, and when none came, he repeated the call. On the third repetition, shapes materialized out of the mist and came toward them.

There were three of them—a young man, a boy, really, two or three years younger than Raisa, and a man and woman of middle age. They shared the same thick black eyebrows and strong straight noses. They wore pale robelike garments that made them difficult to see in the freezing mist. All carried fighting staffs like Amon's.

The young man stood facing Amon. In contrast to Amon's plain weapon, his staff was intricately carved with fish, serpents, and other fantastical creatures. It was small enough to suit his stature and slight build. His attire was more elaborately decorated than that worn by the others, embroidered with pale, silvery thread in a design that mimicked sunlight on wavelets and fish scales.

"Good day, Dimitri," Amon said in Common, extending his hands toward the young man.

"Corporal." Dimitri made no move to reciprocate the gesture, but stood, gripping his staff, his face impassive. Amon tilted his head, studying Dimitri's face, and pulled back his hands, dropping them to his sides.

"Good day, Adoni and Leili," Amon said, turning to the older man and woman. They stood stiff and expressionless, their staffs angled across their bodies.

After an uncomfortable pause, Dimitri bent and laid his staff on the ground next to Amon's. He straightened and took a step back.

Amon settled back on his heels, looking relieved.

The older man and woman followed Dimitri's example, though neither looked happy about it. They flanked Dimitri, standing to either side and a little behind him.

"Shall we speak Common so that we all can understand?" Amon said, extending a hand toward Raisa.

Dimitri looked at his companions, and they shrugged.

"Will you share my fire?" Amon asked, gesturing toward Raisa's small blaze.

The Waterwalkers scowled, as if reluctant to share even this small token of hospitality from them.

Bones, Raisa thought, shivering. They're going to kill us for sure.

Finally, Dimitri ripped free his cloak, threw it down on the ground, and sat on it. The others did the same, arranging themselves cross-legged around the fire.

Amon sat down also, and Raisa sat next to him.

"This is Rebecca Morley," Amon said, touching Raisa's shoulder.

"Are you two espoused?" Leili asked bluntly. Ironically, Common always sounded more formal than the other languages used in the Seven Realms.

"No." Amon shook his head, color staining his cheeks. "She's a cadet. A first year."

"Another soldier, then," Dimitri said.

"Not a soldier," Amon said. "A student only."

"Still a soldier," Dimitri said, looking at Adoni and Leili, who nodded. Raisa's prickling unease intensified. They are his counselors, she thought. He looks to them for guidance. And they hate us.

"You are lord now?" Amon asked Dimitri.

"I am," Dimitri said, self-consciously fingering the intricately embroidered hems of his sleeves.

"What about your father?" Amon asked in his direct fashion. "Where is he?"

"My father died at Rivertown," Dimitri said.

"I'm sorry to hear about Lord Cadri," Amon said. "How did it happen?"

"Why have you come here with soldiers?" Dimitri burst out.

"We're traveling through," Amon said, "on our way to the academy at Oden's Ford. I stopped at Rivertown to ask a traveler's blessing, and found it gone."

"Yes," Dimitri said. "Rivertown is gone. Destroyed by Fellsian soldiers at midsummer."

Sweet Hanalea! Raisa opened her mouth, then closed it again without speaking.

"They told me at the West Wall that there's been trouble along the border," Amon said. "What is going on?"

The older man spoke in the marsh language, his hands slicing the air. Dimitri glanced at Raisa, then translated quickly. "The Queen of the Fells sends us a Dyrnnewater full of poisons. It grows worse by the day. Fish cannot live in it. It kills the plants we gather for food. Our children sicken and die. Yet when we complain, she does nothing. It's been a problem for a long time, but now it's worse than it's ever been."

Amon nodded. "I know. Refugees from the Ardenine Wars have crowded into Fellsmarch. They camp along the banks and empty their slop jars into the river. It's made a bad situation worse."

The river had been bad as long as Raisa could remember. The sewer systems in Fellsmarch had been built hundreds of years ago, during some prosperous and public-spirited season in the past. Now, with the cost of maintaining a mercenary army and dwindling taxes due to the wartime drop-off in trade, there never seemed to be enough money to pay for repairs.

The clans complained that they sent a clean river out of the high eastern Spirits only to have the Vale dwellers use it as a repository for filth.

"If we can no longer feed our families," Dimitri went on, "we have no choice but to take from others, especially those who caused this problem. So we've sent raiders across the border, and taken foodstuffs from Tamron and the Fells."

"And the guard destroyed Rivertown in retaliation," Amon said.

Dimitri nodded. "Yes. I was away at the time. They came down from the fortress at the top of the escarpment, using the road that you and I built. They burned or knocked down all the houses, pierced our boats, destroyed the docks, took all of our nets, our tools, the dried fish and grain we had stored for the winter. They killed everyone who didn't run away, from the oldest crone to the youngest baby. They bound the children hand and foot, and threw them living into the river to drown."

Raisa recalled what Barlow had said. *The Waterwalkers been raiding over the border, stealing livestock and food. We put a stop to it.*

"Blood and bones," she whispered. "I am so sorry."

Dimitri glanced at Raisa, frowned in disapproval, then turned back to Amon. "My mother is dead, and my sisters. Most of the men of the village were killed, my father and his father, my brothers, all of my uncles except Adoni. Those who escaped are all crowded into Hallowmere, by the sea."

Dimitri gestured helplessly. "Those that remain alive will likely starve this winter. We take some fish from the sea, but our boats are not built for the winter storms on Leewater. And our food stores for the winter have been destroyed."

"Dimitri, Adoni, Leili, this cannot stand," Amon said, his gray eyes dark with anger. "I will not let it stand. Do you know who commanded those that attacked you?"

"What does it matter?" Leili said with quiet bitterness. "Soldiers are all the same." She extended her empty arms. "My babies are dead."

"I am lord now, replacing my father," Dimitri said. "Uncle Adoni and cousin Leili are my counselors. We've continued to cross the border and take what we can from the uplanders. We've destroyed the new road, which will make it difficult to move men, horses, and weapons in. But eventually the up-landers will slide down the escarpment and attack Hallowmere, and we expect to be pushed into the sea. We are in a fight to the death. So you understand why we do not welcome soldiers here."

"We're not here for fighting. You know that," Amon said.

"Do we?" Adoni replied, his face hard and impassive.

"Where are the other cadets?" Amon asked, meeting Dimitri's eyes. "Are they still alive?"

"They are still alive," Dimitri said. Raisa's heart rose, until he said, "But not for long."

"You know me, and you know my father," Amon said. He sat very straight, his hands on his knees. "My father saved your father's life. We've never lied to you. All we want is to go on to Tamron, and leave you in peace."

"There is no peace," Dimitri said. "Not anymore."

Adoni leaned toward Dimitri and said something in the marsh language.

"My uncle says my debt has been paid with the lives of my father and uncles. The Fells owes us *gylden* for hundreds of lives. Your deaths will help repay that debt."

"My father had nothing to do with the destruction of Rivertown," Amon replied. "He would never drown a child. He probably doesn't even know about it."

"He is the captain of the Queen's Guard," Leili said in Common. "He is responsible, along with the queen and the army. Perhaps the loss of his son will help him recognize the pain he's caused."

"You and your companions will die honorably," Adoni conceded, "because your father is an honorable man."

"You know I am not your enemy," Amon said, looking at each of the Waterwalkers in turn. "Nor are my cadets. My father has a voice at court. If you let us go, I'll make sure he speaks on your behalf. Killing us won't help anything, and you'll turn him against you. You'll create a debt of honor you can never repay."

Raisa knew what else he was thinking: If you kill the princess heir, there would be no chance of reconciliation. Ever.

"I'm sorry," Dimitri said. "You were my friend. Maybe we can be friends again in the afterlife. But not on this earth. Too many deaths divide us now."

He's given up, Raisa thought. He thinks it's over. He's like a dead person, walking around, waiting to stop breathing. And his people will pay the price.

Raisa stared out into the mist, blinking away icy raindrops and tears of frustration. The fog swirled and coalesced, and a giant gray-white she-wolf sat facing her, its tongue lolling over razor-sharp teeth. Its green eyes gleamed in the firelight, and a rime of glittering ice silvered its fur.

The Gray Wolf—totem of Raisa's line. Meaning risk. Opportunity. A turning point.

I refuse to die here, Raisa said to the wolf. *I'm just sixteen. I have too much to do.*

The wolf shook itself, flinging bits of ice into the fire. The flames sputtered and popped, sending sparks skyward. It bared its teeth, growling, followed by three sharp yips.

Was it some kind of sign? A pathway to follow?

Raisa came up on her knees, leaning forward, hands clenched. "If you intended to kill us all along," she said to Dimitri, "why did you even agree to a meeting?"

They all three stared at her, her fury taking them by surprise.

"You call yourself the leader of your people. If you are, you need to save them."

Dimitri blinked at her. "You don't understand," he began.

"I think I do," Raisa said. "Rivertown was destroyed. Your

115

family was killed. It's an awful thing. You're overwhelmed with sorrow. You feel paralyzed. Anyone would, in your place. But you are not allowed the luxury of wallowing in grief."

Amon gripped Raisa's knee. "Morley, shut *up*," he growled.

"He needs to hear this," Raisa said. "He's going to kill us anyway, so what does it matter if he doesn't like it?" She stood and strode back and forth, pounding her fist into her palm in emphasis. "You *know* we're not your enemies. You *know* we're no danger to you. And you know that killing us won't keep the Fellsian army out of your territory. The only reason to kill us is for revenge, to balance the debt you feel is owed you by the queen of the Fells."

She swung around, facing Adoni and Leili. "It's so easy. Your counselors are encouraging you to do it. They're grieving also, and it'll feel good in the short run. You'll feel like you're doing *something*, when right now you feel helpless.

"But you're responsible for your people, and killing us will do your people harm. Rulers don't get to do the easy thing. You don't get to do what you want to do."

Amon sat frozen, hands resting on his thighs, as if by moving he might set off an explosion. Adoni and Leili stared at her with a mixture of astonishment and annoyance.

"Be quiet, girl," Adoni growled. "We don't need a fledgling upland soldier to lecture us about what we can and cannot do."

But Dimitri raised his hand to quiet his uncle without taking his eyes off Raisa. "I don't get to take revenge, you say. What *do* I get to do?" he asked dryly.

"You get to make the decision that's best for the Fens, regardless of your own desires. Regardless of tradition. You get to do the smart thing. If you let us go, Corporal Byrne will take your grievance to his father and to the queen. He'll be an advocate for you, and I will too."

Raisa realized that promise might be difficult to keep, given her self-imposed exile status. She'd find a way. Somehow. If she survived the day.

She returned to the fire and squatted in front of Dimitri. "What's most likely to benefit your people—murdering us or letting us go?"

"This girl is a witch-talker," Leili said to Dimitri. "Why should we believe her?"

Dimitri laced his hands and tapped his forefingers against his chin, thinking.

Perhaps suspecting that his nephew was wavering, Adoni spoke up. "Lord Dimitri, we could let Corporal Byrne go. That would make Captain Byrne beholden to you. Then kill the rest," he said. He glared at Raisa, as if she might be first on the list.

"That's not acceptable," Amon said. "I'm responsible for my triple. I won't ride away and leave them to die. Do you think my da would welcome back a coward?"

"That's your choice," Leili said, shrugging. "Stay and die with them if you insist."

Dimitri kept staring at Raisa, as if studying her face for clues. Raisa looked past him to where the gray wolf waited in the forest. Dimitri stiffened, blinked, and rubbed his eyes.

The wolf stood, shook itself, and trotted into the mist, its brushlike tail the last thing to disappear.

Dimitri rose abruptly, his face pale and set. "Leili, Adoni, let us talk in private." They walked a little distance away. There ensued an intense discussion.

"Just go," Amon said to Raisa. "I'll distract them so you can get away."

"No," Raisa said. "I'm staying. He needs the chance to make the right decision. If I run, it will look like a trick, and they'll kill you and everyone else."

"Gaah. We're probably surrounded anyway," Amon muttered, squinting into the mist. "You're crazy, you know that, don't you?" he added, without looking at her.

No, not crazy, Raisa thought. I'm angry. I'm sick and appalled by what's been done in the name of the Gray Wolf line.

The three Waterwalkers returned to the fire. Adoni and Leili looked grievously unhappy, which gave Raisa hope.

"I have come to a decision," Dimitri announced. "We will allow you and your cadets to live, Corporal, so you can take our grievance back to your father and he can use his influence with the queen. You both give your word that you will do that?" He looked from Amon to Raisa. "The witch-talker included?"

"I will do everything in my power to see your grievances addressed," Raisa said, then bit her lip, realizing that she didn't sound much like a soldier.

"Where do you find cadets like this, Corporal Byrne?" Dimitri raised an eyebrow. He turned to Adoni and Leili. "Go and bring the other soldiers," he said. "I'll wait with the uplanders." When they hesitated, he added, "As I said. These are not our enemies."

Dimitri's counselors left the campsite, looking back over their shoulders.

Dimitri waited until they were well out of earshot, then said, "One of our raiding parties brought back news from the uplands. They said that the princess heir of the Fells has run off." He looked directly at Raisa as he said it.

Amon shifted slightly forward, putting himself between Raisa and Dimitri.

"Why do you think she left?" Dimitri said, still looking at Raisa.

"Maybe she wanted to find out what was really going on in the world, so she could be a better ruler," Raisa said, shrugging, feeling the heat of Amon's disapproval.

"They say she already goes her own way," Dimitri said. "They say she founded a program to educate and feed poor people in your capital, called the Briar Rose Ministry."

"She does what she can, Lord Dimitri," Raisa said. "Briar Rose is the princess heir's clan name and emblem. Here, I'll show you." Crossing the campsite to where the ponies were tethered, she reached into her saddlebag, careful to move slowly and deliberately. She pulled out a length of silk embroidered with her rose-and-thorn motif. Returning to Dimitri, she handed it to him.

"This scarf bears the emblem of the princess heir. Once the princess returns to Fellsmarch, you can use it as a token. If you ever need her help, or need to get a message to her, send this scarf along with the messenger, and I guarantee you will be heard."

Dimitri stood immobile for a long moment, the fabric draped over his hands. Then he carefully tucked the scarf away, inside his tunic, and inclined his head. "One day, my lady, the princess heir will be queen. And she will owe *gylden* to me." He smiled.

Raisa smiled at Dimitri. "Aye, she will," she said. "And one day, perhaps you'll teach Princess Raisa sticking."

"I'll look forward to it. For now, I'll send my own token to her as a reminder of me." Dimitri picked up his staff, laid it across his two palms, and extended it toward Raisa. "For the future queen of the Fells. I've nearly outgrown it anyway," he added, stretching himself as tall as he could.

Raisa accepted the staff gravely, feeling the balanced weight of it in her hands. "I'll see she gets it. It looks to be just the right size."

Lord Dimitri turned to Amon. "I'm going to give back your soldiers' weapons. But I need your promise that they won't use them on us."

A dozen Waterwalkers emerged from the mist, led by Adoni and Leili, and shepherding Mick, Talia, Hallie, and the other missing Gray Wolves. The cadets collected into a group, looking from Amon and Raisa to their captors, saying nothing.

Garret and Hallie appeared bruised and battered, as if they'd put up a stiff fight. The rest seemed shaken, but otherwise not the worse for wear.

"Return their weapons," Dimitri said. The Waterwalkers passed back swords, daggers, belt knives, bows, and quivers. The marsh dwellers handled the metal pieces with obvious distaste. Raisa slid her new staff into her baldric alongside her sword.

Dimitri drew a rough map in the dirt to show them the way. "The mist should clear as you head south. You'll find the headwaters of the Tamron two days' walk away." He offered them waybread for the journey, but Amon politely declined, no doubt thinking of the Waterwalkers starving at Hallowmere.

They mounted up and turned their ponies south once again, relying on Amon's clan-made pointer stone and Dimitri's directions. None of the Wolves looked back, as if by doing so they might break whatever spell had overcome their captors.

Hallie waited until they were well away before she heeled her horse up alongside Amon's. "What happened back there? I thought you were both dead and we were soon to be, when all of a sudden they untie us and lead us back to camp and treat us like it was all some kind of mistake."

"Morley here explained to Lord Dimitri all about the responsibilities of a ruler," Amon said. His gray eyes studied Raisa with a fierce curiosity, as if he might somehow figure out what kind of magic she'd done.

"Huh?" Hallie looked from Raisa to Amon. "I don't get it."

"It seems Morley's a witch-talker," Amon said, and despite Hallie's questions, wouldn't explain further.

CHAPTER SIX

FLATLAND
DEMONS

Han and Dancer left Delphi early the morning after the card game, without seeing Cat Tyburn again. Han wondered what she would decide to do—stay in Delphi, travel on, or go back home.

The bluejacket at the border had been right about one thing—Arden south of Delphi was a dangerous place. Han and Dancer rode through a landscape scarred by war—burnt-out farmsteads and crops beaten down by the boots of soldiers. If Prince Geoff was meaning to declare victory, like the server had said, he'd have his work cut out for him.

Rough-looking mercenary types and armed soldiers jammed the roads, in and out of uniform, some bearing the unfamiliar signia of the various warring families: the Red Hawk, the Double Eagle, the Tower on the Water, and the Raven in the Tree.

Han and Dancer avoided them all. The last thing they wanted was to be impressed into some lordling's army to die in a stranger's war. They slept in the woods, often without the comfort of a fire, which might draw attention from unfriendly eyes. Their many detours were costing them precious time.

As they traveled south, the hills flattened into high plateaus, then declined into wide plains and stretches of wood where wind, water, and man contoured the land. Even in the woods, Han felt oddly exposed and vulnerable. He was used to the comforting frame of mountains and hills, walls and buildings, defining and shortening the horizon.

Han couldn't shake the uneasy feeling they were being watched and followed. He set trip-wire charms around their campsites, but left off doing that when raccoons kept them up all night. Nothing more dangerous tried to approach them. He put his worries down to the unfamiliar terrain and lingering thoughts about pursuit from the Fells.

Han could see why Arden was called the breadbasket of the Seven Realms. The soil was deep and rich and black, less prone to growing rocks than the rough, bony skeleton of the Fells. Han had hoped they could supplement their waybread and sausage and dried fruit with fresh food from farms along the way. But they found little to forage and less to buy. It was as if some plague from the Breaking time had swept across the fields, taking with it every edible thing.

Although the autumn days grew shorter, and mist shrouded the fields in the mornings, the weather seemed stubbornly stuck in late summer. They traveled just fast enough to stay ahead of the change of seasons.

When they could no longer stand the stench of bodies too long on the road, or stomach another meal of bread and hard sausage, they stopped at inns, avoiding the common room save for their evening meal. They wore their amulets, but kept them hidden under their shirts, hoping to avoid trouble in a realm where magic was forbidden.

At the inns, Han and Dancer paid for candles, retired to their room, and pored over books of charms that Elena had procured for them. In camp, they practiced working with magic, taking advantage of Dancer's limited experience. Through the long hours on horseback, they kept their hands on their amulets, storing up power for the days ahead.

Dancer studied another book on his own—thin and battered, with onionskin pages written in Clan and illustrated with line drawings of amulets and talismans. He drew magical objects and emblems of power in his journal.

He's not given up on being a flash crafter, whatever Elena says, Han thought.

Though he was bone-weary every night, Han often slept restlessly, the serpent amulet cradled in his hands. Some nights he was plagued by bizarre nightmares, images of places he'd never seen, people he'd never met. He never quite remembered these dreams, but he awoke groggy, his head aching, as if he'd continued his studies long into the night.

After the episode at the border, Han was wary of magical accidents, but as he gained better control, there were no more spurts of power. He could plant a thorn hedge anywhere he wanted. Useless, most of the time, but it was the fanciest charm he knew.

Sometimes he was prickled by worry. If this amulet had once belonged to the Demon King, and he had used it as Han was now doing, it might be loaded up with dark, demon magic. Maybe it would drive Han lack-witted, just like its previous owner.

But these worries couldn't compete with the seductive attraction of the flashpiece, with its ability to draw power and give it back transformed. The charms he and Dancer tried were simple and practical. These days, they never needed flint and steel to kindle a fire—they could conjure it out of the air. They studied charms to calm horses and entice fish out of the streams and into their hands. They used travelers' charms to discourage mosquitoes, make knots fast, and keep rain from soaking their clothes.

At times, Han sizzled with impatience, frustrated by their travel delays and worried there'd be too much to learn and not enough time. How long would it take to learn everything he needed to know? And what would he do with the knowledge then? Serve as bravo for the clans, as he'd promised? Battle the Wizard Council on behalf of a queen who'd betrayed him and probably didn't want his help anyway? Or could he find a way to use it for his own purposes?

If only his gift had been freed soon enough to save his mother and sister. Now it seemed like the height of irony—a remedy delivered after the patient had died.

The clan elders didn't care about that. Lord Averill and Elena *Cennestre* had cuffed and bound him, strangling off the magic that now torrented through him. They'd watched him struggle to feed his family on the streets of Ragmarket, and never opened that spigot of power until it suited their purpose. By then, Mam and Mari were dead.

Han would give his loyalty to certain people—like Dancer's mother, Willo, Matriarch of Marisa Pines; Speaker Jemson of Southbridge Temple; the hermit Lucius Frowsley; plus Cat and

Dancer. Otherwise, he'd serve himself, waiting and watching until he could take advantage. He wouldn't play the fool anymore.

As they approached the city of Ardenscourt, traffic on the road thickened. Soldiers swarmed thick as thieves in Ragmarket. Han and Dancer took to traveling in daytime. It was better to be lost in a crowd in daylight than stand out in the dark.

Close to the capital, the farms were larger and seemed to be under some powerful lord's protection—likely King Geoff. Peasants toiled in the fields, harvesting wheat and oats and beans and hay, with armed guards overseeing them. Han wondered if the guards were there to protect the farmers, or to keep them at their work.

Apple trees groaned under the burden of fruit—varieties that Han had never seen before, green and yellow and pink, as well as red. The Red Hawk of Arden flew from estate houses along the road, and soldiers wore the signia everywhere. The newly declared Montaigne king held the capital city and the estates surrounding it in an iron grip, but his influence didn't seem to extend far into the countryside.

They encountered more flatland temples built in the austere style of the Church of Malthus. They passed groups of priests and holy sisters, like flocks of black crows to Han's eyes.

"Their priests are all men, I hear," Dancer said. "Strange."

"What do the sisters do?" Han asked.

"Pray, mostly. Sing and teach. Do good works."

Han and Dancer planned to circle around the city and intersect Tamron Road to the west, but they soon realized that the city was huge, spread out, and sloppy, and it would take them far out of their way to ride clear around it.

That night, they stopped at an inn on the outskirts. It drew a mixed crowd—soldiers and farmers and even a Malthus crow or two.

Dinner was chicken legs and brown bread, with cloyingly sweet southern cider. At home, a fire on the hearth would be welcome this time of year, but on this balmy evening the door stood open and the hearth lay cold.

A half dozen men occupied two tables, loudly demanding food and drink whenever they ran short. They had the look of soldiers, but wore no signia or uniform. One of them, a stocky man in his early twenties with a stubble of beard, had an incandescence about him that said he was gifted and leaking magic.

Han eyed him curiously. The soldier must have an amulet, perhaps hidden under his shirt, but he didn't seem to know the trick of drawing magic off to dim his aura. A good thing for him that only other gifted could see it.

A veiled Malthusian sister sat alone at a table nearest the door. A half-empty plate sat before her, but she kept the barman coming and going, refilling her mug.

The maids of Malthus like their ale, Han thought, amused. He'd seen at least one in every tavern and common room since they'd reached the flatlands.

In contrast, the tall, skinny Malthusian priest huddling in the back corner picked at his supper, engrossed in a large, leather-bound book with onionskin pages. Several oversized golden keys hung from a cord around the priest's waist, his only ornamentation save for elaborate jeweled spectacles dangling from a chain around his neck.

The priest looked up suddenly and caught Han staring at him.

Scowling, he bent his head over the holy book on the table. Han guessed it was a holy book, anyway. It was hard to imagine this sour-faced pudding-sleeve reading a romance or an adventure story. Oddly, the priest didn't use his spectacles for reading text.

Han finished his meal and sat back, relaxed and sociable.

"You ready to go up?" Dancer said, having finished long before Han. As usual, Dancer was eager to go upstairs to read and study charms, away from the crowd.

Han, however, had no desire to leave the common room and hide out in their tiny, windowless room in the attic. It would be stuffy and hot, and they'd have to sit in the dark or pay for candles, since there was no natural light. Plus, one of the pretty servers had winked at him, and he was waiting to see what developed.

"Let's stay a little while," Han said, slathering butter on soft tavern bread, so different from their hard waybiscuits.

Dancer shrugged and nodded, yawning to make his position clear.

The priest had raised his peculiar spectacles to his eyes and scanned the room. When his gaze swept across Han and Dancer, he stiffened and fixed on them, his eyes unnaturally large and owl-like through the lenses.

The priest lowered the spectacles and glared at them. "Sinners!" he said. "Idolators!"

Han and Dancer sat frozen for a long moment. "Does he mean us, do you suppose?" Dancer asked without moving his lips.

"How can he tell we're sinners?" Han whispered, aiming for a look of polite confusion. Was that what the spectacles were for? Identifying sinners?

The priest rose in a swish of fabric and stalked toward them, one arm extended, the other clutching his rising-sun pendant like a wizard might grip an amulet. "Repent, northerners!" he said. "Repent and accept the holy church and ye shall be saved."

Han stood and nodded toward the stairs. Perhaps if they just retired upstairs, as Dancer had suggested, it would calm the man.

"Leave off, Father Fossnaught," the gifted soldier said, grinning. "If you drove out the sinners, this place would lose all its patrons."

Two other soldiers rose and gathered up Father Fossnaught's books and papers, handing them to the priest. "You go on home and pray for them, all right?" one said.

The priest departed, flinging black looks over his shoulder.

"Thank you," Han said to the gifted soldier. "Does he do this very often?"

"Father Fossnaught is harmless—just a bit overzealous in sharing the good news of the Church of Malthus," the soldier said. "No harm done, I hope." He stuck out his hand, and Han took it, wondering if the soldier would notice the sting of wizardry.

In addition to leaking power, the stranger's hand was heavily calloused from weapons. "Name's Marin Karn," he said. "I'll buy another round to make up for your trouble." He gestured toward the bar. "Cider, was it?"

Han nodded, seeing no way out. He wanted to decline, and he knew Dancer did too. If they'd gone upstairs to begin with, the incident would never have happened. But it seemed smart not to offend those who had intervened on their behalf. Particularly since they were soldiers. Particularly since this Karn might know they were gifted.

Karn fetched two mugs of cider from the bar.

"So, seems you two *are* northerners, from your speech," Karn said, pulling a chair over to their table. "What brings you to Arden?"

"We're traders," Han said, following their established story. He took a swig of cider, which tasted more bitter than sweet. Must be the dregs at the bottom of the barrel. "We've got the finest fabrics, beads, and trimwork you'll see in all the Seven Realms. Do you have a special lady friend? We got fancies that would win any lady's heart."

Karn shook his head. "No, no lady friend." He eyed Han speculatively, then leaned close and said, "You wouldn't have any magical pieces, would you?"

Han shook his head. "That an't allowed here in the flatlands."

Karn laughed. "Just checking, my lad. Have to ask. No harm meant."

"You and your comrades," Dancer said. "Are you king's men?" Likely, Dancer wondered if Karn was inquiring after magical pieces in any official capacity.

"Us?" Karn shrugged noncommittally. "We're sell-swords, between assignments, I guess you'd say. We're waiting to see how it all comes out."

Dancer yawned again, resting his chin on his fist, looking even more droopy-eyed than before. He'd downed his cider quickly, probably hoping they could go on upstairs.

Han took another long swallow of cider, draining it nearly to the bottom. There it was again, that bitter taste against the cloying sweetness. His mind seemed fuzzy and unfocused.

He looked over at Dancer, who now lay sprawled over the table, head down, his breathing deep and even.

"Guess your friend's had enough," Karn said. "He drank it up kind of fast."

Dancer *had*, but cider didn't have the kick that . . .

Turtleweed. Han blinked at Karn, clubbed by the realization. It was turtleweed, and lots of it, mixed into the cider. Turtleweed would knock you out in no time.

Gripping the hilt of his knife, Han yanked it free. He tried to rise, but his body no longer responded to his commands. He was overpowered by fatigue, his eyes drooping, shut of their own accord.

"There, now," Karn said, wresting his knife from him. "Guess that cider was stronger than you thought. We'd better help you two home."

"Leave go. We're staying here," Han mumbled in protest. His lips felt numb.

Karn thrust his meaty hand under Han's shirt and grasped the serpent amulet.

"Aaaaagh!" he shrieked, letting go of it and slapping his hand against his thigh.

Han curled protectively around the flashpiece. "Leave it be, you angling lully prigger, or I'll . . ." He trailed off, unable to remember what he meant to do.

Karn made no further attempt on the amulet. Instead, he and one of the other soldiers hauled Han to his feet. Two other soldiers dragged Dancer out the door.

What is this? Han thought, clutching his amulet and ineffectually scuffing his feet against the floor. What do they want from us?

And then he didn't think anything anymore.

★ ★ ★

Han awoke to a crashing turtleweed headache and a sick stomach. Sign of poor-quality product. He'd never dealt in that kind of stuff.

He lay on a straw pallet on a stone floor, covered with a filthy wool blanket. Once his head stopped spinning, he gingerly sat up. It wasn't easy—his hands were bound tightly together behind his back, his ankles bound also. He tested the knots, trying to slide his hands free or rub the cords loose on the stone floor. He got nowhere, ending with bruised and skinned wrists. His wrists were wrapped so tightly his fingers felt like fat, clumsy sausages. He was all dressed up like a warm mark on Temple Day.

Dancer lay facedown a few feet away, similarly bound, still sound asleep. They lay in a dark room, faintly illuminated by the moonlight that sieved through the tightly shuttered windows and under the door. Cool night air leaked through imperfections in the wall and ran along the floor, chilling Han. There was no stink of the city in the air. The rattle of branches overhead and chirp of crickets said they were out in the country.

Han's flashpiece was gone. Somehow they'd found a way to get it off him. He felt a profound sense of loss—as though someone had ripped out his heart. All the power he'd stored away was now in somebody else's hands.

Dancer stirred, groaning feebly. Probably had the same head on him that Han did.

Han scooted up next to Dancer. "Dancer!" he said. "Wake up!"

Dancer's eyes flew open, though it took a few moments for him to focus on Han's face. Then, in that way he had, he settled into calm awareness. "What's going on?" he whispered through cracked lips. "My amulet's gone."

"It was those soldiers in the common room. They wanted our flashpieces. I don't know how they knew we had them."

"One of them was gifted," Dancer mumbled. "That Karn." He closed his eyes again. "I feel awful."

"They drugged us with turtleweed," Han said.

"If all they wanted was our amulets, why are we here?" Dancer's tongue seemed thick in his mouth, his speech still slurred from the drug.

Han shrugged, sending tingling pain through his arms. "Can you get free at all?"

Dancer tested his bonds, and shook his head. Whoever'd dressed them knew what he was doing.

Han scanned the room for anything sharp, anything he could use to fray at the rope. A stone hearth along one wall had possibilities. The hearth was cold, but there might be an iron grate or rough stones he could use to cut himself free.

Han had begun scooting toward the fireplace, when he heard footsteps and voices drawing nearer. A key rattled in the lock, the door slammed open, and three men entered.

One was Marin Karn, the gifted soldier that had drugged and kidnapped them. Karn carried a large lantern, which he set on the mantel, shedding a buttery light over everything. A leather saddlebag was slung over his shoulder, and Han knew immediately that their amulets were inside. He glanced over at Dancer, who nodded, his eyes also fixed on the bag.

The second man was slender, of medium height, with light brown hair and faded blue eyes, dressed for blueblood soldiering. The brooch pinned to his cape bore the device of a red hawk, and his clothing was tailored from the finest fabrics. The sword at his hip was made for business, though, and looked well used.

A few years older than they, he moved with the dangerous grace of a fellscat.

The third man was the Malthusian priest who'd confronted them in the common room. He came and stood, looking down at Han and Dancer as if they were evil and dangerous—fascinating but helpless predators. He reminded Han of some at the market that paid a copper to see a ratty old bear chained to a stump.

Up close, the priest stank of old sweat and fanaticism.

The blueblood pulled off his expensive gloves and slapped them against his palm as he looked down at Han and Dancer, his handsome face pinched with contempt.

"This is them?" The blueblood nudged Han with his booted foot. "These are the northern mages you told me about?"

"Mages!" Karn shouted at Han and Dancer in Common, like a barker hoping his menagerie would make a better show. "Bow before Gerard Montaigne, King of Arden."

Han obediently bent his neck while his mind raced furiously. The king of Arden? Han didn't know much about the nobility, but he had to think the king of Arden didn't sleep in a falling-down farmhouse.

"Are you certain no one knows about this?" Montaigne said to Karn. He spoke the southern tongue, but it was close enough to Common that Han could make it out. "What about your men? Soldiers cannot keep their mouths shut."

"They think these two are northern spies," Karn said. "I said I wanted to question 'em in private. They're out on patrol, so they won't have seen you come in."

"I still don't like this," Montaigne said, his voice brittle and cold. "I told you I wanted nothing to do with sorcery." He shifted his gaze to the priest. "I'm surprised you would be involved in this, Father, given the church's position on magic users."

Father Fossnaught fingered the keys at his waist. "I have made a study of mages and their ways. They are evil, disgusting creatures, yes, but I believe that, properly restrained, they can be put to use."

"We give 'em a choice," Karn put in. "They can repent and use their sorcery for the greater glory of Saint Malthus. Or burn."

Han's skin prickled as if flames were already licking at his flesh.

"The *principia* doesn't share that view," Montaigne said.

Fossnaught twitched. "True, there is a diversity of opinion on whether sorcerers can be saved through any means but the flame. I happen to believe Father Broussard's view is rather . . . shortsighted." He paused, then rolled his eyes heavenward. "Then again, His Holiness also believes Prince Geoff should be crowned at Ardenscourt, as the eldest surviving son of our late king. The *principia* is committed to succession by birth order. I, however, happen to believe that the Maker's hand is in this war. Should you win, and I believe you will, then it must be the Maker's will that you be crowned king."

Montaigne rubbed his chin, nodding. Han could tell the young prince liked this line of thinking. "If I'm going to take this kind of risk, I want to do it with some likelihood of success," Montaigne said. "Yet you bring me a pair of scruffy-looking boys. If they had any magical skill, you'd never have taken them."

Karn cleared his throat. "They don't look like much, aye, but as you said, it's unlikely we could capture a fully schooled mage.

These ones'll be more tractable. Don't know how much training they've had, but their amulets are packed with power."

"What do *you* know of such things?" Montaigne glared at Karn, and Karn shifted his eyes away.

This prince of Arden doesn't know his captain is gifted, Han thought. Karn's kept it from him. With good reason, it seemed.

"If we use a weapon we don't understand, it's likely to explode in our faces," Montaigne went on. "Remember what happened with the fire powder?"

Karn said nothing. He likely knew when to speak and when not to. Han wondered how much the captain really knew about magic and mages, as he called them. Could he have received any training in a place like Arden, where magic was forbidden?

Montaigne chewed on his lower lip. "If the jinxpieces are so powerful, couldn't we just use the amulets and dispose of these two?" he asked, as if Han and Dancer were merely magical wrappings to be thrown away. The prince of Arden either assumed they couldn't understand the flatland speech, or didn't care.

Fossnaught shook his head. "Mages and amulets work together, Your Grace. One's no good without the other."

"Anyway, these mages must have safeguarded their amulets against use by anyone else," Karn added. "The fair-haired boy's jinxpiece blistered my hand when I tried to pick it up." Karn held up his hand. It was wrapped in bandages.

Han didn't look at Dancer, but he knew they were both thinking the same thing—they had no clue how to safeguard their amulets from anyone. He didn't know why Karn couldn't touch his flash, unless Han's stored power was incompatible with Karn's.

Unless it was demon-cursed.

All he knew was that the loss of his amulet had left him with an empty, sick feeling. He felt hollowed out and hungry for the magic he'd lost. How could he have become so linked to it in such a short time? He desperately wanted it back.

"The magelings will turn on us at the first opportunity," Montaigne argued. "We'll never be able to trust them."

Father Fossnaught fished in his carry bag and drew out two pairs of silver manacles and two sets of keys. "These are old magic pieces called magebinders. I bought them off a trader in magical devices. The copperheads made them during the mage wars to control mage prisoners. You put the binders on the mage and you hold the key. If they disobey orders, the key holder can inflict excruciating pain. In time, they're conditioned to obey."

The priest paused. His gaze slid over Han, cold as a butcher's hands in winter, raising gooseflesh on him. "I can demonstrate if you like, Your Majesty."

You can try, Han thought, hoping they'd have to untie him to put them on. He'd worn magical cuffs all his life until Elena *Cennestre* of the Demonai clan removed them. He didn't mean to have any new darbies fastened around his wrists if he could help it.

Montaigne took one of the sets of manacles and examined them as if they were an attractive but dangerous new toy. Without looking up, he said, "That won't be necessary. Leave us, Father. Go back to town. We will let you know what we decide."

Father Fossnaught took a quick breath, as if to argue. Then sighed and bowed his head. "Very well, Your Majesty. I'll be at my lodgings in the cathedral close, awaiting your decision. You can send word the usual way." The priest stuffed the set of manacles into his carry bag and extended his hand toward the prince. "Your Grace, if you don't need . . ."

"I'll keep these," the prince of Arden said.

The priest bowed and left, with many backward looks, unhappy to be leaving his torture toys behind. Clearly wanting a seat at the table.

Montaigne continued to stare down at the manacles. "How would you use these two mages against Geoff's armies, Captain Karn?"

At this, Karn's muddy brown eyes lit up with enthusiasm. "In the mage wars, wizards could flame dozens of soldiers at a time. They could call down fog so the enemy would wander off a cliff. They'd spread fear and weariness among the enemy soldiers until they'd turn tail and run. They'd talk to birds and use them to spy, and use magical force to interrogate prisoners. They'd break sieges by walking through walls."

"That's difficult to believe," Montaigne said, handing the cuffs to Karn.

"There's written accounts from reliable eyewitnesses in the church archives," Karn said. "Father Fossnaught's made a study of it."

"If word gets out about this, it could turn some of the more pious thanes against us," the prince said.

"But Father Fossnaught says—" Karn began.

"Cedric Fossnaught is ambitious," Montaigne cut in. "And changeable as a woman. He hasn't forgiven the church for passing him over when he stood for *principia*. He thinks that a new king in Ardenscourt might lead to his own advancement."

"Nothing wrong with that," Karn said. "We need churchmen on our side."

"It's too great a risk," Montaigne said.

"Begging your pardon, but everything's a risk, Your Majesty," Karn said, picking over the words like a fire walker over coals. "We're losing. Duprais and Botetort are still with you, but Matelon's wavering. Geoff controls the capital and the greater part of the kingdom."

"Whose fault is that, Captain?" Montaigne fingered an elaborate ring on his left hand. "*You* are my strategist, *you* lead my armies, therefore *you* are responsible for the current situation." The prince bit off each *you* like day-old bread.

Karn lifted his hands, palms up. "The thanes are tired. They've emptied their treasuries and neglected their crops for ten long years. They just want the war to be over."

"The war will be over when I sit on the throne of Arden, and not before," Montaigne said. "If the thanes want peace, they should swear to me." He paused, fixing his icy gaze on the captain. "Perhaps you're thinking of going with Geoff as well?"

"No, Your Majesty," Karn said. "I'm a loyal soldier, you know that. Besides, Geoff would never take me on—not after what happened at Brightstone Keep." His face twisted. "It offended his *sensibilities* when I ordered the sacking of the town and the killing of everyone in it. He has his *principles*. If Geoff has his way, I'll swing for it."

Karn's already tried Geoff, Han thought. And that was the answer he got.

Montaigne gazed at Han and Dancer for a long minute, then shook his head. "No. It's bad enough I can't trust the thanes. I'm not going into battle with mages at my back," he said.

"But, Your Majesty," Karn protested, "what should I do with these two?"

"Kill them," Montaigne said, turning away.

"Would you kill us without knowing what we can do?" Han protested in Common. "Don't you even want to see a show? Give us back our amulets and we'll give you sorcery like you never saw before."

Montaigne paused in the doorway and looked back at Han, his face as hard and expressionless as the cliffs along the escarpment. "No doubt," he said. Then he was gone.

Karn stared after his prince for a long moment. Then swore forcefully and flung the magic darbies against the wall.

Han found himself feeling almost sorry for the captain. Karn was trying to win a war for his prince, and his prince wasn't cooperating.

But his sympathy for Karn didn't last long. After glaring down at Han and Dancer as if it were their fault, Karn crossed the room and fetched back his saddlebag.

Kneeling next to them, Karn untied the flap and pulled out three large, leather-wrapped packages. He folded back the leather, exposing their three amulets—the serpent flash, Dancer's Fire Dancer, and the Lone Hunter piece Elena had made for Han.

The Demon King amulet flared up, casting a sick, greenish light over Karn's face, as if it knew it was in enemy hands.

Karn drew an assassin's dagger and, leaning toward them, pressed the tip of it to Dancer's throat.

"All right, magelings," he growled. "Take the hexes off these jinxpieces and tell me how to use 'em."

"There's no way you can use them," Dancer said, canting his upper body backward to relieve the pressure of the blade. "You need us alive."

"Really?" Karn breathed, pressing harder on the blade so blood trickled down. "Are you sure about that?"

"Why should we tell you anything?" Han demanded. "You'll kill us anyway."

"Aye," Karn said. "That's so. But there's different ways to die. Slow ways and fast ways. Hard ways and easy ways. Maybe I'll let you watch while I cut up the savage, bit by bit. Then it'll be your turn."

Karn's mud-colored eyes had gained a feverish glint. The young captain would bring a certain enthusiasm to the task. Han's drug-clouded mind scrabbled for ideas. He had no idea how to make his amulet accessible to Karn, even if he wanted to.

It would do no good to scream or shout for help. Han had been listening hard, ever since he'd awakened. He'd heard nothing but the sound of night insects and the rattle of branches in the wind.

Montaigne and Karn meant to keep their flirtation with magic a secret. They'd carried them out to the middle of nowhere, far from the capital city controlled by Gerard's older brother.

"All right," Han said. "I'll undo the hex. But you got to free my hands." When Karn frowned, he added, "I'll need my amulet, too. I need to hold it. Only the mage that places the charm of protection can take it away."

Karn stared into Han's eyes for a long moment, then nodded grudgingly. "Fair enough. But try anything and your friend's a dead man."

Like that was a threat. They'd both be dead within the hour if Karn had his way. And if he killed Dancer quickly, it would be a blessing of sorts.

Han didn't know if Dancer would see it that way.

Karn dumped Han over onto his stomach and sliced through the ropes binding his hands with his knife, leaving Han's feet bound.

Han flexed his fingers, his breath hissing out in pain as the blood returned. He rolled over and sat up, stretching his shoulders, taking his time, wanting to get functional again before he made his move. Karn gripped one corner of the amulet's leather wrapping and slid it closer to Han. Then he took a fistful of Dancer's hair and pulled his head back, sliding his blade under his chin.

Han gripped the flash with both hands. Power thrilled through him, driving his pain away, replacing it with a savage anger that wanted nothing more than to destroy the man before him. An anger that cared nothing for the knife at Dancer's throat. His heart thudded in his chest. A charm bubbled to his lips, and he opened his mouth to speak it.

The door banged open again. Han turned, extending his hand toward the intruders.

It was Gerard Montaigne, his eyes bulging out, lips purplish in the sallow light from the lantern. And behind him, propelling him forward, was Cat Tyburn, her garrotte wrapped around the prince of Arden's throat, her blade pressed into his rib cage.

CHAPTER SEVEN

ON THE ROAD AGAIN

For a long moment, nobody moved. Then Dancer smashed his head into Karn's chin. Karn lost hold of his knife, and it fell down between them. Instead of fishing for it, Karn launched himself at Cat and Montaigne. The three of them tumbled to the ground in a mad tangle, with Montaigne and Karn both shouting for help.

Dancer located Karn's knife. Gripping it between the heels of his hands, he leaned back against it, sawing away at the ropes. Power rippled unbidden from Han's amulet, and the lantern exploded, sending shards of glass and burning oil flying. The room plunged into darkness, save the illumination from the Demon King jinxpiece. Han slid the chain over his head, tucking his amulet inside his shirt. Using a fragment of glass, he cut his ankles free. Then he slid his hands over the stone floor, searching for the other amulets.

Cat scrambled up next to him. She'd somehow extricated

143

herself from the confusion as Karn dragged the would-be king of Arden toward the door.

"Come *on*," she hissed. "We got to pike off. There's soldiers in the woods, and with all this noise, they're going to come running."

Dancer knelt, leaning forward, also searching for the flash-pieces. "Here's yours," he said, reaching back to hand Han the Hunts Alone amulet, smeared with blood. Dancer must have cut his hands as he groped around on the floor.

Cat stared at the amulet, looking perplexed.

Outside the farmhouse, feet pounded toward them. Montaigne's soldiers arriving.

"Your Majesty!" someone shouted. "What is it? Is something wrong?"

"To me!" the prince of Arden shouted. "I'm under attack by northern assassins."

Soldiers jostled through the doorway, bottling them in.

Desperate, Han slid his hand inside his shirt and took hold of the serpent amulet. Once again, the power seized him. He extended his arm, spoke an unfamiliar charm. Karn slammed into his prince, knocking him out of the way as flame erupted from Han's fingers, engulfing the Ardenine soldiers in the doorway. Han smelled burning wool and charred flesh as the soldiers tried to force themselves back out the way they'd come in. They piled up against the entryway, screaming in fear and cursing those blocking their escape.

Han's heart thudded in his chest. He'd killed before, but that had always been in street fights, blade to blade. Never with magic.

He forced himself to let go of the jinxpiece and turned to find Cat staring at him, openmouthed.

"It's got to be here somewhere," Dancer said, still crouched on the floor.

"Leave it," Han said, tugging at Dancer's arm. "Won't do you any good if you're dead."

Easy for me to say, he thought. I have two amulets.

Dancer finally stood, abandoning his search with visible reluctance, pressing his bleeding hands against his shirt.

"Let's go." The doorway was blocked by a heap of smoking corpses. Han slammed both hands against the window, and the shutters exploded outward. Boosting himself to the sill, he swung his legs over and dropped to the ground. Dancer and Cat slithered out behind him.

Someone shouted, "There they are!" Understandably, no one rushed forward.

They ran for their lives, zigzagging across the farmyard, vaulting over chicken coops and around outbuildings until they found the welcoming shelter of the trees.

Fright lent them a speed the prince of Arden's soldiers couldn't match. They passed from the forest into open farmland, leaping over furrows, crossing fields studded with cornstalks and edged with hedgerows and stone walls. Even when they could no longer hear the sound of pursuit, they ran on, following a dirt track that merged into a larger road several miles farther on.

Finally, they crawled behind a tall hedge to recover their breath. Han sat slumped, head drooping, willing his heart to slow down. He felt shaky and weak, tingling all over, as though he'd been chewing razorleaf.

Dancer looked worse off than Han—pale, trembling,

perspiring. He propped his head in his hands as if he couldn't hold it up on his own.

"How'd you do that?" Cat demanded, getting in Han's face as if *she* were the one who deserved answers. She seized his wrists, turning his hands palms up. "How'd you learn to throw flame like that?"

"What are *you* doing here?" Han retorted. "I thought you didn't want to come." Then it came back to him, that feeling of being watched that had plagued him since Delphi. "You been following us, haven't you? I thought I heard someone sneaking around camp a couple of times."

"Well, good thing I did," Cat said. "Seeing as I saved your sorry . . ." Her voice trailed off. She stared at his chest, eyes wide, then reached her hand toward Han's flash.

"Don't touch it," he said, tucking it inside his shirt.

"That's what the demons was looking for," Cat whispered. "In Ragmarket. They kept asking about a bit of bagged flash, a magical piece, shaped like a snake, with—"

"When were you talking to demons?" Han demanded. "And why would—"

"Blood and bones!" Cat interrupted, staring at the two of them as if they'd just grown horns. "You're bloody jinxflingers is what you are. It an't possible."

"Do you two know each other?" Dancer said, pressing the heel of his hand against his forehead as if it hurt.

Cat dropped to a half crouch and backed away from them, eyes slitted, a blade in each hand. She seemed genuinely terrified.

"Leave off, Cat," Han said gently. "And put your blades

away. We are wizards, true enough, but we an't going to hurt you."

Cat quit backing away, but she didn't come any closer, either. She ran her tongue over her lips and pointed a blade at Dancer. "Who is he, anyway? I never heard of no copperhead jinxflinger."

"It's a long story," Han said, not yet sure what questions he wanted to answer. "Cat Tyburn, meet Hayden Fire Dancer. Dancer's my friend from Marisa Pines Camp. I know Cat from Ragmarket. We used to run a canting crew together."

Cat and Dancer eyed each other as Han's two worlds crashed together in this foreign place.

"He's a *copperhead*," Cat blurted. "What you doing with *him*?" As if Dancer's being a copperhead overshadowed the fact that they were wizards.

"He's my *friend*," Han said. "I've spent near every summer with the clans since I was little."

Except the three summers he'd spent with Cat, as streetlord of Ragmarket.

"How did you find us out here?" Han asked Cat, to change the subject.

"I saw those soldiers drag you out of the inn, and figured you was in trouble," Cat said, still glaring at Dancer. "So I followed you." She snorted. "I couldn't believe it. The great Cuffs Alister falling for turtle'd cider."

A revelation struck Han. "You were the Malthusian sister who drank like a teamster," he said, recalling the veiled dedicate in the common room. In the last several common rooms, now that he thought about it.

"Least I didn't go sliding under the table like a 'prentice in his cups," Cat said, smirking.

"Well, thank you for rescuing us," Han said. "You probably saved our lives."

"No *probably* about it," Dancer said, smiling at Cat. "Thank you. That was quick thinking. You're very good with a strangle-cord."

"So," Cat said, still looking at Han and ignoring Dancer, "I think you need looking out for. I think you need better help." She curled her lip at Dancer, then shook back her mass of curls. "You planning to set up a new crew in Ardenscourt or what?" Scrunching her hair together, she tied it with a length of cloth. Her Ragger scarf. "Looked like there'd be lots of fat purses and not much competition. Trust me, nobody'd bloody-up against a jinxflinger for territory."

She never believed we were going to Oden's Ford, Han thought. She assumed I was going back to the Life and cutting her out.

"Look," he said. "Dancer an't my crew. Like I said, we're going to Oden's Ford, and it an't to dive pockets. We're going there to school."

"Why don't you come with us?" Dancer said, all out of the blue, even though he didn't know about Jemson's offer to Cat. "All kinds of people go to school there, and there's all kinds of subjects. There's got to be something you're interested in."

Han and Cat both stared at him.

"I don't need your pity, copperhead," Cat snarled. "You think just because you're tight with Cuffs Alister you can—"

"Shut it," Han said. "You can come with, but you got to get

along with Dancer, and you got to go to school if you do. Don't think we an't grateful you saved our lives, but that's the deal. Take or leave."

"You'd choose him over me?" Cat said, her eyes wide and amazed.

"He an't the one asking me to make a choice."

Cat shuddered, wrapping her arms around herself. The declining moon's angled light only partially illuminated her face, glittering on the tears running down her cheeks.

Cat Tyburn? Crying?

"Hey, now," Han said. "It can't be bad as all that."

"I'll come," she said, swiping at her eyes with her sleeves and sniffling. "I'll go to the Temple School. I got nowhere else to go. Everybody's gone. I can't stay in Ragmarket, nor anywhere in the city."

Han stared at her, speechless, once again crushed by guilt. In a way, he was responsible for her. He'd been the cause of all her losses.

Still, his instincts pricked him. Why would Cat want anything to do with him, when she had him to blame for the loss of everything she had—the Raggers, her territory, Velvet. She should hate the sight of him. And Cat wasn't the forgiving sort.

Unless, like she said, she didn't have a choice.

"All right," he said. "Good that's settled. Now we got to go. Soon as they give up hunting us out here, they may be looking for us to go back to the inn. We want to get there before they do, collect our horses, and be on our way." He wasn't leaving his pony behind, not after he'd waited a lifetime to own one.

Dancer had been quiet all through this, but now he shook his head. "You two go ahead. I'm going back. I can't just leave it there."

"Leave . . . oh. Your amulet." Han put his hand on Dancer's shoulder, and Dancer twitched irritably, as if he already knew what Han would say. "You can't go back," Han said. "They'll kill you."

"I can be in and out of their camp before they know I'm there," Dancer persisted. "I'll meet you back at the inn. If I don't come, you two go on without me."

"Don't you think they've locked it up again?" Han said. "Don't you think they'd expect you to come back after it? We got no idea how many soldiers are with them. Do you want to end up fighting in the Ardenine war?"

"What am I supposed to do at Oden's Ford without an amulet?" Dancer raised his hands, palms up. "Carry water and build fires? Clean the latrine?"

Han felt guilty having two amulets when Dancer had none. The Lone Hunter amulet was made for me, he thought. I should give Dancer the Waterlow piece.

But he didn't want to. The Waterlow amulet seethed with power—he'd been packing it full for weeks. The Lone Hunter flashpiece seemed dark and empty in comparison—like an unconsecrated temple.

But since he hadn't connected with it, perhaps it would bond with Dancer instead.

Besides, whenever anyone else tried to touch the serpent flash, they got burnt.

Han lifted the Hunter amulet from around his neck and dangled it in front of Dancer. "Try this. I've not used it. Most wizards aren't matched with custom amulets. They're lucky to get one at all."

Dancer stared at the spinning amulet, scowling like a trader confronted with a paste diamond in a setting of gilded tin. He extended a cautious finger and touched it. It flared up in greeting as power rippled between them.

Dancer sighed, shaking his head. "I'll have to start over," he said. But he took the Hunter amulet from Han, dropped the chain over his head, and tucked the jinxpiece under his shirt. Immediately, his aura dimmed as the amulet began taking in power.

Would Karn be able to make use of the Fire Dancer flash? I hope they burn themselves up, Han thought.

He climbed a tree to get a better view. The lights of Ardenscourt faded against the rising sun to the east. He guessed they were a few miles west of the city.

He climbed back down. "It'll take them a while to sort things out back there. We can be back to the inn by breakfast time," he said. "Once we're in the city, they won't dare come after us in daylight. Let's go."

CHAPTER EIGHT
ODEN'S FORD

It took more than a week for the Gray Wolves to reach the border of the Kingdom of Tamron. The spiderwebbing waterways of the Fens eventually coalesced into the broad and lazy Tamron River. It meandered south, wrapping around islands and sandbars as if it didn't really care where it was going.

Waterwalkers poled rafts and flatboats up and down the river at will, there being little current to fight. The Wolves traveled mostly at night, staying well away from the riverbanks, and making wide circles around Waterwalker villages. After their experience at Rivertown, they did not know how they would be received.

They slipped across the border one night, waiting until after sunset. They needn't have troubled themselves. The keep that frowned over the river road on the Tamron side was abandoned—occupied only by feral cats and armies of mice, living amicably together. The stable yard was overgrown with brambles and grasses. Some of the stonework had been cannibalized by scavengers.

"Tamron must've sent their armies south and east, to reinforce the border with Arden," Amon said, kicking at a rusted bucket lying in the weeds. "Seems they're not worried about the Waterwalkers down here."

They slept that night in the shelter of the ruined castle. Amon directed Raisa to a corner of what must have been the officers' mess, and planted himself and his bedroll next to the door. The other Wolves found sleeping space in the courtyard.

Raisa could see stars above where portions of the wooden roof had rotted away. It was good to have sturdy walls around her, after their experiences in the Fens, yet she tossed and turned, unable to sleep. Once again, she second-guessed her decision to leave the Fells. Homesickness lay like a cold stone under her breastbone.

The mountains called to her, all the dead queens in their tombs of stone. *Raisa,* they whispered. *Raisa* ana'*Marianna* ana'*Rissa and all the other* ana's *back to Hanalea. Come back home.*

I refuse to cooperate in the re-enslavement of the Gray Wolf line, she thought.

Finally, she rose and walked to the doorway and stood over Amon Byrne, where he lay cocooned in his blanket. He rolled onto his back and opened his eyes.

"What's the matter?" he whispered. "Why are you up?"

"Why can't I ever sneak up on you?" she demanded.

Amon sat up and rubbed his eyes with the heels of his hands. "Why don't you try it in the daylight?"

Raisa snorted. "If I can't do it when you're fast asleep, how could I expect to do it when you're awake?"

"I'm just saying it would be more convenient in the daylight."
He yawned.

Oh. Right. Raisa stuffed her hands in her pockets. "I'm
sorry. I didn't mean to wake you. It's just I can't sleep." She
stared down at her feet in the heavy wool socks that were
scarcely needed in this strange southern climate.

"Hmmm." He raked his hand through his tousled hair.
"Here. Sit," he said, patting a stone bench next to the door.
Raisa sat. He slid out of his blankets, wearing only his breeches,
and sat next to her.

She took his hand between her two and leaned her head on
his shoulder. She traced the veins on the back of his hand with
her forefinger. His hands were large, blunt-fingered, capable. She
loved his hands.

A voice whispered in her head. *I will lean on Amon Byrne for
the rest of my life.*

After a brief silence, he said, "If it means anything, I think
you made the right decision. Leaving the Fells, I mean."

Raisa blinked up at him. "How did you know that's what
was bothering me?"

"Lucky guess," Amon said, looking away and shrugging his
shoulders. "You're not one to run from a fight, and you can hold
your own with most anyone in a fair go. But how could you
hope to fight your mother and the High Wizard both?"

"But my mother's the queen," Raisa said. "How can I expect
others to bend their knees to me if I rebel against my liege ruler?
How can my people trust me if I run away?"

Amon gazed down at their joined hands. For once he didn't
pull away. "You pick a battle you can win, and choose the time

and place of it. Don't let the enemy choose."

"Is that what they teach you at Wien House?"

"It's what my da says. The Bayars wouldn't have risked pushing this marriage and enraging the clans if they weren't sure of the outcome."

Raisa sighed. Somehow, out here in the lonely dark of this peculiar autumn, what had happened back in Fellsmarch Castle on her name day seemed like an overwritten melodrama starring somebody else.

"They could be wrong. The Bayars, I mean."

"Aye, they could be," Amon said, his voice measured. Meaning he doubted it.

"She does resist Lord Bayar sometimes," Raisa persisted, somehow compelled to defend her mother. "Maybe it's more a matter of influence than control."

"Maybe. Still, you'd be married to Micah Bayar if you'd stayed."

Micah. Raisa looked up at the stars, focusing, trying to dispel the memory of Micah's face, of the kisses that had sizzled through her like flame through paper.

"Let's talk about what will happen when we get to Oden's Ford," she said, suddenly eager to change the subject.

"I don't suppose you've reconsidered the idea of going to the Temple School?" Amon said this with little hope.

Raisa sighed. "Except for my time at Demonai Camp, I've studied art, music, and languages all my life. I need to learn something else."

She looked up into his face, willing him to understand. "Going to Oden's Ford is risky, but it's also an opportunity.

None of the Gray Wolf queens has gone there, not recently, anyway. I'll learn things my mother can't teach me. The queendom is under siege, and we're running out of time." Raisa suddenly realized she was gripping Amon's hand really hard, and let go her death hold a bit.

Amon looked sideways at her. "Because of what happened with the Bayars?"

Raisa shook her head. "It's not just them. I feel like the sand is washing from under my feet." She laughed bitterly. "I sound like my mother, the melancholy queen. But, unlike her, *I'm* not willing to trade sovereignty for protection." She paused. "The problem with the gift of prophecy is you're never sure if it's a true vision or just the doldrums setting in.

"Lord Bayar is right about one thing—we're going to be under assault from the south as soon as the Montaignes quit fighting each other. I'll never be a soldier, but I need to know more about diplomacy, politics, and military strategy. I need to know my enemies better."

"So you want to go to Wien House."

She nodded.

The moon freed itself from a veil of clouds, and light spilled into the ruins.

"Micah and Fiona Bayar will be at Mystwerk House as first years," Amon said, raising an eyebrow. "The Manders, too."

She sighed. "I guess I'll run into them sooner or later."

"Maybe later, if we're lucky." He rubbed his nose. "One advantage of Wien House is that it's on the opposite side of the river from Mystwerk. Warriors, engineers, and accountants—the practical arts—train on one side of the river. Wizards, healers, and the temple artists train on the other side. There's not much mixing between."

"Really?" Raisa said, surprised. "Why not?"

Amon smiled, his white teeth flashing against his sun-dark skin. "Any red-robed wizard newling who wanders onto the Wien House side is likely to be pitched into the river. It's mostly southerners on our side, and they aren't keen on anything magical."

"Wouldn't they think twice about tangling with a wizard?" Raisa said.

"You'd think." Amon nodded. "But there are strict rules about magical attacks within the academy. Any kind of aggression, actually. You've heard of the Peace of Oden's Ford, I guess."

Raisa nodded. "It's amazing they can enforce it. And since the school's between Arden and Tamron, I'm surprised neither has tried to take it over."

"Arden and Tamron would both love to have the academy, with all its wealth and knowledge," Amon said. "Arden disapproves of Mystwerk because it trains wizards. The Church of Malthus wants to shut Mystwerk down, and they've tried to overrun the school before. But the faculty and students fight to defend it. You've got the most powerful wizards, the best military and engineering minds in the Seven Realms. Nobody's messed with them in a long time." Raisa waited, but Amon seemed determined to make a long story short.

"Do you think getting into Wien House will be a problem?" Raisa asked.

"My da said he'd write recommendations to the masters of the Temple School *and* Wien House. He used to teach at Wien House, so he has some influence." Amon paused, as if debating whether to go on. "Taim Askell is the master of Wien House, though, and he could be difficult."

"Difficult? How?"

"Let's just wait and see," Amon said. "I don't want to call down trouble that might pass us by." He looked up at the sky. "Promise me you'll go to Temple School, though, if you can't get into Wien House?"

"Let's just wait and see," Raisa said. *I'll get in*, she told herself. *I'm not wasting my time at Oden's Ford.*

"If you're recognized, you may have to leave at a moment's notice," Amon said, tightening his grip on her hand.

She nodded. "I understand. But I don't see where I could go that would be safer. Not Arden. Tamron's a possibility, I guess," she said, thinking of Liam Tomlin.

"What about farther south? Bruinswallow or We'enhaven?" Amon said.

"You're the one who suggested Oden's Ford in the first place," Raisa said. "Besides, I don't *know* people in Bruinswallow or We'enhaven. That's my problem. I haven't *been* anywhere; I don't know anyone outside of my own realm except the people who came to my name day party. I could end up someplace where they sacrifice foreign princesses to their gods." She paused, but Amon didn't smile. "I can't put myself under someone else's control. And I want to stay close enough to get a message to my mother."

Amon's eyes narrowed. "You can't mean that, Rai. It's too dangerous."

"She needs to know I'm still alive," Raisa insisted. "And that I still love her, and that I'm coming back. I don't want her to have any doubts about that."

"How are you planning to send a message in a way that doesn't lead directly back to you?" Amon said. "Here I'm worrying about your running into Micah, and you're planning to stand up and wave at Lord Bayar and say, 'Here I am!'"

"I'm not writing to Lord Bayar," Raisa growled.

"Same as," Amon retorted. "Besides, because of the war it's not all that easy to send mail from Oden's Ford to the Fells."

"I don't know how I'll do it!" Raisa snapped. "Why is it that everything I want to do is dangerous? Everything worthwhile, anyway. Some chances are worth taking."

Amon muttered something under his breath.

"What was that, Corporal?" Raisa demanded. "I couldn't quite hear you."

Amon clenched his jaw and stared straight ahead, his dark eyebrows drawn together.

"What?"

"I *said*, Your Highness, that the difference between you and me is that if you get yourself killed, you don't have to blame yourself every day for the rest of your life."

Raisa's cheeks warmed as the blood rushed to her face. "Do you really think anyone is out to kill me?" she said softly. "Isn't it more likely that I'll be carried back to the Fells to marry Micah if I'm recognized and taken?" She shrugged. "If that happens, I'll deal with it. As long as I'm alive, I'll find a way. I promise you this: *I will not be a captive queen.*"

Amon looked up at the sky, the silvery moonlight washing over his face, gilding his chest and arms. He seemed to be struggling over whether to speak.

"You mentioned prophecy before," Amon said finally. "I just

can't shake the feeling that you're risking more than a bad marriage." He cleared his throat and gestured toward her bedroll. "Best get some sleep, Your Highness. We've a long way to go tomorrow."

In contrast to the Fells, where much of the land was too rocky and steep to farm, all of Tamron seemed to be tamed and under cultivation. Great orchards stretched down to the river, the arching branches of the trees loaded with fruit—peaches, apples, and strange orange and yellow fruits that made Raisa's mouth pucker when she bit into them.

Fields of wheat, beans, corn, squash, and pumpkins were centered by great manor houses and studded with the huts of the crofters who labored in the fields. The houses were sprawling, elegant structures with ground-floor windows, not built for defense. Tamron had been at peace for as long as anyone could remember.

It was hard to believe that a war raged just a few hundred miles to the east.

Amon had visibly relaxed since they'd crossed the border, becoming almost chatty for a Byrne. There was little hunting to be had, so they bought provisions from markets in the villages along the way. Amon always made sure they paid a fair price for everything.

Raisa gained a little weight back, requiring no nagging to devour the rich, fresh, southern food. What she gained was mostly muscle, because the daily workouts continued. Raisa trained regularly with her new staff, and found it surprisingly effective, even against a swordsman. Her bladework was improving, too, although she'd never be a champion, given her size.

As they followed the Tamron River south, she was struck by how geography, weather, and terrain drove the economies of nations, creating haves and have-nots.

The industries that thrived in the north relied on materials readily available there—precious stones, gold and silver, wool, furs and leather. The Vale was the only sizable stretch of land that was arable.

So the clans had become masters of commerce, buying and selling goods produced by themselves and others. But that made the Fells vulnerable in times of war, with trade disrupted. It made it difficult to keep the people fed.

When the Seven Realms were joined together, goods, money and people flowed freely among them, making the whole stronger than its component parts.

Traveling through Tamron, Raisa thought of Prince Liam Tomlin, heir to the throne of Tamron, who'd attended her name day party. It was only two months ago, but it seemed a lifetime had passed since their flirtation in the Great Hall had been interrupted by Micah Bayar. What might have happened had Micah not hauled her away to what was intended to be a clandestine wedding?

Liam had claimed he was looking for a rich bride. Having seen a little of Tamron, Raisa was beginning to realize that the heir to this kingdom would bring a lot to the table himself. She had no interest in giving up her queendom, but how would it be, she thought, to marry the interests of the Fells and Tamron together? Prior to the Breaking, they had been united, as two of the Seven Realms ruled by the Gray Wolf queens.

Raisa was determined to seize control of her matrimonial

future, to develop her own plan. There was a difference between marrying for the good of the Fells and becoming a tool of everybody else's agendas.

As they drew closer to Oden's Ford, the road became congested with traffic—wagons carrying produce, grain, even pigs and chickens to market. There were students, also, and here the variety was greatest. Some rode in great carriages, with escorts of armed men, servants, and baggage-wagons behind.

"First years," Amon said, grinning. "Newlings. They're in for a big surprise. They call Oden's Ford 'the great leveler' for a reason. Everyone gets the same space—a bed with a drawer underneath. They'll have to haul most of that lot back home, or find a place to store it outside the academy."

Some students came on horseback, singly and in groups, on mounts ranging from blue-blooded pacers to farm stock, from healthy to spavined. Others came afoot, with road-worn shoes and packs on their backs. Hired wagons rattled by, students jouncing around inside them, eyes pinched shut against the dust.

Inns along the way were packed full. When the Wolves could find a table for supper, they were surrounded by scholars from all over the Seven Realms, even Bruinswallow, We'enhaven, and the islands. The clamor of languages had Raisa straining to test her skills. But they seemed to speak more rapidly than her tutors did.

The Gray Wolves encountered friends along the way—fellow cadets on the road back to Wien House. As a newling cadet, Raisa attracted considerable interest. Several boys struck up conversations with her. One Tamric soldier was particularly persistent, plying her with ale and flattery, until Amon's relentless glare drove him away.

"He seemed nice," Raisa said, watching him beat a hasty retreat.

"I know him," Amon said bluntly. "And he's not."

Stores in the small towns, and peddlers along the road, displayed goods students might need—paper in many colors, quills and blotters; leather-bound encyclopedias many inches thick that the hawker claimed contained all knowledge.

A storekeeper hovered by a rack of reading glasses meant for eyes weakened from hours of study. Another offered jars of pigments, rolls of paper and canvas, brushes in all sizes, wooden blocks, and small sharp knives for carving images for block printing.

It was nearly dusk when they crested a small rise and the academy lay before them. From that distance, it might have been a fortress bisected by the Tamron River, protected by high stone walls. Temple spires, gold-leafed domes, and tiled roofs protruded above the walls, gleaming in the dying sun like lavish icing on a stone cake.

Traffic on the road ahead had dwindled. Savvy students had arrived before suppertime and were no doubt already at table. As if in honor of this thought, Raisa's stomach growled loudly.

Amon reined in with difficulty. His horse, Vagabond, was eager to go forward, already anticipating dinner and a barn ahead.

Raisa was less sure of what her reception would be as an unexpected add-on. She hoped for a long hot bath. She and Switcher smelled a lot alike. If she'd ever hoped to impress Amon Byrne with her newly acquired glamour and beauty, that chance was gone forever. He'd seen her in every kind of ugly.

Amon, of course, seemed well suited to life on the trail.

Living rough lent him a kind of rugged, stubbly patina that, if anything, made him more attractive.

"It's getting late," Raisa said, urging Switcher up next to Vagabond. "Maybe we should find an inn tonight and go over to Wien House in the morning."

"We'll have to stay in the dorms tonight," Amon said. "The inns will be full, with classes beginning in just a few days. We've come after dark on purpose—there's less chance we'll bump into someone we know outside the gate or on the Mystwerk side of the river."

"You know I'll be recognized sooner or later," Raisa said, keeping her voice down so the others wouldn't overhear. "We'll just have to deal with it."

"Later is better," he muttered. He gazed down at the town, stroking his horse's neck. "This works really well as long as nobody knows you're here. Once they do, it's going to be impossible to protect you."

"Most of my subjects have never seen me up close." She smiled ruefully. "Those who have wouldn't recognize me without a tiara on my head."

He didn't smile back.

Amon twisted in his saddle to face the others. "Stay here and rest the horses. I'll go down and check things out." Not waiting for a reply, he drove his heels into Vagabond's sides, and they clattered off down the road, descending into the valley.

Amon was gone for two hours. When he returned, he wore a rather grim, resigned expression. "We're good," he said, the words not matching his demeanor. "I've spoken to Master Askell, and arranged lodging at the dormitories for tonight. Let's go."

As they descended the long hill to the river, Raisa leaned close to Amon. "What's going on?" she asked. "What did Master Askell say?"

"He wants to meet with you," Amon said, rubbing the back of his neck.

"That's good, isn't it?"

"Depends."

They did not enter the academy by the main gate, but circled around to the postern gate on the south side. Two cadets ushered them through, and locked up behind them.

Switcher followed after Vagabond without much guidance from Raisa, freeing her to look around as they crossed the academy commons.

The school was the size of a small city, but had more green space than any city Raisa had ever seen. Ancient stone buildings studded the lawns, connected by covered galleries paved with brick and twined with night-blooming flowers. The intoxicating fragrance cascaded over them, carried by the warm, moist air.

Lights blazed in the kitchens and dining halls. Most students were still at dinner, though a few had begun walking back to their dormitories, chatting and calling to friends across the commons in all the languages of the Seven Realms. Others trickled down the main road toward the river, unburdened by schoolwork, since classes hadn't started.

"What are these buildings?" Raisa asked, pointing.

"This is the Mystwerk side of the river," Amon said. He gestured to an elaborate stone building that sprawled over several acres. "That's Mystwerk Hall, the oldest building in the academy. Supposedly the academy was founded when a wizard built a hut on the riverbank and began taking in apprentices."

Raisa studied Mystwerk Hall, tilting her head back and taking in the massive bell tower. Was Micah Bayar somewhere inside?

How long had Micah waited for her at the West Wall? Had he given up his plans to come to Oden's Ford in order to hunt for her?

They passed elaborate herb gardens quilted with flowers, some familiar, some not.

"Those are the healer's gardens," Amon said, noticing Raisa's interest. "People come here from all over to train as healers and to be treated in the Healer's Hall."

Ahead, a stone bridge arched high over the water, lined with shops and vendor stalls, most shuttered for the night. The taverns were still open, and clusters of students spilled onto the street.

"The bridge and the shops along Bridge Street are kind of a borderland, where students from both sides mingle," Amon said. He pointed at Raisa with his gloved hand. "So *you* need to stay off Bridge Street."

Amon led the way onto the bridge. Raised voices poured out of an open tavern door to the right, followed by two students locked in a wrestling match. One wore a dun-colored uniform, the other red wizard robes. More students spilled out of the tavern and joined the rainbow of House colors.

"Must be a philosophical disagreement of some kind," Amon said, carefully circling the mob.

"What about the Peace?" Raisa asked.

Amon laughed. "The provost guards handle fights between students." He pointed toward three stern-looking men in drab gray uniforms striding across the street behind them, making for the struggling students.

"They're thick out here, especially after dark, and you go before the rector if you get caught," Amon said. "Serious or repeat offenders get booted from the academy, and there's no appeal. Students usually try to work things out themselves."

They reached the far end of the bridge and descended into the streets on the Wien House side. The buildings here were of newer construction, though still hundreds of years old, built of the same gray stone that must have come from a quarry nearby. The dormitories were less elaborate, more utilitarian, yet there was a stark, simple beauty about the architecture that appealed to Raisa.

The warrior academy was a complex of buildings, a citadel consisting of parade grounds, weapons foundries, dormitories, stables, classroom buildings, and pastures for livestock.

"All academy students stable their horses over here," Amon said. "Whether in Wien House or not."

They passed several long, low buildings that, from the smell, had to be stables. Reining in next to one of them, they dismounted. Raisa removed Switcher's saddle and tack, and rubbed her down. A cadet directed them to a row of stalls. They made sure their mounts were watered and grained before they shouldered their saddlebags and walked over to a large stone building. *Wien Hall* was engraved over the doorway.

A clark sat at a table in the entrance hall with a great ledger in front of him. "Amon Byrne reporting with his company from the Fells," Amon said. "I've already spoken to Master Askell."

The clark nodded. "Welcome back, Commander. Master Askell says you'll be staying in Grindell Hall. All of you." The clark leaned forward, whispering to Amon.

Commander? Raisa's overtired mind couldn't grapple with that. Instead, she idly studied the names and dates carved on either side of the entrance—a list of class commanders that dated back to the Breaking. Noticing a familiar name, she focused, looking closer. *Byrne* surfaced at regular intervals over the past thousand years. Most recently, Edon Byrne, Amon's father. And Amon Byrne.

She sensed Amon's presence behind her, a prickling between her shoulder blades. "There are a lot of Byrnes up there," she said, pointing.

"It's kind of a tradition." He took her saddlebags from her and handed them to Mick. "The rest of you, go get settled at Grindell," he said. "Pick up extra linens for Morley and me, and put Morley's things on the third floor. Talbot and Abbott, you're in with Morley. Once your beds are made up and your things stowed, go on over to the dining hall. Don't wait for us."

He turned to Raisa. "You come with me, Morley. Master Askell is ready for us."

Do we have to go see him *now*? Raisa thought. Weariness had overtaken Raisa's hunger, and she wished she could just fall into bed. Aloud, she said, "I was hoping to get a bath first. Could I at least wash my face?"

"Better to be on time," Amon said. "He'll care more about your appearance if he agrees to admit you."

The other Wolves collected blankets and sheets from a small storeroom and left the building through a side door. Raisa and Amon clumped up a long stone staircase to the third floor. Amon rapped on a thick wooden door at the top of the stairs.

"Come," a deep voice said.

Taim Askell was standing in front of his desk when they entered. He was tall, maybe a little taller than Amon, but probably outweighed him by half. His bulky, muscular frame overwhelmed the room, though the office was a good size. His face was creased and lined by long years of sun and weather, and there were crinkles at the corners of his eyes that said he had smiled at some time in the past.

He wasn't smiling now.

A faculty robe lay folded across the back of his chair; otherwise, the room was neat and uncluttered, everything in its place, save a packet of papers spread over the desk surface.

Bookshelves lined the walls, packed with matching volumes in gold-stamped black leather—histories of military campaigns. A map of the Seven Realms covered the wall opposite the door, and a framed map of Carthis in sepia ink hung behind his desk.

"Master Askell," Amon said in Common, pressing his fist over his heart in salute. "Commander Byrne reporting as ordered, with the applicant Rebecca Morley, sir."

Raisa copied Amon's salute, wondering just how much Master Askell knew.

"Be at ease, Commander, and . . . Candidate Morley," Master Askell said in Ardenine-accented Common. "Sit down," he said, gesturing at two straight-backed chairs. It was more order than invitation.

Raisa sat bolt-straight on the edge of her chair, resting her hands on her thighs, trying to look taller and more substantial. More deserving of admission.

Askell did not sit. Instead, he loomed over the two of them

like the Breaker on the Day of Judgment. As if he didn't mean to give them more than a few minutes of his time.

"This won't take long, I assure you," Master Askell said, reinforcing Raisa's initial impression. "I have made it a practice to interview every applicant who seeks entrance to Wien House, particularly those who request special privileges."

"Special privileges, sir?" Raisa glanced at Amon, who stared into space, a muscle working in his jaw. "I'm not sure what you mean, sir." Raisa meant to err on the side of too many sirs than too few.

"Exactly what is it you expect from us, Morley?" Askell folded his arms.

His hostile tone startled Raisa into speech. "I would imagine that my expectations are similar to those of any other cadet, sir," she said. "I hope to benefit both from study under the Wien House faculty, and through interaction with a diversity of students."

"Is that so?" Askell tilted his head. "And how, exactly, will your presence here benefit Wien House? And the world at large?"

Raisa blinked at him, her weary mind too sluggish to respond. "Um . . ."

Askell plowed on as if he hadn't really expected an answer. "Commander Byrne tells me that you come from the nobility, that though you are female, you are your family's lineal heir, as is the—ah—*custom* in the north," Askell said.

From his expression, Raisa guessed that he disapproved of that custom.

"We attract many applicants from noble families. Many more than we can possibly accommodate. Some families see the military as a means of developing character or addressing certain physical inadequacies. Others see it as a way of disposing of n'er-do-well sons or less than promising daughters."

Worn out as she was, Raisa's temper began to smolder. "I assure you, Master Askell, sir, my parents did not send me here for any of those reasons," she said stiffly.

Askell raised an eyebrow. "So it seems. You come without a letter of introduction from your parents, which is unusual. Perhaps you ran away to join the army, then. Perhaps you see this as a means of rebellion against them."

"I did not run away to join the army, sir," Raisa said. "I am here to seek an education that will prepare me to carry out my obligations to my family and the Fells."

"We *do* have a letter of recommendation from our alumnus Edon Byrne." Askell paused, as if expecting Raisa to comment, but she said nothing. "And your own commander has asked for certain accommodations for you. This raises immediate concerns. Most candidates wait until they are admitted to request special treatment. Do you really think Wien House is a good fit for you?"

"Master Askell, perhaps I—" Amon began, but the master shook his head.

"I asked Morley, Commander," Askell said, without taking his eyes off Raisa. "I need to make sure that your presence here won't be a distraction that adversely affects the education of the other cadets. We have a responsibility to them as well as to you. Our students are organized into cohesive units. Instances of favoritism work against that."

Raisa looked straight at Askell. "I am curious, sir, about the accommodations Commander Byrne has requested on my behalf," she said. "Since he did not choose to share them with me."

For a long moment, Askell didn't answer, as if Raisa's response was not what he expected. The master stalked to the sideboard, grabbed up a teapot, and set it on the hearth to heat.

He turned and leaned against the mantel. "Commander Byrne has asked that all Fellsian cadets from his command—and you—be lodged together in Grindell Hall, when it is our policy to mix cadets from the different realms together in the dormitories as well as in class. It is also unusual to house first years like yourself with fourth years like the commander.

"Further, he has asked that a unique curriculum be tailored for you—one that crosses school boundaries to combine military science, rigorous physical training, geography, diplomacy, history, and finance. In fact, he has proposed a curriculum that would likely occupy you for all of your waking hours and many of your sleeping ones."

"What?" Raisa said, making no effort to hide her surprise. "I had no idea, sir, that Commander Byrne had taken this degree of interest in planning my education." She turned and stared at Amon, who did not meet her eyes. Seeing the spots of color on his cheeks, she realized what it had taken for him to spend his influence with Askell in trying to secure special treatment for her. It was not the way he operated.

She turned back to Askell. "However, hearing it, sir, I think it sounds perfect for me."

"You are coming late to the academy," Askell said. "The other cadets your age have been here for three years already. It would be a challenge for you to master the usual curriculum, let alone one so . . . demanding."

"I am used to hard work, sir," Raisa said, lifting her chin.

"I'm not totally untutored. I fostered with the Spirit clans for three years in the Fells."

"Did you, now?" the master said, his face displaying a flatlander's disdain for the clans. "I fail to see how that applies to your admission to a military academy."

Edon Byrne says I ride like a Demonai warrior, Raisa was tempted to say.

"If I may, that is the reason I proposed a somewhat different curriculum for Morley, sir," Amon said. "As you know, much of the first three years here at the academy is physical training—horsemanship, wayfinding, tracking, survival skills. There is considerable overlap with what Morley learned in the upland camps. Morley has also been training hard for the past month in flatland weaponry. I think you'll find that—"

"If it could be done in a month, we would be that much more efficient, now wouldn't we, Commander Byrne?" Askell said, emptying a paper of tea into the teapot. Using a rag to protect his hand, he carried it over to his desk and set it on a battered trivet.

Finally, he sat down in his high-backed chair and looked at Raisa as one might a child who overreaches. Raisa had seen that look often, and it never failed to annoy her.

"Is it really your intention to be a soldier, Morley?" Askell asked. "Wouldn't it make more sense for you to study the softer sciences? Healing, art, and philosophy are all important topics. That's a more typical course of study for those of your station."

"My *station* or my *gender*, sir?" Raisa said. "You've said Wien House is full of thanelings and dukes. I can think of only one way in which they are different from me."

173

"There are women in Wien House," Askell said stiffly. "Surely, Commander Byrne has told you as much."

"There are women, aye," Raisa said, her voice quivering with anger. "And they're all from the north, and likely the daughters of soldiers, right? No gently raised ladies?"

Askell looked at her for a long moment, then shook his head. "No gently raised ladies," he admitted. So at least he was honest.

Raisa stood, her fists clenched at her sides. "To answer your question, no, sir, I don't mean to be a soldier. But kings, dukes, and lords have been sending their heirs to Wien House for more than a thousand years—not to make them soldiers, but to make them better leaders.

"I've been stuffed full of philosophy and art and the softer sciences, as you call them. If I could stitch or sing or recite my way out of a crisis, I'd be well prepared. I came here because this is said to be the best place to get an education in the Seven Realms. I came here to fill in the gaps in my education, to prepare for the times I'll be making decisions all by myself, when knowledge of leadership, engineering, and military science may make the difference between success and failure."

Raisa glanced at Amon, who sat motionless, save his gray eyes flicking from her to Askell and back again. "What Commander Byrne has proposed sounds like just what I need. But I'll train as a simple soldier if that's what I have to do to get an education. I'll live wherever you assign me. I ask no accommodations from you. If I fail, I fail. But maybe I'll learn something in the meantime. Sir."

Raisa bowed to the master, saluting him as Amon had done. "Thank you for your time, sir. I'll leave you to discuss this with

Commander Byrne." She backed from the room, knowing she'd probably ruined any chance she had of staying at Wien House.

Furious tears stung her eyes as she banged down the stairs. She paused on the second-floor landing to collect herself before descending the rest of the way. When had admission to Wien House become so important? Two months ago she'd had no plans to come to Oden's Ford at all. Was this just a childish desire for anything denied her? Was this something she hadn't wanted until Askell resisted?

Then again, two months ago she hadn't known of Gavan Bayar's treacherous plans to subvert the Næming and seize power by marrying his son to the future queen of the Fells. She needed to return well armed for the battles that lay ahead.

That Amon Byrne had turned into a truly devious person. When had he hatched this new scheme for her education, and when had he planned to tell her about it? It was arrogant on his part, yet she couldn't help being touched by it.

What would she do if Askell refused to admit her? She didn't have much choice. She needed to stay within the sanctuary of Oden's Ford. But if she crossed the river to the Temple School, it would be that much more likely she'd be seen by Micah Bayar or his friends. Plus, she would lose the protection of the Gray Wolves.

Raisa asked the clark on the first floor how to get to Grindell Hall. Surely they'd let her sleep there one night, even if they booted her out the next day.

By the time she reached the dormitory, the rest of the Gray Wolves had eaten. They'd brought plates back for Raisa and Amon, but Raisa had lost her appetite. She huddled in an overstuffed chair next to the cold hearth in the common room long after the others had gone to bed, nursing a cup of tea and waiting for Amon to return.

Finally, she heard his familiar footstep. He paused in the doorway, a tall silhouette, looking in at her. "I thought you'd be in bed," he said.

"What did Askell say?" Raisa demanded.

Amon came forward into the light and knelt next to her chair. He closed his rough hand over hers, and that strange, wild energy flowed between them. Time seemed to telescope, and it seemed she could look ahead, this same scene repeating itself long into the distance, a future that would find them growing older together.

A prophesy? Raisa's skin prickled, and her heart accelerated. What did it mean?

"What is it about you?" Amon whispered, a bemused look on his face. "Have I told you lately that you are amazing, Your Highness?"

"Not lately," Raisa replied, swallowing hard. "Or ever."

"I'm sorry I didn't tell you about my idea," Amon said. "I figured Master Askell would flat out say no, and I didn't want you to be disappointed. I thought you might be more willing to go to the Temple School if you didn't know I'd come up with an alternative."

"What did Askell say?" Raisa repeated.

"Dimitri was right. You are a witch-talker," Amon said, shaking his head. "Master Askell has approved your curriculum and your housing. You start day after tomorrow."

CHAPTER NINE

THE
ROAD WEST

Han was glad to leave the capital of Ardenscourt behind him. The West Road ran straight as a taut bowstring across the plains between Ardenscourt and the Tamron River. They made good time, since there were no mountains to work around, only the occasional river or stream to navigate. But in some places the bridges had been destroyed, and they had to travel far up or downstream to find a crossing place. Often makeshift ferries served travelers along the east-west road.

The evidence of the ongoing war surrounded them— burned-out farmhouses, salvos of foot soldiers on the march, massive keeps locked up tight with battle flags flying, large encampments of soldiers. Repeatedly, Han's party left the right of way, hiding themselves in the trees to avoid mounted patrols flying the myriad colors of the warring thanes.

They came upon battlefields, sometimes dislodging crows and carrion birds from the decomposing bodies. The scavengers circled overhead, complaining rudely, then settled again as soon as they passed. Several times they passed gibbets bearing the stinking fruit of recent executions.

It's a good season for crows, Han thought. There was no way they'd be in time for the opening day of classes, delayed as they were by their late start and many detours.

Cat wasn't happy on horseback. The horse Jemson had lent her was an ill-favored, lazy beast, nearly as bad-tempered as Ragger. Cat clung to his back like a sticker burr, totally uncomfortable, impossible to dislodge. Things went better once Han convinced her to switch to the spare pony. They used Cat's horse for baggage.

Cat's superior street skills did little good in the countryside, which made her sullen and briary. She wasn't used to being second best at anything.

Han and Dancer traded off teaching Cat woodcraft, such as tracking and bow hunting. She had quick, accurate reflexes, and she'd always been good with blades of all kinds. When their hunting was successful, she quickly learned to skin and dress the carcasses.

She seemed subdued, very different from the Cat Han remembered from the Raggers. In the past, it was Cat's pride and obstinacy that got her into trouble. Now she seemed snappish, like a dog that's been kicked too many times.

She displayed a persistent prejudice against Dancer for the crime of being clan. It seemed ironic, Cat being from the Southern Islands, that she'd soaked up Vale attitudes. Sometimes people that get beat on just want to beat on someone else.

They continued to travel by night. As dawn approached,

they'd find a sheltered place to lay up for the day. Han and Cat would set out a few snares, while Dancer built a fire and set up camp. They'd eat, catch a few hours sleep, then prop up and pull out their books.

Dancer switched off between his Demonai flashcraft book and the book of charms. Han committed charms to memory, then struggled to make his amulet do what he wanted. Sometimes he succeeded, sometimes he failed, but at least there were no more aggressive spurts of power or bizarre, self-destructive behavior.

He'd just as soon get that out of his system out here in the middle of nowhere.

As long as they stuck with reading, Cat would stay. Sometimes she brought out her basilka and played—sweet, melancholy tunes that could bring a person to tears, even if you didn't know the words. Dancer would often leave off reading and lean forward, wrapping his arms around his knees, eyes closed, just listening.

But if they started practicing charms, Cat would stalk out of camp and stay away for hours. She made it plain that she wanted nothing to do with magic.

Dancer still disliked the substitute amulet, though he continued to load it with power. "This doesn't feel right," he said, poking at it. "It's like there's something coming between me and the amulet . . . something that doesn't belong."

Han shrugged. "Maybe they're all like that," he suggested. He hesitated, then pressed his fingers against the Waterlow piece. "Sometimes it seems like this one has knowledge and power embedded in it already. I thought maybe it was because of . . . because of who I am. Or because of who owned it before."

Dancer frowned. "You think it's cursed? Or you think you're cursed?"

"Maybe both," Han muttered. What if it was true—what Elena had told his mother? What if he *was* cursed because the blood of the Demon King ran in his veins? His family fortunes had certainly fallen over the past thousand years—from king of the Seven Realms to starveling street thief.

"Why? Who owned it before?"

Startled, Han looked over to where Cat sat cradling her basilka. He'd forgotten she was there.

Han didn't want to lie to Cat, but he also didn't want to spook her any more than she was already by telling her he was using the Demon King's old amulet.

"Well," he said, "it used to belong to Lord Bayar. The High Wizard."

Cat blinked at him. Then stood, setting aside her basilka. "It seems like it brought you a whole lot of trouble," she said. "Maybe you should give it back." She turned and disappeared into the woods.

Han and Dancer stared after her.

"Well," Dancer said, "for what it's worth, I don't think you're cursed. If I did, I'd stay away from you." He tilted his head, gazing at Han's amulet. "As for the flashpiece, it's more likely it's because the thing's extremely powerful, and you don't know what you're doing. At least wait until you get a little training before you decide."

CHAPTER TEN
CADET

Raisa opened her eyes to darkness, but she could hear that Talia and Hallie were already up. A flare of light, and then the lamp was lit. She closed her eyes against the glare, wishing she could go back to sleep. But if she did, she'd miss breakfast. And she would need breakfast to get through the morning. After four weeks of classes, she knew that much.

With a shuddering sigh she pushed back the blankets, swung her legs off the bed, and stood in her smallclothes, yawning and stretching. Her spare uniform jacket was draped over a chair back to dry.

Cadets wore buff uniforms that required washing nearly every day in the sodden autumn weather. When they marched on the parade ground, mud splashed up their breeches to their knees. Because of that, or because of the drab color, students from the other side of the river called them *dirtbacks*.

Raisa poked at her jacket as she passed by. Still damp. Nothing ever dried in this miserable climate. She thrust away memories of a life in which clean clothes magically appeared whenever she needed them. With several ensembles to choose from.

Somebody had been washing those clothes, she thought. And doing the mending, and all the hundred little tasks she now had to do herself—and to military standards.

Amon had arranged it so that there was no dorm master in residence at Grindell, and Raisa, Talia, and Hallie could share the room on the top floor. This meant that they all had to share the dorm master's duties—keeping the common areas and wash-rooms clean, and maintaining a supply of fresh linens for the beds. As the weather cooled, they hauled wood for the fireplaces from the quartermaster's depot along the river.

Hallie was done in the washroom already; that girl was amazingly efficient. She just skinned her hair back and tied it with a cord, washed her face, and she was done.

Raisa fluffed her cap of hair and regarded her reflection glumly in the polished metal mirror. Would long hair have been easier? She could have tied it back. But thick as it was, it would dry just as slowly as her jacket. She scrubbed her face with cold water, then slid into her damp uniform, making a face as the clammy fabric touched her skin.

She'd be hot soon enough.

Raisa walked out into the sitting room, where Talia was sprawled in a chair, knees draped over the arm, the lamp close by her, reading. She looked up from her book and smiled, marking her place with a finger.

Talia was a mixed-blood, like Raisa—her mother was clan and her father was Valeborn—a member of the Queen's Guard.

182

She always rose early to read the Temple Book before class. Either that or one of her moonspinner romances that would put a blush on a fancy's face.

Talia was a person of diverse interests.

"You two ready?" Hallie called from the door. "If we don't hurry, all the sausage will be gone again."

At least Hallie and Talia had quit calling her "Lady Rebecca" after they'd heard her swearing like a teamster when Switcher stepped on her foot.

The three of them barreled down the stairs, nearly toppling Mick, who was hopping around the common room, trying to darn his socks while wearing them.

"Bad idea," Raisa called as she shouldered open the door.

"That fool's just hoping somebody will offer to do it for him if he looks pitiful enough," Hallie said. "He's going to have holes in his socks for a good long time."

Snickering, they crossed the dark, soggy quad to the dining hall, where sleepy cadets were already lining up for breakfast.

At least I don't have to do my own cooking, Raisa thought as she plopped a dollop of porridge into her bowl, adding molasses and milk and, yes, two sausages. One advantage to drilling at the break of dawn—there was still meat left.

She carried her tray to the long table, sat down, and began shoveling in the porridge. It was a bad way to start the day, but she refused to leave any of it behind when the bells rang for first session.

This term she was enrolled in a History of Warfare in the Seven Realms lecture and recitation; a finance class full of clarks with ink-stained fingers; courses on military strategy and weaponry; and an intensive on the Ardenine language. Plus, she had been assigned to drill daily with the first-year cadets. That was right after breakfast.

"So, Rebecca," Talia said, squeezing in next to Raisa. "Do you like any of these, then?" She pointed her spoon toward the cadets at the next table. "What about that one on the end? With the red hair. Barrett. I hear he's a lively one."

Barrett was in her History of Warfare class. Raisa surveyed him appraisingly, chewed, and swallowed. "Not my type," she said, shaking her head.

"How about Sanborn, then," Talia said, pointing at a well-built boy with straight black hair and skin that was close to Raisa's own bronze color. "He's from the down-realms—We'enhaven, I think. They say they're calm and steady."

Raisa yawned hugely. "I don't know how you have the energy for romance."

"You're too bloody picky," Talia said. "It's not like you have to *marry* them."

"Leave her alone, Talia," Hallie said. "Maybe there's someone back home she's pining for. Some young lord or a rich merchant. She comes from quality, you know. She may be aiming higher than Barrett or Sanborn."

"That doesn't mean she can't have a sweetheart at school," Talia persisted.

Talia was on a matchmaking mission. She and Pearlie Greenholt, the Wien House weapons master, were madly in love, and Talia wanted to share the joy with everyone.

"Just watch yourself, Rebecca," Hallie advised her. "Talia and Pearlie—they're moonspinners. They don't have to worry about making babies."

The word *moonspinners* referred to members of the Temple of the Moon back home in the Fells—women who chose other women over men. Talia was a member; had been since she was twelve. Pearlie wasn't officially—she was Ardenine.

Hallie stood. "Listen to Talia, and you'll end up with a baby in your belly." She patted her midsection for emphasis and walked back toward the food line, her broad back very straight.

Hallie was the single parent of a two-year-old daughter, Asha. She'd had to leave her back in Fellsmarch, with her parents. She was an old soul—not prone to romantic musings.

Hallie needn't have worried. Raisa deftly parried all of Talia's hints and suggestions. She couldn't very well tell Talia that she was in love with their commander.

So much for all her plans to play the field before marriage.

Raisa genuinely liked Hallie and Talia. She enjoyed their company and admired their grit and determination. Talia loved whom she loved, not caring that spinners were frowned upon in the down-realms. Hallie was determined to further her education even though she missed her daughter terribly.

They'd become friends despite all the secrets that divided them.

Having female friends was new to Raisa. Relationships at court were competitive, politically charged, with everyone jockeying for a position next to those in power. No one could be trusted, all motivations were suspect. Amon had been her only real friend, and now that relationship carried its own baggage.

It was no wonder Hanalea had walked about in disguise. It was the only way to find out what people were really like.

The session bells clanged through the dining hall. Raisa carried her bowl and spoon to the scrappers and crossed to the door.

"Give Pearlie my love!" Talia called as she exited into the autumn darkness.

Cadets were already running circuits on the parade grounds when Raisa arrived. She peeled off her jacket and set it aside, knowing she'd be sweating before long.

A half hour of running, and she was drenched. Then they drilled with weapons as a group. Wielding pikes, they charged back and forth across the field in a line ten across, screaming like banshees until Raisa was hoarse and her arms so heavy she could scarcely keep her weapon from dragging on the ground.

This was flatland warfare, and alien to Raisa's eyes. There was no room in a mountain pass for lines of soldiers to maneuver together. Clan warriors battled as individuals or small groups in an alternating attack-and-retreat fashion. But that kind of fighting required cover, and there was no cover in the flatlands.

The drillmaster finally called a halt, and Raisa handed off her pike to Pearlie, who stacked them in the racks. "Talia sends her love," Raisa said. Pearlie blushed and smiled, her face radiant with pleasure. Talia was Pearlie's first real girlfriend.

"Gaah," Raisa muttered, snatching up her jacket and heading for the bathhouse. Love everywhere, and none for me.

The sun was just rising as she crossed the quad to Wien Hall for her first class—the History of Warfare, taught by Taim Askell.

She'd been surprised that the master taught a course for newlings. Askell was a remarkably good teacher—passionate about his subject and knowledgeable, with the kind of practical experience many academics didn't have. He peppered his lectures with real-world examples, many from his own past. He'd fought in battles as far away as Carthis, using all kinds of weaponry and tactics.

Raisa had studied the history of the Seven Realms with her tutors at Fellsmarch Castle, but this was a new kind of history, focused on warfare, and enlivened by the diversity of the students in her class. They came from all over the Seven Realms, and Raisa soon realized that there was more than one truth to know about the past.

Due to the lack of natural barriers, there'd always been more interchange between Arden and Tamron, We'enhaven and Bruinswallow; even the island realms. The southern realms shared customs, languages, faiths—the same basic worldview.

The Fells had become isolated, consumed with its own problems. As a result, the mountain peoples were the subject of much speculation, fascination, and misinformation.

What little the flatlanders did know about the Fells came through the traders who traveled out of the mountains, selling metalwork, jewelry, and other upland products; and buying the foodstuffs that grew in the deep soil and warmer climate of the flatlands. Clan traders were exotic, romantic figures that were good at spinning tales.

Raisa was the only Fellsian student in most of her classes, even the military ones.

Like usual, Raisa had arrived for class from the bathhouse at the last possible moment, and so was forced to sit in the front row as Askell strode to the podium. She hurriedly set out her ink and paper. She always took copious notes in Askell's class.

He spread his lecture notes and surveyed the class, as he always did. Today his gaze lingered on Raisa a little too long. She straightened and met his gaze directly.

"This morning we will discuss the use of magic in warfare," he said. "And so this lecture will pertain particularly to Fellsian charmcasters and the Spirit clans, though it also applies to some elements in Carthis."

A murmur ran through the class, like a stiff wind through the aspens.

Raisa tapped her pen on the table, surprised at the master's use of proper northern terminology for the gifted peoples of the Fells. Most Ardenines referred to wizards as blasphemers, idolators, and mages, and to the clans as heathens and savages.

As if cued by her thoughts, a newling cadet from Tamron raised his hand. It was Barrett, the one who Talia had pointed out at breakfast.

"Do we really need to spend time on this? No one here will ever use such tactics." The cadet's demeanor suggested that Askell had proposed a session on devil-summoning or torture techniques.

On second thought, the topic of torture techniques would have been better received.

"Newling Barrett, shall we assume that you have the gift of predicting the future?" Askell said. "Can you promise everyone here that they will never use magical tactics, and that they will never be at war with anyone who uses them either?"

"Of course not, sir," Barrett spluttered. "But it seems unlikely that—"

"It's the unlikely tactics that will be your undoing," Askell said. "Not the ones you are prepared for. Would that our enemies were so cooperative." His gaze swept over the class again. "Any other objections? No? Then let's discuss the odd and symbiotic relationship between the Spirit clans and the charmcasters who invaded from the Northern Islands—a relationship fraught with conflict over the past thousand years."

For once, Raisa was ahead of her classmates. But she soon realized that Askell knew a lot more than she did about the use of magic during the wizard wars of conquest, and by the Demon King at the time of the Breaking. After a thousand years of peace in the north, it had not been a priority in her education.

But could it be, in the future? What would happen if war broke out between Arden and the Fells? Raisa looked around the lecture hall. A good third of the students in her class were Ardenine. How could she make use of Fellsian assets to turn aside an invasion from the south?

A sudden silence pulled her out of her reverie. She looked up to find everyone looking at her. Including Askell.

"I—I'm sorry, sir. I guess I was . . . distracted," Raisa said, mentally pummeling herself. She had to get better at responding to her assumed name.

"Now that Newling . . . ah . . . *Morley* has rejoined us, I'll repeat the question," Askell said. "Someone asked whether an amulet loaded with charmcaster magic could be used by someone else—gifted or not. I, frankly, don't know. I thought perhaps that you might be able to answer that question, being a northerner."

"I . . . I don't know for sure, but I don't believe so," Raisa said. "I've heard that the power accumulated in an amulet can only be used by the wizard who put it there."

"Thank you, Morley," Askell said. "So we've seen that the

tactics used by Alger Waterlow, known as the Demon King, were both innovative and devastatingly effective."

Some of the students made the sign of Malthus to protect against demon magic.

Askell rolled his eyes. "I wouldn't rely on Saint Malthus to protect you from magical attack," he said. "Now, then. Some scholars suggest Waterlow may have traveled to Carthis and trained under sorcerers there. I can find no primary sources to support that. We do know that just prior to the Breaking, he was well fortified on Gray Lady with Queen Hanalea and an arsenal of weapons. He might have held off the armies of the Seven Realms indefinitely, save that he was betrayed by someone inside."

Askell looked up from his notes. "Surround yourselves with trustworthy people," he said. "If you don't, all the weaponry and tactics in the world can't save you."

When the lecture was over, Raisa collected her notes and stuffed them into her carry bag. Then walked up the aisle to where Askell was gathering his materials together.

"That was excellent, Master Askell," Raisa said, smiling. "Thank you. I learned so much. You have an amazing knowledge of a topic that we don't talk about at home."

Askell stopped shuffling papers and gazed at her for a long moment. "Thank you, Newling Morley," he said dryly. "Suddenly it all seems worthwhile."

Raisa blinked at him. "Sir," she said. "Have I done something wrong? To make you dislike me?"

Askell sighed. "Newling Morley, *dislike* implies a certain degree of interest, a certain engagement or focus, as on an adversary."

He shook his head. "No. I don't dislike you particularly. Nor do I like you."

Raisa held Askell's gaze for a long moment. "Thank you, sir," she said finally. "I am reassured." She saluted him, her fist pressed to her chest, turned, and walked out of the hall.

At least, if it ever came to war between Arden and the Fells, Ardenine arrogance would work in her favor.

CHAPTER ELEVEN

MYSTWERK HOUSE

Han and his party finally reached Oden's Ford one afternoon in late September, four weeks after classes had begun. They entered the eastern gate of the academy in a driving rain, on the Wien House side. The guards at the gate gave them directions to the Mystwerk House quad on the far side of the bridge.

The main road wound its way around and between the buildings of the academy. Han scanned his surroundings with interest. As the bells in the temple towers bonged four o'clock, students in hooded rain cloaks burst from doorways, hurried down covered galleries, and splashed through puddles between the buildings. They all seemed to be in a hurry.

Stone pillars identified the colleges—Factor House, Merchant House, Isenwerk House—all designed and built for the business of learning. Each school centered on a grassy quad, and consisted of classroom buildings, libraries, and dormitories. The academy reminded Han of Southbridge Temple, but on a larger scale.

The dormitories were impressive, too—three and four stories tall, built of brick and stone, with great stone chimneys and arched doorways.

Oden's Ford was like a small city, without the gritty, ugly bits. Even in the rain, it seemed illuminated, its glittering stone buildings set like jewels into green lawns, their flower borders like the embroidery on ladies' dresses. Everything was still green and lush, though autumn was well under way back home in the mountains.

"The bridge should be up this way," Dancer said, as they passed the building marked Wien Hall. "The stables are just ahead, on this side of the bridge, but the Temple School and Mystwerk are on the other side of the river. I've heard it's not wise for the gifted to linger on this side."

"Why not?" Han asked, as Dancer urged Wicked forward, cutting between two long, low buildings that smelled of hay and horses. As they passed between the stables, horses within whinnied a greeting and Ragger answered with a challenge.

"Wien House cadets and Mystwerk students don't mingle," Dancer said. He turned to Cat. "After we leave off our horses, is it all right if we go to Mystwerk quad first, then over to the Temple?"

Cat shrugged and rolled her eyes, like she'd be willing to wait forever. "Maybe I can share your crib," she said to Han. "Even if I'm at the Temple School."

"We'll ask," Han said. He had no idea what the rules were, or how many students shared a room. An awful thought struck him. Maybe all the newlings slept in the same room. Maybe he'd be sharing with the Bayars. He'd never be able to close his eyes.

"Hunts Alone!" Dancer's warning shout broke into his reverie. Han looked up to see that a girlie in a hooded rain cloak had turned across the courtyard in front of him. With her face turned away from the weather, she hadn't seen them. He reined in, hard, splashing water over her.

She shook the water from her cloak and glared up at him. "Look where you're going, will you? You nearly ran me over." He caught a brief glimpse of her face in the shadow of her hood before she spun around and hurried away, moving at a near run, head down against the driving wind and rain.

Han stared at her back, rendered speechless by surprise. Then said, "Rebecca?"

She disappeared between the buildings.

Memories slid through his mind like scenes from an unfinished play: Jemson's study at Southbridge Temple, Rebecca touching his bruised face with cool fingers, saying *Who did this?* like she was ready to go to battle for him; Rebecca, huddled in a corner of his crib in Ragmarket, glaring at him, daring him to make a move. And finally, strutting out of Southbridge Guardhouse, proud as any queen, leading a dozen freed Raggers.

"What is it?" Dancer asked, looking after the fleeing girlie. "Who's that?"

Han shrugged. "My mistake. She looked like someone I knew back home."

Cat snorted. "Trust you to go making eyes at a girlie as soon as we arrive." Dismounting, she led her pony toward the stable doors.

Han hesitated, still staring at the spot where the girlie had disappeared. Even if it wasn't Rebecca, girlies didn't usually run away from him.

It probably didn't help he'd dumped water on her.

It was just as well. His life was complicated enough. Han swung down to the ground and followed after Cat.

After leaving off their horses, they crossed an arching stone bridge lined with shops and taverns that were just opening their doors. Han could smell roasting beef, bacon, and sausage.

They'd ridden straight through lunch that day, in their haste to get to the Ford before dark. Han's stomach rumbled, and he wondered if they should stop or chance getting something to eat at the dormitory. Dancer and Cat walked on, though, and Han followed after, but not without some longing backward looks.

Mystwerk Hall was the size of the cathedral temple in Fellsmarch, a sprawling building that had been added onto with no obvious plan in mind. The wings of the building warred with each other, divided in front by the original temple, circling around for a back-alley fight in the rear. The temple was topped with a tall stone bell tower pierced with tall windows, like narrowed eyes.

Any one part would have been beautiful on its own, but taken together they created a brittle tension that appealed to Han.

An older student occupied a desk in the front hall of the building, his head bent over a spidery manuscript, one hand twisting a lock of his tightly curled hair. He was from Bruinswallow, maybe—and his robe was edged with gold thread.

Han and his friends hesitated in the doorway, waiting to be acknowledged, but the young man seemed engrossed in his reading and didn't look up.

"The fancy work means he's a proficient," Dancer whispered, fingering his own plain sleeve.

"What's a proficient?" Han asked, wishing he knew more about what he was getting into.

"He's passed two sets of exams. First, you're a newling. Then a secondary, then proficient. If he passes his thirds, he'll graduate as a master and he can be faculty," Dancer said. "Three years of reading, writing, and teaching, and he can go for a dean."

Dancer had been studying up on Oden's Ford for months.

He cleared his throat loudly. "Excuse me," he said in Common.

The proficient looked up distractedly, as if his mind still traveled a distant road. "Oh. Sorry. I'm Timis Hadron, proficient on duty," he said in accented Common. He looked them up and down, taking in their travel-worn appearance. "Did you just get in?"

"I'm Hayden Fire Dancer," Dancer said, "and this is Hanson Alister. We're new fall term students for Mystwerk House. I'm sorry we're late; we had some trouble traveling through Arden."

Hadron nodded. "You are not the only ones. Three other newling Mystwerk students arrived yesterday, and two more have yet to arrive. It is unfortunate that the Peace doesn't extend into Arden, yes?"

He pulled a register book toward him and scanned the names. His finger stabbed down at the page. "Ah, yes. Dean Abelard has inquired about you several times. She will be relieved to know you're here." He glanced over at Cat, who was shifting from one foot to the other. "And this is . . . ?"

"This is Cat Tyburn," Dancer said. "She's not enrolled in

Mystwerk, but we hoped she could stay with us."

"No servants allowed," Hadron said, making a notation in his ledger without looking up. "They should have told you when you enrolled."

"I an't no servant!" Cat snapped, slapping her hand down on the register book.

"No sweethearts, either," Hadron said. He looked up, startled, when Cat seized hold of the front of his robe, jerking him forward. She glared down into his face.

Cat was tense. Han could tell. "Cat. Leave off," he said, putting his hand on her arm. "He an't the enemy."

Grudgingly, Cat relaxed her hold on the fabric and stepped back.

"Or bodyguards," Hadron continued, tapping his quill against the manuscript.

"Cat is a newling at the Temple School," Han said.

"Really." Hadron sat back in his chair and regarded Cat with interest. "I apologize, Newling Tyburn. Newlings at Mystwerk often arrive with an entire staff of servants and expect us to find housing for them. They are astonished when we say no. If you're a temple newling, you'll stay right in the temple itself."

"Don't want to stay in the temple," Cat muttered. "Can't I stay here?"

Hadron shook his head. "Newlings stay in assigned housing." He paused. "Congratulations on gaining admission to the Temple School—it's very competitive."

Cat just fumbled with her scarf, retying it around her hair.

"You'll like it, believe me," Hadron went on. "It's the best housing on campus. Much better than where they'll be."

He nodded toward Han and Dancer.

"Maybe they could come stay with me, then," she muttered.

"Don't worry," Dancer said. "It'll be all right. It can't be far away. We'll be together a lot."

"Like I'd want to snuggle up to you," Cat said, folding her arms across her chest.

While they talked, students trickled through the entry hall in twos and threes, their red robes swishing across the stone floor. They eyed the newcomers curiously, pointing and whispering, fingering their amulets.

Han glanced down at his clan travel garb, soiled from the road, and felt out of place. Straightening, he put his shoulders back, his street face on.

"Let us make arrangements for the two of you, shall we?" Hadron said to Han and Dancer. "You've left your horses back at the stables, yes?" When Han nodded, Hadron pushed a pen-and-ink map across the desk toward them.

"You Mystwerk newlings will be in Hampton Hall dormitory, here." He pointed, then looked up at them apologetically. "Not the best accommodations, since you are among the last to arrive, but you'll be out of the rain. The dorm master will have linens for you, and show you your room. The dining halls are here." His finger stabbed down on the map. "Curfew is ten o'clock on class days, later on temple days. All newlings are expected to be inside their dormitories by then unless they're meeting with a faculty member or participating in a sanctioned discussion group or event."

Cat curled her lip, making no attempt to hide her amazement at this long list of rules, but Han kept his face blank. He'd been running the streets since he was a *lytling*. Mam had long ago given up on telling him when to come and go.

He'd find his way around the rules.

"The dorm masters will have your schedules posted. You'll be expected to attend classes tomorrow. I'll let Dean Abelard know you're here. She and the other faculty will advise you as to what assignments you'll need to catch up with the other students."

Hadron pulled his manuscript back toward him. "Is there anything else?" he asked, politely dismissing them.

"We're set. Thank you," Han said, and led the way out of Mystwerk Hall.

"I an't going to stay in no temple," Cat growled, before they'd even descended the wide stone steps of the hall.

"You got no choice if you want to stay here," Han said. "It's a long way back to Fellsmarch."

"Why not at least try it?" Dancer said. "You can always quit. Meantime, you get housed and fed; you're out of Fellsmarch, and you're out of the war."

Cat didn't honor that with an answer.

Han knew better than to push her. "That must be the Temple School," he said, pointing to a stone building with soaring towers just across the quad. "It *is* close. Let's stop at our dormitory and take a look at your crib. Then get something to eat."

Hampton Hall looked to be one of the oldest buildings on campus—a four-story stone structure shaded by massive oak trees, the stone walkway worn down by the tread of millions of feet over thousands of years.

The common room smelled of damp wool and wood smoke.

Two students hunched over a table next to the fire, playing royals and commons. They looked up as Han, Dancer, and Cat entered, running their gaze over the three of them. Wrinkling their blue-blood noses, they returned to their game.

The dorm master Dilbert Blevins was a middle-aged, harried-looking individual with bloodshot eyes and a runny nose, who acted as though they'd come late on purpose.

"I'm warning you, boys, there's not much left, so I don't want to hear you complaining about it," he said, as soon as they introduced themselves. "I heard enough complaining already." His fishy gaze slid over Cat, her duffel bag over one shoulder, her basilka slung across the other. "You can't be having girlies up in your rooms," he said.

"We know," Han said, thinking they might as well be living in the temple. "She promised to . . . help us arrange things."

"Hmmpfh," Blevins said. "Well, if she's going up, I'm going up with you." He eyed their spare belongings. "That's it? Well, least you didn't bring everything you own, like *some* people."

That's where you're wrong, Han thought. This *is* everything I own.

Blevins handed Han and Dancer each a stack of books and thrust bundles of linens into their faces. He led the way up a steep staircase that wound up and up. On each landing, a narrow window pierced the thick stone, admitting the smeared, dismal light the rain allowed. Rendered clumsy by the weight of multiple bags, Han nearly stumbled over the uneven steps.

All the way up, Blevins kept up a continual litany of complaints, mostly about students with high expectations.

Han steeled himself for the worst. No matter how bad it is,

he thought, I'll make it work. I won't spend much time in my room anyway.

The stairway to the fourth floor was even narrower than the previous three, as if the top floor had been an attic now converted into living space. The landing was roomier on this floor, but the ceilings at either end of the hallway sloped under the peaked roof.

Blevins led the way down the dark hallway to the right, finding his way as if by instinct. At the end of the hall there were two doors, one on either side. Drawing a large key from the pocket of his robe, Blevins unlocked both doors and pushed them open.

"Doors stay unlocked at all times so the dorm masters can get in for inspection," he said, glaring at Cat in case they'd missed his point.

Han's hand closed around his amulet. "Unlocked? But what about—"

"Students should leave their valuables to home," Blevins said. "First years are two to a room, but being as you're some of the last students to arrive, and being as these rooms are smaller than most, you each get your own. Washroom's on the third floor."

"We both have our own room?" Han rocked back on his heels in surprise.

"Don't get too excited," Blevins said, swiping at his nose with his sleeve.

Han glanced into each room. Identical in size and furnishings, they were tiny and slope-roofed, set into gables, really, with leaded glass windows opposite the doors.

Han chose the room on the left and set his duffel bag and linens down on the straw-ticking mattress that graced the bed.

Cat made as if to follow him in, and Blevins barked, "Girlies stay in the hall."

The air was stale and stuffy, even this late in the season, and Han knew it would be impossibly hot in the summertime.

A small hearth pierced the outside wall, with a pile of seasoned wood stacked next to it, but Han couldn't imagine it would ever be needed for heat.

The bed took up most of the limited floor space. He could lie on his back across the bed with his head on one wall and his toes on the other. A trunk at the foot of the bed would easily hold Han's worldly goods. The desk and straight chair tucked under the window would take best advantage of natural light for studying. There was a pitcher and basin for washing, and a braided rug on the stone floor.

Han didn't like that there was only one way in and out, via the stairs, but the window looked large enough to slide through. He'd test that once Blevins had gone. He pushed the sash open a few inches, admitting fresh, rain-washed air and a few drops of rain. He ran his fingertips over the real glass in the windows. A slate overhang kept most of the wet out, but might also make it difficult to get to the roof above.

Han grinned, shaking his head. All in all, it was the plushest place he'd ever stayed. He was amazed that mere students were allowed to live in such a place, and sleep one to a bed, let alone one to a room.

He pulled open the bag Blevins had given him. Inside were cotton sheets and blankets, a plump feather pillow, a hunk of tallow soap for washing, and two Mystwerk robes in deep crimson wool (one size to fit all, apparently). He stroked the fine fabric and set the robes aside for trying on later.

Han returned to the hallway, where Dancer waited with Cat and Master Blevins, who, it seemed, wasn't going anywhere as long as a girlie remained on the fourth floor.

"Where can we get some supper?" Han asked Blevins, who looked all pinch-eyed, as though he still expected to take abuse about the rooms.

"The dining hall is across the courtyard, next to the kitchens," Blevins said. "Serves ever'body at Mystwerk and Temple. They'll have your names. Meal times is posted down in the common room, and if you get there late, you go hungry."

Han turned to Cat and Dancer. "Let's go back to the bridge tonight, after we go to the Temple School," Han said, aware of the weight of clan money in his pockets. "I feel like celebrating."

"Lots of Mystwerk students like The Crown and Castle," Blevins said. "They serve a hot supper and a fair jack of ale at a good price."

They descended the steps from the dormitory, leaving the covered galleries to shortcut across the quad toward the temple towers.

Classes had dismissed for the day, and the campus now swarmed with students despite the steady rain. Most wore utilitarian boiled-wool cloaks over their scholars' robes, their books and papers tucked underneath out of the wet. A few glowed with power—those drew Han's eye. Most headed for the dining halls, but a few better-dressed students broke off and walked toward the bridge.

The temple also looked to be one of the oldest buildings on campus. It stood next to the river, surrounded by formal gardens and pavilions that ran down to the waterside. The front of the building faced the temple quad, the arched doorway leading to the sanctuary and classrooms. If it was like Southbridge, the side wings with broad porches likely housed the dormitories.

Students and dedicates sat on the porches, under the shelter of the roof. Some were curled up in wicker chairs, reading; others treadled spinning wheels or bent their heads over stitchery. A circle of students sat on cushions around a master, who smeared paint onto a canvas.

The common room for the dormitory lay just beyond the side door off the porch. A Temple student sat at a desk under a wall of mailboxes, a cloth spread out in front of her, an array of tiny tools and bits of precut wood laid out on the cloth. She was doing marquetry—inlaid pictures made of exotic woods.

She looked up and smiled at Han and his friends as the door slapped shut behind the three new students—a smile as sunny as Cat's face was cloudy. She wore white robes, but her volume of hair was bound by a scarf in familiar brilliant colors.

Han's heart lifted. She was a Southern Islander, like Cat. A good sign, right?

"Welcome to the Temple School," she said, her voice carrying the lilt of the islands. "The Maker bless you."

"And you also," Cat said automatically. She'd spent that much time at Jemson's school.

"My name is Annamaya Dubai," the girl said. "How may I help you?"

"I'm Cat. Um. Tyburn," Cat said, poking at the rug with her toe. "Speaker Jemson, he put in a word for me." She looked aside, distracted, as the notes of a flute floated in from the porch.

Annamaya rose in a rustle of fabric. She was nearly as tall as Han—big-boned and sturdy. She rushed forward and flung her arms around Cat as if she were her long-lost rich cousin, even though Cat was soggy from the rain and filthy from the road.

Cat stood frozen, too stunned to move.

"Caterina! Thank the Maker! We've been so worried."

Caterina? Han looked at Dancer and raised an eyebrow. Who knew?

"Dean Torchiere will be so relieved," Annamaya bubbled, words pouring from her like water from an open spigot. "Your room is all ready for you, though you can change it if you like. It's right next to mine, with a garden view. We're so excited to have you here. We can't wait to hear you play. Perhaps we can schedule a recital once you're settled in. I see you brought your own basilka. Do you play anything else?"

Cat stood immobilized, like a fellsdeer trying to decide whether to flee a hunter or hope to go unnoticed.

Annamaya rushed on, not waiting for an answer. "I'll show you your room. This is the girls' wing, so it's right upstairs." She slid Cat's bag off her shoulder and onto her own, then took hold of Cat's arm. Han could tell Cat wanted to snatch it back.

Annamaya started up the stairs with a stunned Cat in tow. Han and Dancer hesitated at the bottom, but Annamaya looked over her shoulder and waved them up. "Come see where Caterina's staying."

Han and Dancer followed the two girlies up the broad, shallow staircase to a gallery that ran toward the back of the building.

"This is like a palace," Han whispered to Dancer. Actually, he'd never been in a palace, but he guessed it would look like this—with marble floors and carved banisters and high ceilings and glittering crystal sconces on the walls that burned continuously. It was like Southbridge Temple, only bigger and fancier. Much bigger and fancier. Still, it seemed soothing, not intimidating, with its cool surfaces and large open spaces.

They turned the corner into a back hallway, walking between rows of doors. Annamaya chose one on the right and pushed it open.

The room was larger than the ones assigned to Han and Dancer, though still cozy, the walls painted a deep blue. The large bed had a roof on it, covered in brilliant striped fabrics. Music stands and a desk and drawing table filled a windowed alcove. A large bookcase stood against the left wall. At the rear, two tall doors stood ajar, leading to a balcony overlooking the gardens and the river beyond. A breeze came in through the doors, carrying the scent of rain and flowers. In good weather, the sunlight would pour in.

Han had thought his room was plush. It was nothing next to this.

Cat stood frozen in the doorway, staring. Then spun around to confront Annamaya. "This some kind of a joke?" she demanded. "This how you fun the riffraff? Because it an't funny, it's mean."

Annamaya's face scrunched up in dismay. "You don't like it? I know it's small, and the washrooms are down the hall, but . . . well, to me, the garden view is worth it."

Han walked to the rear doors and looked out over the gardens. Then turned to look at Annamaya. "You're serious, right? This *is* her room. No fooling."

Annamaya nodded, practically wringing her hands. "You could stay here for now, and at least freshen up. I can ask the dorm master and see what else is available."

"What I got to do to have this room?" Cat asked, drawing her brows together suspiciously. "What kind of place is this? Who else lives here?"

"Just you," Annamaya said, looking puzzled. She glanced at Han and Dancer for clues. "We—we aren't allowed to have anyone stay in our rooms. Just so you know."

She bustled around the room, pointing out its features like a trader at market, while Cat stood chewing her lower lip, saying nothing.

"If you need more linens, there's a closet down the hallway. And when you're ready for your bath, just see the dorm master, and she'll—"

Cat held up a hand to stop the pitch. "It's good," she croaked. "The room's good. It's all good. I like it. Thank you."

Annamaya tilted her head, looking unconvinced. Afraid Cat was just being polite.

"All right. If you're sure. Now, the schedules for first years are posted in the common room. I'll fetch you in the morning and take you to see Mistress Johanna. Do you need directions to the dining hall or—?"

"We're going to go to Bridge Street tonight," Han said.

As they crossed the quad toward Bridge Street, Cat slumped along, looking miserable.

"You all right?" Han asked. "Annamaya seems . . . friendly."

"Why they put me in a palace?" Cat said. "I'll never sleep a wink in that place. I'd be afraid of getting the sheets dirty."

"They must get students from all over," Dancer said. "You'll get used to it."

Cat groaned. "What you suppose Jemson said to them about me? I don't want to have to live up to whatever tale he told."

"Knowing Jemson, he told the truth," Han said. "He wouldn't set you up."

"He's a dreamer," Cat muttered. "He always think you better than you really are."

Han shrugged. "He *is* a dreamer. But he'd say you got to have dreams."

The Crown and Castle, the tavern Blevins had recommended, stood at the near end of the bridge. It did seem to be a popular place—the common room was crowded, and wonderful smells emanated from the kitchens. The patrons were mostly Mystwerk students; Han spotted several red robes draped over chairs.

Han claimed a corner table. "I'm buying," he said, remembering that he had a specific reason to be celebrating.

"*You're* buying?" Dancer tilted his head. "Why is that?"

"It's my name day," Han said. "I'm seventeen today."

Dancer's confusion cleared. "Right. It's September. I forgot." He grinned. "Happy name day, Hunts Alone," he said, clasping his hand.

Han didn't want his name day to go by unrecognized this time. His sixteenth had passed without celebration, his last with Mam and Mari. There'd been no money for the traditional name day parties. Since then, he'd chatted with death too many times to count.

Han looked at Cat, and again thought of all the dead Southies and Raggers. He'd be an old man on the streets now. Most streetlords never reached seventeen.

"From now on we're celebrating all our name days," he proclaimed. "When's yours?" he asked Cat.

She shrugged. "I don't know. Don't know how old I am neither, so don't ask."

"Pick a day, then," Han said. "After solstice, maybe. We'll need a party then."

They ordered up bowls of ham-and-bean soup and black bread all around, with great mugs of cider. The soup was delicious, with bits of meat and a rich, oniony broth. Cat and Dancer toasted Han multiple times, slamming their mugs down on the table for emphasis. With each round, the toasts got sillier, more extravagant.

"To Han 'Deatheater' Alister, Scourge of the Seven Realms!" Dancer proclaimed.

Han raised his mug, but couldn't help looking about to see who might have overheard. No one seemed to be paying attention to their little party.

Though most of the other patrons were no older than Han, they had the blueblood look, with finely tailored cloaks, soft leather boots, and too much fur for the weather.

The rich handle money differently than the poor. They use it carelessly, slapping it down as though it came from an unlimited supply. They kept the server on the run, fetching pitchers of ale.

Han glanced over at Cat, who surveyed the scene over the rim of her cider mug. There'd be easy money to be made here for a street runner with skills.

But this was a chance for Cat to be something different. Han knew from experience how hard it was to leave the game. When he'd given it up, he'd been threatened by his enemies. They either didn't believe he'd changed, or hoped to take advantage of it. He'd been tempted by his friends, made edgy-jumpy by his rejection of the Life and the void he'd left behind him.

The serious drinkers soon arrived from dinner in the dining halls, the rain driving them off the porch and inside. They churned through the throngs by the door, bellying up to the bar. As the tavern grew more jammed, there were no more tables to be had. Newcomers leaned against the walls, juggling mugs of ale and plates of stew and roast beef.

Han ordered another round of drinks and a cinnamon cake for them all to share.

He felt at ease in taverns—they'd been his second home growing up, a place to get away from whatever squalid place he was living in. There was always action in taverns—warm marks and natty lads, streetlords and fancies who worked the trade.

Han would have to develop new habits if he was going to succeed here. He'd have to learn to sit in the library come dark-man's hour. So his seventeenth name day felt like an ending as well as a beginning.

Han glanced over at Cat, who'd been stuffing herself with seconds. Though her bowl was still half full, she'd stopped eating to stare toward the door, fingering her curls the way she did when she was agitated.

Han followed her gaze. Three wizards had walked in together, their auras illuminating the gloomy taproom. They stood with their backs to Han, shaking the rain from their expensive cloaks and looking around.

"*This* is the best tavern in town?" the tallest one said, freeing a mane of black hair from his hood. "It's going to be a long year."

The cold, blueblood voice struck a chord in Han. His feeling of well-being evaporated.

The other two snickered. "Maybe the food is good," the stockier one said hopefully. He pulled off his hood, revealing russet hair.

Han's skin prickled. He squinted at the newcomers, fingering his amulet, wishing they'd turn around so he could see their faces.

"At least the help here is more attractive than at the Four Horses," the tall one said, turning to ogle a server threading her way through the crowded room. He spoke with the precision of someone who knows he's had too much to drink, and is accustomed to managing it. "I think the Four Horses was named for its barmaids."

"Naw," the more slender one said. "It's named after what they put in the cooking pot." His slurred speech suggested he was deep in his cups, too.

The pretty server swept past with a tray. The tall wizard seized her arm, nearly spilling the ale she carried. "You, there," he said. "We need a table for three."

She swung around to look at him, scowling. "Do you *see* a table for three anywhere?" she snapped.

"Clear someone off, then," the wizard said. "We don't mean to eat standing up."

"You'll have to wait your turn, like everybody else. Now let go my arm and keep your flaming wizard hands to yourself." She struggled unsuccessfully to pull free.

The wizard half turned to Han, and the light from the lantern washed over his face, the hard planes and angles—familiar, graven into Han's brain. Memory shuddered through him.

It was Micah Bayar and his cousins, the Mander brothers, Miphis and Arkeda. That was who'd set fire to the sacred mountain of Hanalea and launched a train of events that had ended with the deaths of Mari and Mam and the destruction of his old life.

Micah was the son of Gavan Bayar, the High Wizard of the Fells, who likely still hunted him. Micah was brother of Fiona Bayar, who'd chased him and Dancer across the border into Delphi. Han took hold of his amulet, gripping the intricately carved stone. It hissed against his damp palm.

"I'll let you go when you find us a table," Micah said, yanking the server toward him. The tray went down, ale splattering waist high and tankards rolling across the floor.

Magic flooded through Han, making his head spin. He shook his head, trying to clear it, then surged to his feet, his chair crashing to the floor behind him. Dancer said, "Hunts Alone! Wait!" in a low, urgent voice, but Han ignored him. Han pushed forward, and the crowd parted in front of him until he stood in front of Micah and the server.

"Let go of the girlie, Bayar," he said.

Micah's bleary black eyes swept over him with disinterest, then widened and focused. Startlement splashed over his face. He looked down at the knife Han clutched in his right hand. Then back up at Han.

"Alister," he whispered. "But . . . it can't be. You can't . . . you're not . . ."

"Bayar," Han said. He did not smile. Anger blazed in his gut like brandy. He could hush Bayar, here and now. It would be easy. No one in this place would stop him. He'd be well away before they even reacted. The trick was to make eye contact with any would-be heroes, then walk away slow until you got outside, then—

"Blood of the Demon! You're burning me! Let go!" the server said, ripping her arm free from Micah's grip. She stood, blinking back tears, staring at the blistered handprint on her upper arm.

Micah seemed as surprised as she was. "I—I'm sorry," he stammered. "It was an accident. I didn't mean—"

"Just shut it," Han said. "She don't want to hear it. You Bayars like to go after them that can't defend themselves. Like barmaids and ragpickers and *lytlings*."

His words rang out loud in a sudden quiet, and the apology drained from Micah's face. Micah's cousins moved up on either side of him, though they stayed a step behind.

They won't go down on the bricks for him, Han thought. Micah Bayar wouldn't last long as a streetlord.

The crowd rippled as the server turned and fled, forcing her way to the door.

"I don't know what you're talking about," Micah said. His eyes strayed to the departing serving girl, then wrenched back to Han. "I didn't mean to hurt her."

"Why don't you try me instead?" Han said, waving his knife slowly back and forth in front of Micah's face, a blademan's trick. He kept his other hand wrapped around his flash as the patrons melted back.

"Hunts Alone," Dancer said behind him, his voice soft and steady so as not to startle him. "Remember why we're here. He's not worth it."

213

Han released his grip on the amulet, but kept the knife in play.

"Did you follow me here?" Micah demanded. "If you did, I'm warning you—"

"I go to school here, same as you," Han said.

Micah blinked at Han stupidly, the drink slowing him down. "You? Do you even know how to read and write? They can't have lowered the standards that much."

"Well," Han said, "they let *you* in."

Anger wiped the sneer off Micah's face. "You're a thief," he snarled, his black eyes glittering. "A thief and a murderer. We've been looking for you all over the Seven Realms." His gaze dropped to Han's amulet. "That amulet belongs to my family, and you stole it from me. Now give it over."

Micah reached for Han's amulet. Han made no move to stop him. As Micah's hand closed on it, flame jetted from the jinx-piece, and Micah jerked his hand back, swearing and sucking his burnt fingers. Twice more he tried, and twice more the serpent amulet prevented him from taking hold of it.

The crowd tittered nervously.

"But . . . how did you . . . ?" Micah stared at the amulet, looking betrayed.

"Who's the thief, Bayar?" Han said, again cradling the flash-piece in his hand. "Who does it belong to, really? How far back should we go? I'm a rank angler, next to you. You come from a whole family of thieves and murderers."

His knife hand rippled with flame, and Han pressed his lips together, damming up the charm that threatened to pour out, unbidden. Not knowing what it might be.

"You're not a wizard," Micah said, still focused on the amulet.

"How can you even touch it? What have you done to it?"

"Are you *sure*?" Han whispered. "Are you *sure* I'm not a wizard?" He wrenched his hand away from the amulet and extended both hands toward Micah. Power collected under his skin, shimmering through his fingers, illuminating Micah's astonished face.

"When did *you* get to be a wizard?" Arkeda Mander wailed, as if Han had somehow talked his way into their blueblood club.

Staggering backward, Micah groped inside his collar for his flash, reaching his other hand toward Han.

Unwilling to chance the Waterlow amulet, Han grabbed a fistful of Micah's cloak and pulled him forward, pressing the blade of his knife into Micah's throat.

"Let go of your flash or I'll cut your throat," Han murmured.

Micah dropped his hands, his eyes nearly crossing as they fixed on the blade.

"Hunts Alone!" Dancer repeated. "No."

"Better study up, Bayar," Han said, his face inches from Micah's. "I'm in Mystwerk House, too. Better study up in a hurry if you want to keep up with me."

He said it knowing that issuing a magical challenge to Micah Bayar was probably one of the stupider ideas he'd had in a very bad year.

But it was that or cut his throat on the spot, in front of dozens of witnesses. His fury had ebbed. He'd not survived seventeen years on the streets by being stupid.

The front door banged open, and the server marched in, leading four provost guards in gray uniforms. "It's them, Max," she said, pointing at Han and Micah. "They're the ones."

Han stepped away from Micah, returning his knife to his

sleeve. He and Micah shoved their hands into their pockets, the picture of innocence.

Max pulled out a small notebook bound in leather. "Anyone else hurt?" he asked, licking the end of his pencil and glaring around.

Nobody made eye contact or said a word.

Kind of different from the bluejackets, Han thought. Armed with a notebook instead of a club.

Max singled out one student slumped over a table in the middle of the room. "Hurd! What did you see?"

Hurd shrugged. "Didn't see anything. Didn't see any fighting." He glanced at the server nervously, then away. "Not that I think Rutha was lying. I just didn't see it. Must've been sleeping." He yawned hugely and laid his head back down on the table.

Max looked at Han and Micah. "Names?" he said.

"No need for names, is there, sir?" Han said, shrugging. "Nothing really happened. Just a bit of loud talk and hand waving."

Max snorted. "*You* say. Rutha, which one burnt you?"

"The dark-haired charmcaster there. The fair-headed one came to help me."

Han's eyes shifted from Max to Rutha. He couldn't believe it. For once he wasn't getting the blame.

Max glared at Micah. "Name?" When Micah didn't reply, he added, "You don't give your name, we'll take you to the provost gaol for the night."

"Micah Bayar," Bayar said, grinding the words between his teeth.

"Where are you staying?" Max continued.

Micah rolled his eyes toward the ceiling. Either he didn't want to say where he lived, or it was a commentary on the accommodations. "Hampton Hall."

Han and Dancer exchanged glances. Bayar was lodging in the same dormitory as them—the worst one on the quad. Which made sense, since he'd come late also. What had he been up to, that he was so late to school?

"You a first year or what?" Max asked.

"*Yes*," Micah said. "I'm at Mystwerk House. I just arrived from the Fells this morning. If you're taking names, you should know that my father is—"

"*You* should know that we don't tolerate fighting here at the Ford," Max said, plowing right over Micah's words. "No matter who your father is. Newlings don't know better, but they learn fast or they're gone. You'll need to learn to control your temper and keep your hands to yourself."

Like a street player, Max paused and swept his gaze over his captive audience, then fixed it back on Micah. "I'm giving you fair warning. Any more trouble from you and you'll go up before the rector. An' the rector's not afraid to expel you neither, if you're too stupid to learn to mind your manners."

Max leaned in toward Han and Micah. "Magical assaults is a different matter. Use your amulets to attack somebody, and there's no hearing. You're out. Understand?"

Han swallowed hard, glad he'd resisted the temptation to let fly with his amulet. Likely this was a speech Max had given many times before to upstart blueblood first years accustomed to getting away with bad behavior at home.

"I'm not the one who should be answering questions. He's a thief!" Micah said, pointing at Han. "He stole my amulet."

"Already?" Max asked, flipping to a new page in his notebook. "When did that happen? I thought you said you just got here."

"It happened back at home," Micah said. "My cousins saw the whole thing."

The Mander brothers nodded in unison, like puppets lashed to the same strings.

"I was there too," Dancer said, moving forward out of the shadows to stand on Han's right side. "And I remember it differently."

Bayar seemed even more startled to see Dancer. "*You*? What are *you* doing here?"

"Same as everyone else. I'm here for school," Dancer said. He'd let go of his amulet, and now he too glittered with accumulating power.

"But you're *clanborn*," Bayar said, wetting his lips, seeming more unnerved by Dancer's presence than by Han's. "You're not . . ." He stopped. He was probably going to say, *You're not gifted*, when the evidence in front of him was plain as day. "But that's impossible," he said, disgust twisting his features. "Congress between copperheads and the gifted is forbidden."

"For someone who just got here yourself, you sure got a lot of opinions, Micah Bayar," Max said, stowing his notebook away. "We don't have jurisdiction outside the Ford. I don't care what happened back home. You got to leave it behind."

By now, Micah had mastered himself. Whatever else you could say about him, he was a quick learner. He turned to

Rutha, the server, who stood by watching. "I apologize for your injury and my rude behavior," he said, inclining his head. "It was inexcusable. Please, see a healer and send the bill to me at Hampton Hall."

Rutha nodded, sniffing. "Just watch yourself from now on."

"You can depend on it," Micah said. He turned to Max. "Sir," he said, "I apologize for this incident. You won't have any more trouble from me."

"Good," Max said, looking mollified. "See that I don't. Now you two shake hands, and I'll be about my business."

Han looked Micah Bayar directly in the eyes and smiled, a streetlord challenge. He extended his hand. After a moment's hesitation, Micah gripped it. Power flamed between them, a magical duel that ended in an impasse.

Micah leaned in close to Han and said, "Better watch your back, Alister. Now I know where to find you, and I've got plenty of time." He let go of Han's hand, and took a step back.

Micah swung his cape about his shoulders, fastening it at the neck with an elaborate clasp. His gaze swept over Dancer and locked on Cat, still huddled at the corner table. Micah smiled— a long, slow smile—and bowed sardonically. She twitched and hunched her shoulders, scowling.

Now that Han thought about it, Cat had been surprisingly shut-mouthed during his face-off with Bayar. After what had happened to the Raggers, was she scared of wizards now?

Still smiling at some private joke, Micah nodded to Han. "Alister," he said. "I wish you luck." Gesturing to the Manders to follow, he walked out of the tavern.

CHAPTER TWELVE

RAISED FROM THE DEAD

Raisa was waiting for Amon in the common room of the dormitory when he returned from his late recitation. Maps of the Seven Realms lay scattered across the table in front of her. She was supposed to be writing an essay on how geography had shaped the great battles of the past, but she was having trouble concentrating. In fact, all she'd managed so far was a title. "How Geography Has Shaped the Great Battles of the Past."

It was still pouring rain, and Amon looked weary and worn down as he stripped off his wet cloak. Five days a week he had patrol duty at 6:30 a.m., and his late recitation on Modern Weaponry ran until ten p.m.

"Blood of Hanalea," he grumbled, hanging up his cloak. "It takes a special talent to make weaponry boring." He yawned hugely. "Do you think you remember what you hear in your sleep?" He sloshed the teapot to check the water level, then put it on to boil.

"He's alive," Raisa said, practically bursting with the news. "I saw him. Cuffs Alister."

"What?" Amon flopped down in a chair and tugged off his boots. He inspected his feet, wrinkled his nose, and began peeling off his socks.

"Cuffs Alister," Raisa repeated. "He's here."

Amon stopped peeling and looked up, frowning. "What are you talking about?"

"I was walking across the courtyard near the stables and he nearly rode into me."

The socks dropped to the floor. "What would Alister be doing in Oden's Ford? That doesn't make sense." Amon leaned forward, hands on his knees, his face hard and intent. "Did you speak with him? Did he recognize you?"

Raisa shook her head. "Well, no. As soon as I recognized him, I ran away."

"You ran *away*?" Amon lifted an eyebrow. "You didn't think that might raise his suspicions?"

"Well, yes," Raisa said, feeling irritated. "I didn't know what to do. I never expected to see him here. *You* told me he was dead."

"He's *supposed* to be dead," Amon said, as if Cuffs had pulled a nasty trick by being alive. He paused, chewing on his lower lip. "You sure it was him?"

She scowled at him. "I *know* it was him."

The teapot shrilled. Amon pried himself out of his chair and crossed barefoot to the hearth. "Want some tea?" he asked, spooning leaves into a cup and pouring for himself.

"It was *Cuffs Alister*," Raisa repeated stubbornly, ignoring

Amon's question. He poured a cup for her anyway and set it on the table in front of her.

He looked slightly less agitated, and Raisa knew he was convincing himself she'd been mistaken. "It's been raining all day," he said, sitting back down. "So I'm guessing he was cloaked and hooded up."

Well, yes, Raisa thought, unwilling to say it aloud. But I know what I saw. His fair hair had badly needed cutting, and his blue eyes were as brilliant as she remembered in his appallingly handsome face.

The last time she'd seen him, he'd been covered in cuts and bruises, his arm splinted, courtesy of the Queen's Guard. Now his face was marked by a different kind of injury—pain and loss and betrayal—and layered with a new wariness.

"Sometimes it's hard to tell one person from another when they're wrapped up like that," Amon persisted.

Raisa rubbed her forehead, trying to recall every detail. Now that she thought about it, the boy she'd seen in the stable yard was riding a clan pony. He'd been dressed in expensive trader garb—a boiled-wool cloak and fine clan leatherwork boots.

That didn't make sense. Alister was a slum dweller—where would he learn to ride a horse? Where would he get one? And why would he be dressed as a trader?

Raisa's certainty began to crumble. Did she want Alister to be alive so much that she'd conjured a ghost? Had a stranger's resemblance to Cuffs brought him to mind?

"Even if he *were* alive, what would he be doing here?" Amon said, his voice a constant drip-drip-drip against her hopes.

"I don't *know*," Raisa said, too stubborn to concede. "Maybe he's going to school, too. Or maybe he's just hiding out here until things settle down in the Fells. Like me."

"He's not like you, Rai," Amon said. "He's a thief and a killer, and you're—"

"You're right, of course. There's *nobody* like me," Raisa said, wrapping her arms around her knees and feeling sorry for herself.

Amon raked his fingers through his wet hair so it stuck up in all directions. "Why do I get the impression you hope it *was* him?"

"Well," Raisa conceded, "I hope he's not dead." Ever since she'd heard that Alister had been murdered, she'd felt hollowed out and guilty. She'd failed him, like the queen had failed all the desperate residents of Ragmarket and Southbridge.

"If you're going to hope, then hope that he's alive and happy someplace far from here," Amon said. "Eventually you're going to be recognized, but I'd like to put it off as long as possible." He pulled a sheaf of papers from his carry bag and wedged them onto a free corner of the table.

"Alister doesn't know who I really am," Raisa said. She blew on her tea to cool it, and took a cautious sip. "So he can't give me away."

Amon rolled his pen between his fingers. "I'll look into it," he conceded. "I'll see if anyone by that name is enrolled at Wien House or Isenwerk. If he came here for school, it seems most likely he'd be going as a soldier or engineer." He bent his head over his work and began scratching notes. "Unless you think he's going into orders. Speaker Jemson seemed impressed with him."

Amon Byrne was actually making a joke.

Raisa watched him for a long moment, then slumped in her

chair. "You're right. I was probably mistaken."

Amon kept working, so Raisa turned back to her own task, squeezing sentences out with great effort and little enthusiasm, like paint from an empty tube.

She tried to ignore the dull ache beneath her ribs that might have been disappointment.

CHAPTER THIRTEEN

CHARMCASTING FOR BEGINNERS

Han scrubbed at his eyes with both hands and set the book of simple charms aside. He was a decent reader—he'd been the best in his class at the school at Southbridge Temple—but this vocabulary was totally foreign to him. It didn't help that he'd risen before the sun, after a sleepless night, driven by worry. It was only his first day of classes, and he was already drunk with fatigue.

Taking hold of his flashpiece, he walked the perimeter of his room, stumbling over words as he tried to reproduce the spoken charm. When he'd circled the room twice, he stopped in the center and looked around.

Nothing happened. No gush of flame charred the walls (a good thing). No shimmering net of protection settled over the doors and windows (maybe a bad thing). The book had described it as a charm of protection against those who meant him harm.

How would he know it worked if there was no enemy to try it out on?

An enemy lived two floors below. And he still hadn't decided what to do about it.

He'd already sat through a lecture from Dancer on the topic, the night before, when Micah left the tavern and Han wanted to follow.

"Leave him be," Dancer had said, getting in his way. "You don't know how well armed he is, or what he knows. Don't start a fight unless you know you can win."

"The fight's already started," Han said. "It started on Hanalea." *But the war began with Mam and Mari*, he added silently.

"He has an amulet, and he probably knows how to use it," Dancer said. "Unlike us."

"You heard what he said," Han argued. "He's coming after me. Better if I hush him first." It was what he knew, the law of the streets, kill or be killed. "He'll be dead before he can squeak out a charm."

Dancer put his hand on Han's arm. "And if you do that, who do you think the provosts will suspect? If you wanted to kill him you shouldn't have faced off with him in public."

Han scowled, but didn't argue the point. He knew Dancer was right.

"If you go after him, I'll have to back you. We'll both be expelled," Dancer said.

Han shook his head. "No. I never asked you to—"

"Right now he knows less about you than you do about him," Dancer interrupted, knowing he was gaining ground. "You surprised him. He's off balance. He'll wait until he has more information before making his move. You can use that time, Hunts Alone."

But Micah won't be sitting idle, either, Han thought. Could he stand to walk around with that constant prickle between his shoulder blades?

He'd rather have a chat with Micah in a back alley and ease his own mind.

Dancer's voice cut into Han's thoughts. "I'm back from breakfast," he called from the doorway. "I brought something for you."

Han looked up in time to catch the napkin-wrapped bundle Dancer tossed at him. Pulling back a corner, he saw that it contained a biscuit with cheese and ham tucked inside. "Thank you," Han said, taking a big bite.

"I saw Cat in the dining hall," Dancer said.

"How was she?" Han asked, hoping a night's sleep had improved her mood.

"Well," Dancer said, "she still looked kind of witch-fixed. That Annamaya from last night was there. She'll take her to her classes and help her get her books together."

After they'd left the tavern the night before, they'd walked Cat back to the Temple School. By then she seemed to have run out of arguments. It worried Han, since he'd never known it to happen before. They left her standing at the door, arms wrapped around herself as if she hoped she could fold up and disappear.

Han hated to leave her there, but he'd already done enough walking around to know that there was no way to make a living on the down low within the walls of the academy. The provost guards were everywhere, the common spaces were brightly lit, and there'd be no cheap places to throw down for the night. It would be like trying to run a canting crew out of the castle close.

She had to make it work.

The bells in Mystwerk Tower sounded once. It was time to be on their way.

Han slid his book into his carry bag and rooted through it one more time. It contained the books of charms Elena had given him, a thick book of charms by someone named Kinley he'd got from Blevins, a sheaf of clean paper, and his writing box. At Southbridge Temple he'd never brought any books to class, because he didn't own any. Nor paper, pencils, or ink, save those supplied by Jemson once he got there.

At Southbridge, none but Jemson cared if he showed up or not. He'd had no problem holding his own. The other students came from the streets too. They talked like he did—using the flash patter street slang they'd all grown up with.

This was different. His classmates would have been raised in families of blueblood charmcasters. They'd been exposed to spellwork since they were *lytlings*. They would have had training before they were even allowed to have amulets, and access to whole libraries of charmcraft.

"We're going to be late!" Dancer broke into Han's fog of worry. Dancer had put on his school robes and slung his carry bag over one shoulder.

"Coming." Han pulled his red robe over his head, poking his arms through the sleeves and pulling it down so it covered his clothing. He liked having the robe on—it made him feel more like he belonged.

They descended the stairs, Han hiking up the hem of his robe to keep from getting his feet tangled in it. It would take some getting used to.

It was a fresh, clean morning, still peculiarly warm, but with less humidity than before. Sunlight slanted across the lawns, sparkling on the dew-spangled grass. Students crowded the walkways in their multicolored robes, still yawning and blinking away sleep. Han finished his biscuit as they walked.

The classroom was on the second floor of Mystwerk Hall, overlooking the Tamron River. Stone risers were arranged in a semicircle around a raised central podium. When Han and Dancer arrived, students were settling into their seats, fishing books and papers out of their carry bags. There were fifteen students in all, arranged like candies in a box, all in the same red wrappers.

Han paused in the doorway, scanning the room. He spotted Bayar and the Mander brothers in the back row, left side, bunched together like sour grapes.

Micah was sprawled in his seat, hands braced against the table in front of him, head tilted back, black eyes fixed on Han, his falcon amulet prominently displayed on the outside of his robe.

Well, Han thought, at least they were all here instead of tossing his room for the jinxpiece he'd taken from them.

If they looked, there'd be nothing to find. Han had a thief's chariness about leaving money in his room, so he carried his purse on his person. The jinxpiece hung around his neck, and his books were in his carry bag.

Han smiled, nodded, and waved at Micah, all but blowing him a kiss. He found himself a seat to the right, in the second row, where he could keep an eye on Micah. Dancer settled into the empty seat beside him.

In the academy overall, the majority of students were flat-landers. From what Han could tell without the clue of clothing, most in this class were northerners. There were three olive-skinned charmcasters, likely mixed-bloods from Bruinswallow or the Southern Islands. Two were very pale, their hair almost white—they might be from the Northern Islands, where wizards had originated. Some had hair streaked with wizard red.

None from Arden, of course. And none but Dancer carried clan blood.

Han touched his own pale hair, perhaps a gift from Alger Waterlow.

Like Micah, the other students wore their amulets on the outside of their robes—like a gang mark display. It was their one chance for making show. The jinxpieces varied widely. Some were huge and ornate, like jewel-encrusted incense burners from the temple—worth a fortune in materials alone. Others were small and plain—silver and gold in simple shapes, often images from the natural world. Some mimicked animals and plants, and looked almost alive—glowing with elegant clan craftsmanship. Many were probably heirlooms, handed down through families of charmcasters, recharged by clan artists for this new generation.

When he'd worked the streets, Han had dealt in bagged flash, the street name for magical pieces like these. He'd pinch them from careless shop owners or lift them from houses. Fortunately, he'd never tried to take one directly off a wizard. He now real-ized that it would have been easier to yank out a tooth and slide away unnoticed.

The magical element of a jinxpiece was called flash. At first Han had assumed that the fancier the amulet, the more flash it had—the more powerful it was. In his dealings with fences he'd found out that wasn't always true. The materials they were made of had more to do with the wealth of the wizard than the power of the piece.

Han pulled his serpent amulet free and let it rest on the front of his robe. It was more than a thousand years old, and only middling showy, but it was likely the most powerful piece of flash in the room.

Dancer exposed his amulet also, the Lone Hunter he'd borrowed from Han. Han wondered if the amulet Elena had made for him was permanent or temporary. That would be worrisome—the knowledge that his amulet would eventually lose power. He was beginning to understand why wizards were unhappy with the clans' power over them.

Han looked over at Micah whispering with his cousins. It made him twitchy. Han wasn't used to sharing territory with an enemy. You drove him out, or he drove you out. You hushed him, or he hushed you, and life went on. For one of you.

The side door opened, and a wizard in a wheeled chair rolled into the room. Though the sleeves of his robe were decorated with master's bars, he looked to be only three or four years older than the newling students. He had cinnamon hair, pale skin, and a bitter expression, as if he expected to be disappointed.

When he reached the base of the podium he swung forward two arm canes and levered himself out of the chair.

The foam of voices gradually settled into an awkward silence as the master struggled up the steps to the lectern and spread a sheaf of papers and a battered-looking book atop it. His amulet glittered in the sunlight cascading through the windows, a large quartz crystal shaped into a castle keep.

He didn't call the roll, but his gaze whispered over the assembled students, resting on Han and Dancer for a long moment.

"You are—ah—*Dancer* and Alister, I presume," he said, looking down and sorting through his papers. "I am Master Gryphon. I have the perilous and unfulfilling task of teaching spellcasting to newlings. How fortunate we are that this year's newling class is so . . . exceptionally diverse. I feel quite . . . in context."

Han stared at the master, unsure whether they'd just been insulted or if he was poking fun at himself.

Gryphon raised his eyes from his papers. They were a startling blue-green color, and when Han met his gaze, cold trickled down his spine. Despite the master's unhealthy pallor, it was a handsome face, a poor match for the graceless body.

"Proficient Hadron tells me that the two of you traveled through Arden to come here. Arden is a dangerous place for anyone these days, but especially for charmcasters. Which raises the question: are you two stupid, unschooled, or merely foolhardy?"

Well. That was an insult for sure. Han couldn't help looking at Micah, who gazed up at the ceiling, a faint smile curving his mouth.

Han kept his street face on. "I've had better ideas," he said, shrugging.

Surprise flickered across the master's face as some of the other students snickered. Then Gryphon's gaze dropped to Han's amulet, and his eyes widened. He looked up into Han's face, studying him with a fierce intensity.

"Interesting that you would choose such a dangerous road, Alister," he said finally. "It seems that you are not afraid of the dark."

Han suspected he was not talking about the road through Arden at all.

"Well," Han said, meeting that blue-green gaze, "sometimes there's no choice."

"There is always a choice," Gryphon said. Flipping open a thick book, he said, "Speaking of journeys, I asked you to read from Kinley, the twelfth chapter, where he discusses the challenges of traveling in Aediion. Kinley instructs us that . . ."

The door to the classroom opened, and two more students filed in. Han stared, along with everyone else. It was Fiona Bayar and lovelorn Wil, who'd chased him and Dancer across the border into Delphi.

They looked travel-battered and cranky, so Han assumed they'd come directly to class after ditching their baggage at their dormitories. Wil's face was bronzed by the sun, but Fiona was pale as ever, as if the sun wouldn't presume to penetrate her icy skin. She'd taken her hair out of the braid, and it billowed in long waves past her shoulders.

She wore traveling clothes: a roughspun sweater, corded jacket, and canvas breeches that showed off her long legs. No student robes.

Fiona ran her chilly gaze over the room. When her eyes settled on Master Gryphon, they widened in surprise. "Adam!" she cried, as if the entire class weren't looking on. Turning to Wil, she said, "Look, Wil, it's Adam Gryphon, of all people."

Blood of the demon, Han thought. My spellcasting teacher is

pals with the Bayars. It's no wonder my feet are in the flame.

Striding forward, Fiona extended her hand toward Master Gryphon as if she expected him to kiss it. "Father told me you'd entered orders, but I had no idea . . ."

Master Gryphon had turned a deep raspberry red color, an amazing transformation. He made no move to take her hand, but seized the podium in a white-knuckled grip. "It's *Master* Gryphon, Newling Bayar," he said. "And though I am on faculty at Mystwerk House, do note that I've not taken vows, nor do I intend to."

Fiona pulled back her hand, realizing that there was no kiss in the offing. "Really? I must have heard wrong. It did seem like a good option for someone in your . . . situation."

"A good outcome for a cripple, you mean?" Master Gryphon said softly. "Perhaps so. How fortunate that you and Newling Mathis made it here safely. Next time, please wear appropriate attire to class. Now, take your seats so that we can proceed with our lesson. This constant influx of students has put us behind."

That acid tongue is sweeter now, Han thought.

Fiona flung her hair back over her shoulders and turned toward the risers to look for a seat. Her gaze fell on Han and Dancer in the second row. She froze, going even paler than before. "*Alister*," she whispered. "I don't believe it."

Wil took her elbow. "Come on, Fiona," he said.

Fiona didn't move. "What are you *doing* here?" Leaning forward, she extended trembling hands toward Han as if she were itching to close them around his throat.

Han rested his hands on the table in front of him, forcing himself not to make any defensive moves. "Your brother can fill you in," he said, jerking his head toward Micah. "Now, d'you mind? If you come to class late, the least you can do is sit and shut it. I came here to learn something." He tapped the cover of his book and raised his eyebrows.

Fiona continued to stare at Han as if she couldn't believe her eyes.

Wil tugged at her arm. "Let's sit," he said quietly.

Fiona finally allowed Wil to tow her to a seat in the back row.

She had barely settled into her seat, when Gryphon barked, "Alister! What does Kinley tell us about the risks and benefits of traveling in Aediion?"

Welcome back the acid-tongued master.

Han swallowed hard, sweat popping out all over. "I don't know," he said.

"No?" Gryphon sighed. "That *is* disappointing. Then, define *Aediion* for us."

"I'm sorry. I . . . ah . . . I've not done the reading." Han admitted. Instead, he'd been busy laying charms of protection around his room.

Somebody snickered. Out of the corner of his eye, Han could see Micah's smirk of amusement. He could feel Fiona's eyes boring into him like hot pokers.

"No?" The master tch'd. "*Here* to learn, but not, apparently, *ready* to learn. Do you expect me to do all the work?"

"No." Han shook his head.

"Do you expect me to shovel knowledge into the gaping maw of your untried mind?"

"No."

"No, what?"

"No, sir," Han said.

Gryphon leaned forward, speaking softly, but still loudly enough that everyone else could hear. "Are you certain you really belong here, Alister?"

"Yes, sir," Han said, meeting the master's eyes defiantly.

Gryphon paused, then, still glaring at Han, said, "Darnleigh? Risks and benefits?"

"Aediion is the world of dreams," said a solemn, brown-haired boy whose wizard stoles were finely embroidered with boars' heads. "With proper training, support from a powerful amulet, and a close connection with another person, it is theoretically possible to communicate across distances. That's the benefit."

"Theoretically, you say? Don't you believe it?" Gryphon cocked his head.

"It is uncommon enough that some scholars say it is only a myth; others say that this was common before the Breaking, but rarely heard of since."

"What are the risks that Kinley describes?" Gryphon prompted him.

"Well, Aediion can be enticing," Darnleigh said, "because a skilled charmcaster can shape it to his hopes and desires. It's possible to get lost in it, and never return to the real world. Also, you can become trapped if your amulet runs out of stored power. Finally, Kinley says that if you are killed in the world of dreams, you die in real life."

"What could kill you in a dream, Stefan?" a pale-haired Northern Islander asked, rolling her eyes. "I've had a lot of nightmares, but I always wake up alive."

"Magic," Darnleigh said, tapping his forefinger on the page. "Only magic can kill you in Aediion."

"What evidence does Kinley present?" Gryphon asked. "Why should we believe that he is telling the truth? Silverhair?"

"We shouldn't," the Northern Islander scoffed. "Kinley repeats legends from centuries past without question. His books are full of mythological monsters, like watergators and dragons, that no one's ever seen."

"Couldn't they have once existed?" Gryphon said. "Perhaps they were destroyed in the Breaking. If so, is it possible that remnants of the high magic that was common before the Breaking persist in the hidden corners of the world?"

"There are no hidden corners these days," Silverhair said. "No secrets anymore."

"Kinley used primary sources," Darnleigh said. "His sketches are based on eyewitness reports. He even conducted his own experiments to verify what he heard."

"Experiments that no one has been able to duplicate in modern times," Silverhair countered.

"Perhaps the problem is the tools we use now," Darnleigh said, touching his amulet. "These are much more limited in scope than the amulets of old magic. The copperheads refuse to provide us with the tools that we need. We'd have to buy old flash on the down-low market, or use heirloom pieces."

The debate heated up, swirling around Han, leaving him feeling ignorant and unread. His classmates would have heard these arguments since childhood. They shared a common anger and frustration that they'd missed the golden age of wizardry.

Han pressed the heels of his hands against his forehead,

feeling out of his depth. He'd heard nothing of Kinley on the streets of Ragmarket.

Gryphon argued both sides of the question, refueling the discussion when it lagged. He didn't pick on Han again. Maybe he figured his point had been made. The master also left the Bayars in peace. It seemed they'd be given plenty of time to study up.

Gryphon didn't call on Dancer either, ignoring his raised hand.

Han fought down his anger. It was just a different kind of battle, one he'd have to learn to win. Since when had life ever been fair?

Though Gryphon clearly knew his stuff, Han couldn't help comparing him to Speaker Jemson. Jemson's love of history cascaded over you until you were neck-deep and drunk with it. But he made sure all his students stayed afloat.

You can't control what Gryphon does, Han thought. What can you control?

You can come to class prepared, he thought. No matter what.

Gryphon allowed the debate to go on for a while longer, then raised both hands, palms out, to bring it to a halt. "All right, then, let's try an experiment of our own," he said. "Please turn to page 393."

The passage was entitled Portal to Aediion and consisted of lines of spellwork, like free verses trickling down the page.

"Now, choose a partner—preferably someone you already know," Gryphon said. "If you need a partner, raise your hand."

Han turned to Dancer, who shrugged his assent.

Arkeda paired off with Miphis, and Fiona with Wil. Micah was left without a partner, since there was an odd number of students in the class.

"Newling Hayden," Gryphon said, all of a sudden noticing Dancer. "Perhaps you should pair off with someone more experienced, like Bayar." He nodded toward Micah. "I can work with Alister."

Dancer shook his head. "No thank you, sir. I know Alister. I'll stay with him."

"If you insist," Gryphon said, with a sour expression. "You're with me, Bayar."

Micah shrugged his indifference, but Han thought he looked relieved.

Is Gryphon just picking on me again? Han wondered. Did he want to be matched with me for some reason? Or did he want to match Dancer with Micah?

Or did it mean nothing at all?

"This should be easier than communicating across a distance. Face each other and take hold of your amulets," Gryphon directed. "At the risk of being disappointed, I will assume that you have all stoked them with power in preparation for class."

Han had done that, at least, storing magic during the long journey to Oden's Ford.

"Now choose a location, a place you both know," Gryphon said. "And don't all go to The Crown and Castle. I want to hear about different places."

Dancer leaned toward Han. "The fishing hole on Old Woman Creek," he suggested. That was a place on the lower slopes of Hanalea they both knew well, where Han's former employer Lucius Frowsley spent most of his time.

A place that, as wizards, they were now forbidden to go.

"Read over the entire spell," Gryphon said. "Memorize it,

239

since there's no guarantee that Kinley will be available to you in Aediion. The first three lines open the portal; the last three allow you to close the portal and return to reality."

The master gave them a few minutes to do that, waiting until they all looked up from their texts. "All ready now?" Heads nodded around the room. Some of the students looked pale and worried, some leaned forward eagerly, others rolled their eyes, like this exercise was a stupid waste of time.

"Read the first three lines to open the portal," Gryphon said. "Quietly, now, so as not to distract your colleagues. Should you both be successful, you will meet your partner in the dream world. Notice your surroundings, because what you see is a reflection of you. Notice also that you can shape your appearance as you wish. Exchange messages with your partner and immediately return to the classroom. I repeat: don't remain in Aediion longer than a few minutes. Once everyone has completed the exercise, you will report on your experiences." He paused. "I know that some of you are skeptical of Kinley's work, but I expect you all to expend some effort here."

Taking hold of his amulet, Han read through the opening lines of the spell, while all around him he heard others whispering the words in a splash of accents.

For a moment he was engulfed in a swirling black nothingness. Then sunlight broke into his thoughts, streaming down through glittering yellow aspens, sparkling on the waters of Old Woman Creek. Leaves swirled and danced on the current. Han shivered; it was cold, colder than Oden's Ford, and moments later he found himself wearing a fringed and beaded buckskin jacket of clan design, fleece moccasins on his feet.

Amazed, he fingered the soft leather.

Was it real? It seemed very real—the wind swirling over Hanalea smelled of snow. It lifted the hair from his forehead and set aspen leaves chattering over his head.

He looked up the creek. Dancer walked toward him, dressed in leggings and the loose, soft, doeskin tunic he favored, carrying a fishing pole and a fish basket.

"What do you think?" Han said. "Is this it?"

Dancer shrugged. "Let's see if we both remember it the same when we leave."

They stood for an awkward moment.

"Gryphon said to exchange messages," Han said. "I'll say something to you, and then I'll see if you remember it later. You do the same." He thought a moment. "Cat Tyburn is sweet on you," he said, keeping a straight face.

Dancer cocked his head. "*Really*? Why do you say that?"

Han wasn't sure just why he'd said it, except that he knew Dancer wouldn't forget it. "She's shy," he said. "She has trouble speaking her mind." Right.

"Fiona Bayar fancies *you*," Dancer retorted. "She can't take her eyes off you."

They both burst out laughing. Han's spirits rose. It felt good to be back in the Fells, on familiar ground, even if only in the dream world.

"We'd better go back," Dancer said.

Han took hold of his amulet, ready to speak the closing charm, when the air before him rippled like the surface of a pond as the wind catches it. It coalesced and hardened, displacing light, until the image of a person stood before him.

It was young man, a half-dozen years older than Han, expensively dressed in blueblood style. His hair was soot-black, his eyes a brilliant blue. Sunlight glittered on the many rings on his fingers.

The stranger blinked, looking about, and a triumphant smile spread across his face as if he'd done something extra special.

Han glanced aside at Dancer, but as he did so, his friend shimmered and dissolved, blinking out like a cinder in the dark. "Dancer!" Han said, taking a step toward the spot where he'd disappeared.

"You there! Wait! Don't go yet," the stranger said, in Fellspeech.

"Who are you?" Han said, backing away, thinking that nobody should be showing up here that he didn't invite. "How did you get here?"

Was it someone from his class, intruding? Han didn't recognize him, but that didn't mean anything. Gryphon had said that you could change your appearance, so it could be anyone in disguise, even one of the Bayars. Micah and Fiona likely had the most powerful amulets in the class, next to his own.

Could Micah find his way to a place he'd never been? Then again, the first time they'd met was on Hanalea.

"You can call me Crow," the stranger volunteered. He brushed a hand through his hair as if preening his feathers. "And you are . . . ?"

"Tell me how you got here, or get out," Han said, a knife magically appearing in his fist. Amulet or not, he'd still go to knives if he got in a jam.

He balanced lightly on his feet, ready to jump one way or

the other, recalling Darnleigh's words, moments before in the lecture hall.

Kinley says that if you're killed in the world of dreams, you die in real life.

"Please," Crow said, "hear me out. I promise, it will be worth your time." He took a step forward.

Han took a step back. "I'm warning you, I'm rum with a blade."

"It's wise to be wary in your situation." Crow kept shifting— from formal dress to plainer garb, to a dean's robe. Either he couldn't decide what suited him, or he liked to dress up. "I, at least, gave you a name," he went on. "That's more than you have done. Do you belong to Aerie House?" There was something in the way he said it, something that set off alarms in Han's head.

Han hesitated. "Aerie House?"

"The Bayar family. Are you one of them? Everything taken together, I would guess not." He studied Han's face. "Ah," he said, smiling. "I see you are not. In fact, they are *not* your friends."

Han struggled to reclaim his street face.

"Then, tell me, how did you gain possession of that amulet?" Crow said, his eyes fixed on Han's jinxpiece.

"You going to tell me why you're here?" Han demanded. "And stay still, will you?"

Crow finally settled in his blueblood garb. His jacket looked made to measure, with glitter-thread sewn over, and trailing sleeves. Han guessed he was handsome, if you liked the type.

Crow extended his empty hand toward Han, palm out, as if feeling his heat. "You are quite powerful, you know." He tilted his head, appraising Han. "And you *are* well favored. Even rather handsome, despite your speech."

Who was he to judge Han's looks and speech? And why should Han care? "I an't a fancy, if that's what you're thinking," Han said. "No offense."

Crow laughed. "I hope not," he said, as if it were a very funny joke.

"Did you steal your amulet from them?" Crow said, looking back at the amulet. "If so, I must say, I am impressed. What do you mean to do with it? Do they know you have it? Do you have a plan?"

Han said nothing to this torrent of questions.

Crow shook his head. "No plan? That's not good. The *Bayars* no doubt have a plan. Better think ahead, or you're not going to keep that amulet for long."

"I won't answer any questions until I know who you really are," Han said.

"I understand." Crow chewed on his lower lip, thinking. "Very well. I can tell you this much. I'm on faculty here at the academy. I've been looking for a student to mentor, someone capable of mastering higher level magic. I also need someone who is not afraid to bend the rules a bit. The fact that you are here, and your possession of that amulet, tells me that you might be the person I have been looking for."

He raised his hand when Han opened his mouth to speak. "I'm not going to tell you any more than that until I know I can trust you. It's still possible that you are in league with my enemies."

"How do *you* know the Bayars?" Han asked, fingering his

amulet, still unsure whether to stay or go.

"Let's just say we are political rivals," Crow said. "I need gifted allies. In return, I'll help you protect yourself against them."

"Help me how?" Han asked.

Crow took another step toward Han, looking intently into his eyes. "I can teach you how to use that amulet. I can teach you marvelous things." Crow's eyes glittered, his voice low and coaxing, almost pleading.

"Keep your flash gammon to yourself," Han said. "If you want to talk to me, come see me in real life. I'm going back," he added, summoning up the returning words.

"We *have* to meet in Aediion," Crow said. "It's not safe for us to be seen together."

Han stared at him. "What do you mean?"

"You have no idea how vulnerable we are." Crow drew a quick breath as though he meant to say something else, then looked aside, distracted. "We're out of time," he said. "Do not tell a soul about our meeting. No one, do you understand? If the Bayars hear about this, they will kill you and seize your amulet to prevent our meeting again." He paused to let the words sink in, then added, "I will meet you a week from tonight, midnight, in Aediion. Mystwerk bell tower is a private place. Do you know where that is?"

Han blinked at him, a thousand questions elbowing their way forward. "I know where that is," he said. "But what makes you think I—"

"We cannot be seen together," Crow repeated. "Aediion is the only safe place. Rebuild your amulet in the meantime. If you can't come a week from tonight, come the next week. Or the next. I'll wait for you each week until you come. Open the portal at midnight. And come alone."

He shimmered and blinked out.

Han was suddenly conscious of a terrible pain in his head. He groaned and opened his eyes, looking into Gryphon's grim face.

He thought for a moment he might be sick, but that passed. He looked down at his amulet and saw Gryphon's hand wrapped around it, just below his. The master was gripping it so hard his knuckles were white, and his face shone with sweat.

"Let go," Han said feebly, tugging at Gryphon's fingers with his other hand.

"You first," he said. "I don't want you slipping away again."

Reluctantly, Han loosed his hold and wiped his sweaty hand on his breeches. He lay on the stone floor in the lecture hall, his head pillowed on somebody's coat. Beyond Gryphon he saw a circle of faces—the other students in the class.

Micah Bayar scowled as if sorry that Han had rejoined the living. He didn't see Fiona.

Gryphon touched Han's forehead with hot fingers, then finally let go of the amulet. "You're out of danger," he said. "The Maker protects the impaired, it seems."

The master sat on the floor, his canes next to him, his robes hiked up to his knees. Gryphon's lower legs were scarred and shriveled, the flesh leathery and dark, as though they had been burnt. Iron braces extended from his ankles past his knees.

Gryphon followed Han's gaze. Scowling, he yanked the fabric down to cover himself.

"What happened?" Han said, sorry to be caught staring. "In Aediion, I mean," he rushed to add.

"We've established, beyond any doubt, that you are a fool, Alister," Gryphon said. "You've managed to drain both your amulet and yourself completely. That's why you needed my help to get back. I hope the journey was worth it."

The doors to the classroom slammed open, and a tall, angular woman marched in, followed by Fiona. The stranger's hair was straight and chin length, a steel gray streaked with wizard red. Her robes were edged with heavy embroidery, and the multiple velvet bands on her sleeves said she was a high up.

"What's going on, Master Gryphon?" she demanded. "Newling Bayar tells me there's a student in trouble."

"Dean Abelard!" Gryphon gripped his canes and struggled to rise to his feet, seeming embarrassed to be caught on the floor.

"Can I help?" Dancer asked, squatting next to him. When Gryphon nodded, Dancer slid his hands under the master's arms and lifted him up. Gryphon shook him off as soon as he was upright. Dancer handed him his double canes.

"There's no trouble," Gryphon said. "Newling Alister delayed too long returning from Aediion."

"From Aediion?" Dean Abelard stared down at Han, biting her lower lip. "Really?"

Gryphon nodded. "He is recovering now."

Scrunching her robes in her hands, Dean Abelard knelt next to Han. She pressed the back of her hand against his cheek. Her hand felt blazing hot against his cold skin.

"Get the boy some water," Abelard commanded, and somebody rushed away to fetch it. Moments later, a cup appeared, and Han drank it dry.

Someone knelt next to them, knees pressing into Han's hip.

He turned his head. It was Fiona, lips parted, her pale eyes fixed on his face.

"What's the matter with him?" she said, leaning forward, her hair brushing Han's cheek. "Will he survive?"

"If he's lived this long, then, yes, I expect he will," Abelard said. "It was good you came to fetch me."

She reached for Han's amulet, then jerked her hand back as if startled when she saw the design.

"An interesting choice, Alister," she murmured, straightening her wizard stoles. "We need to talk about that. Among other things." And then, without taking her eyes off his face, she said louder, "Master Gryphon, dismiss your class."

Gryphon turned to face the gawking students. "Newling Alister has demonstrated for us all the price of carelessness and arrogance combined with ignorance. Do take note." He paused, to let that sink in. "For tomorrow, I want two pages from each of you about your experience in Aediion to share with the rest of the class. Class dismissed."

The other students collected their things. Han felt the vibration of feet and the touch of eyes as they shuffled out. Fiona didn't move, as if hoping to be overlooked.

"You too, Fiona," Gryphon said. "And you, Hayden. Out."

Fiona's knees were removed from Han's side as she stood. He heard her walk away, a door opening and closing.

"I'll wait and see Alister back to his room," Dancer said. "Or Healer's Hall. Wherever he needs to go."

Abelard looked up at Dancer, taking in his stubborn expression. She sighed. "All right. But step outside a moment, please. We need to speak to Alister in private."

Dancer shook his head, his blue eyes fixed on the dean. "I'm not—"

"It's all right," Han said, waving him off. "I'll be fine." He *was* beginning to feel a little better. A trickle of heat in his middle said his magic was building up again.

Abelard waited until the door closed behind Dancer before she spoke.

"So, Alister," she said softly, closing her fingers around his wrist. "Tell me all about it." Power flowed into him. It was hard to resist, depleted as he was.

"Tell you about what?" Han asked. When she continued to stare down into his face, he said, "All I remember is, I felt dizzy, and then I must've passed out. I don't think anything really happened. Magical, I mean."

"Alister partnered with the copperhead that was just here," Gryphon said. "His friend returned after a few minutes, but Alister stayed until I dragged him back by force. He was using power like mad. He'd drained his amulet almost completely."

Abelard frowned. "How long was he gone?"

The master hesitated. "About fifteen minutes."

"Fifteen minutes!" Abelard straightened and stared at Gryphon. "He's a *newling*, Master Gryphon. A child, magically speaking. Why didn't you put a stop to it sooner?"

Gryphon looked like he wished he could get out from under Abelard's flinty gaze. "I had partnered with another student, since there was an odd number in the class."

"You should *know* better than that," Abelard exploded. "How can you supervise the students if you are attempting travel in Aediion yourself?"

Gryphon held the dean's gaze. "It was irresponsible. A mistake on my part." He paused. "It will not happen again, I assure you."

Abelard turned to Han. "Did Master Gryphon warn you about the consequences of staying too long?" Abelard asked.

The way she said it, Han wasn't sure who was on trial—him or Gryphon.

Han shifted on the hard floor. "He told us to come right back."

"Did he tell you why it was so important to return quickly?" Abelard continued.

Han looked at Gryphon, whose gaze was fixed on the ceiling. "We talked about it. If you drain your amulet it's hard to come back."

"If you drain your amulet, you *cannot* come back," Abelard said. "You remain in the dreamworld forever, while your body lies abandoned. You are *dead*."

Well, that was news. Han felt a little queasy. "So you believe in what Kinley says about the dreamworld? I mean, it sounds like most people don't even think it exists."

Abelard nodded. "I believe travel in Aediion is rare, but possible. It could be a very useful tool, if we could master it." The dean fingered a strand of her silver hair. "We do this exercise every fall with the first years. When the students report tomorrow, most will have tried and failed. Some will make up stories, suggesting success. Others—nonbelievers—won't have even tried.

"But every so often we encounter students like you and . . . Hayden, who succeed. Most are smart enough to follow directions. Your friend closed the portal on his own and returned. You stayed in Aediion too long. That's a dangerous business, Alister."

"What makes you think I succeeded?" Han asked, feeling pinned under the gaze of the dean and the master.

"You were using prodigious amounts of power," Abelard said. Her sharp, pointed face wore a hungry look that Han mistrusted. "Your amulet is depleted."

"Maybe it was because I didn't know what I was doing," Han said. When in doubt, experience had taught him to deny, and keep denying. "I didn't do the reading. When my charm didn't work, I just kept having at it. I guess I lost track of time."

"You claim you didn't go anywhere?" Abelard said.

"Not that I remember," Han said.

Abelard scowled at him, rolling her eyes.

Han was usually a rum liar, but he couldn't seem to amuse these two.

"*Whatever* happened," Gryphon said fiercely, "you need to follow my directions, or you're out of here."

"Master Gryphon is right," Abelard said. "If you persist in taking chances, endangering yourself and others, I will have you expelled and your amulet confiscated. Do you understand me?"

Han closed his hand around his amulet. You can try, he thought, gazing at her straight on.

To his surprise, Abelard smiled. "I don't know that name. Alister," she said, giving him another good look-over. "And your speech is . . . unusual. Where do you live? What is your house? Perhaps I know your family."

"I'm from Ragmarket," Han said. Once he got started, the words just tumbled out. "Used to live on Cobble Street, over the stable, before it burnt down. I'm sort of between houses now, since my family's dead. My mam was Sali Alister, my sister's name was Mari. Mam was mostly in laundry, but her sideline was ragpicking. Heard of them?"

Wordlessly, Abelard shook her head.

"You will," Han said, looking the dean in the eyes.

Abelard cleared her throat. "It's possible that your amulet was responsible for your success," she said. She reached out and fingered the serpent flash cautiously, as if it might bite. It must have been totally drained of power, since it didn't react to her touch at all. Han shivered, resisting the temptation to snatch it out of her hand. It was as though she'd reached into his chest and took hold of his heart.

"Where did you get this?" Abelard leaned in close.

"I bought it in the clan markets. Secondhand," Han said.

"I thought it might be a custom piece," the dean said. "One with . . . extra capabilities, since you're so friendly with the copperheads. That would explain a lot."

"You think I could afford a custom piece?" Han said. "Friends is friends until it comes to a trade. That's how it works in the markets."

"Not many charmcasters would choose a piece of this design," Abelard said. She paused. "Do you know who else carried an amulet like this?"

"I got no idea," Han lied. He felt weary and besieged, stripped of his usual charm.

"It's a reproduction of the amulet carried by the Demon King," she said.

Han produced a look of surprise. "Huh. Maybe that's why it went so cheap."

"Do you have a special interest in dark magic, Alister? Is that it?" Her voice was velvety soft.

"I want to learn about all kinds of magic," Han said. "That's why I'm here."

"There are those who will make assumptions about you based on that amulet, Alister," she said. "People who believe that all pathways should be open to those who seek knowledge. Those that believe that the end justifies the means."

Abelard stood abruptly so that now she was towering over him, a black silhouette against the light from the windows. She bent and reached her hands down to help him up and settle him down into a chair. She was surprisingly strong.

"Call in his partner," she murmured to Gryphon.

Gryphon called, "Newling Hayden!"

When Dancer came back in from the corridor, Abelard said, "Hayden, Alister and I have been talking about his experiences in Aediion. What do you remember?"

Dancer's eyes flicked from Han to Abelard, as if he suspected he was walking into a trap. Han tried to send him a message with his eyes.

"Well," Dancer said, "I don't remember much."

"Blood and bones of the Demon King!" Abelard exploded. "Just tell me what you *do* remember." When Dancer glanced at Han again, Abelard gripped Dancer's chin and wrenched his head around. "Look at *me*, newling."

Dancer fingered his amulet as if for reassurance. "Beforehand, we agreed to meet back home, in a place we know on Hanalea. So we—"

"What would you know about Hanalea?" Abelard interrupted.

"It is forbidden for wizards to go there."

"I was born on Hanalea," Dancer said calmly.

"You're Spirit clan, aren't you?" Abelard said as if she hadn't been talking behind his back. "I've never seen any gifted come out of the camps before."

"I'm mixed-blood," Dancer said, without elaborating. "So after I spoke the charm, I saw Han walking toward me. He was kind of flickering, like someone you see by firelight, and his clothes kept changing." He paused. "I guess I must have been dreaming."

"And . . . ?" Abelard prompted. "Then what happened?"

"Well, we talked some. Then I . . . ah . . . woke up."

The dean's eyes narrowed. "But Alister did not return with you?"

Dancer shook his head. "When I opened my eyes, Han was slumped over the table. I waited for him to wake up. Everyone else was awake, except Micah Bayar and Master Gryphon. Fiona went to find you. Then Master Gryphon woke and came to help."

Abelard reached toward Dancer's amulet, and it brightened in response. She drew her hand back again. "Unlike Alister, you've not totally depleted your amulet. You were either smart enough to follow directions, or you never went there at all."

She smiled a brittle smile. "Alister. I often work with exceptional students, even newlings. Plan to meet me in my office four weeks from today. I'll see what I can find out about you in the meantime." She walked to the podium and picked up the Kinley, riffling through it.

It was their signal to leave so she could have a solitary chat with Gryphon.

Bones, Han thought. What could the dean find out about him in a month? And what would she do with that information?

"Hayden, take Alister back to his room and see that he rests a while," Gryphon said. "He'll need to restore power to his amulet before class tomorrow. Don't forget your pages. And may I suggest you both do the reading for next time," he called after them as they walked toward the door.

As they crossed the grassy quad, Dancer kept one hand under Han's elbow, steadying him. Han pulled free. "I'll live," he said.

"You're cold as the Dyrnnewater, you know that, right?" Dancer said. "You're always hotter than me, but there's nothing there." He shook his head in amazement.

"Was it real?" Han asked, scuffling through a pile of leaves. "Did we really meet on Old Woman Creek?"

Dancer nodded, looking sideways at him. "You said Cat was sweet on me."

"And you said Fiona Bayar lusted after me." Han raised an eyebrow.

"She does, Hunts Alone," Dancer said, grinning. "Truly."

"So Abelard wants to work with me and not you," Han said. "I wonder what that's about."

"I'm a copperhead," Dancer said. "That's what it's about." He rolled his eyes. "I'm not exactly heartbroken."

"If she teaches me anything useful, I'll pass it along," Han said. They walked in silence for a few paces. "Did you see anything else?" Han asked. "Before you closed the portal?"

Dancer shook his head. "Like what?"

"Somebody else showed up, just as you left. A blueblood

wizard a little older than us. Called himself Crow. You didn't see him?"

Dancer shrugged. "No. Was it someone from class?"

"I didn't recognize him, but he had to have been from Mystwerk, anyway," Han said. "He said he was faculty here."

"How would he find us on Hanalea? Don't you have to be able to visualize a place before you visit it in Aediion?" Dancer said.

Han shrugged. "I got no idea. I don't know how this works. But maybe somebody overheard us saying we were meeting there." Maybe I *should* go back and read the text, he thought.

"So what happened?" Dancer said. "Did he say anything?"

Han remembered what Crow had said. *Do not tell a soul about this.*

No reason he had to do as Crow commanded. "He said he wanted to partner up with me against the Bayars. He offered to teach me magic. Then Gryphon yanked me back."

Dancer looked at Han for a long moment, his brows drawn together. Finally he said, "Well, you were lucky, Hunts Alone. Fiona went after Abelard because Gryphon and Micah were out almost as long as you. We were beginning to think nobody was coming back. I was about ready to open the portal and go back after you when they woke up. Gryphon rushed over and revived you."

"Huh," Han said. "Well, if Gryphon really went to Aediion, he must be stoked, then. He still had plenty of power on board, and I was nearly out."

"How did you leave it with Crow, then?" Dancer asked.

Han snorted. "I didn't say, one way or the other, but I an't a fool. Seems chancy to take lessons from someone I don't know in a place where I don't know the rules."

Just like Oden's Ford, he thought.

The bells in Mystwerk Tower sounded the end of the first class period, meaning they had fifteen minutes to walk down-river to their next class at Healer's Hall. Something about amulets and talismans.

"I'll walk you back to Hampton, and then go on to class," Dancer said.

"I an't going back to Hampton," Han said, turning onto the gallery along the river. "I don't want to miss class. We're behind enough already."

"But Master Gryphon said—"

"We won't tell him, all right?"

But Crow's words still sounded in his mind, like a phrase of music he couldn't forget.

I can teach you how to use that amulet. I can teach you marvelous things.

CHAPTER FOURTEEN
DEAN'S
DINNER

When Han returned to Gryphon's class the next day, he made sure he did nothing to call attention to himself. His amulet was still low on power, though he'd stoked it all night long. He kept a hand wrapped around it all morning, and it greedily sucked him dry.

His report on his visit to Aediion was as sketchy as anyone's. Gryphon smashed his lips together tight, but said nothing after except "Thank you, Alister. That is, indeed, a remarkable story."

Micah and Fiona provided equally vague reports.

Han read and studied Kinley like a fiend, searching for answers. He couldn't ask Gryphon because that would only draw the master's attention. After the incident with Abelard, they left the topic of Aediion for good. The master continued to pick on Han in class, regularly descending on him like a predator bird with broken wings and a savage bite. It was as if he blamed Han for getting him into trouble with Dean Abelard.

Han stayed up late every night, preparing for class, trying to make himself less vulnerable to attack. The threat of humiliation was incredibly motivating.

The rest of the class suffered too, just not so often as Han. Gryphon reduced Darnleigh to tears, ridiculed the Mander brothers, and treated Dancer like an idiot. Even the Bayars came in for tough questioning at times, though it seemed to Han that Gryphon's verbal blade was blunted in their case. Especially with Fiona.

Twice during the next week, Dean Abelard came into the class and sat at the back of the room. She tapped her fingers on the desk in front of her, her face grim and unsmiling in the faint glow from her amulet. During those sessions Gryphon floundered, often losing his train of thought.

Micah and his cousins spent little time at Hampton Hall, so Han rarely saw them except in class. They preferred The Crown and Castle, where they held court nightly with Fiona and Will and a large crowd of Mystwerk newlings Micah was tight with. It made sense. Most of Han's class came from the Fells; they'd likely been cozy since childhood.

Han forced himself to go into The Crown and Castle now and then, just to make show, even though the taproom went silent when he entered, and Micah's mates made a point of grabbing their purses and guarding their amulets if he came anywhere near.

Seven weeks into the term, the newlings were notified that Dean Abelard would host the first Dean's Dinner at Mystwerk Hall on Temple Day. All Mystwerk students, proficients, and faculty were expected to attend.

Han didn't look forward to coming under Dean Abelard's

eye again. His face-to-face with her was only a week away. He still clung to the frail hope he could get out of it.

As Han dressed for dinner, he was glad for the red robe of anonymity he pulled on over his clothes. He'd bathed, scraped the stubble from his face, combed his hair, and shined up his amulet with a chamois. He couldn't think of how else to prepare.

Mystwerk Hall was ablaze with lights as Han and Dancer walked across the quad, the entryway spattered with red robes. For once it wasn't raining, though a brisk wind from the north said the weather was changing.

Servants wearing Mystwerk livery directed them into the Great Hall.

At the front of the room, long tables glittered with plates and cups and silver—more of each than seemed needful, when there wasn't even any food set out.

Great banners hung from the cavernous ceilings—wizard house emblems, including the familiar Stooping Falcons of the Bayars.

What would his banner be, if he had one, Han wondered.

Although everyone wore the requisite red robes, most were decorated—with stoles bearing the signia of their wizard houses, and with the badges and embroideries denoting their academic ranks. Many wore jewelry beyond their amulets—gaudy rings on their fingers, heavy gold chains and wrist-cuffs. Even in his red plumage, Han felt underdressed, like the plainest of sparrows.

Han located the Bayars amid a cluster of students on the far side of the room. As he watched, Micah glanced at Han, then said something that set the others to snickering. Fiona was facing Han also, and she looked up and caught his eye. She held his gaze for a long moment, her face as hard and cold as marble, then turned toward Wil.

Han felt the familiar prickle of danger between his shoulder blades. Straying onto blueblood turf was like walking the streets of Southbridge without a gang mark or a reputation to protect you.

Touching his amulet for reassurance, he put his street face on.

Drinks were on offer at a bar in one corner, so he and Dancer headed that way, sliding past clusters of students and faculty.

As they passed, conversation washed over them. Han caught snatches of it—the words "Ragmarket" and "slumlord" and "copperhead" struck his ears like sour notes.

Han scanned the array of glittering bottles, casks, and barrels at the bar. Not just ale and cider, but brandy, wine, and whiskey, too. Han thought of Lucius Frowsley, back home on Hanalea, and wondered if his distillery was still in business, and who carried product for him now.

Han and Dancer both ordered cider. This dinner would be tricky enough to navigate with a clear head.

Adam Gryphon entered the room in his wheeled chair, maneuvering expertly through the crowd toward the bar.

Too bad he can't use that chair all the time, Han thought. But the academy was riddled with steps, curbs, cobblestones, and other hazards.

Someone tugged at Han's sleeve, and he spun around, nearly spilling his cider.

He faced a girlie with extremely pale skin and short-cropped, spiky black hair streaked with wizard red. She wore a red robe sewn over with proficient trim. Her hands were loaded with rings, and much of her visible skin was covered in bright, metallic tattoos, like painted-on jewelry. The design seemed to ripple and move on its own.

"They're talismans and wards," the girlie explained, brushing her fingers over a symbol on the back of her hand. "To protect against hex magic."

"Ah," Han said, trying to think of the right thing to say. "Is someone trying to hex you?"

She nodded, then stood on tiptoes so she could stage whisper in his ear. "I'm Mordra deVilliers," she said. As if that explained it.

"I'm Han Alister," Han said. He nodded toward Dancer. "And this is Hayden Fire Dancer."

"I know," Mordra deVilliers said, looking from one to the other, her eyes wide and solemn. "Is it true you're a thief and a murderer?"

Han just looked at her.

There was no trace of judgment in her face, only avid curiosity. When he didn't answer right away, she rushed on. "They say you're a notorious criminal, and that you tried to murder Lord Bayar." She turned to Dancer. "And they say that *you* are a copperhead spy."

Dancer glanced at Han. "Who told you that?" he asked.

Mordra tilted her head toward the Bayars' corner.

"So." Han rubbed the back of his neck. "What do *you* think?"

"Well," she said, nodding at Dancer, "you *are* a copperhead." She turned to Han. "And *you* sound like a street person, even if you're not dressed like one." She scanned his face. "And you *do* look rather ruthless, with those scars and all."

How did he sound like a street person? Han wondered. He hadn't even said that much.

"Should you be talking to us, then?" he asked. "Could be chancy."

Mordra shrugged. "They don't think much of me either, because I'm from the down-realms. Even though my bloodline is pure, and my father's on the council. Dean Abelard favors me, though, because I have considerable talent." She extended her arm, displaying the trim on her robes. "I'm the youngest proficient ever."

"You must be rum clever," Han said.

"If you're smart, she'll take notice of you too," Mordra said. "Doesn't matter who you are." She glanced at Dancer, and shrugged. "Unless you're a copperhead, of course."

This Mordra may be smart, but she'll say anything that comes into her head, Han thought.

"Maybe I don't want to be noticed," he said.

"Oh, you want to be," Mordra said. "Dean Abelard offers special classes for Mystwerk students with potential."

"What kind of classes?" Han asked.

Again, Mordra went up on tiptoes, grabbing onto his arm to keep her balance. "Forbidden magic," she breathed, her warm breath tickling his ear. "Powerful spells."

An icy voice cut into their conversation. "Shut up, Mordra."

Startled, Mordra jerked back, nearly falling. Han looked up to see that Fiona had somehow made it all the way across the room without his noticing.

"*You* shut up," Mordra said, recovering herself and balling up her fists.

"You're always spewing nonsense like a newling in his cups," Fiona went on, rolling her eyes. "Alister is a street thug. He has no interest in your pathetic fantasy life."

"Actually, it was fascinating," Han said. "Mordra was just saying that—"

"Never mind," Mordra interrupted. "Where are you sitting?"

"Wherever there's room, I guess," Han said. Far from the Bayars and the dean, he thought to himself. And maybe Mordra, too. She might be the only one willing to talk to him, but her chatter was wearing him out.

"You're assigned a seat—didn't you know? I'm at the dean's table," Mordra said.

"How do you know where you're sitting?" Han asked. It always seemed like he was missing information that everyone else knew.

"There are little cards at the places," Mordra said. "You should walk around and find yours. It's almost time to sit down."

Han's place turned out to be at the dean's table, too. With both Bayars, Adam Gryphon, another proficient, and another master. So much for avoiding notice.

Dancer was seated at a nearby table with several of the Bayars' crew. They squirmed and leaned away as if he smelled bad. Dancer sighed and put on his trader face.

It was as if the dean had decided to make everybody miserable on purpose.

Han was seated between Mordra and Fiona, with Micah across from them, next to Master Gryphon.

Fiona sat rigid, staring straight ahead, as if she could pretend Han wasn't right next to her.

Fortunately, servers arrived in a hurry with soup, ladling it into bowls in front of each person.

It was a thin broth, with a bit of greens floating in it. Not much of a supper, Han thought, surprised. He'd expected a more lavish spread. Spooning some up, he blew on it to cool it off. It tasted smoky and salty, like dried mushrooms and onions.

I hope we get seconds, he thought. Or at least some bread to go with. He took a few more bites, then noticed that nobody else was eating.

Across the table, Micah gazed at him, fingers templed, one eyebrow raised. Mordra leaned over. "You're supposed to wait until everyone is served and the dean has welcomed us," she said in a whisper loud enough to be heard at nearby tables. A titter rolled around the room.

Han put his spoon down, feeling the blood rush to his face.

It turned out that soup wasn't supper. It was what came before supper. Supper was roast quail and potatoes and carrots and little cakes and fruit soaked in brandy set aflame and three different wines and sweet spirits in tiny cups.

Nobody else brought their cider to the table.

Though he tried to follow along with what others were doing, every so often, Han would pick up the wrong fork or eat things in the wrong order, or use the wrong sauce on the wrong thing, and Mordra would correct him in her player's whisper, sending the room into silent convulsions of laughter.

The only ones not laughing were Dean Abelard, Dancer, Mordra, and Fiona.

Fiona?

All through dinner she drank wine but ate very little, pushing the food around her plate with a scowl on her face until the servers took it away. She drummed her fingers on the table and shifted in her seat.

Sitting next to me takes away her appetite? Han thought.

Several times, Master Gryphon leaned across the table and tried to engage Fiona in conversation, but she seemed distracted, as if she scarcely heard him.

Finally she leaned across Han to speak to Mordra. "Just stop it!" she hissed, as Mordra opened her mouth to speak when Han went to butter his roll, likely with the wrong knife.

"What?" Mordra blinked at her.

"You of all people should not be correcting anyone's manners!" Fiona went on, her voice brittle as steel at solstice. "*You* are a disaster."

Mordra thrust her chin out. "I was just trying to—"

"Stay away from Alister, or you'll be more of a pariah than you already are," Fiona warned.

"Both of you shut it!" Han exploded, slamming his hands down on the table, rattling the china and sloshing wine out of glasses. "It'd be easier to eat in the middle of a tavern brawl than to sit between the two of you."

The room went dead silent.

Fiona scraped back her chair and stood. "Dean Abelard, please excuse me. I'm not feeling well." She swept out of the hall without a backward glance.

Han looked across the table to where Micah sat staring at him, eyes narrowed in appraisal. Gryphon gazed after Fiona until she disappeared through the doorway, then fixed his uncanny eyes on Han, his face pale and furious. Dean Abelard propped her elbows on the table, resting her chin on her hands, a faint smile curving her lips.

Han stopped eating then, too, unwilling to chance more lessons from Mordra. She rattled on, and he answered in short sentences.

Finally, the endless dinner was over. Students and faculty collected into chatty groups. Han and Dancer left the hall by the back door in order to avoid contact with anyone.

"We have to do this every month?" Han muttered, the rich meal like an anvil in his middle. "Bloody bones."

"Fiona Bayar and Mordra deVilliers were *fighting* over you?" The wind rattled branches overhead, and Dancer turned his collar up. When Han glared at him, he added, "It looked like it to me."

"I got no idea what that was all about," Han said. "Fiona doesn't want anyone to talk to us. Maybe she wants to isolate us more than we already are."

"Maybe she wants you for herself," Dancer said.

"Ha." They walked on in silence for a moment. "I wonder who goes to Abelard's classes," Han mused. "I wonder what she's up to."

As they rounded the side of Mystwerk Hall, light flared under the gallery, catching Han's eye. He squinted, making out a robed silhouette amid the shadows, an angular face illuminated from below.

Overhead, stone cracked with a boom that set Han's ears to ringing. Without looking up, he launched himself into Dancer, sending both of them flying to a sprawling landing on the grassy quad.

Han rolled to his feet. A jumble of roof tiles and broken stone littered the ground where they'd stood moments before. Palming his knife, he charged toward the gallery, running a zigzag course so as to make a difficult target. But nobody was there.

"What is it?" Dancer said, just behind him. "What did you see?"

Han shook his head and put his finger to his lips. He looked back toward the walkway.

It appeared that a large second story gallery had broken off and shattered on the cobblestones. Some of the pieces were bigger than his head. Any one of them could have killed them had they struck true.

As they watched, a crowd of students and faculty rounded the corner and clustered around the fallen masonry. They didn't notice Han and Dancer hidden in the gloom.

Neither of the Bayars were there.

Han touched Dancer's shoulder and jerked his head toward their dormitory.

All the way back, Han kept his knife in one hand, his amulet in the other, his senses on alert for an ambush along the way.

Blevins looked up as they passed through the common room. "Dinner over already?" he said.

"Has anyone else come back from dinner?" Han asked.

Blevins shook his head. "You're the first."

They climbed the stairs to the fourth floor. Han closed the door at the top of the stairs and rechecked his magical barriers. Soft-footing it down the hallway to his room, he eased the door open. No one there. Crossing to the window, he looked out. Excited voices still floated from the crowd around the rubble near Mystwerk Hall.

Han turned around, to find Dancer in the doorway.

"Somebody was standing under the gallery on the far side of the quad," Han said. "He cast a charm right before the gallery came down on us."

"Are you sure?" Dancer asked. "The wind might have loosened one of the cornices. It's been howling all day."

"Whoever did it wanted it to look like it was the wind," Han said.

"You didn't see who it was?"

Han shook his head. "Somebody tall, in wizard robes."

The light from the amulet had momentarily illuminated their attacker's face, but it had extinguished so quickly he couldn't be sure who it was.

He had a guess, though. Fiona would have had plenty of time to get into position. Or Micah could have hurried out the front door in time to be waiting for them when they came around the building.

They'd been lucky this time—but who knew how long their luck would hold?

CHAPTER FIFTEEN

FRIENDS
AND ENEMIES

Amon did review the roster of students in Wien House and Isenwerk, newling cadets and secondaries, but there were no Alisters listed. Cuffs could have been enrolled under an assumed name, but if he'd just arrived at Wien House, surely Raisa or Amon would have spotted him again in the dining halls or libraries. When that didn't happen, Raisa grudgingly conceded that she'd been mistaken.

"Just remember: stay off Bridge Street," Amon said.

As weeks went by, Raisa began to relax in her identity as newling cadet. She'd never fool anyone who knew her well, but to anyone else, a cadet's tunic and chopped-off hair seemed to be a remarkably good disguise for a princess. She encountered a few of her countrymen in the dining hall and on the quad, but no one recognized her.

Taim Askell was as good as his word. The curriculum he and Amon had cooked up for Raisa kept her running from early morning until she fell into bed exhausted on the top floor of Grindell Hall. Not even Hallie's snoring could keep her awake.

She couldn't complain. She'd asked for it—no—demanded it. And now she was paying the price. There were no daydreamy sessions of stitchery or chamber music or painting landscapes in the garden. There were no lazy afternoons gossiping over tea on the terrace.

There was no terrace.

The lack of a dorm master at Grindell Hall might have encouraged rule-breaking, but they were all too exhausted for that. As fourth-year commander, Amon strictly enforced curfew on his fellow cadets, though he was rarely on the premises himself. Raisa was always half asleep by curfew anyway, trying to read a few more pages before she doused her candle. Some nights she did fall asleep, draped across her desk, her face mashed into the pages of her history book. Maybe some of it would soak in through her skin.

She stayed off Bridge Street, even though she was sorely tempted when Talia and Hallie invited her to go out with them. She told herself she didn't have time to go to taverns anyway. At least that way she could avoid Talia's relentless matchmaking.

She quickly grew to dread her recitation in the History of Warfare. Lectures by the masters and deans were scheduled three times a week, with recitations every day. The recitations were moderated by proficients, who led discussions and administered oral and written examinations. So they had a lot of power, especially over newlings.

Her history recitation was led by an Ardenine proficient named Henri Tourant.

A younger son of a thane, Tourant had apparently decided that an academic post provided opportunities he wouldn't have at home—opportunities to bully and humiliate students during the day and pursue other pleasures at night.

Tourant was a tyrant, and he had a typical Ardenine attitude toward women—arrogant and condescending. He made his opinion clear early on—women should be enrolled elsewhere, not wasting the time of the faculty in Wien House and the other, more manly academies. A thousand years since the Breaking, and Arden still couldn't seem to get over the fact that they had once been ruled by a woman.

Tourant was a small man—in stature and in every other way. He had thin, cruel lips and curling brown hair that he wore long. It was already thinning on top, though he was only a few years older than Raisa. His face was rather reptilian, with a receding chin and a pointed nose.

He was also something of a dandy, and often removed his scholar's robes to display his finery.

Tourant strutted back and forth at the front of the classroom, doing most of the talking during what was supposed to be a discussion. He rarely stayed on topic and seemed to have only a nodding acquaintance with the facts. A real discussion would have been helpful, but Tourant's recitation was a waste of time.

Raisa mostly sat in the back row and did homework. But today the topic was magic in warfare, and she had trouble keeping her mind occupied elsewhere and her mouth shut when Tourant rattled on, spewing misinformation like a broken waste pipe.

I'm learning self-restraint, Raisa thought, keeping her

clenched fists hidden in her lap. A valuable skill.

It got worse. A rather wild-eyed temple dedicate from Arden proclaimed that the Demonai warriors went into battle naked. "Though they are fabulously rich, the northern savages wear all of their wealth as jewelry," the dedicate went on. "They fight in the nude save for massive gold collars and bracelets that proclaim their status. And quivers for their arrows."

"Now that is something I would like to see," Tourant said, grinning. His gaze slid over Raisa, cold and nasty as a demon's kiss. "You're a half-blood, Morley, right? Ever go into battle naked? Is the idea—to distract the enemy?"

Raisa pushed away an image of Reid Nightwalker galloping through the trees in the buff. "If you think about it, sir, you'll realize that can't be true," she said, choosing each word before she spit it out. "Anyone who goes naked in the mountains would be cold and uncomfortable even in summer. In a northern winter, he would freeze to death."

"They are accustomed to the cold," the dedicate said. "They don't even feel it."

"We *are* accustomed to the cold," Raisa said. "Much more than flatlanders. But there are limits. The clans are famous for their metalsmithing, so they do wear jewelry. But they also wear leather and fur and woven fabrics, too," she said, recalling the great looms in constant use in the lodges.

"Some say the savages grow heavy fur in the winter, like wolves," Tourant said, as if it were a matter of real debate among scholars. "That's why they call them the wolf queens." This was met by a scattering of laughter, but many of the students shifted uncomfortably in their seats. "Is that true, Newling Morley?"

"That's not true!" A statuesque girl with coppery skin and a Tamric accent spoke up without being called upon. She wore Isenwerk robes and elaborate jewelry. "My family deals with clan traders all the time. The one who calls on us is well educated and fully clothed; certainly not a savage—though he does drive a hard bargain."

"Well, now, Newling Haddam," Tourant said, winking at her. "Sounds like you're sweet on him. When you say he drives a *hard bargain*, what exactly does that mean?"

Haddam flushed angrily and opened her mouth to speak, but Tourant pointed at another student, who was eagerly waving his hand. "Gutmark. What do you think?"

"The queens of the Fells are witches," a solemn boy from Bruinswallow said. "They charm the men into letting them rule."

"The queens of the Fells rule for the same reason that the kings of Tamron and Bruinswallow rule," Raisa said. "Blood-lines, history, education, and ability."

"There's demon magic in the northern mountains," a Southern Islander said. "That's where the Demon King come from, and that's where he died, and his bones, they infect the land to this day. The soil blisters your feet, and plants just wither in the ground."

"Plants grow there," Raisa said. "Just not the same plants that grow here. Where do you think all your medicines and scents come from?"

"Sorcery," the Ardenine dedicate said, with a pious shudder. "I wouldn't wear those wicked perfumes. They cloud the mind and lead to sins of the flesh. After I graduate I am going to be a missionary. I'm going to go and live with the mountain savages and help civilize them and bring them the true faith," she said.

Raisa tried to imagine this naïve girl facing off with her father, Averill Lightfoot, Lord Demonai, and attempting to civilize him. Her grandmother, the Matriarch Elena *Cennestre*, would devour her alive.

"Well, good luck to you," Raisa said, rolling her eyes. Then flinched as a voice boomed from the back of the room.

"Proficient Tourant, have you ever been to the Fells?"

Everyone swiveled to find Master Askell standing in the back of the lecture hall.

Tourant colored. "No, sir, it's hardly I place I would—"

"Who has been to the Fells?" Askell said, looking down over the rows of seats. "Stand up."

Raisa slid out of her chair and stood. She was the only one.

"No one else? Not even briefly?" Askell said. Everyone stared at the floor. "Anyone have friends, relatives, business associates from the north?"

This time Haddam stood in a rustle of fabric, glaring at Tourant.

Askell sighed. "Sit down, Morley and Haddam." They did. "As master of Wien House and faculty here at Oden's Ford, I like to think that I play the most important role in your education. But that's not true. What makes Oden's Ford so effective is the diversity of its students, who come from all over the Seven Realms.

"Smart cadets will embrace this opportunity. They will shut up and listen to the experts among them, those who speak from personal experience. In future, whether you meet them again in war or peace, you'll be better prepared to do your job. Those that rely on evidence will succeed. Those that embrace myths, innuendo, and rumor will fail. Do you understand?"

"Yes, sir!" rolled through the hall.

Askell smiled faintly. "Carry on, Proficient Tourant," he said, then turned and walked out the door.

Raisa turned back in time to catch Tourant's poisonous glare. Well, she thought. I've made an enemy.

After that she saw a lot more of Master Askell in her classes. Especially the recitations. Raisa would notice a shift in Tourant's attitude and demeanor, and look up from her note-taking to find the master leaning against the back wall of the classroom.

She'd turn away from the chalkboard in her finance class and Askell would be conferring with her teacher in the back of the room. At the end of language recitation, she'd spot him sitting among the students, and wonder how long he'd been there. He would often slip in unnoticed during the heat of discussion or in the midst of an oral examination. He'd leave again when he'd seen whatever it was he'd come to see.

Raisa's performance in the physical part of soldiering continued to improve, but she realized she'd never be adept at it. She was too small and lightweight for most flatland weapons, even though she'd been remade with a layer of muscle. She was a decent archer and a skilled rider. She excelled at geography, wayfinding, and survival skills, courtesy of her training in the camps.

She was also good at finance, a benefit of her time in the clan markets.

She liked sharing a room with Hallie and Talia. As they spent more time together, they began to treat her more like a peer and less like a breakable object.

Hallie seemed like a grown-up compared to her fellow Wolves. She was big, loud, strong, and gregarious, but she would go silent and sad when conversation turned to her daughter. She had a small sketch of Asha that she pulled out and studied several times a day, as if afraid she'd forget what her daughter looked like. She sent letters every week, and small gifts, never knowing if they reached their destination.

Raisa asked Hallie to see Asha's picture one night when they were both up late, studying for exams.

"She's beautiful," Raisa said, examining the drawing of a solemn-looking girl with enormous blue eyes and a halo of fine, pale hair. "Who did the drawing for you?"

"It was Corporal Byrne's sister, Lydia. He asked her to make it when I signed up for school and joined the Wolves."

"It must've been a hard decision. Coming here, I mean," Raisa said.

Hallie shrugged. "I was in the regular army—the Highlanders—when I found out I was expecting." She looked at Raisa. "I an't a fool, I was taking maidenweed, but it's hard to keep a schedule when you're in the army, traveling all the time.

"I came home to have my girl, but I needed to work to support her. All I know is soldiering, but I hated going back to the army because I'd be away from her all the time. I thought of joining the bluejackets, but you need schooling for that these days." She hesitated, as if deciding how much to share. "I thought I'd have to try and find a good streetlord, join a crew. Only, if anything happens to me, Asha's on her own. I keep her and my mam and pap, both."

These people make gut-wrenching choices every day, Raisa

thought. And I thought life among the working class was simple.

"Then Speaker Jemson at Southbridge Temple said there was something called the Briar Rose Ministry," Hallie went on. "He said he could get me money to pay my fees at Wien House if I could get in."

The Briar Rose Ministry! Raisa's head came up. "Really?" Impulsively, she gripped Hallie's hands. "Oh, that's wonderful news!"

Hallie squinted at Raisa, tilting her head. "Well. Right. So you can guess the rest. I got in and here I am. And every Temple Day I buy a rose from the flower girl on the bridge and leave it on the altar for the Princess Raisa. And when I get back home, I hope I'll be assigned to her service. I can be with Asha and I can keep the lady safe."

"Maybe it will happen," Raisa said, clearing her throat.

"Maybe it will." Hallie tucked Asha's picture away.

In class, Raisa studied battle strategies developed by Gideon Byrne centuries ago. Lila Byrne had designed the prototype of a double-edged rapier that was still in use today. Dwite Byrne had made innovative use of mounted soldiers at a time when the cavalry had fallen into disuse.

Raisa and Amon had this in common: they both felt the pressure of being the living heirs of an ancient dynasty of accomplishment.

Amon was skilled with weapons, and performed well in his course work, but he wasn't the biggest or strongest or richest of the cadets in his class at Oden's Ford. He didn't win over his classmates by buying ales and ciders for them on Bridge Street, then staggering home arm in arm with them in the small hours.

He radiated a calm focus—like he knew who he was and where he was going. He was a steady mooring in a sea of change. He was honest and he kept his word, and he was unrelentingly fair. It made people want to follow him.

I can learn from him, Raisa thought. I tend to stir people up, not settle them down.

Amon continued to train her in sticking, using the staff Dimitri had given her. Some days it was all she saw of Amon— he left the dormitory before she crawled out of bed, and she was usually fast asleep when he came home. As class commander, he attended endless meetings and participated in the governance of the school. That was the story, anyway. It still seemed to Raisa that he avoided being alone with her.

Yet sometimes she'd look up, even at dinner, and find those gray eyes fixed on her.

"I thought this place was called the great leveler," she said to Amon as she closed the book on another long day. It was now eight weeks into the term, the most exhilarating and exhausting eight weeks of her life.

Amon looked up from his engineering drawing. "It is."

"Then why did Master Askell agree to put us all in the same dormitory? And why did he approve a special curriculum for me, if everyone is treated equally?"

"They are," Amon said. "Until they're not." He returned to his work until the pressure of her glare made him look up again. He sat back, rolling his quill between his fingers. It had become a habit. "Master Askell knows who you are," he said. "I told him."

Raisa nearly spit out her tea. "What? Aren't you the one who said it was so important that nobody know who I am?"

Amon nodded. "Right. It is. But I needed to convince him that we should all stay here in Grindell Hall, which is against policy. Though you're technically a first year, I wanted you in with fourth years." The quill landed on the floor, and he bent down to get it. "I didn't want to be lying awake at night, wondering if you were safe in a dormitory across campus. I wanted someone in authority to know, in case this goes wrong."

"You trust him?"

"Aye. I trust him."

Raisa recalled her interview with Master Askell. "That's why he gave me such a hard time. He expected me to be temperamental and demanding."

Amon nodded. "Right. He only agreed to what you wanted because he expected you to wash out right away." He grinned, looking pleased with himself. "He doesn't know you like I do."

"He's been coming to some of my classes," Raisa said.

"He does that all the time anyway, but especially if he has a question about a particular student." Amon hesitated, then plunged on. "Taim Askell is the heir to a noble Ardenine family. Remember when he asked you if you'd run away to join the army? That's exactly what he did. He sailed across the Indio to Carthis and fought in the wars over there, working his way up from foot soldier.

"When he came back to the Seven Realms, he decided he needed schooling to become an officer. He came here. My da was his class commander. Askell thought my da was a jumped-up cake-eater, promoted beyond his abilities. Da thought Askell was an arrogant know-it-all who should shut up and learn something."

"So what happened?" Raisa asked.

"Da never said, but the story goes they met off campus to fight it out, and beat each other up pretty bad. Then Askell shut up and learned something, and he and Da wrote a book about the Carthian wars that helped Askell get a teaching job here later on. It's in the library, if you want to take a look."

"What was it like, coming here to school under Askell?" Raisa asked.

"He gave me hell the first two years," Amon said, grinning. "I saw a lot of him in my classes, too. But it ended with him making me class commander."

CHAPTER SIXTEEN
A MEETING WITH THE DEAN

In the days following the dean's dinner, Han was so focused on charmcasting that he fell behind in his other classes. He had to prioritize, with so much to learn. He was especially keen to learn charms that would keep buildings from falling on him.

Because they were newlings, the Bayars, the Manders, and Han shared every class. They were a constant distraction.

The class on healing seemed useless to Han. The clans had hired him to kill, not to heal, and the people Han would have liked to heal were already dead.

Master Leontus was a gifted middle-aged healer with missionary zeal and a shiny bald head who did his best to interest his students in his chosen profession.

It was a tough sell. Most charmcasters were weaned on power and privilege—not tenderhearted to start. And poor Leontus was cursed with relentless honesty.

"Gifted healers take on the illnesses and injuries of their patients.

This involves considerable pain, suffering, and expenditure of power." Leontus paused and looked over his spectacles. "But there are strategies that can be used to minimize the damage to your body and regain strength after a healing session. With proper care and education, there is no reason why a gifted healer cannot achieve a normal life span."

As Leontus rambled on about the sacrifices and rewards of the healing trade, his students daydreamed about more appealing topics, or did their homework for other subjects. Han's attention repeatedly strayed during lecture and recitation.

The lectures on amulets, talismans, and magical materials were delivered by a wizened old clansman named Fulgrim Firesmith. Firesmith reminded Han of the insect carcasses he sometimes found along the trails in summer—brown, crispy, and shriveled.

Creation of magical objects was the province of the clans, outside the abilities of wizards. So it was more of a history class than anything else—a survey of magical devices of the long-ago past compared to those available today. It only stoked the frustration of students who resented the limitations of modern magical tools.

Firesmith's lectures were terminally boring yet hard to ignore. Firesmith was deaf as a post, so he yelled out his lectures full volume.

He taught from an ancient text so fragile that he had the students parade past to view its yellowed pen-and-ink drawings rather than risk lifting it from its stand.

Han felt a relentless urgency, an impatient desire to focus on material that could be immediately applied. He already had a powerful amulet. He wanted to know more about the charms and hexes that would enable him to use it. He would have preferred to double up on the charmcasting classes and forget the rest.

Not that he fancied spending more time with Gryphon.

His mind kept drifting to Crow and his offer of mentorship. Learning spellcasting from Crow seemed far more appealing than suffering under Gryphon. If Crow could be trusted.

Dancer, however, seemed fascinated with Firesmith and his dusty old books. He scribbled lines and lines of notes and asked detailed questions about theory and craft until Fiona rolled her eyes and smothered yawns behind her hand.

"Are you really interested in all that?" Han asked Dancer as they crossed the quad for the midday. It was raining again, a dreary, cold downpour from a fish-belly sky. A bone-chilling wind drove raindrops into their faces like needles of ice. "I couldn't stay awake. There's so much to learn, and there's nothing practical we can we do with that."

"I *am* interested," Dancer said, scuffling through soggy leaves. "Remember? Before all this happened, I'd hoped to apprentice to Elena *Cennestre* to be a flash metalsmith."

"I know." Han swung around to watch a pretty girlie splash across the lawn, laughing, lifting her skirts to expose a fine pair of legs. She ducked under one of the galleries and disappeared. He turned back to Dancer. "Have you ever made anything magical?"

Dancer nodded. "When I was younger. Simple pieces, but they seemed to work."

"But . . . now you're a charmcaster," Han said. "And wizards can't . . ."

"I'm still clan," Dancer said, lifting his chin. "I don't care what the Demonai say. I haven't given up on my chosen vocation."

"But . . . how would you learn to work with magical materials?" Han said. "Elena won't teach you, even if you have the gift of flash metalsmithing."

"Firesmith says the library here has the best collection of texts on magical materials in the Seven Realms," Dancer said.

They climbed the steps to the dining hall, taking shelter under the porch roof. Dancer shook his head, flinging water in all directions, then stepped to the side, out of earshot of the other students streaming into the hall.

"But clan artists learn by apprenticeship," Han said. "Firesmith won't teach you either, if he knows what you're up to."

"He doesn't *want* to know what I'm up to," Dancer said. "He's thrilled to have a student that's actually interested. I signed up for a special project with him next term." Stuffing his hands in his pockets, he strode on. "I'll teach myself if I have to."

Dancer has a hard spine in him that would be easy to overlook, Han thought. He chooses his battles and plays to win.

Just then a Southern Islander in Temple dress spotted them. She broke away from a group of her fellow students and strode across the porch toward them.

It was Cat Tyburn, but Han might not have recognized her had she not opened her mouth. Her mass of wiry curls had been tamed down and woven into a long plait that fell over her left shoulder. She wore white trousers and a long white overtunic split up each side for easier walking. She was cleaner than Han had ever seen her—except for the stained leather belt she'd strapped on overtop, her knife jammed into it. She still wore silver in her ears and nose and on her fingers. Between that and her blade scars and the thief marks on her hands, it was an odd marriage of sacred and profane.

They hadn't seen her in two weeks, though not for lack of trying. Several times they'd visited the temple dormitory, but had been told she was unavailable. And she hadn't come to see them, either.

Han stumbled into speech. "Cat, you . . . uh . . . you're . . . I don't think I've ever—what happened to you?"

"They stuck me in a bath, and while I was scrubbing off, they stole my clothes and left me with these." She tugged at the hem of her tunic. "They told me I had to stay seques . . . holed up in the Temple School for a fortnight, and think about my vocation." She made a face. "It don't take that long. It's not like I got a lot of choices."

As they got into line in the dining hall, Cat continued her litany of complaints. "The sun an't even up when this bell starts clanging and we get out of bed and go to morning meditations. Then it's bells, bells, bells, and class, class, class all day. For hours. Reading and writing and mathematics." She pinched two apples and an orange off the line and stuffed them into her carry bag. "After lunch is better. There's music class and dance and drawing."

Ladling soup into bowls, they carried them to a long table.

Cat used her belt knife to whack off hunks of brown bread from a loaf in the center of the table. "I liked the school at Southbridge. You only had to go when you felt like it."

"How often did you feel like it?" Dancer asked, dunking his bread into his bowl.

"I was there near every month," Cat said, slathering her bread with butter.

"She means *once* a month, on the day they gave out cinnamon bread," Han said, and received a scowl from Cat.

"*You* an't been there for years," Cat retorted. "Not since you was streetlord."

Well. He'd been there the one time. He'd been beaten half to death by Mac Gillen and his bluejackets and had taken refuge with Speaker Jemson in the temple. Corporal Byrne had tried to take him prisoner, and Han took Rebecca Morley hostage. It seemed a lifetime ago.

"I'm not used to sitting in a classroom either," Dancer said. "In the camps, we learn by apprenticeship—one teacher, one student."

"Why'd you come here, then?" Cat asked, keeping her eyes fixed on her bowl. "I an't seen no other copperheads here."

"They don't teach clan vocations here," Dancer said. "There'd be no point."

Cat shrugged. "From what I heard, you all spend your time stealing babies, hexing animals into monsters, and making poisons and witch pieces." She licked butter off her bread. "It's no wonder people don't like it when you come down to the flatlands."

"Shut up, Cat," Han growled. "Don't rattle on about things you know nothing about."

"The clans are gifted in magical materials, healing, and earth magic," Dancer said to Cat. "High magic—the kind wizards use—that's not a clan vocation. That's why I had to come here." His face remained untroubled, as if Cat's digs and insults slid right off him.

"Some people say Southern Islanders ought to stay in the islands," Han said, feeling the need to stick up for Dancer, since he wouldn't stick up for himself. "We all got to make the best of it. There must be something about the Temple School you like."

Cat gnawed on her fingernail. "I do like the music," she said grudgingly. "All you want. There's basilkas and flutes and harps and organs and harpsichords. Choirs singing. Recitals all the time. Mistress Johanna gave me *another* basilka all to myself, said I could keep it long as I'm at school. She said they got masters can give me lessons on any of the other instruments, too. My choice." She crammed a handful of grapes into her mouth. "She keeps pestering me to do some recitals. Play in front of people. I don't know if I want to do that."

That Mistress Johanna is smart, Han thought, if she already figured out that the way to Cat was through music.

"You've been accepted and come this far," Dancer said. "You should take advantage. I'd love to hear you play."

Cat twitched irritably, twisting a lock of her hair between her thumb and forefinger. "I just don't know how long I'm going to be here. No point in getting all tangled up in something that won't last. People begin to think they own a piece of you."

Han flung his napkin onto the table. "There's nothing you're in a rush to get back to, is there? That's why we're all here. We got nothing and nobody at home."

"You got no idea who I am or why I'm here," Cat said. She stood and stalked out of the dining hall.

"That's true enough," Han said, looking after her, shaking his head. He turned to Dancer. "You don't have to put up with her ragging about the clans, you know."

"She's all right. It's nothing worse than what I've heard in the Vale." Dancer pushed his bowl away. "Want to go to the library now?"

Han shook his head. "Later. After dinner, maybe. I'm going to stop by Hampton and drop off my books, then I have to go see Abelard." He rolled his eyes. "I an't looking forward to that."

Han crossed the quad to Hampton Hall. The dormitory seemed deserted, all the students either in the dining hall or in class. He loped up the four flights of stairs to the top floor. When he reached the landing, a stench hit his nose. Excrement. Pressing his sleeve over his face, he looked up and down the corridor. The door to his room stood open. Drawing his blade, he soft-footed down the hallway, his other hand planted firmly on his amulet. Keeping his body canted to one side, he eased his head around the door frame and looked into his room.

It had been completely trashed. His clothing had been dragged out of his trunk and sliced to pieces, his books yanked from the shelf and shredded, his lamp smashed on the floor, the oil soaking into the wood. His bedclothes were ripped from his bed, torn apart, and scattered. It appeared that a number of brimming chamber pots had been dumped on top.

A gout of anger flamed up in him.

The protective charms he'd laid had done no good whatsoever. And he knew exactly who was responsible. Someone who knew Han would be down in the dining hall. Someone Han didn't remember seeing there.

Micah's words came back to him. *I know where you live, Alister, and I've got plenty of time.*

Turning, he swung around the corner into the stairwell,

heading for Micah Bayar's rooms on the second floor. Two steps down, he tripped and went flying, head over heels down the stairs, slamming into the wall at the bottom of the first flight and bouncing down a second flight of stairs.

Han should have been dead, but he knew how to take a fall. He bounced once or twice on the way down, which slowed him down some, and he managed to wrap his arms around his head before landing painfully on his right shoulder on the landing at the bottom, his head hanging over the top step. He'd narrowly missed tumbling down the third and final flight. His knife flew out of his hand and landed with a ping down below.

He blacked out momentarily. When he came to, the wind was totally knocked out of him and black spots swam before his eyes. His right arm was numb, his shoulder aflame with pain. Blood trickled into his eyes from a gash on his forehead.

Han heard footsteps approaching, but for the moment, he couldn't move.

"Is he dead?" somebody asked, his voice trembling with fear and excitement. "He's got to be. I never thought—he really landed hard." Han recognized his voice. The thin Mander . . . Arkeda.

"Let's hurry before somebody comes." Someone bent over him, groping at his neckline. The plush Mander . . . Miphis.

"Don't touch it," a third person muttered in Fellspeech. "Roll him over and lift it by the chain." Unmistakably Micah Bayar.

The spots cleared and Han saw a pair of fine blueblood boots next to his head. He grabbed the groper's calf with his good hand and yanked. Miphis shrieked and went down, thudding down the last flight, landing hard on the stone floor at the bottom.

Han screamed like a mad tom, curling his body protectively around his amulet. He heard swearing, running feet, doors slamming, Blevins bellowing out questions that grew louder as he got closer until he was kneeling next to Han and screeching in his ear.

"Great hounds of the demon, boy, what happened to you?"

Han spit out blood from his bitten tongue, along with a fragment of tooth. Rolling onto his side, he sat up, cradling his right arm close to his body, supporting his elbow with his left hand.

The black spots returned as the weight of his arm pulled on his collarbone. Leaning back against the banister, Han said, through bloody lips, "Fell down the stairs."

"I told you boys not to race up and down them steps," Blevins said. "They got loose boards and they're all different sizes. It's lucky you didn't break your fool neck."

Yeah, Han thought. Lucky me. He looked up toward the third floor, down to the first, though moving his head was painful. The staircase was empty save for him and Blevins. Miphis had managed to get up, then, and leave on his own.

"Did you see anyone else on the stairs?"

Blevins shook his head. "No. Why?" The dorm master mopped at Han's forehead with a filthy handkerchief.

"Someone made a mess of my room. I was . . . coming to tell you."

Blevins's face flushed pink-purple. "You boys got to learn that pranking just leads to misery, you hear me? You got to work these things out among yourselfs."

The message was: don't count on me to intervene. Not that

Han expected or wanted it. He was used to fighting his own battles.

This is more than a prank, Han thought. And I'll find a way to stop it myself. I have to if I'm going to survive.

"Could you find my knife?" Han asked. "I think it's down below. It was knocked loose when I fell."

The dorm master descended the steps, returning a few minutes later with Han's knife. Han slid it into its sheath and eased to his feet, still leaning against the railing.

"Anything broke?" Blevins asked.

"My collarbone. Maybe." Han trailed off, mumble-minded from the pain.

Blevins grabbed Han's left elbow as if he thought he might fall. "We got to get you to Healer's Hall, then. Let's hope Master Leontus isn't out this evening."

"Just a minute. I want to take a look. See if there's a loose board or something." Over Blevins's protests, Han hauled himself back up the stairs, gritting his teeth against the pain in his shoulder and arm.

Ah. Someone had stretched a heavy cord knee-high across the stairs just below the fourth-floor landing, where a person wouldn't see it if he was in a rush. Drawing his knife, he cut it free and stuffed it into his pocket before he went back down to Blevins.

"What I thought," Han said. "Loose board."

Fortunately, Master Leontus was in his office. It was very different from the matriarch's lodge. There were none of the bundles of herbs and jars of unguents that Willo kept handy. No tools for extracting the essences of plants. No patients convalescing in back rooms. Everything was scrubbed up and orderly, plain and empty, save a shelf of books of healing charms. Peculiar.

The wizard healer diagnosed a broken collarbone, a fractured cheekbone, a split scalp, and various bumps and bruises.

Blevins left to tell Dean Abelard that Han Alister was with Leontus and so would not be able to make their appointment.

That was one bit of good out of it, anyway. Like they said about summer fever—it might kill your friends and family, but it was bound to kill off some enemies, too.

But Abelard sent back word that she wanted to see him anyway, soon as he was done.

Han laid back on a table so Leontus's proficient could wash the blood out of his hair and clean out the wound in his forehead. It had bled like crazy, but he'd had worse. One more scar to add to the collection.

Bluebloods back in Fellsmarch hired wizard healers, but they never set foot in Ragmarket. Being healed by wizardry was a peculiar business. Leontus laid hands on Han's collarbone, and a cool flow of magic seemed to wash the pain away. Han felt better and better while Leontus looked worse and worse. The wizard paused when Han guessed they were about evens.

"How do you feel, my boy?" Leontus asked, trying for heartiness. He'd lost color, his eyes had clouded, and his skin glistened with sweat. "Maybe not perfect, but . . . ?"

"You did a rum job, thanks." Han felt guilty asking him to do more. "I'm sure I'll heal up good on my own now."

"Let's put this arm in a sling for a few days; keep the pressure off the mending bone," Leontus said.

As the healer applied the sling, Han asked, "Do you ever use herbs or plant remedies? Seems like that might help ease some of the . . ." His voice trailed off when Leontus curled his lip in a sneer.

"If you are speaking of copperhead remedies, they are dangerous and unproven," Leontus said sternly. "They have no place in legitimate healing."

Well, then. Han had some willow bark back in his room he could take for the pain. At least, he used to. No telling where it was now, or if it was still safe to use.

"Can a wizard heal himself?" Han asked. That would come in handy, considering how things were going. It might make it worth paying attention in Leontus's class.

Leontus shook his head. "No," he said brusquely. "Wouldn't be much need for healers, then, would there? Here, take a look in the glass and see what you think." He turned a table mirror so Han could see his face. He had a fat lip, and his right eye was blackened and nearly swollen shut. His cheek was all bruises, but no longer dented. It looked like it would heal up all right. Han ran his tongue around the inside of his mouth, found his broken tooth. Least it wasn't right in front, in case he ever smiled again.

"You'll be stiff and sore in the morning," Leontus said. "You also need to rest and build up your magic again." He brushed the back of his hand across Han's undamaged cheek. "You're used up. It's not unusual. The patient's magic contributes to healing."

The winter sun had already set as Han limped across the quad toward Mystwerk Hall and his meeting with Abelard. Students collected in little groups between the buildings, shivering in the raw wind.

Ignoring his screaming muscles and joints and his aching

head, Han put his shoulders back, lifted his chin, and tried to make a good show, in case somebody was watching. But he felt like an empty vessel—fragile and vulnerable. Genuinely scared.

If he'd been killed in the fall, it would have been put down to an accident. He'd been careless, and he couldn't afford that. There were countless other accidental ways to die. Bayar and his cousins only had to get lucky once. If he didn't find a way to defend himself, it would be a very long year.

Or a very short one.

Abelard's offices were luxurious, a suite of rooms on the top floor of Mystwerk Hall, overlooking the river. The proficient in the outer office went in to announce Han, then ushered him into the inner office.

The dean was seated behind a massive desk, leafing through a stack of papers. On the wall behind her hung a banner emblazoned with an open book, flame gouting from its pages. Thick We'enhaven rugs covered the polished wood floors, muffling sound to a whisper.

She allowed Han to stand there a while before she looked up.

Her eyes widened when she saw his face. "Demon's blood, Alister, what happened to you?"

"I fell down the stairs," Han said. "Didn't Master Blevins tell you?"

"Really." She leaned forward, her sleeves puddling on the surface of the desk. "Care to tell me about it?"

"Stairs are tricky at Hampton," Han said, sitting in the available chair without waiting for an invitation. "All it takes is one little misstep."

Abelard gazed at him a while longer. "You're not one to

complain, are you, Alister? And you know how to keep a secret. That's good." She put her papers away, taking her time. Then said, "I've looked into your background, as I promised. And it seems what you told me is true—as far as it went. You do come from Ragmarket. You're a criminal, in fact—a thief and a murderer. The queen of the Fells has put a price on your head for trying to kill the High Wizard."

Han just looked back at her steady. I can't be the first murderer to attend Mystwerk Hall, he thought. Murderers probably get extra credit.

She leaned in again, lowering her voice. "Did you really try to kill Gavan Bayar?"

"He had it coming," Han said, knowing that the dean had already made up her mind about him anyway.

Abelard sat back, resting the heels of her hands on her desk. "I can tell you're not stupid, so I'm wondering why you'd take that kind of risk."

"It was him or me," Han said. "Next time I'll aim better."

Unexpectedly, the dean laughed. "You have no remorse at all. I like that."

I'm not the one should be sorry, Han thought.

The dean just sat and looked at him for another long moment.

"Well, then," he said, scooting to the front of his seat. "You got the goods on me fair. Is that all? That healing has wearied me out, and I'd like to go lie down a while."

Abelard raised both hands as if to push him down in his seat. "Not so fast," she said. "I have something to discuss with you—an opportunity."

"Opportunity?" Han settled back in his chair. "What do you mean?"

"The political situation in the Fells is becoming untenable," Abelard said. "The truce between the Gray Wolf line, the savages, and the Wizard Council is dissolving. We wizards are prisoners of restrictions from another time, based on a tragedy that probably never happened."

"The Breaking, you mean."

Abelard nodded. "The limitations on magic and magical weapons, the restrictions on wizards politically, it makes us weak—too weak to defend ourselves. Many of us believe that the wars in Arden will spread to the rest of the Seven Realms. Here at the Ford we are particularly vulnerable, having no barrier of mountains to protect us."

"I've heard that," Han said, wondering why the powerful dean of Mystwerk House was delivering this little speech to the likes of him.

"The Valefolk and the copperheads must be forced to see reason. There will be a need for wizards with your particular skills in the near future," Abelard said.

"My particular skills?"

Abelard steepled her hands. "Those willing to spill blood if need be. Those who are . . . experienced in that line of work."

Han cleared his throat, thinking he must have misunderstood. "You're looking for an *assassin*?"

"I need someone with the flexibility to do whatever is required." Abelard rose and walked to the wall of windows, looking out over Mystwerk quad. "You would seem to be uniquely qualified—bright, powerful, and totally without scruples."

These are dark times, Han thought, when everybody's in the market for a killer.

Abelard turned back toward Han, and must have read resistance in his face. "Don't worry. You will be well compensated, and no one will dare attack you openly while you are under my protection. I intend to return to the Fells within the year. If you prove capable, I will take you with me." She paused, then added delicately, "I hope your attachment to that mongrel copperhead won't prove to be a problem."

Not for me, Han thought. No way I'm throwing in with you.

"I've left the Life," Han said. "As you can see, it's all I can do to manage my classes and reading and studies. I an't interested in politics."

"That's good," Abelard said. "That way you'll do as you're told." She paused, and when he didn't respond, went on. "Come now. I won't be sending you out with a list of people to kill. We'll start with some special training. I work with a select group of talented students. I would like you to join us."

Han sat up straight, resting his hands on his knees. This must be the group Mordra deVilliers had mentioned. "What do you mean, you work with them?" he asked.

"I provide them with instruction that goes beyond the usual curriculum, and introduce them to powerful magical tools. They will be the core of our wizard army and will play a pivotal role in the struggle to come."

"Who else is in this group?" Han asked.

"Mostly fourth years, proficients, and masters," Abelard said, shifting her eyes away. "It's an unusual opportunity for a first year."

"Are there any other first years?" Han persisted.

Abelard heaved an exasperated sigh. "The Bayar twins," she said.

"That's a deal breaker," Han said, putting up his hands. "Thanks just the same."

Abelard shook her head. "Hear me out. Politics among wizards is complicated. We have some common goals—to defeat the clans and protect ourselves from the fanatics in the south. Thus we need a well-trained gifted army. But we are not of one mind when it comes to other issues, such as who should be High Wizard, who runs the council, and who controls the queen."

"Like I said, I'm not really interested in politics," Han said.

"You should know that the High Wizard and I are not allies. We are rivals, in fact. The Bayars have wielded too much power for too long. I intend to bring them down."

Han's head came up, and he stared at her. A turf war within the wizard aristocracy?

The dean smiled thinly. "Don't look so astonished. You'll report directly to me. I am not without influence. If our arrangement works out, I can offer you some protection when we return to the Fells. You *would* like to go back home, wouldn't you?"

"Why would you teach special classes to Micah and Fiona if you're at odds with their father?" Han asked.

"The simple answer is that the High Wizard insisted. They are likely here to keep an eye on me." The dean's mouth twisted. "The more complicated answer is that we need large numbers of well-trained wizards to meet the external threats from the clans and from Arden. So I might do something contrary to my own interests in the short run for the greater good."

"For the greater good of wizards, you mean," Han said.

"Of which you are one, I believe," Abelard said dryly. "In the long run, I need someone without an agenda of his own who can dispose of gifted adversaries if need be."

Han pushed up from his chair, feeling a little sick. "No thanks."

Abelard leaned her head back and looked down her nose at him. "Did you think you were being given a choice?" she said softly.

Han was already turning toward the door, but he swung back around to face her. "There's always a choice."

"You can cooperate with me, learn everything you can, and act on my orders. Or be expelled from Mystwerk House and sent back to the Fells for hanging."

"Expelled?" Han blurted, his mouth going dry as ashes. "For what?"

"Had we known we were harboring a wanted criminal, we would not have admitted you in the first place."

Well. It *was* a choice—between two nasty options.

"Why are you so interested in me?" Han asked. "Why would you drag someone kicking and screaming into your crew?"

"Because it's unlikely you work for Gavan Bayar," Abelard said. "Or ever will. He will never forgive you for trying to kill him. Ever. You'd better hope that I win."

Just because you're the enemy of my enemy don't mean you're my friend, Han thought. But he kept shut on that.

"Despite your upbringing, your language, your history, there's also something almost aristocratic about you," the dean said. "Maybe it's only arrogance, but I think you could learn to maneuver at court, with a little training. I don't need a street thug. I need someone who can move in those circles."

She also wants a tool, Han thought. Someone who will never be accepted by her blueblood friends, someone who has to depend on her handouts for survival.

He eyed Abelard, thinking fast. He'd never been one to make long-term plans, and lately his life had been all about buying time. He needed time at Oden's Ford to build his skills in wizardry, and protection from his many enemies.

The extra classes couldn't hurt, either. Abelard could provide that, at least until she found out he'd been playing her. When that happened, he'd still be better off with more weapons.

How many times can I pledge my services before my gang lords catch on?

"All right," he said, shrugging. "I'm in."

Dean Abelard smiled. "I knew you were a smart boy," she said.

"On one condition."

Abelard lifted her plucked eyebrows, registering amazement. "Which is?"

Han meant to make his point with the Bayars. He needed to prevent retaliation after.

"The Bayar twins and their cousins have been dogging me because of what I did to their father," Han said. He touched his swollen cheekbone. "They tried to kill me this afternoon—for the second time. I an't the most patient person. I need you to put a stop to it. Unless you want me to hush them right now, which I will do if need be."

Abelard raised both hands. "No. Absolutely not. There's no way I can bring you back to court if their killings are linked to you."

Well, you're a cold one, Han thought.

"I will let them know in no uncertain terms that you are under my protection," she said. "They won't cross you again."

"Good." Han rubbed the back of his neck. "But wait until they come to you about me, all right?"

She scowled. "What possible reason could there be to—"

"I need to teach them a lesson first," he said. When Abelard opened her mouth to protest, he added, "Don't worry. They'll survive. And I won't do aught that can be tied back to me."

Lacing her fingers across her torso, the dean gave him a good look-over. "Just don't get caught. If you do, you're on your own."

Han smiled. "No worries." He stood. "Is there anything else?"

"I meet with my group on Wednesday evenings, here in my office," Abelard said. "Be here at seven."

CHAPTER SEVENTEEN

IN MYSTWERK
TOWER

When Han arrived back at Hampton, Dancer met him at the top of the stairs. "Bad news. While we were out, somebody made a mess of—what happened to you?" he demanded when he got a better look at Han's face. "Did she hit you or what?"

Han blinked at him out of one eye, uncomprehending. "Did who hit me?"

"Dean Abelard. That's where you've been, right?"

Han nodded. "I just came from there. She didn't hit me, though. I took a tumble down the stairs. Had to go to see Leontus."

"What? How did you—?"

Han extended the length of rope toward Dancer. "Them that scowered up my room left this tied across the staircase."

Dancer's face went hard as amber. "Master Blevins, does he know about this?"

"He knows I fell down the stairs. They were trying to lift my amulet when he come running. Else I might be dead."

"Who was it?"

"Micah and his cousins. They left in a hurry when Blevins came." Han swayed, taking hold of the newel post to stay upright. The walk back had nearly done him in.

Dancer stuck out a hand to steady him. "Come on and sit down before you fall down the stairs a second time."

Han followed Dancer down the hallway to his room. The bed was stripped, the linens piled in the corridor, and the broken bits swept up.

"Thought I'd start on it, anyway." Dancer gestured to a chair. "Sit."

Han felt bad allowing Dancer to do all the work, but he was just too busted to argue. "This an't going to happen again," he said. "Just so you know."

"Mmm," Dancer said skeptically, carrying an armload of Han's slimed clothing out to the hall. "Are you thinking Blevins might—"

"Blevins won't do anything. He doesn't run the whole campus, anyway." The college town he'd thought was so safe now seemed perilous. "It's got to be me."

"Us, you mean." When Han said nothing, Dancer said, "What are you planning to do? Your protection charms didn't work, and we can't stay here all day and all night."

"I'm going to meet with Crow in Aediion. Tomorrow night. See what he's got."

"I think that fall must have jostled your brain loose," Dancer said, tossing clean sheets over a fresh straw mattress.

"I don't have a choice. I won't roll over for Bayar. He needs a good basting, and I'm going to give it to him."

"You're not in Ragmarket anymore," Dancer said. "This isn't a gang war."

"That's what you think." Han worked the fingers of his captive arm.

"Remember what happened last time you went to Aediion? At least if you fall down the stairs, there's someone around to help."

"No one can help if I'm dead." Han fingered his swollen eye.

"If you go after them with magic," Dancer countered, "you'll get expelled."

"It has to be me, and it has to be magic, because that's where he thinks he has the advantage."

"That's where he *does* have the advantage." Dancer dipped a brush in soapy water and began scrubbing down the walls.

"I mean to change that." Han watched Dancer for a few minutes. "I'll clean your room for a month," he offered. "Soon as I'm out of this sling."

Dancer wrinkled his nose. "You owe me a year after this," he said. "And if you insist on going to Aediion, then I'm coming with you."

Han shook his head. "He said to come alone."

"You need someone to watch your back," Dancer said.

"He may not even show," Han said. "It's been a month."

"I hope he doesn't," Dancer said.

Han stayed in his room all the next day, resting and replenishing his amulet, building it up for his meeting with Crow. After that, and some of Dancer's willow bark, Han felt well enough to walk downtown with Dancer after classes to buy some new clothes to replace those that had been ruined. That took some time. For one thing, Han wasn't used to buying new. There were too many decisions—fabric, cut, color, style.

For another, the tailor took her time. She was a curvy Tamron girlie with kohl-lined eyes and lips the color of crushed strawberries. At first she goggled at Han's pounded appearance, but soon she was taking measurements of every possible part of his body and gushing over what a made man he'd be when she was done with him.

Her hands lingered on his shoulders and hips and thighs somewhat longer than necessary. She compared the blue of the velvets to the blue in his eyes. As she draped fabric over his torso, she leaned in and whispered, "Come back alone for your fitting."

She was pretty enough, and it was an offer he might have welcomed in the past. Now the girlie's pursuit of him just made him feel weary and besieged.

You *are* beaten down, Alister, he thought. You need a tonic.

By then it was too late to eat in the dining hall, so he and Dancer walked to Bridge Street. They went back to arguing about Aediion over dinner. Dancer was as stubborn as any rock, and the debate continued as they walked to the Bayar Library.

"All *right*!" Han said, exasperated. "We're meeting in Aediion, in Mystwerk Tower. I've never been there, so we'll have to go there for real in order to find it in the dream world. We'll leave about eleven fifteen. That gives us time to get in and get settled. You stand watch while I cross over. If I don't come back, you come after me."

Dancer reluctantly agreed.

Han beat back the worry that he wouldn't be able to return to Aediion. And that Crow wouldn't be there if he did.

Bayar Library was an ornate stone building on the riverbank, linked to Mystwerk Hall by arched stone galleries that sheltered students from the weather. The library reminded Han of the family that built it—intentionally intimidating.

It resembled a palace of learning, with its elaborately carved stairway railings and thick granite windowsills, its massive hearths ablaze late into the night. There were five main floors, meant for first-, second-, and third-level students, plus two with reading and conference rooms for masters and deans. Even higher were the stacks, reachable only by pull-down staircases and reserved for dedicated scholars.

Han ducked self-consciously under the Stooping Falcon signia engraved over the door, as if at any moment he might feel those extended talons sink into the skin on the back of his neck, and the razor-sharp beak tear into his flesh.

In the first-year reading room, the newlings shared access to magical texts so rare that even wealthy heirs of the wizard houses couldn't afford their own. When Han and Dancer walked in, Han saw that Micah Bayar, Wil Mathis, and the Mander brothers had already claimed the prime turf next to the fire, their books and papers spread over a large round table.

A proficient sat by the door, ready to answer questions, issue passes, and make sure that those who used the reading rooms didn't distract others from their work.

Micah was bent over his books as if he were studying hard. He slowly turned the pages, occasionally writing notes in an elegant leather-bound journal.

Miphis Mander stared into space, chewing on his pen. When he saw Han, his jaw dropped and his pen fell to the floor. His mouth opened and closed like a beached fish.

Just then, Fiona walked in from the adjacent room, carrying a large book, her finger marking a place in it. She wore a bored expression that transitioned to puzzlement as she ran her eyes over Han, taking in his bruised face and arm sling. She looked at Micah, then back at Han, and frowned.

She wasn't in on it, Han realized. I thought they shared everything, but she didn't know about this plan. I wonder why.

Miphis elbowed Micah. Micah lifted his head, looking annoyed, like he was about to bark at his cousin. It was almost—*almost*—worth yesterday's humiliations and injuries to see the astonishment on Micah Bayar's face when he laid eyes on Han. Astonishment that he quickly wiped away.

Their eyes met, locked together. "Blood and bones, Alister, what happened to you?" Micah said, touching his own cheekbone with his forefinger. "Fighting again?"

Miphis tittered, his eyes shifting from Han to Micah.

"Fell down the stairs," Han said. "Nearly broke my neck, in fact."

"Perhaps you should watch your step next time," Micah said, stretching lazily.

Fiona's puzzlement turned to fury. She cocked back her arm and pegged the book at her brother's head. He just managed to duck in time. It whizzed past him and smacked into the wall with tremendous force.

The proficient looked up, glaring, but decided not to intervene when he saw who it was. Wil Mathis fetched the book and handed it back to Fiona. She sat down next to Wil and opened it, spots of color on her pale cheeks.

Fiona had a rum arm. Han made a mental note to remember that.

He also wondered what could be going on between the two Bayars.

Han and Dancer took a table in a corner. They each chose a book, taking notes on the assigned chapters, then recopying them for the other.

Several times, Han looked up to find Fiona watching him fixedly, her pale blue eyes going nearly purple in the flickering candlelight, her hands clenching the book on the table in front of her.

Well, have an eyeful, girlie, Han said to himself, massaging his aching head. I can't help how I look. This is your brother's doing.

That was the thing. In the blueblood world, your enemy dined and danced with you, talking pretty to your face while reaching around to stab you in the back.

At ten, Han put his other work aside and pulled out Kinley to reread the chapter about Aediion. He'd never planned on going back; now he had to study up quick.

At eleven o'clock, Micah swept up his books and papers and stowed them in his book bag. Pulling on his cloak, he slung the bag over his shoulder and stopped by the proficient's desk for a walking pass, since it was past the ten o'clock curfew.

It seemed Micah was done for the night.

Struggling to concentrate, wondering where Micah had gone, Han read and scribbled until the bells in Mystwerk Tower bonged quarter past eleven. Catching Dancer's eyes, Han slid his papers into his carry bag, laying Kinley on top. Dancer collected his books and papers also.

Han stood, stretched painfully, and fumbled one-handed into his wool cloak, draping it over his carry bag.

He nodded at the proficient, who'd looked up from his book when Han and Dancer stood. "Guess we'll head back to the dormitory," Han said.

Dancer went to get their passes from the proficient. Miphis Mander leered at Han and whispered, "Careful on your way out. That first step is a bone-breaker."

"Pardon me?" Han said. "Did you say something?" He stepped in close to Miphis and leaned down as if to hear better.

Miphis snickered, seemingly drawing courage from Han's maimed state. "I said, careful out there. That . . . he—hey!" He sucked in his breath as Han's knife sliced through his breeches from waist to ankle—quick and slick so nobody saw before the blade disappeared. Miphis clutched at his trousers with both hands in an attempt to keep decent.

"Lucky for you I'm a rum blademan leftie or right," Han said under his breath. It was a bit of a brag, but not much. More loudly, he added, "*You* be careful out there. It's a bit brisk to leave your arse hanging out like that."

Those at nearby tables turned and stared. Fiona half rose from her seat, then settled back down.

Han guessed Miphis wouldn't be reaching for his amulet, since he had both hands busy.

Dancer had their passes. Han picked up their lantern and carried it into the hallway. Instead of walking out the door, they climbed the wide staircase to the third floor and ducked into a side room. Han shuttered the lantern while Dancer threaded a rope through the carry handle. Unlatching the window shutters with his good hand, Han threw them open, feeling the chill night air in his face.

Sneaking in and out of places was a skill that Han had mastered at a young age. All his life, people had been trying to keep him inside places he didn't want to be, or out of places he needed to get into.

Still, it wasn't easy being a one-armed cracksman. He was glad Dancer was along.

Boosting himself onto the wide sill, Han poked his legs through and dropped the few feet onto the roof of the galleried walkway. When he landed, a tile broke loose and dropped to the stone walk below, shattering into a thousand pieces and sounding loud as a scream in the dead of night. He froze, but no one came running.

You're out of practice, he thought. And his bound arm affected his balance.

Dancer followed with the darkened lantern. They light-footed it along the gallery roof, a story above any provost guard or nosy proficient patrolling down below. The roofed walkways made a network of secret pathways that could take him unseen to most anywhere he wanted to go.

No one else seemed to be out past curfew, save two cloaked sweethearts who had stowed themselves in the corner where the gallery met Mystwerk Hall. They folded into one another, holding hands and whispering.

Han felt a pang of regret, thinking of Bird. He wondered

if she ever thought of him. No. She'd made it plain enough she never wanted to see him again.

The lovers didn't notice Han and Dancer passing over their heads like undead spirits.

They had to crab sideways along the wall to where a window opened into Mystwerk Hall. Han fished his blade from under his cloak and slid it between the shutters, tipping up the latch inside. He pulled the shutters toward him and peered into an empty classroom. Resting his rump on the stone sill, he turned and slid through, dropping feetfirst to the floor on the other side. Dancer handed down the lantern, then followed.

This is likely not what Leontus meant when he told me to take it easy, Han thought, trying to ignore the nagging ache in his arm and shoulder.

Carefully uncovering one pane of the lantern, Dancer peeked out of the door of the classroom. He stood and listened for a moment, head cocked, then motioned Han into the corridor.

They followed the corridor until they found a staircase up. Han liked stone staircases—they never creaked. They climbed past the proficient and master floors, circling wide around lighted offices and laboratories.

The belfry door was locked, but easily managed with a narrow iron slider that Han had brought along. This door led to an even narrower staircase—wooden this time. It twisted upward, the walls brushing Han's elbows on either side.

Rats skittered up the stairs ahead of them, sliding into hidden crevices to either side. At the top of the stairs an unlocked door lead into the bell chamber.

Unshuttering the lantern, Dancer set it in the corner, and they looked around. Bell pulls dangled like ghost tails from the four huge bells that provided the cadence of Han's life these days. A ladder leaned against one wall, allowing access to the bell mechanism.

Han circled the room, noting every detail so he could return from Aediion. He settled into the corner and retrieved the copy of Kinley from his carry bag.

Dancer leaned back against the wall a short distance away. Pulling out a sketchbook, he rested it on his lap. "When should I begin to worry?" he asked.

"Give me half an hour," Han said.

"That's too long," Dancer objected. "You don't know how much power you've been able to store up. Try a shorter time at first."

"I can be dead in five minutes," Han said. "I either do this or I don't. I got a lot to learn and not much time."

Still, he was nervous, sweating, despite the chill wind that leaked through the walls of the belfry. He took deep breaths, trying to settle into a calm place.

This time, Gryphon wouldn't be available to haul him back if he stayed too long. Hopefully Dancer could stand in if need be.

Watch your back, Bayar had said. *I know where you live and I've got plenty of time.*

Han's resolve hardened. He settled Kinley onto his lap and thumbed through to the chapter on Aediion. Looking around the room, he stowed away images to anchor him there. Then took hold of his amulet and spoke the spell that opened the portal.

Again, the rush of darkness. When the light returned, Han was standing on the main floor of the belfry. Moonlight poured through the arched windows, inscribing bright patterns on the wooden floor and illuminating the dust that hung in the air. The dust coalesced, took shape, and organized itself into Crow. As if he'd been waiting eagerly for him.

"Thank the Maker," Crow said, looking vastly relieved. "I was beginning to think something had happened to you. I didn't know whether to keep coming or . . ."

"I'll hear you out," Han broke in. "I'm not making any promises."

Crow waved away Han's words. "I've no doubt that once you see the potential for . . ." He stopped abruptly, eyes narrowed. "What *is* that you're wearing?"

Han looked down at himself. He was clad in clan leggings and shirt, bearing no evidence of his recent injuries. Was that how he saw himself?

"Try this," the blueblood said. Han's clothes reorganized themselves, taking on color and trimmings until he stood dressed in a deep navy blue velvet coat and a snowy linen shirt with lacy cuffs that draped over his hands, narrow black trowsers with a silver-buckled belt, and black leather boots. The clothes were finer than any Han had ever owned.

Crow grinned. "Much better. And, to finish . . ." He pointed.

Han looked at his hands, now weighed down with rings, the stones shifting from rubies to emeralds to diamonds. If they were real, they'd be worth a fortune.

"Hey!" Han said, shaking his hands as if he could fling off the baubles. "Get those off or I'm gone." And just like that, the jewelry evaporated and his clothes shifted to a plain gray coat and black breeches. The clothes still felt different, though, made of finer, softer fabrics and cut closer to his body.

"There, now," Crow said, sighing and rolling his eyes. "You look like a flatland cleric. Is that what you want?"

"What I want is for you to leave my clothes alone," Han said through gritted teeth. "I an't here to play dress-up."

"You should dress like who you aspire to be," Crow said. "It's all part of the game." Crow extended his arms in front of himself, admiring his lace sleeves and the many rings on his fingers, like a ragpicker trying on the dress-up clothes bluebloods threw away. The only plain thing about him was his amulet, a black crow carved out of onyx, with diamonds for eyes.

"I told you. I an't a fancy, and don't want to be," Han said, already sorry he'd come. He didn't like that Crow could change their surroundings at will. Putting his back to the wall, he conjured up a blade and made sure that his amulet was exposed and ready for use.

He looked up to find Crow stifling laughter at his efforts. "Why not a sword, instead?"

Han clutched a massive sword in his fist. Its blade extended nearly to the ceiling, running with blue flames.

Crow grinned. "Would you like . . . some armor as well?"

Instantly, Han was weighed down by a heavy gold breastplate, his arms enclosed in chain-mail gauntlets.

"Perhaps that's a bit overdone," Crow said. The sword and armor went as quickly as they came.

Han glared at Crow. He'd not come here to be toyed with.

Maybe I should step out and close the portal right now, he thought. He took hold of his amulet. It glowed through his fingers like a fallen star.

"Please forgive me," Crow said, taking a step forward and

raising both hands. "Here's my point—your blade's no good here. It's an illusion. I'm not saying that illusions cannot be extraordinarily powerful. But the only way to hurt someone in Aediion is through the direct use of magic."

That's what you say, Han thought. It all looks rum convincing to me.

"Are you at least willing to tell me your name now?" Crow said.

"My name's Alister," Han said. He waited for Crow to reciprocate with an actual name, but he didn't. He seemed distracted, his attention caught by every little sight and sound—the clatter of horse hooves over the cobblestones outside, the flames on the hearth, the pattern on his velvet sleeves. He was like a small child, examining everything as if it were fresh and new and fascinating.

A peculiar cove, all the way around. This was who he was partnering with?

"Where do you come from?" Han said. "You sound like a northerner, but I an't seen you around campus."

"Doesn't it stand to reason that I would assume a different guise in Aediion if I did not wish you to recognize me in the real world?" Crow said. "There is always the chance that I've misjudged you, that you will betray me if you know who I really am."

Which meant he could be anyone.

Han closed his hand more tightly around his amulet. Maybe this is what he's really after, Han thought. My amulet. Crow was just stringing him along until he had the chance to take it. Well, Han wouldn't lie down like an easy mark.

As if Crow had read Han's thoughts, Crow's amulet changed so it was identical to Han's. "There, you see? I am not lusting after your amulet. I have my own," he said.

In the dream world, it was easy to go all mumble-minded about what was real and what wasn't.

"Look," Han said. "You said you could teach me magic."

"I can," Crow said. "What I can teach you will make you the most powerful charmcaster in the Seven Realms." He walked to the arched window and gazed out, then turned and rested the heels of his hands on the sill. "But there's a price," he said.

Ha, Han thought. Here's where the Breaker demands my soul in payment. Well, he'd dealt with connivers before. He knew when to walk away from a bad deal.

"What's your price?" Han asked, feigning indifference.

"I will not invest my time in someone who will never make full use of the gift of knowledge I offer," Crow said. "If we are to be allies, I shall expect improvement in every aspect of your life—your speech, your manners, your . . . attire." He flicked his hand toward Han, taking in his clothing.

Han stared at him, taken by surprise. "You want *me* to turn into a bleeding blueblood? That's your price?"

Crow studied his hands, twisting the elaborate ring on his right forefinger. "Our time in Aediion is limited as is. I don't want to spend it showing you how to navigate in society. Surely you can find someone else to teach you those skills."

"Look," Han said, "I don't got time to learn the things I need to learn, let alone studying pretty speech and manners."

Crow stepped close to Han, leaning in so they were nearly nose to nose. "Don't underestimate the Bayars. You have been lucky so far, but it's only because they've underestimated *you*. They will destroy you if you don't learn to meet them at their level. It's more than spellcasting. It's more than a powerful amulet. It's politics, and the law, and winning powerful people to your side. That requires you to be articulate, at least."

"Why do you care if they destroy me?" Han said. "It's no skin off you if I lose."

"Let's just say it's a grudge match," Crow said, turning to look out of the tower windows. "I hate Aerie House," he said softly. "They destroyed everything I care about."

We have something in common, then, Han thought. If he's telling the truth.

Still, the blueblood was right, now he thought on it. Han had to learn to fight on their turf. If he didn't, he would go down quick. He recalled the humiliating experience of the dean's dinner. It might be worth his time to avoid a repeat performance.

"All right," Han said. "I'll look for a teacher. But if you're going to help me, it can't wait until I learn to talk pretty. The Bayars have come after me twice now. Third time's the charm."

Crow stiffened, his blue eyes brilliant against his pallor. "They've come after you? What do you mean?"

"They've been trying to kill me and take the amulet. I need to put a stop to it."

Crow shook his head, a quick, dismissive movement. "No. I will not allow this," he said, pounding his fist into his other hand. "I've finally found someone I believe I can work with, and I won't let them . . ." He trailed off, as if belatedly recalling that Han was there. "We will stop them," he said, his face hard and resolute. "I'll show you a charm that will destroy them and never leave a trace to connect it with you."

"No," Han said, surprised that Crow would take his possible murder so hard. "That an't what I want. I do that, I'll be climbing the deadly nevergreen in no time."

"You'll what?" Crow stared at him.

"They'll send me back home for hanging," Han said. "Anyway, killing an't all that impressive. Any fool can kill you if they want to make a name and don't care what it costs. That's why even smart streetlords go down, sooner or later."

Han slid back his sleeves, finding that he liked the feel of the soft wool. "Killing is one way to handle a rival, but it also shows respect. It shows he's important enough to have a chat with. A better way is to humble him. Make him look a fool. Show him that the price for coming after you is his reputation."

Crow blinked at Han, looking as astonished as if one of the bricks in the wall had gotten up and given a pretty speech.

"I could hush that lot if I wanted to. I don't need your help for that," Han went on. "That's one thing I'm good at. But I don't want to. I just need to make them sorry they came after me, so they don't try it again. So I can get on with my business."

Crow furrowed his brow as if surprised that Han had plans of his own. "*Your* business? Which is?"

"*My* business," Han repeated. He could keep secrets as well as Crow. "I want to use magic to scare off the Bayars. I want something nobody's seen before, so I won't be suspected nor expelled."

"Hmmm," Crow said, rubbing his chin and regarding Han with grudging respect.

"Don't think too long, all right? I got to do something before they come after me again. Meantime, I need to keep them out of my room. I want something that won't kill anybody, but will keep them out," he repeated for emphasis. "Got anything like that?"

"Of course," Crow said, rolling his eyes. "To clarify: Do you want to exclude specific people? Or everyone but you?"

"Specific people. I also need to know how to get through any protective charms they've laid down."

Crow extended his hand, and lines of flaming spellwork appeared on the stone wall of the tower. "That's the incantation," he said. "You need to speak it at each entrance to your room—doors and windows. Anchor it to your enemies with this line, using their hair, blood, or flesh." More spellwork appeared. "Not only will this keep them out, but it will mark them so you can tell if they've tried to cross your threshold."

"Mark them? How?" Han asked suspiciously.

Crow smiled crookedly. "Boils and pustules," he said. "Lots. Now, here's how to disable charms of protection they may have laid. It's very versatile, and you don't need to know what charms they used." He reviewed more spellwork.

Han studied it over until he was sure he had it down. But the hard knot of suspicion in his stomach wouldn't go away.

"I'm taking a big chance here," he said. "If I snabble their rooms, and your charm doesn't work, I'll be in a world of trouble." He waved his hand. "Show me something. I want to see you do magic in the real world."

Crow thought for a moment, then said, "Fair enough. But we'll have to leave Aediion in order to do that." He walked straight toward Han. Han backed away, but he came up against the wall. The other wizard kept coming until he seemed to *slide* into Han, chilling his bones like an icy wind out of the Spirits.

"Now speak the charm to close the portal," Crow said inside his head.

Han took hold of his amulet and spoke the charm.

Again, the passageway through the darkness.

Dancer looked up, startled, as Han opened his eyes. The slant of the light told Han he was back in Mystwerk Tower—the real one. He wore his regular clothes, the sling supporting his right arm. His collarbone throbbed, suddenly painful.

Dancer scrambled to his feet. "Hunts Alone! What happened? Why did you come back so soon?"

"This requires very little power, which is all you have," Crow whispered in Han's ear. "Use the same anchor charm with this one, too."

Han's fingers described a charm, and conjure words spilled out of his mouth as Crow spoke through him.

For a moment it seemed that nothing had happened. Then Han heard a rush of sound, thousands of tiny movements all around him. The walls of the belfry seemed to come alive, with bright eyes and whiskered faces and rodents' teeth.

Rats and mice poured from every crevice and crack, swarming out onto the floor and rolling toward him like a furry gray sea capped with flickering wormlike tails.

Han heard a flapping sound overhead, and clouds of bats dropped from the highest reaches of the belfry, soaring down toward him, opening triangular mouths, exposing needle-sharp teeth.

"Aaah!" Reflexively, Han threw up his left arm to protect his head and face. Leathery skin brushed over him. Bats smacked into him and dropped to the floor, straightening their wings, looking bewildered.

Dancer seized hold of the lantern and swung it in a wide arc, forcing the rodents back. Han joined him in his corner, and they put their backs to the walls.

Rats and mice slipped past Dancer's lantern, swarming over Han's feet, sinking their razor-sharp teeth into his ankles. The magic *was* real. The magic had crossed over. And it was anchored to him.

Han danced from one foot to the other, trying to shake off the rodents climbing his breeches. He extended his hand, meaning to channel power into the teeming hordes. Then he remembered he was in the wood-and-stone bell tower of Mystwerk Hall and risked setting it aflame in the process.

Taking hold of the amulet again, Han spoke the thorn-hedge charm, spinning in a circle. A thicket of thorns arose all around them, so tight and impenetrable that the rats impaled themselves on the thorns. Dancer stomped the few rats that had slipped through while Han swatted at the bats that still spiraled down from above.

"Good job," Crow said in Han's ear, his voice low and amused. "Very creative. Now make them go away." He followed up with the charm, spoken through Han's lips.

The heaving sea of rodents drained away into the walls, as though someone had pulled a stopper plug. Moments later, Han and Dancer were alone in the bell tower, surrounded on three sides by a thorn hedge, ringed by rat corpses.

Han's heart pounded, his shirt soaked with sweat. He slid down the wall until his backside hit the stone floor.

Crow whispered in his ear again. "Tomorrow night. Midnight. Same place. And, please . . . build up a little more power in your amulet next time. We have lots to do and we need to work fast."

And then he was gone.

"Hunts Alone?" Dancer knelt next to him. "What in the name of Hanalea's blood and bones was that all about?"

Han scraped his damp hair off his forehead and sat thinking until his breathing steadied and his heart slowed. He looked up at Dancer and smiled. "I think I know how to solve our burglar problem," he said.

CHAPTER EIGHTEEN
ABELARD'S CREW

Abelard's crew of exceptional students met in the dean's office, familiar to Han from his previous visit. Chairs ringed a polished wood table in a plush meeting room with a view of the river. Refreshments were set out under the window.

Han made it a point to arrive early. Master Gryphon came early also, so he could get into the room and settled before everyone else arrived. Han was surprised to see Gryphon, since he and Abelard didn't seem to get on. Maybe his family had clout too.

Timis Hadron, the proficient who'd greeted Han the day he arrived, circled the table, arranging writing materials and books in front of each seat.

Mordra arrived soon after. Han was relieved when she took a seat next to Master Gryphon instead of him. He didn't care to be lectured in manners again in front of a crowd.

The Bayars walked in with Abelard. The dean must have briefed them on their new classmate. Micah pretended to ignore Han as he found a seat on the opposite side of the table, by the door. Fiona's eyes brushed over Han like icy fingers, making his skin pebble up.

He wondered what Abelard had said to them. *Don't worry, he's my hired bravo?*

Fiona and Mordra exchanged daggery glances, then ignored each other.

"Good evening," Abelard said, taking the empty seat at the head of the table. "I've invited Hanson Alister to join our gatherings. Although Alister is a newling, I think you will find that he brings a special range of skills to share with us."

Resting a proprietary hand on Han's shoulder, Abelard pointed out each of the members in turn. "Timis Hadron is a proficient, though he'll soon take his master's examinations. You know Master Gryphon. You met Proficient deVilliers at dinner, and, of course, you already know Micah and Fiona Bayar."

Abelard walked to her seat at the head of the table. "Alister, each week, one of our members presents on a topic in advanced charmcasting, and leads the others through a practical demonstration, if possible. Of course, some types of magic are impossible to trial safely. Others we cannot master because we no longer have the tools that were used when the techniques were developed."

Han nodded.

"Some of these techniques are, in fact, forbidden by the Næming. For that reason, it is imperative that nothing of what we do here is discussed outside our small circle. Do you understand?"

Han nodded again, knowing that his life would hang by a thread once Abelard found out that he was working for the clans.

"We will expect you to contribute to our series eventually," Abelard said. "Alister has special expertise in the area of travel to

Aediion," she said to the others. "He has agreed to share it with the rest of us."

I don't really remember agreeing to that, Han thought, but he kept shut.

"Now, let's continue our discussion from last week," Abelard said. She nodded to Timis Hadron. "Proficient Hadron, if you would, please."

Hadron spread out some notes on the table. "As most of you know, I've been researching evidence for the existence of the Armory of the Gifted Kings," he said.

"Excuse me," Han said, wondering whether he should raise his hand. "Armory of the Gifted Kings?"

Fiona straightened, twisting a lock of her hair between her thumb and forefinger. Micah glared up at the ceiling.

"The Gifted Kings of the Fells accumulated a vast collection of magical pieces and weapons," Hadron said. "It disappeared around the time of the Breaking. The weapons may have been destroyed by the Spirit clans to keep them out of wizard hands. Some say the Demon King hid them away, meaning to retrieve them later. A third theory is that they were confiscated by one of the wizard houses that laid siege to the Demon King's stronghold on Gray Lady."

Did Han imagine it, or did Hadron glance at Micah and Fiona when he said that?

"We've been searching for the armory since the Næming and the restoration of the Gray Wolf line," Abelard said.

Hmmm, Han thought. If anyone held the keys to the magical storeroom, it'd be the Bayars. They'd owned at least one forbidden amulet—the one Han now wore.

Hadron went on to review the sketchy evidence he had collected. "So I think we can say with confidence that the armory existed at one time," he concluded. "The question is, does it still exist, and if so, where is it? Here we need to dig deeper."

As Hadron continued, Han looked up from his note-taking to see Fiona, head down, hand flying across the page. Micah, too, seemed transfixed, his black eyes focused on Hadron, his face pale and intent.

Were they worried that Hadron might uncover its location? Did they plan to report back to Papa? Or was it possible that they didn't know where it was, either? Maybe they were as eager as anyone to find it.

Maybe Han could beat them to it. He scribbled faster, splattering ink across the page.

"Most of the focus to date has been on libraries and temple records in Fellsmarch," Hadron said. "But evidence suggests that many records that predated the Breaking were carried here to Oden's Ford for safekeeping. So there could be materials archived in the Bayar Library that would help us locate the armory."

"That would be like finding a flea on a dog," Gryphon said. "Have you seen what's up there?"

"What would you suggest we do, then?" Abelard asked Hadron, ignoring Gryphon.

"Mordra and I will be here over the summer," Hadron said. "We could begin a methodical search of the stacks in Bayar Library."

Mordra wrinkled her nose at that suggestion, but Hadron didn't see. "Any of you who are staying on are welcome to help," he said. No one volunteered. He cleared his throat.

"Think about it, and let me know."

"Thank you, Hadron," Abelard said. "Given the constant litany of complaints about the lack of powerful weapons at our disposal, it is my expectation that those of you who stay on for the summer will join Proficients Hadron and deVilliers in their research." She swept her gaze over her crew. When no one objected, she continued. "Now deVilliers will report on the topic of magical possession." The dean nodded at Mordra.

Mordra tapped her finger on the stack of pages in front of her. "Possession is a magical technique that first achieved prominence during the War of the Conquest, when the mainland was invaded by wizards from the Northern Islands. It also proved useful during the Reign of the Gifted Kings, both for keeping the peace, and in counterespionage activities."

Mordra looked around the table, as if to make sure she was the focus of everyone's undivided attention. Han's eyes fixed on the tattoos on her arms. They wriggled and swam against her skin. He looked away.

"Eventually, the Spirit clans developed talismans to defend against possession, which limited its effectiveness. Still, it was commonly used up until the time of the Breaking, when the tactic was forbidden by the Næming. The Demon King was said to have used it to eliminate pairs of rivals. He would possess one, then induce him to murder the other. Thereafter, the first would be executed for the crime."

Hmmm, Han thought. Great-grandfather Alger was rum clever. I wonder how Great-grandmother Hanalea got the best of him.

"You see before you three common variations on the spellwork used to activate the possession charm," Mordra went on. "These represent degrees of possession. In some cases, the possessor merely precipitates actions the possessee would not undertake on his own. In others, possession is complete, and the possessing wizard has total control of the—ah—subject. Once possession has taken place, it is easier to subsequently accomplish. The possessor must be in close proximity to the subject. It is most successfully used on an unwitting target, who can therefore raise little defense.

"We are reasonably confident of the authenticity of the spell lines we've unearthed from the archives." Mordra went on to demonstrate the spoken charms and gestures used in casting the spell. "You should know that no one has used these incantations successfully since the Breaking. Modern amulets don't seem to support this kind of magic." Her shoulders slumped, and when Han scanned those around the table, they wore matching glum expressions.

"No offense meant," Gryphon said, "but does it make sense to spend so much time on spellwork we are unlikely to be able to use?"

"Why don't we try it?" Han said. "What have we got to lose?"

Heads turned, all around the table.

"Master Gryphon is right," Han said. "It's like passing out warm sugar cakes and telling us not to take a bite."

"What do you suggest, Alister?" Abelard said dryly.

"Let's pair off," Han said. "See if anybody can make it work." He paused, then added, "I'll go with Micah." Lacing his fingers across his chest, he cradled the serpent amulet and slid a smile across the table to Bayar.

For a long moment no one said anything. Abelard looked

from Han to Micah, as if trying to divine Han's intentions.

"All right," the dean said, shrugging. "Why not?"

"I choose Hadron," Mordra said. Han wasn't sure if she was aiming to stay away from Fiona or cozy up to an almost-master.

"No!" Micah said, pressing both hands flat against the tabletop. "I will not team up with Alister. He can work with someone else."

Abelard's lips tightened. "Newling Bayar, we discussed this, and . . ."

"Maybe you have your reasons for inviting a street thug to our gatherings," Micah said, his face bone white and furious, "but you should remember that this gutter-whelped thief attacked my father and nearly killed him."

Eyes widened all around the table. Some shifted away from Han.

"What's the matter, Micah?" Han said, tilting his head back and looking down his nose at the High Wizard's son. "Are you afraid?" He fingered the Demon King's amulet.

Micah stood. "I merely believe that if one associates with filth, eventually the stench rubs off." He inclined his head to Abelard. "Dean Abelard, if you will excuse me." Turning on his heel, he walked out. Fiona stared after her brother, then looked back at Han, eyes narrowed in appraisal. She looked almost . . . impressed.

The others also sat frozen, sliding wary looks at Han. He guessed that no one else would be eager to pair up with him, either.

Abelard looked up at the clock on the wall. "Our time is up," she said as if she were glad of it. "Too bad. Next week, Master Gryphon will lead a discussion of glamours and their use in warfare."

Chairs scraped back as Abelard's crew beat a hasty retreat.

CHAPTER NINETEEN
CAUGHT IN THE ACT

The spidery diagram swam on the page, and Raisa's eyes practically crossed as she forced herself to focus. *Earthwork fortifications used against pirates along the Indio after the Breaking.* She faced yet another test in history of warfare.

At least the term is almost over, she thought.

Pushing her book aside, she glanced around. It was almost dinnertime, but the common room was empty save for her. This was Amon's only night free of obligations. Raisa meant to intercept him and have an actual conversation. He'd been less available than ever these past few weeks. Almost furtive.

Speaking of furtive. Lifting the blotter, Raisa pulled a few scribbled pages from underneath and reviewed what was left there.

Mother,

Please know that I am well and safe, and I hope this finds you well also.

I know you were under considerable pressure in the days leading up to my name day, and that you truly believed that a marriage to Micah Bayar was the best way to keep me safe.

After reading it over, Raisa scratched through *a marriage to Micah Bayar* and substituted *the marriage you had planned for me.*

That way, if the letter fell into the wrong hands, it might have been from any daughter or son who had fled an unwanted marriage.

I beg you to consider that what seems safest may turn out to be most dangerous. It may be that the danger you saw coming was the marriage itself—a danger to me, and a danger to you as well.

I long to come home and present my case in person if we can find a way to do that safely. I will get this letter into my father's hands somehow, and hope that he will get it to you. If that should happen, please keep it among us three. There has been one attempt on his life already.

If we begin a dialogue, perhaps we can work out a way for me to come home, which is what I want most in the world. Though it may be selfish, I can't help but hope that you are missing me, as I am missing you. Please know that I love you, and while love may not be sufficient to heal the breach between us, it is a place to start.

Hallie and Talia came stomping down the stairs, and Raisa pushed the letter into her carry bag.

"You coming to dinner?" Hallie asked. "I hear it's ham and cabbage."

"I'll wait for Corporal Byrne," Raisa said. "And walk over with him."

Hallie and Talia looked at each other. "I'm not sure he's coming to dinner," Hallie said, rubbing the side of her nose with her forefinger. "I think he has plans."

Plans?

"Come with us," Talia urged. "We'll go out somewhere after. Don't be a hermit."

Some undercurrent in their speech set Raisa's teeth on edge.

"I'll be over in a few minutes," she said lightly. "Save me some ham."

They walked out the door with many backward looks, their faces set and anxious.

A few minutes later, Amon descended the stairs. He wore his dress blues, with creases in his trousers and his hair neatly combed off his forehead. He nearly stumbled when he saw Raisa, but kept his feet and continued to the bottom.

"Hello, Amon," Raisa said. "You're looking handsome."

He looked down at himself, then tugged at the hem of his uniform jacket to straighten it. "Right. Well. Thank you."

Raisa pushed up out of her chair and went and stood in front of him. "I hoped we could go to dinner together, maybe have a chance to talk. I never see you anymore."

He stood frozen, like a schoolboy caught out in a prank, his gray eyes fixed on her face. "We're both busy, Rai. It stands to reason that we wouldn't—"

"Let's go to dinner, then," Raisa said, taking his hands in hers.

He swallowed hard, the long column of his throat jumping. "I can't. I . . . have something I need to do."

Raisa's instincts screamed that persistence would lead to heartbreak. But she couldn't help herself. "I'll come with you, then. And, after, maybe we—"

"No," he said. "Not tonight. I—we can't." He looked as miserable as she'd ever seen him.

"But it's your only night off." Raisa knew she sounded desperate, and didn't care.

He nodded. "I know. I'm . . . sorry," he whispered, his face pale and strained.

Raisa cast about for something—anything—that might change his mind. That might make him stay. "Well," she said, swallowing down the dull ache of longing. "Then take this with you, and think of me." She kissed her first two fingers, then, standing on tiptoes, reached up and pressed them against his lips.

Seizing her wrist, he pressed her hand against his cheek, smooth from recent shaving. He closed his eyes, took two shuddering breaths, and let her go.

"Good-bye, Raisa," he said, his voice thick and unfamiliar. "Go on to dinner. I'll be back late." And he was gone.

Raisa stood frozen for a heartbeat, then grabbed her cloak and slipped out the door, following after him.

Fortunately, the streets were crowded, packed with cadets heading back to the dining halls for dinner, or walking toward Bridge Street and the eateries there. Amon walked fast, so Raisa had to trot to keep up. Once, he swung around and looked back, but she managed to duck into a doorway.

Raisa soon realized that he was heading for Bridge Street, and when he started across, she hesitated briefly to tug her hood over her head before stepping onto the bridge. It was the first time she'd crossed it since the day she'd arrived.

Amon made one stop, at the flower seller's on the bridge, where he bought a small bouquet of mixed flowers.

Raisa forced down despair. A voice in her head whispered, *Go back!*

But she didn't.

Amon hurried on as if he knew the way, turning onto the quad that separated Mystwerk Hall and the Temple School. The winter-seared lawn bloomed with a mixture of red Mystwerk robes and white Temple garments. Raisa pulled her head back into her cowl like a turtle into its shell.

What if he goes into Mystwerk? Raisa thought. Crossing the bridge is risky enough. I can't follow him in there.

But Amon stepped onto the stone walk that led to the Temple School, turning off to the entrance at the far right. In front of the heavy wooden door, he paused long enough to take a swipe at his hair, then raised the knocker and let it fall with a clatter.

Raisa had remained on the main walk, off at an angle, so she couldn't see who came to the door. But Amon bowed at the waist and extended the flowers. Then he stepped inside, closing the door behind him.

For a long moment Raisa stood frozen on the walk, unsure what to do next. The broad porch was crowded with dedicates and students, so she couldn't very well go up and listen at the door. But perhaps if she circled around . . .

Fortunately, the ground floor was lined with tall windows and glass doors, spilling light into every room. Raisa crept along the perimeter of the building, between the shrubbery and the foundation, peering into every window. Though some were probably at dinner, Raisa saw dedicates and students reading, relaxing, doing stitchery, painting, playing instruments, and the like.

This is what everyone had intended for me, Raisa thought, fingering her dun-colored uniform tunic.

In the rear was a parlor, a cheerful fire in the fireplace and trays of cookies and sandwiches set out on tables. Amon was there, sitting in a chair by the fireplace, his back very straight, his hands on his knees. Across from him sat a girl in temple dress, dark-skinned and pretty, with masses of long curly hair—a

Southern Islander. She clutched the nosegay in one hand, and every so often she raised it to her nose and took a sniff.

Two other couples shared the room, and a rosy-faced dedicate sat in a far corner, keeping an eye on the young lovers.

Amon's face was in profile, but Raisa could see the girl's shy smile and her large dark eyes, and hear the murmur of their conversation.

Any fool could see that the girl was in love with Amon Byrne.

Raisa's eyes burned with hot tears. Was this possible? Honest, straightforward Amon Byrne was . . . *cheating* on her? She tried to ignore the voice in her head that said it wasn't cheating if there hadn't been a relationship to begin with.

You don't lie to your friends, Raisa said to herself defensively. He'd gone out of his way to hide this from her.

And then, as if in a bad dream that turns into a nightmare, she saw Amon stiffen, squaring his shoulders under the blue wool. He slowly turned his head so that he was looking right at Raisa. For a long moment she was petrified, unable to move, and they stared at each other. Then, cheeks flaming, she dropped below the windowsill and scrambled backward like a crab, out of the shrubbery.

She stood upright and fled toward the front of the building. She'd gone only a few yards when a hand closed tightly around her upper arm, jerking her sideways.

Raisa twisted around to face another Southern Islander in temple dress, this one as unlikely a candidate as she'd ever seen. The multiple piercings in her nose and ears were pegged with silver. She clutched a wicked-looking knife in her free hand.

Even worse, she looked oddly familiar.

"Who you spying on, dirtback?" The girl gave Raisa a little shake.

"N—nobody," Raisa said, trying to pull free. "Let go, that hurts!"

"I want to know who you are and what you . . ." The blade-wielding Temple student's eyes narrowed in recognition. "I *know* you," she said. "I seen you someplace."

"That's not surprising. I go to school here, too," Raisa said, grabbing at dignity with both hands. "I just wanted to see what it's like in the Temple."

"You're from the Fells," the dedicate said, avidly studying Raisa's face. Then her eyes widened in astonishment. "You was the girlie with Cuffs Alister. You the one walked into Southbridge Guardhouse after the Raggers."

It was Cat. Cat Tyburn, the streetlord who had replaced Cuffs as leader of the Raggers. Alister's former girlfriend.

It was no wonder Raisa hadn't recognized her at first. Cat looked different—almost cared-for—like a weedy, thorny garden that some gifted gardener had taken on. Her eyes were brilliantly clear, not cloudy like before, and she'd put on weight.

What was she doing at Oden's Ford?

"I don't know what you're talking about," Raisa said. Her mind flashed to her sighting of Cuffs Alister by the stables. Could there be a connection? It didn't matter. She had to get away.

In desperation, she rammed her fist into Cat's middle, hoping she wouldn't get her own throat cut in the process.

Fortunately, Cat was distracted and hadn't seen the blow coming. She crumpled, dropping the knife. Raisa took off running again, this time clearing the Temple close and the quad, and turning onto Bridge Street. She ran like she was being pursued by demons.

CHAPTER TWENTY

STAR-CROSSED

Raisa ran all the way to Grindell Hall.

She charged through the common room, drawing puzzled stares from Mick and Garrett, who were playing cards, and Talia and Hallie, who hadn't gone out after all. She loped up the stairs, into her room, slammed the door, and flopped facedown on her bed.

A few minutes later, she heard the door open softly. "Rebecca?" It was Talia.

"Go away," Raisa said into her pillow, wishing she had a room to herself. Wishing she were a princess again, so she could order people around.

Of course Talia didn't go away, but came and sat on the side of the bed.

"I thought you were going out," Raisa muttered.

"We decided not to," Talia said, stroking Raisa's hair. "Did you follow him?"

Raisa nodded, her face still pressed into the pillow. "How long have you known he was seeing someone?"

"A while. He hasn't kept it a secret . . ."

"From anyone but me," Raisa finished. She wished she could disappear. Was it that obvious she was in love with Amon? How could she ever face any of them again?

Talia pressed her hands into Raisa's shoulders, digging deep into the muscles, working free the knots. "He didn't want to hurt you."

"I see. So he discussed it with the triple, and you all agreed that—"

"No, no, *no*." Talia's hands stilled themselves. "It wasn't like that at all. He's not a very good liar, and he's so bloody honorable. He's been absolutely miserable, if you haven't noticed."

Raisa could hear the love in Talia's voice. Every member of the Gray Wolves loved Amon Byrne. They had that in common.

The door opened and closed again, and Raisa twitched irritably.

"There, now," Talia said. "Hallie's brought you some tea is all."

"I'll get you something stronger if you'd like," Hallie said. "I got some brandy will put you out like a doused candle."

Raisa shook her head. She needed a clear mind.

"We didn't know what had been between you," Talia went on. "Or if any promises had been made, but—"

"None," Raisa said bitterly. "There was nothing. We were friends, that's all."

I used to think I was good at reading people, she thought. I loved Amon, and I was convinced he loved me back, or that I could make him love me if I could just break through the barriers of class and duty.

Could they ever be friends again?

She didn't even have the energy to be worried about running into Cat Tyburn. Just then, getting her throat cut seemed like an easy out.

For the next hour, Hallie and Talia soothed her, plied her with tea, and tried to feed her dinner. Much of the time they just sat with her, holding her hands, saying nothing. Amid the heartbreak and self-blame, Raisa felt propped up by their presence. Maybe this was what it was like to have real friends.

Finally, she heard the creaking of the stairs, and recognized Amon's step.

"We'll stay if you want," Hallie said quickly. "No matter what the corporal says."

Raisa shook her head. "We need to talk. We've needed to talk for a long time."

He knocked on the door.

"Come in!" Talia said, and Amon pushed open the door. He stood looking at the three of them, his expression haggard and grim.

Talia and Hallie kissed Raisa on opposite cheeks. "We'll be downstairs if you need us," Talia said. And they left, circling Amon, giving him the hard eye.

Silence coalesced around them. Raisa sat up in bed, her back against the wall, her arms wrapped around her knees.

Finally, Amon fetched the chair from Raisa's desk and set it next to the bed. He sat down in it. "I'm glad you got back safely," he said. "I should have come after you straight away, as soon as I saw you'd crossed the bridge."

"Well. That would have been awkward," Raisa said, resting her chin on her knees. "This isn't going to be about me crossing the bridge, is it?"

He shook his head. "No. It's not going to be about that." He toyed with a heavy gold ring on his left hand. The ring with the circling wolves.

Raisa almost wished it would be. She'd rather fight with him than have this conversation. "Who is she?"

Amon looked up. "Her name is Annamaya Dubai," he said. "Her family is from the Southern Islands, as you could probably tell. Her father is military—he's a mercenary in the Fells. He's one of the few stripers in the regular army that my father trusts."

"How did you meet her?" Raisa asked.

"My father and her father set it up. They thought we would be well matched."

It sounded like they were a pair of carriage horses.

"Well," Raisa said, nodding, "she *is* tall."

"Stop it, Rai," Amon said. "I'm not apologizing for seeing her. I'm apologizing for keeping it a secret from you. You can beat on me all you want, but leave her out of it. She's sweet, and hard-working, and well-read. She's an excellent harpist—very talented. And she's great with horses. She's lived in a military family all her life, so she'll understand what that's like—that my first duty is to the guard."

Then it hit Raisa like a fist in the face. Her heart began to pound so hard that it seemed Amon must be able to hear it.

"You intend to marry her," she whispered.

He nodded, his gaze fixed on the floor. "Not till after I

341

graduate from the academy. But the plan is we'll announce our betrothal when we return to the Fells in the summer."

"*What?*" Raisa's voice rose. "You're getting married, and you never *told* me?"

He looked up at her, his gray eyes swimming with guilt. "I have no defense. It was wrong, and I know it. I just didn't have the courage to tell you."

The conversation was like a series of body blows. She wanted to hurt him back.

Well, clearly she's everything one could want in a wife—a horsey harpist, Raisa wanted to say. But when she looked up at Amon, his expression was so bleak and hopeless that the words dried up on her tongue.

"You don't love her," she whispered.

"I didn't say that."

"But you don't. I can tell. Don't try to lie to me; you're no good at it."

He gazed at her, and Raisa could tell he was debating giving it a try anyway. Then he shrugged his shoulders. "I'll be a good husband to her," he said.

And he would, except for the minor detail that he didn't love her.

Well, Raisa thought, if he's going to marry anyone he doesn't love, it's going to be me.

"Before you go through with this, there's something you should know," Raisa said crisply. "It's important that you make an informed decision."

From Amon's expression, he might have been facing a firing squad. "Rai, please. Before you say anything, there's something I should have told you before now. I wanted to tell you, only . . . Da said I shouldn't because we—"

"No. Hear me out," Raisa said. "And then you'll get your turn." She took a deep breath. "Amon, you're my best friend. You always have been. You're the most honorable person I know. And apparently you're not the kind of person to get involved with a girl when you know it can't go anywhere."

He kept his gray-eyed gaze locked on her face. "No," he said quietly. "I'm not that kind of person."

She took his hands, rubbing her thumbs across his palms. She needed that physical connection to maintain her courage. "Me, I accepted that we could never marry, but I was willing to take you on whatever terms . . . you would offer." She smiled. "That's what we do, the Gray Wolf queens—we take what we can get when it comes to love. That's why they call us witches and harlots in the south."

Amon closed his eyes, his lashes dark against his sunroughened skin. His hands tightened on hers. "Your Highness, please don't say things you'll regret later. I don't want things to be awkward between us."

"No," Raisa said. "I think I'd regret *not* saying them. And things are already as awkward as they can be." She paused, and when he said nothing, went on.

"So. I know that I should make a political marriage, one that benefits the Fells and the line. But . . . it's a new day. The Fells has never sent a princess heir to Oden's Ford. Here I'm learning to let go of old ideas and embrace new ones. There has to be a way to make it work."

"Make what work?" he whispered like a dying man who

exposes his throat, waiting for the killing stroke.

"I love you," she said simply. "I'm asking you to marry me."

Raisa couldn't have said what kind of response she expected, but not an expression of mingled desire, grief, and despair.

"You don't understand," Amon whispered, shaking his head. "I can't . . . we can't . . ."

"I know we're young," she said quickly. "I didn't want to marry so soon either. But if we marry, that takes a marriage to Micah Bayar off the table. We can go back to the Fells together, and that will stifle talk of putting Mellony on the throne. I think the people would welcome a marriage to a native born, rather than a foreigner."

The clans especially would welcome a Byrne. They respected Amon's father, Edon Byrne. And the Byrnes weren't magical or beholden to a foreign power.

It made so much sense, she had to make him see it. It was what she wanted, and practical, too. But Amon just stared down at his boots.

"I know there are obstacles," Raisa said quickly. "My mother won't approve. Maybe your father feels the same way. But . . . we can win them over."

You could learn to love me, she thought. I'll teach you.

"It's not that simple," Amon said, gently withdrawing his hands from her grasp. "I'm not free to marry you."

Raisa's heart stuttered. "What do you mean, you're not free?" A terrible thought crowded into her mind. "Do you mean—because you're already betrothed?" She fixed on the gold ring on his left hand, similar to her own.

"No," he said. "I'm not betrothed." He twisted the ring,

sliding it up and down on his finger. "Is it my turn? Can I speak now?"

She nodded, even though she had a terrible feeling she wouldn't like what he had to say.

"You know that the office of Captain of the Queen's Guard is a legacy title in my family," he said. "By Hanalea's decree a thousand years ago."

Raisa nodded. Legacy titles weren't unusual, though more common among the nobility than the military.

"It typically goes to the first-born of each generation. The successor is selected by the previous captain to serve the new queen when she ascends to the throne." He paused, as if waiting for a response from Raisa, but she said nothing.

"I've been chosen to serve as your captain," he said. "Da and I discussed it before we came south."

"Oh!" Raisa said. "Well, then." Now she thought about it, she couldn't imagine anyone else she'd rather have by her side. "That's wonderful news," she said. "Why didn't you say anything before?"

"Well, it's unusual to select a captain before the princess heir takes the throne. It's threatening to the current queen. She might worry that the princess heir, in collusion with her personal guard, will try to take the throne early."

"Oh!" Raisa said. "Well, I suppose . . ."

"Once the choice is made, it cannot be undone, save by death of either party. That's another reason to wait until the princess is crowned queen."

Where did all these rules come from that I never heard of? Raisa wondered. Just one more example of information that should have been passed to her by Queen Marianna.

Still, it seemed that Amon was straying off topic.

"But why are you telling me this now? The role of Captain of the Queen's guard works with the role of consort. It makes a lot of sense, if we could just persuade—"

"It's not just a legacy. There's a magical piece," Amon said.

"A magical piece?" Raisa shivered, her skin pebbling as if a draft had come in through the window. "What do you mean?"

"Well, you know how the High Wizard is linked to the queen of the Fells, so that he or she cannot do anything contradictory to the interests of the Gray Wolf line?"

"Of course," Raisa said. "Though something seems to have gone amiss with our current High Wizard," she added darkly.

"The captains are linked too," Amon said. "There's a ceremony, with a speaker presiding. Once the link is made, it's permanent. It prevents treason and assures the captain's commitment to the survival of the line."

Raisa struggled not to gape. The Byrnes were the most unmagical people she knew. They always seemed like the plainspoken voice of reason against the drama of wizardry, the hardwired sorcery of the clans, and the seductive words of the speakers.

Being linked to Amon could only be a good thing, right? Was it possible they could be bound any tighter than they already were?

"So you'll undergo this 'linking' ceremony when I become queen?" Raisa asked.

Amon shook his head. "It's already done. Before I left the Fells. My da thought I should, since you were leaving the Fells and passing through a war zone. And because, like you said, there may

be a magical threat against the sovereignty of the current queen."
He held up his left hand, showing her the ring on his middle finger. She focused on the wolves circling the heavy gold band.

"I'm already bound to you, Raisa. For good. Forever."
Something in his expression told her this was a mixed blessing.

Raisa tried to swallow down her astonishment. "Did you
really need to hold the ceremony early?" she asked. "The last
thing I want is for people to think I'm plotting against my own
mother. And I don't see why your father thought he had to
prevent your turning traitor on me."

"Well, there are advantages. Sometimes . . . I can predict
what you're going to do, and anticipate danger to you in time to
prevent it. I can sense where you are, in an imperfect way."

A memory came to her, that day in the western Spirits when
they'd been attacked by Sloat and his renegades. She'd stood hidden in the woods, watching Amon work out with his staff. He'd
turned as if he'd sensed her presence, and said, "Rai?"

And earlier today, when she'd been spying in the window,
he'd turned and looked at her.

It was suddenly hot in the upstairs room. Raisa slid off her
bed and went to throw open the shutters. Then came and sat
down on the edge of the hearth.

"Well. Thank you for telling me this. Finally. I still don't see
how it relates to—"

"A match between us is a danger to the line," Amon said.
"That's how it relates."

"That—that—that's not true," Raisa stammered. "It can't
be." And then, when he said nothing, added, "What makes you
think so?"

"Ever since the ceremony, if we . . . if we kiss, or if I'm tempted to . . ." He threw up his hands. "I'm warned away. Prevented."

"Warned away? You mean . . . you mean by *magic*?"

"Yes."

"What happens?" Raisa asked sarcastically. "Does lightning strike, or—"

"I feel sick and dizzy. Then excruciating pain. I feel faint. And . . . I have to stop." He shrugged.

"When has this happened?" Raisa asked.

"Well, that time on the road, when we were sharing a tent, and you . . . ah . . . rolled onto me. And then when we kissed, right before Sloat and his bunch showed up."

Thinking back, she remembered Amon's response both times. He'd actually looked ill—pale and perspiring, gasping for breath.

"How do you know it's not your own scruples at work?" Raisa said. "Maybe it's not the line at risk, but the vaunted Byrne honor. You know that love between us is forbidden, so . . ."

"You think I'm lying?" Amon drew his dark brows together. "You think this is some kind of scheme to put you off?"

"If you are, there's an easier way," Raisa said. "Just tell me you don't love me, and I'll let the matter drop."

"What?"

"What I said. Just say, 'Rai, I don't love you and I never will.' It's that simple."

"Raisa, this is getting us nowhere."

"Say it!"

Amon raked his hand over his head, and his hair flopped back

348

down on his forehead. Pushing up from his seat, he began pacing back and forth.

"Well?"

Amon kept pacing, like a fox in a box trap.

"Will you sit down? You're making me edgy."

Amon came back and sat down next to her. Staring down at the floor, he mumbled, "I can't say it."

"Why not?"

"Because it's not true." He looked up at her, tears pooling in his eyes, his voice ragged and barely audible. "I do love you, Rai. I wish I didn't, but I do. Are you satisfied? Does that make it better or worse?"

Raisa was momentarily speechless.

"Oh," she finally said, in a small voice. They sat side by side but not touching, lost in their own thoughts. Across the river, the temple tower clock bonged once.

"Why didn't you tell me before?" Raisa said through numb lips.

Amon rubbed away tears with his thumb and forefinger. "About the magical barrier or about loving you?"

"Well. Both."

"No one ever tells the queens about the magical part," Amon said. "Only Hanalea knew, because she started it. Though we link to an individual, we're really linking to the line." Amon shifted his gaze to Raisa. "There may be times that we act against the interest of an individual queen to preserve the line."

Which would make him a traitor of sorts to an individual queen, Raisa thought.

"Why did you tell *me,* then?" Raisa asked. "After all these generations?"

"Well, as you said, a new day," Amon said. "We're both breaking the rules. But mostly because you're so bloody persistent. I thought if I ignored you and avoided you, you'd give up and find someone else."

"I won't accept this," Raisa said. "There has to be a way around it. You are not allowed to marry someone you don't love. I forbid it."

"I have to marry, Your Highness. And so do you."

To continue the bloody line, Raisa thought. "What about Lydia? She's married."

"She doesn't have children yet," Amon said. "There's no one in the next generation to take over, when I . . ."

Raisa's breath caught in her throat as the realization struck her. She turned to glare at Amon. "Your father did this on purpose, to keep us apart. He knew we'd be traveling together to Oden's Ford, and he knew the temptation would be too great."

Amon's eyes said yes, even though he didn't say it aloud. "Whatever he did, he did it for the line," Amon said. "That's what he's committed to, more than family, more than anything else."

"I hate your father," Raisa said through stiff lips. "I'll never, never, ever forgive him. He had no right to make that decision for us."

They sat glumly staring at the floor for a while.

"Listen," Raisa said. "Let's try it. Kissing, I mean. Like an experiment."

"This is hard enough already," Amon said. "What do you think this has been like for me? I'm flesh and blood, you know."

"Just this time. Please. I am not going to give you up without a fight. Maybe what happened before was a coincidence. Or maybe it had to do with that particular situation. The danger to the line was probably Sloat, and not anything to do with us."

Amon sighed. After a long pause, he nodded. "You're right. I guess we'll never know if we don't try it. Maybe something's changed."

Raisa turned to face him. Amon's expression mingled wariness and hope. She extended her hand and cupped it under his chin, now rough with early morning stubble. She felt him swallow.

Leaning forward, she pressed her lips against his, gently at first, then more firmly. She reached her other hand around his neck and pulled him closer, fingering the cropped hair on the back of his neck, tracing the bone and muscle there. She pressed against him, feeling his heart accelerate against her chest.

He slid his arms around her, pulled her tight against him in a desperate embrace.

Something rippled between them, and Amon began to tremble. A violent shudder went through him, then another. He broke away and doubled over, clutching at his middle. Sliding sideways to the floor, he lay there writhing and gasping for breath.

"What's the matter?" Raisa said, though she already knew.

"Blood of the demon," he whispered. He raised his arms, covering his throat as if to ward off unseen attackers.

"Amon!" Raisa knelt beside him, pressing her hand to his forehead. It was clammy and cold, pebbled with sweat. "N—no," Amon said, turning his head from side to side, dislodging her hand. "I'm sorry. Don't . . . touch me. Please."

Raisa snatched her hand away, and Amon doubled up in misery, moaning, "Sweet Hanalea, forgive me," he cried, his face contorted in agony, tears seeping from the corners of his eyes. Convulsions rolled through him like waves breaking on a steep shoreline. "Sorry," he whispered. "I'm sorry."

Raisa ran and pulled her pillow from the bed and tucked it behind him so he wouldn't smash against the brick hearth. She covered him with her cloak, because now he seemed to be shivering.

Gradually, the seizure eased. Amon's body relaxed, his eyes fluttered shut, and he slept.

Raisa put another log on the grate and sat with her back to the fire, close to Amon but not touching him, watching him sleep. She felt cold and numb except for a dull ache under her breastbone, and her eyes were finally dry.

The new dawn found the princess heir awake, exhausted, and completely empty of dreams.

CHAPTER TWENTY-ONE

A VERMIN
PROBLEM

A few weeks after Han's first meeting with Abelard's group, Han and Dancer walked back to the dormitory after supper.

Dancer sat down at his worktable and opened up one of Firesmith's books. Spools of gold wire, bars of silver, and semi-precious stones surrounded him. He'd spent a trunkload of money on flash materials. It was good they'd managed to sell off their trade goods at the markets.

Han pulled out his journal and looked over the notes he'd scribbled down from his sessions with Crow. He didn't want to be caught unprepared. He wished he could take notes in the dreamworld and carry them back with him. Maybe he'd ask Crow about it.

"You meeting with Crow again?" Dancer asked, reeling wire off spools and braiding it together. He made no attempt to hide his disapproval.

"I don't have a choice," Han said. "I'm learning a lot. You know that." Han always shared what he learned with Dancer.

"If any of it works," Dancer said. "Those charms you used on the Bayars—has anything come of that?"

Han shrugged. "I haven't heard anything. But at least I got in and out of their rooms without a hitch." He'd waited till dark-man's hour, then ghosted down to the second floor. Disabling their protective charms using Crow's instructions, he slipped into their rooms and took hair clippings in order to anchor his charms to them.

"I'd think between your regular classes and what you're getting from Abelard, you'd have more than enough to do," Dancer said. "You must be stuffed full of knowledge by now."

"You should talk," Han said, gesturing at Dancer's project. "You spend all your spare time on flash, and holed up with Firesmith."

"At least I know who Firesmith *is*," Dancer said. "And I don't have to go to Aediion to meet with him." He shook his head. "I hope you know what you're doing."

Just then they heard someone clumping up the stairs.

"Blevins," Han said.

Dancer tossed a blanket over his metalsmithing equipment.

The dorm master's head and shoulders appeared in the open stairwell. He glared around, struggling to catch his breath. One good thing about being on the fourth floor was that Blevins never came up there unless he absolutely had to.

"What's all this furniture doing on the landing?" he demanded, waving at the little common area they'd created.

"We're airing it out," Dancer said.

"Hmpfh," Blevins grunted. "They an't filled with vermin, are they?"

"Vermin?" Dancer raised his eyebrows. "Why do you ask?"

"Seems we have a vermin problem on the second floor," Blevins said. "Three of the rooms is infested with rats and mice. Every time I think we got them cleared out, a whole flood shows up again. They must be coming from somewhere."

"It can't be just three rooms," Han said, careful not to look at Dancer. "You see one mouse, you know you got a problem everywhere."

"Them boys must be doing something to attract them is all I can say," Blevins muttered. "I moved them into different rooms while I was trying to smoke 'em out of theirs, and the critters followed 'em like a swarm of bees."

"Who?" Dancer asked Blevins, with a puzzled frown. "What boys?"

"Newling Bayar and the Mander brothers. They been trouble from the day they moved in. Always demanding this and that, never satisfied. Now this."

"Before you know it, we'll be infested," Han said, making a face. "If they're the cause, couldn't you move them out of this dormitory?"

Blevins rubbed his chin. "Well, there's some rooms opened up elsewhere, now some newlings have washed out. I'd love to be rid of them. But who'd take 'em?"

"Maybe you don't have to mention their—ah—problem," Han said.

Dancer still wore his trader face, though the corners of his mouth twitched. "I'd sleep better if I knew they were gone," he said. "I can't abide mice and rats."

The next day Han returned to Hampton to find Micah and his cousins in the process of moving out of the dormitory. Han paused at the edge of the quad and watched. Even at that distance he could see that Arkeda and Miphis were covered in large red pustules, as if they'd caught some virulent disease. Micah's complexion was clean and clear, however.

Han smiled at their predictability.

When Micah spotted Han, he set down his belongings and strode toward him, his cloak kiting behind him. Han broadened his stance and waited, arms folded.

"I'm moving out," Micah said. "We've arranged better quarters elsewhere."

"I see that," Han said. He nodded toward the Mander brothers. "Please. Take the vermin with you."

Micah flushed angrily. "Leontus managed to disable whatever hedge-witch hex you used. He said he'd never seen anything like it. I went to the dean and told her you had to be behind it, and she demanded proof."

"She wouldn't take your word for it?" Han shook his head. "I'm amazed."

"Instead of expelling you, Abelard warned me not to touch you," Micah said. "She said that if you came to any harm, *I* would be expelled. What did you tell her? Why would she side with *you*?"

Han shrugged. "Maybe she doesn't think I'm capable of hexing you, being gutter-whelped and all."

"At least I fight my own battles, Alister," Micah said.

"Really? And exactly *why* did you go cackling to the dean?"

Han gestured toward the poxy Manders, who stood well out of reach, staring at them. "You didn't send your cousins on an errand last night while Dancer and I were out? They look—I don't know—*guilty* to me. Maybe they won't be so eager to follow orders next time."

"Do you think this is some kind of joke?" Micah said. "Whatever you're trying to accomplish, you can't win."

"I'm not joking," Han said. "I am absolutely serious. And I *am* going to win."

It seemed like Bayar was going to say more, but he looked up and saw Cat walking across the quad toward them.

Turning on his heel, Micah strode back to the dormitory, retrieved his belongings, and followed his cousins.

Cat grabbed Han's arm. "What happened?" she demanded, her fingers biting into Han's flesh. "What did Bayar want? What did he say?"

"He's moving out," Han said, seeing no reason to get into it. "That's all." He smiled at her. "How was your recital?" he asked. "I'm sorry I couldn't be there."

"It doesn't matter," Cat said, gazing after Micah. "None of it does." And she walked away, shoulders slumped as if she carried the weight of the world.

CHAPTER TWENTY-TWO
THE WAKING DREAM

Han fingered his amulet, his mind picking over the words of the charm.

"Well?" Crow stood, arms folded, tapping his foot impatiently. "Are you going to try it again or not?"

"I'm getting low," Han said. "Maybe I better try it after I cross back."

"If I don't *see* you do it, then how will I know you've done it right?" Crow said. "It's not safe for you to experiment unsupervised. Now, if you don't have the stamina for it, then . . ." He shrugged.

"Is that all you know? Attack charms? Shoulder taps and nasties? I feel like I'm stuffed full of them." Some days it made Han want to scrub out his insides.

Crow rolled his eyes. "What other kinds of charms do you want to learn?"

Han cast about for an alternative. "I don't know—love charms?"

Crow appraised him, head tilted. "Surely you have no trouble meeting your physical needs, Alister," he said. "Anything beyond that is illusion—a fable sold to fools and romantics."

Han raised his eyebrows. "You are a cynical cove, you know that?"

"Look," Crow said, his chilly blue eyes fixed on Han. "You must prioritize. Aerie House will come after you again. They will keep coming until you resolve this issue permanently."

"The vermin charm worked," Han said. "Micah Bayar and his cousins moved into a different dormitory."

"Of course it worked, Alister," Crow said. "I just quarrel with your choice of tactics. You do not respond to an attempt on your life with a slap on the hand. Or a joke." He closed his eyes, collecting himself. "I don't think you truly apprehend the danger you're in. I've invested too much time in you already. I don't want to start over with someone else."

"I know what I'm doing," Han said. "I just need them to stay out of my way."

Crow folded his arms. "You can't afford to be fastidious."

It's not that, Han wanted to say. *I've killed before. And it was up close and personal and messy and necessary. I didn't leave a magical trap for my enemies that hushed them clean and neat when I was far away.*

When Han didn't respond, Crow went on. "They *an't* going to ever leave you alone, you know, as long as you hold the amulet. And when the Bayars murder you, it *an't* going to be my fault."

"I'm *looking* for a teacher, all right?" Han said, irritated by Crow's needling. "But it an't—isn't that easy to find one." He didn't want anyone at Mystwerk to know he was taking blue-blood lessons. It wasn't like he had any real friends beyond Dancer and Cat.

To change the subject, Han said, "What do you know about the Armory of the Gifted Kings?"

Crow gazed at Han, expressionless. "Why do you ask?" he said finally.

"We talked about it in class. Do you think it actually existed?"

Crow shrugged, fussing with his double-buttoned cuffs. "I am convinced that it once existed. Whether it still does is open to question."

"Some people say the Bayars have it," Han said.

"Some people are fools," Crow said. "If the Bayars held the armory, there would be no opposing them."

"I think they're looking for it," Han said, watching for Crow's reaction.

Crow's gaze flicked to Han's amulet, then back to his face. "If so, we'd better hope they don't find it," he said.

"You're Abelard," Han said suddenly, hoping to take Crow by surprise. "Aren't you?"

That was his latest theory, and it made sense. Abelard was faculty, she was full of learning, and she opposed the Bayars. Plus, she wouldn't want to be seen paying extra attention to Han Alister. It was suspicious enough that she'd included him in her tutoring sessions. This way she could cut him loose at any time without risking his telling on her.

Crow could be short-tempered, unreasonable, intimidating, pompous, and impatient. Like Abelard.

Or Gryphon, Han thought, once again undecided. Crow was bitter and sarcastic—just like Gryphon.

Crow's flat expression didn't change. "I don't know why it's so important that you know who I am." He rolled his eyes. "The charms are real, aren't they? They work, don't they?"

"Yes." Han nodded. "They work." It was true. Crow's charms worked very well, in Aediion and out. So well that Han's masters were amazed by his rapid progress.

"If I guess who you are, will you tell me?" Han said.

Crow smiled—he could be a charmer when he tried. "You are relentless, Alister. I like that about you."

Abelard, Han thought again. "What kind of name is Crow for a blueblood, anyway?" he said.

"You know how crows are," Crow said, his smile fading. "They pick over the bones of the dead." He stood, head down, as if lost in memory, the light through the window extinguishing itself in his hair.

What'd they do to you, Crow? Han wondered. Could it possibly be worse than what they did to me?

Crow might be bitter, but he was also focused, determined, persistent, brilliant, hardworking, thorough, and incredibly knowledgeable.

Crow still sometimes crowded into Han's head without permission, to demonstrate some difficult bit of spellwork. It may have been convenient for Crow, but it left Han feeling invaded. Crow often did it when Han was nearly drained of power.

Sometimes after their sessions, Han felt like he'd been drinking turtle'd cider. There were huge holes in his memory—time passing that he couldn't account for. He felt as though his mind had been trampled and reshaped.

I've got to find out how to keep him out of my head, Han decided. But it was unlikely that Crow would show him that trick.

They always met in the same place—the Mystwerk Hall bell tower. Dancer had kept watch for Han the first few times, but Han had shooed him off after that. Dancer had his own work to do. He couldn't be sitting up every night, holding Han's hand.

Han found a new crib among the dusty stacks high in Bayar Library, where they kept texts and records so old and strange that no one ever used them. He set up a back room with a pallet and dragged a table up from three floors below. It was easier to get to than Mystwerk Tower, and he didn't have to worry about the bell-ringers stumbling across his empty body. It amused him to lay claim to a bit of Bayar Library.

Three or four nights a week Han slipped away to his hideaway, crossed into Aediion, and worked like a slave until his amulet was totally drained.

It posed a problem since his daytime classes required power. It was all he could do to replenish his flash between late-night sessions. Gryphon never missed an opportunity to take a poke at him when his depleted amulet failed to produce.

Crow seemed to have unlimited energy. Of course he did. Han did all the work.

In the mornings he'd often wake bone-weary; half-remembered dreams still circulating in his head, feeling like he'd worked all night. Sometimes he failed to wake on time. He'd go straight to class from the library in the same clothes he'd worn the day before. Several times he'd been late to Gryphon's class, which, unfortunately, was the first of the day.

When Han stayed away all night, Dancer assumed he was seeing a girlie and didn't want company. Wrong, Han thought. I'm living like a dedicate.

He and Crow would agree on a four-hour session and Crow would keep him for six. He'd keep at it until Han's amulet was wrung dry and Han was limp and dizzy, then complain that Han needed to pack in more power the next time.

Crow's barbs always rankled because Han *was* hungry for knowledge. He'd never worked so hard in his life. We could get a lot more done, Han thought, if we could trust each other. If we didn't spend so much time carping at each other. It's like we both want to be gang lord.

"Alister!" Crow's voice broke into his thoughts. "You're in a stupor."

"Sorry. I'll see you tomorrow night, then," Han said. "Thank you for the lesson." Taking hold of his amulet, he spoke the closing charm.

And opened his eyes to find light streaming in through the library windows.

He sat bolt upright, swearing. What time was it, anyway? The last thing he needed was to be late to Gryphon's class. Again.

As if to answer his question, the bells in Mystwerk Tower began to sound. *Bong-bong-bong*, he counted to eight.

Bones. He was in trouble.

He didn't have time to pick his way across the roofs. He barreled down the narrow staircases, circling around and around to the ground floor. Fortunately, there was no proficient on duty yet. He plowed through the front doors and smashed right into Fiona Bayar, nearly knocking her to the ground.

He grabbed hold of her arm to keep her upright. "Sorry, I . . . ah . . . didn't see you."

Mam was right, he thought. You *are* demon-cursed.

Fiona was nearly as tall as Han, so she looked him straight in the eyes. "Just because you're late to class, Alister, doesn't mean you can run people over," she said. She looked down at his hand on her arm, and he let go quickly.

Han jerked his head toward Mystwerk Hall. "Come on. We're late as is."

"What were you doing in the library?" she asked.

"Getting an early start on my reading."

"The library isn't even open yet."

"That way it's nice and quiet." Han began walking, not looking back to see if she was following.

"Your face is improved," Fiona said, trotting to catch up. When he said nothing, she persisted. "The sling is gone, so I assume your broken arm is healed?"

"Collarbone, actually," Han said. It gave him twinges now and then.

"What exactly happened?" she asked as they entered Mystwerk Hall.

"I tripped on the stairs."

Fiona snorted.

"No, really," he said. "Ask your brother." They mounted the steps to the lecture hall.

"That should never have happened," Fiona said. "My brother

doesn't always think things through."

Han grabbed the rail to keep from stumbling. Was she saying she was sorry?

"Our father won't be happy when he hears," Fiona went on, as if listening in on his thoughts. "He wants you brought back alive for questioning before you're hanged for murder."

"Hey now, fair's fair," he said as he opened the door to the lecture hall. "If I do the dangle stretch for murder, then so should Lord Bayar."

His voice seemed to echo through the quiet lecture hall. Heads turned. Micah Bayar left off slouching and sat forward, hands braced against his knees, staring at them.

Gryphon had been speaking, but his voice drained away into a charged silence as Han and Fiona made their way to separate seats. "Newling Alister, Lady Bayar. You are late."

And some demon spirit made Han say, "Sorry, sir. Lady Bayar needed help with her homework."

Fiona shot an incredulous look at him from across the room.

Gryphon gazed at him for a long moment, his surreal turquoise eyes standing out against his pale face. "You, Alister, have been late four times in the past two weeks. It seems you would rather sleep in than come to class. Perhaps you think this is a waste of time. Perhaps you believe you've gone far beyond our flimsy efforts."

"No, sir, that's not true," Han said. "It's just I've been up late, working and—"

"Then summarize chapter nine for us." Gryphon thrust his head forward like a predatory bird.

"Chapter nine." Han wet his lips. He hadn't opened Kinley,

in fact. He'd been up all night with Crow. "I'm sorry, sir," he said. "I haven't read it."

"No?" Gryphon raised an eyebrow. He scribbled something on a piece of paper, folded it, and pushed it to the front of the lectern. "You are excused from this class for the balance of the term. Please take this note to Dean Abelard's office. Fifth floor."

Dean Abelard's office was three floors up from the lecture hall. Han dragged his feet all the way like a small child sent for a whipping. He'd seen the dean in their study group, week after week, but he'd avoided any more one-on-ones with her.

Of all his classes, Gryphon's was the one he wanted to stay in. Charms, spellwork, use of amulets—aside from Abelard's study group, it seemed in line with his purposes. He was learning from Crow, but he didn't want to have to rely on him for his magical education. He wanted to go beyond defense and killing charms.

When the proficient ushered him into Abelard's office, the dean was finishing up a bit of correspondence. "Sit, Alister," she said, waving him to a chair.

He sat.

Abelard sat back in her chair, resting her hands on the edge of the desk. "Well? What is it this time? Aren't you supposed to be in class?"

He handed her the note. "Master Gryphon booted me from class for being late."

Abelard scanned the note. "I see. Do you have anything to say for yourself?"

"I *was* late. I overslept."

"Hmm." She dropped the note on the desk. "I understand

that your attendance in class has become erratic. You are constantly late. And yet your performance on examinations and practica is far superior to that of your peers. How do you explain that?"

Han shrugged. "I work hard. That's why I overslept. I was up late."

"Then you arrive in class exhausted, your amulet nearly depleted," Abelard said.

"I try to load it up. Maybe I'm just not all that powerful." Han looked down at the desk.

"Perhaps you are not being challenged in your classes?" Abelard tapped her fingers against Gryphon's note.

"No, that an't it. I get a lot out of Gryphon's class. I meant to be on time. I just miscalculated."

"Who else are you working with, Alister?" Abelard said softly. "Is someone mentoring you?"

Han conjured a puzzled look. "My teachers are the same as everyone else's. Gryphon, Leontus, Firesmith . . ."

"Don't lie to me," the dean said, eyes glittering. "I have the power to make your life very, very difficult."

"I read a lot," Han said. "Ask anyone. I'm always in the library." He looked up at her. "If I'm going to play bravo for you, I need to study up if I want to stay alive."

They gazed at each other for a long moment, and Abelard looked away first. "Would you like me to rescind Master Gryphon's order?" she asked, pulling a pot of ink toward her and picking up a pen.

Han shook his head. "No, thanks."

Abelard tilted her head. "Why not?"

"Gryphon's right," he said. "I can't be late to class all the time. It was fair, what Gryphon did, even if I don't like it."

Abelard leaned forward. "If you're concerned that Master Gryphon will be angry if I intervene, let me assure you that—"

"But I would like to come back to class in the spring term," Han interrupted. "Maybe you can put in a word for me on that."

"Of course," she said, making a note.

"Good." Han smiled. "Is there anything else?" He made as if to get to his feet.

"I want you to teach the study group next term," Abelard said abruptly. "The topic will be travel to Aediion."

Bones. "Dean Abelard, I don't think that's—"

Abelard raised her hand to stop his speech. "I understand that your success may be due to your amulet. Still, I would like you to coach the other members of the circle. If even a few of us can master the technique, it would be most useful for communication throughout the Seven Realms. One day soon we may have better tools in our arsenal."

"It's a waste of time," Han protested. "Master Gryphon's already covered that, and likely everyone in the study group has tried it."

"I'm not giving you a choice," Abelard said. "You'll have plenty of time to prepare. But be ready in the spring."

Han stuffed down more arguments, and nodded. "All right."

Abelard still gazed at him, tapping her long fingernails on the desk blotter. "Alister, you are difficult to read. Clearly you carry wizard blood. You look like a pureblood. You haven't mentioned your father. Is it possible your mother coupled with—"

"No," Han said, suddenly desperate to get out of her presence.

"It an't possible. My father was a soldier, and he died in Arden."
He stood. "If there's nothing else . . ."

"That's all." Abelard dismissed him with a wave of her hand.

"What happened with Dean Abelard?" Dancer asked when they
left Fulgrim's class and walked toward the dining hall.

"I'm out of Gryphon's class till end of term," Han said.
"That's just another week. She'll get me back in for spring."

Dancer nodded. "Could be worse."

It *is* worse, Han thought. His head ached and swirled with
worry.

"If you slept at Hampton, I could make sure you got up,"
Dancer offered.

"It an't your job to nanny me," Han growled. He felt as fragile as a pane of glass, shattered into shards that no longer fit
together.

"I'm your friend," Dancer said, matching Han's longer strides.
"It's my job to help you if I can. Like you would help me."

Han sighed. "I'm sorry. You're right. Thank you. Maybe we
can try that after winter break."

Cat was waiting for them in front of the dining hall. Two or
three times a week, at least, Han ate lunch with Cat and Dancer.
At first he'd felt like a referee, deflecting Cat's digs and insults.
But that died down as Cat realized that slinging slurs at Dancer
was unsatisfying. They just slid off him.

Cat seemed to be thriving. She'd stopped displaying her
knives on the outside of her tunic, though Han knew she still had
some hidden away. Her eyes were clear of turtleweed and razorleaf and the effects of too much drink.

I'm glad we convinced her to come here, Han thought. Whatever else happens, that's one thing I did right.

Just now, Cat was all crinkle-faced, as if she had a secret she was bursting to tell, or a question she was dying to ask, but couldn't decide how to spring it. They carried their plates over and sat at their usual table by the window.

Han didn't have the energy to pry it out of her, so he ate his meal in silence, rubbing his forehead with the heel of his hand.

And Dancer wouldn't ask. He pretended not to notice, though there wasn't much he didn't notice about Cat. Instead, he launched into a long description of the talisman he was making with Master Firesmith, something that would protect a dwelling from flame.

Cat rolled her eyes and looked at Han, as if hoping to change the subject. "What's wrong with you?"

"I've been booted from Gryphon's class for the rest of the term," Han said.

"That's *it*?" Cat squinted at Han, as if she didn't believe him.

Han shrugged. "That's why I'm here. To learn wizardry."

"I thought maybe your blueblood girlie broke your heart," Cat said, smirking.

This caught Han's attention. He looked up at Cat. "What blueblood girlie?"

"Well, I *knew* you was walking out with someone, because you're out nearly every night, leaving me with this copperhead all the time." She jerked her head toward Dancer. "Last night, I finally figured out who it was."

"Who?" Han asked, mystified. He glanced at Dancer, who looked just as puzzled.

"Rebecca," Cat said triumphantly.

"Rebecca who?"

Cat gave him a "This is me, remember?" kind of look. "Rebecca Morley, you snake. I saw her outside the Temple School last night."

"She's here? In Oden's Ford?" Han stared at her. His heart thudded against his ribs so loud it seemed like the other two would hear it.

"Well, that's where the Temple School is, an't it?" Cat drew her brows together. "You an't been seeing her?"

Han shook his head. "No. I didn't even know she was here."

"Oh." Cat grimaced and dug into her potatoes, as if that were the end of that.

Han's mind raced. He thought he'd seen Rebecca outside of the stables, the day they'd arrived at Oden's Ford. He'd dismissed it because it didn't make sense.

"You're sure it was her?"

Cat nodded, chewing.

"Why was she there?" Han asked. "Is she going to the Temple School?" It was possible, though he would've thought she'd go to Southbridge or the Cathedral School back home.

Cat shook her head. "She was wearing a dirtback uniform."

"She's at Wien House? That's not likely." Though she could be fierce, Rebecca was small and lightweight. Not really soldier material.

"I can't help that," Cat said, scowling. "That's what she wore."

"What was she doing at the Temple School?" Han asked.

Cat shifted in her seat. "Well, glad I cheered you up, anyways," she said. "You don't look so hangdog as before."

"Cat."

"She was . . . she was spying on that Corporal Byrne."

Corporal Byrne was here too? "She was *spying* on him. What was he doing?"

Cat gave up. "Corporal Byrne has been walking out with Annamaya. You met her, remember? At the Temple School? He's been coming by regular, twice a week. They never do anything but hold hands, all formal-like." She rolled her eyes as if to say, What's the point?

"So I'm coming up the walk to the dormitory, and I see somebody crawling behind the shrubbery, peering in the parlor window. I look through the window and see Corporal Byrne sitting with Annamaya. And the girlie was Rebecca, spying on them."

"The Corporal Byrne from Southbridge, right?"

"That's the only one I know."

Han couldn't picture *that* Corporal Byrne cheating on Rebecca. Or keeping two girlies on the line.

"Did you say anything to her?"

"Annamaya?"

"Rebecca."

"Just asked what she was doing there. And like that." Cat didn't meet Han's eyes.

"Well?" Han said impatiently. "What did she say?"

"Said she was going to school here."

"Did you say anything about me?" he asked.

Cat scowled at him. "Why would I say anything about you? You think the whole world's sniffing your butt?"

Han threw a black look at Dancer, who was grinning.

"I thought maybe she was cheating on you with Corporal Byrne, and that's why she was spying on him cheating on her," Cat went on. "She run away before I could ask."

"Why would she run away?" Han asked. Cat could talk an awful lot without ever telling you what you needed to know.

"How should I know?" She paused, then added reluctantly, "Well. I did have my knife out."

Han and Dancer looked at each other.

"Your *knife*?" Dancer said, furrowing his brow.

"Well, I saw her sneaking around, and I didn't recognize her at first, and I didn't know what she was up to, and then I kind of forgot I had it out."

"I can see how that could happen," Han said dryly.

"I talked to Annamaya about it, and she says her and Corporal Byrne are going to get married. Only not for a long time. Me, I think if you're going to get married, you might as well get it over with."

Han cleared his throat. "Do you know where she's staying? Rebecca, I mean."

"I don't know. You might try Grindell Hall. Across the river. That's where Corporal Byrne stays."

CHAPTER TWENTY-THREE
A MEETING OF EXILES

Raisa found out that there was a downside to having friends—they were always trying to cheer you up when all you wanted to do was feel sorry for yourself.

The weeks after Raisa followed Amon to his rendezvous were a painful blur, and then the end-of-term exams began. Raisa was too busy to mope, and Hallie and Talia were too busy to notice. But as the Gray Wolves finished their exams, it freed up time for moping. And noticing. The end-of-term parties began, which would culminate in the solstice celebration.

Raisa wasn't sure what Hallie and Talia had told the other Wolves, but conversations often stopped when she came into a room. Each tried to help in his or her own way. Garret offered to share the flask of whiskey he kept under a floorboard, and Mick tried to give her a clanwork saddlebag Raisa had long admired.

Now Raisa was the one who stayed away from Grindell Hall

as much as possible. When Amon was in the dormitory she would keep to her room. When they had to be together, she was polite and cooperative and calm.

She wasn't angry at him, but she couldn't abide the bleak and guilty expression on his face, as if he wanted to say something, but couldn't find the words. Or the significant looks exchanged among the others.

She might feel sorry for herself, but she didn't want to be pitied.

Once, when the others were out, Amon tapped on the door of her room. "Rai," he said. "I can't stand this. Come out and talk to me."

"I can't right now," she said, keeping her voice steady and light. "I'm studying."

"Rai," he said again, and she knew he was resting his forehead against the door. "Please. You're my best friend."

"And you're mine. But I just can't do this right now, all right?" A sob somehow lodged in her throat, and she couldn't speak, so she sat, fists clenched, breathing deeply, until he went away.

Early solstice eve, the common room was filled with talk of plans for the parties that would be going on that evening, culminating in fireworks. Amon, it seemed, would be watching from the Temple close with Annamaya. He puttered about in the next room, pretending not to listen as the others tried to talk Raisa into going out.

"Come with us," Talia urged. "Pearlie is meeting us over on Bridge Street. We'll have dinner and stake out a good place to watch the fireworks."

"You've been working like a slave all term," Hallie added. "I'm leaving for home tomorrow, so it'll be our only chance to go out together."

Hallie was the only Gray Wolf who would be traveling home during the solstice break. Although the travel there and back would take longer than the visit, for her it was worth it to spend the holidays with her daughter.

Raisa waited until Talia went to the washroom, then pulled Hallie aside. "Hallie, would you be willing to carry a letter back to the Fells to my mother?" she said quietly. "I've got it mostly written, and I can finish it up and put it on your bed to take with you."

"Well, a'course," Hallie said. "But how will I find her? Where does she stay?"

"Lord Averill is friends with her," Raisa said. "If you take it to him, he'll make sure she gets it. And if there's an answer, you can carry it back to me." Raisa paused. "But make sure you put it right into his hands. No one else's. All right?"

"I got it," Hallie said, nodding.

"And please don't mention it to anyone else," Raisa said. Especially Amon Byrne, she thought.

Hallie shrugged. "If that's the way you want it. Now, what about dinner? I know you're not one to go to taverns, but it's a holiday, after all."

Raisa shook her head. "Thank you for asking, but I'm going to eat in the dining hall, do some reading, then go to bed early." She yawned extravagantly. "If I'm still awake at midnight I'll walk out into the quad and watch from there."

"We'll stay, then, and have dinner with you here," Talia said.

"We can keep you company. Maybe you'll change your mind about the fireworks."

"No," Raisa snapped. "I am *fine*. Please don't ruin your plans because of me."

She looked up. Amon stood in the doorway, his gray eyes shadow-dark with pain.

And so they left, with many backward looks, but no more attempts to sway her.

Raisa walked over to the nearly empty dining hall. For once there was plenty of meat, and also spun sugar cakes and solstice cookies, iced to look like little suns. She walked back to Grindell and recopied her letter to Queen Marianna. After leaving it on Hallie's bed, she spread her books out on the table in the common room and opened *A Brief History of Warfare in the Seven Realms*. Despite the title, it was eight hundred pages long. Good thing she didn't have to read the long version.

She'd no doubt have Tourant again the next term for recitation in History of Warfare II. Assuming she managed to pass part one. It seemed impossible that she should fail a subject that she found so fascinating. She wished Master Askell administered the exams instead of Tourant.

Raisa opened her book and soon lost herself in reading. Several of the chapters on the use of magic in warfare referenced Hanalea, who had used a three-pronged approach after the Breaking to fight off pirates, bandits, and invasion from the south. The warrior queen had been an innovator, a risk taker. Her legacy endured to this day.

What kind of legacy would she, Raisa, leave? One of grief and disappointment?

Raisa sat back, rubbing her eyes. The dormitory was as quiet as a tomb. Outside, the temple bells bonged out the hour. Nine o'clock.

Suddenly, she couldn't bear the notion of sitting alone in her room on this most festive of nights—a night without curfews. We're welcoming a new year, she thought. A time for new opportunities. Maybe a night to take a chance.

It wouldn't hurt to get some air, she decided, yanking her cloak from the peg on the wall.

Once out the door, Raisa turned toward the river. She could hear the music from Bridge Street, where the fireworks would begin in a few hours. Would it be so risky to go just this once? She could find Talia and Hallie and raise a glass, at least. It had been so long since she'd seen fireworks. It was a shame not to spend Hallie's last night with her.

As she walked toward the river, she couldn't shake the twitchy feeling that someone was watching her. But when she turned around, she saw no one. There were lots of people in the streets, more and more as she neared the river.

There were evergreen boughs tied around lampposts and lanterns hung along the streets to guide the light back into the Seven Realms. The temples were brightly illuminated, festooned with glitternet and candles to drive off the dark. Within, the speakers and the temple choirs sang hymns to the Maker and drank from wassail bowls, just like at home. Raisa's spirits lifted a little.

As she threaded her way through the narrow, stone-paved streets of the old town, gray wolves loped along on either side of her, yipping and whining as if trying to get her attention.

She stopped, looked around. Saw nothing. Tried to settle her galloping heart.

Wolves sometimes meant a turning point. Maybe this solstice night signified new opportunities.

Your days of playing games are over, she told herself, trying not to think of Amon. She couldn't marry—or even *be* with—Amon Byrne. That path was closed to her. What other path could she take?

She could marry outside of the Fells. Tamron's Liam Tomlin had made it plain he was interested—but to what purpose she didn't know. Liam might be the best marriage option from a political standpoint, but she needed more information to know for sure.

It didn't hurt that Liam was younger and handsomer and more appealing than any other princeling she was likely to be matched with. She didn't love him, but he was infinitely preferable to Gerard Montaigne, who sent shivers down her back.

She could do as her mother intended and marry Micah Bayar, which would precipitate a cascade of consequences, possibly including war with the clans. But she was stronger than her mother, more obstinate. The magical tethers put in place by the speakers might protect her. A union between the Gray Wolf line and the Wizard Council would be potent. The guard and the army would remain loyal to the queen. Probably.

She could marry clan royalty, as her mother had. That would please the clans and infuriate the Wizard Council. It would reinforce the third leg of Gray Wolf power. Reid Demonai was a possibility, and there were likely candidates at some of the other camps.

Hanalea hadn't married for love. No one ever heard anything about the consort she'd married after the Breaking. She'd focused on saving her queendom. It was an example to follow.

Raisa was in such a fog of strategizing that she nearly ran smack into a brick wall. She looked around, realizing that the music had faded. She'd strayed into a labyrinth of brick alleys. She turned back the way she'd come, and found someone blocking her way.

"Well, look who's wandering about alone on solstice eve," he said. "No one to walk out with on the holiday?"

It was Henri Tourant, staggering drunk and stinking of ale, dressed in his usual garish fashion.

Raisa froze for a long moment, debating strategy. Finally, she nodded at him and said, "Proficient Tourant, happy New Year. May the sun come again." She tried to brush past him to the street.

But he grabbed her arm, yanked her back toward him, and shoved her up against the wall, his arm pressed against her throat.

"Let me go!" Raisa tried to shout it, but the pressure against her windpipe made it difficult to generate much volume.

The alleyway swam with gray wolves, ruffs bristling at their necks. Their howls reverberated against the walls to either side.

"Perhaps you'd like to walk out with me," Tourant slurred. "I am . . . available."

Raisa pried at his arm with both hands. "Let go, I said."

"You need to learn to keep your opinions to yourself," he said. "You got me in trouble with Master Askell, and now I'm not teaching next term."

"Perhaps," Raisa gasped, made reckless by fury, "it could be a time for reflection on what a cretin you are."

It was not the smartest move. Tourant's arm pressed harder against her throat, as if to cut off the breath that powered those opinions. Her head began to spin.

What was it Amon always said? *If someone grabs you in the street, hit hard and fast, because you may not get a second chance.*

Bracing herself against the brick, she brought her boot heel down with all her weight on one of Tourant's ridiculous velvet slippers. Bones cracked.

He howled in pain, releasing his hold enough so that she could drag in a breath. Then he slammed her head against the wall. She saw stars.

"I despise northern women," he said, giving her a shake. "You're harlots and whores, all of you. I'm going to show you how we treat harlots in the south."

And he smashed his face against hers in a drunken kiss, using his body to hold her upright against the wall.

He pressed his hands to either side of her face, holding it steady. She gripped the pinky finger on his right hand and snapped it back, breaking it. He screeched and staggered backward, cradling his injured hand, and she slammed her foot into his kneecap. Now he crumpled to the pavers, rolling back and forth and baying in pain.

Raisa knew she was lucky that drink had slowed Tourant's reactions; she knew she should just run away, but she couldn't help herself. All the anger and frustration of the past weeks came due. She drew her knife and pressed it into Tourant's throat.

"When they told you about northern women, did they mention that they carry knives?" she said.

Tourant shook his head. Carefully. "No," he whispered.

"You touch me again, you arrogant Ardenine swine, and I swear on the blood of Hanalea the warrior, I will *geld* you. Do you understand?"

Tourant nodded violently, sweat beading on his forehead. Raisa backed away from him, turned, and ran down the alley toward the street.

Someone was standing in the entry of the alleyway, a tall figure silhouetted against the streetlights. Raisa's heart sank. Was this one of Tourant's Ardenine cronies, come to pitch in?

"Get out of my way," she warned, striding forward, "or you'll get the same treatment as him."

"Including the gelding?" he said in Fellsian. "I've heard of thieves dropping a glove, but that's severe."

Fear turned to confusion. He was Fellsian. Not Ardenine. "Dropping a glove?"

He made a chopping motion at his wrist. "The queen's peculiar justice. Makes it hard for a thief to earn a living any other way."

Recognition shivered over her. She squinted into the darkness. "Who are you?"

"Me, I'd never cross a northern girlie. I know all about the knives." His voice was familiar, but his features were still hidden in shadow. "I meant to yank that bacon-faced dirtback off of you, Rebecca, but I guess you didn't need my help."

Her steps slowed to a stop while her heart accelerated to a pounding cadence. "Alister?" she whispered. And then, louder, "*Alister*, is that you?"

"Come out into the high street and see." He took two steps

back so the light from the lamps washed over his features.

She walked forward, out of the alley, raised her head, and looked into a pair of blue eyes she thought she'd never see again. Her heart swelled almost to bursting, and she struggled to breathe, to force air past the lump in her throat.

"Blessed Hanalea, it *is* you," she whispered, her eyes stinging with tears too sudden to prevent.

"Hello, Rebecca," Cuffs Alister said, then rushed to add, "Hey, now. Don't look so peaked. I an't a spook, if that's what you're thinking."

"But I heard you were dead," Raisa said, almost accusingly. "They found your bloody clothes on the riverbank."

Cuffs shrugged. "I needed to get the bluejackets off my back. So I faked it." He smiled, an oddly painful smile. "Guess it worked."

Resurrection seemed to suit him. He was dressed more finely than she remembered. Not extravagantly, but his clothes looked new, of good-quality fabric. They fit him well, revealing a tall, spare frame and broad shoulders under a wool cloak.

Last time Raisa had seen him, his hair had been shaggy, dyed a dirty brown, and he'd been wearing clan garb. Now his hair had been recently cut. It glittered like spun gold under the street-lights. It was like one of those old romances where the pauper swaps out his rags and becomes a prince.

His face was different, too. Last she'd seen him, he'd been bruised and battered from the beating the Queen's Guard had given him. Now she saw he had high cheekbones and a long straight nose with a little bump on it, as though it had been broken. There were shadows carved into his features that hadn't been there before, a history and an expectation of pain.

"What are you *doing* here?" Raisa asked, her bubbling questions bursting into speech.

"I go to school here. Same as you." Cuffs looked over her shoulder, into the alley. "Let's slide off now, before your friend finds his courage again." He paused, tilting his head. "Or do you want to call the provosts?"

He probably wasn't in the habit of calling on the law.

Raisa imagined that messy scene, the crowd it would draw, and shook her head.

"Then let's go." He directed her left, toward the river, with a hand between her shoulder blades. There was a buzz to his touch, a heat and a tingle, almost like . . .

"Would you like to walk up to Bridge Street?" he asked. "We could tip a cider and talk."

Raisa practically skidded to a halt. Cuffs looked down at her as if worried he'd overstepped. "I mean, unless you got other plans. It's just . . . I wanted to talk to you."

"I'd rather not go to Bridge Street," Raisa said. "After all that's happened, I don't want to be out among people."

"Well, then," he said, scraping his fingers through his hair. "I could walk you back to Grindell."

Alarm bells rang out in her head. "How do you know where I live?" she demanded.

"Well, I . . . ah . . . followed you from there to here," he said.

"You were *following* me?"

He raised both hands, looking around the crowded street as if worried about being overheard. "I'll explain. When we talk."

Raisa imagined going back to her dormitory and the prying eyes of the Gray Wolves. Not to mention the possibility of encountering Amon Byrne.

Likely no one would return there for hours. Still, there was no guarantee. "I want to talk to you too, but we can't go back to Grindell."

To Raisa's surprise, Cuffs asked no questions. "We could go to my place, and use the common room there," he suggested. "I stay at Hampton Hall, across the bridge."

"Hampton? I don't know that dormitory. Which quad is it on?"

He cleared his throat but kept his eyes fixed on her face, as if he didn't want to miss anything. "Mystwerk House."

"Mystwerk! But that's . . . the school for wizards." Her head ached from the banging against the wall. Maybe she'd misunderstood.

"A lot has happened," Cuffs said. Fishing under his cloak he pulled out a glittering jewel on a chain—a serpent carved from green translucent stone. He closed his hand over it. The stone glowed through his fingers, taking on power.

Raisa took an involuntary step back. "You're a wizard?"

He nodded, almost apologetically, and quickly tucked the amulet away again.

"But—but—how can that be?" Her voice rose, and Cuffs flapped his hands, trying to shush her. "Who sent you here?" Raisa demanded. "Did you come here to find me?"

"No," he said. "Like I said, I came here to go to school. It's . . . complicated. I'll explain, but"—he looked around again—"not in the middle of the street, all right?"

"Well, I can't go to Hampton," she blurted, undone by this revelation. "I don't want anyone at Mystwerk to see me with you."

He flinched, his expression closing tight, and she realized he'd taken it the wrong way: he thought she was ashamed to be seen with him.

"I didn't mean it that way," she said, touching his arm. "I mean—is there someplace we could go where we could talk in private?" she said. "Just the two of us?"

He raised his eyebrows, studying her face as if to read her meaning in it. "Well, I got a place in the library over on the Mystwerk quad," he said. "It's kind of hard to get to, but it's private, anyway."

"In the *library*?" That seemed safe enough. "But isn't the library closed?"

"Not to me." He smiled the wicked smile that had charmed her from the start. "But we got to trust each other. I got to trust you won't tell anybody about it. And you . . . well, you'll see."

In order to get there, they'd have to cross forbidden Bridge Street.

Maybe it's time to take a risk, she repeated to herself. She looked about, and the wolves were nowhere to be seen.

"All right," she said. "Let's go." Cuffs watched silently as she pulled her hood over her hair and wound her scarf over her face, though the rain had dwindled.

Bridge Street was filled with revelers, many drinking on the street, raising their cups to the return of the sun. Music poured from doorways, and feathered puppets cavorted in impromptu balcony performances. Raisa gazed around, wide-eyed. There was Hanalea the Warrior, all in creamy white, slaying the red-plumaged Demon King.

Cuffs took Raisa's hand and plowed through the mob, breaking trail for her. Raisa felt the hot sting of wizard power through his fingers.

This is a dream, she thought. A solstice dream. They said what you dreamed on solstice always came true.

"Hey, Alister!" someone called from a tavern porch. "Who's the girlie? Aren't you going to introduce us?"

Cuffs shook his head and kept going. And then they were off the bridge on the Mystwerk side, the second time she'd crossed the river since the day she'd arrived. Last time it had led to heartbreak. This time . . . who knew?

Ahead, Raisa could see the bulk of Mystwerk Tower, its illuminated clock showing ten of the night. Two hours until fireworks. Covered galleries connected the buildings and crisscrossed the quad, protecting students from the torrential southern rains.

At the end of the bridge Cuffs turned down a side street, then a narrower alley. Raisa's apprehension spiraled. *We got to trust each other*, he'd said. What if she'd escaped from one jam only to walk into another?

One side of the alley was a wall of rough stone. Cuffs paused long enough to tie the hem of his cloak around his hips so it wouldn't tangle his legs. He directed Raisa to do the same. Then he skinned up the side of the building like a cat, disappearing onto the roof.

"Hey!" she whispered, looking up, blinking against the mist. "What are you . . . ?"

He leaned over the edge, extending his hands. "Here. Give me your hands."

She stretched her arms up, standing on tiptoes, trying to extend her small height. Gripping her about the wrists, he yanked her into the air and set her onto the roof beside him, keeping hold of her wrists. Power rippled into her like a potent drink.

"You can let go of me now," she whispered, setting her heels and trying to pull free of his grip.

"Careful," he whispered. "It's slick from the rain." He tugged her away from the edge and released his hold. "Promise you won't fall and break your neck?"

She nodded mutely, rubbing her elbows.

He looked south, over a sea of connected roofs. "We can walk the galleries to the library, but you got to walk soft, all right?"

She followed him as he trotted confidently to a gallery roof that led to the next building. He ducked down as they crossed the gallery, so as not to be spotted from below, and she mimicked his posture. They crossed the roofline of the next building. Slate tiles rattled under their feet, and Raisa's heart pinged in her chest, but it was still windy, and no doubt that small noise was lost.

On the far side of the roof, Cuffs leaped nimbly down to the gallery roof below, amazingly soundless. He turned and opened his arms to receive her. "Jump."

She jumped, and he caught her, taking a step back, crushing her to his chest, her face mashed against his wet shoulder. Again she felt the heat of wizardry—his cloak was practically steaming, smelling of hot, damp wool. He slid his hand between them, into his neckline, and the heat subsided somewhat.

"Sorry," he said. "I still get leaky sometimes if I don't draw it off."

On hands and knees, they climbed a steep gable on the far side of the gallery. She began to slide on the wet slate, and he caught her arm to steady her. Raisa looked around when they reached the peak, trying to regain her bearings. They were atop one wing of what must have been the library.

"Down here." He leaped down into the space between two angled rooflines, where they would be hidden from view from the street. Raisa slid down the slope on her rump, landing with a splash at the bottom. By now she was soaked to the skin.

"Demon's blood," she grumbled, struggling to her feet.

A small leaded-glass window pierced the sloped roof. Cuffs forced it open. "I'll go first." He slid through the window feet-first, and she heard the soft thud of his landing. She looked through the window and saw him standing just below, looking up at her, light and rain splattering down on him. "Come ahead."

She slid over the sill, and he caught her arms, steadying her as she hit the floor.

Cuffs dug in his pocket, produced a candle, and kindled it with his fingers. He let it burn a moment, then dripped wax onto a tin plate. Sticking the candle upright in the wax, he set it on a table.

The room was lined with bookshelves, silvered with dust. The table, however, had been wiped clean. It was stacked with paper, a pot of ink and a quill, and books with markers stuck in at various places. On one wall there was a small fireplace grate with a stack of wood next to it. Blankets lay tangled in a corner, with a feather pillow on top.

He sleeps rowdy, she thought, remembering the night they'd spent in Ragmarket. It seemed too intimate a thing to know about him.

So much had happened since. It seemed a lifetime ago.

"You're right, this *is* hard to get to," she said.

"It an't so bad when it's not raining," he said. "When the library's open, I use the stairs."

"You must not have guests very often."

"You're the first."

Cuffs peeled off his cloak and hung it on a hook next to the fireplace. He ran his hands over the wool, and it sizzled dry under his touch. Then he loaded wood onto the grate and kindled it with a gesture and a word.

He's showing off, Raisa thought. Performing wizard tricks. He kept reaching into his shirt and breathing out charms. Where had he learned to do charmcasting?

Mystwerk. Of course.

Cuffs stood and turned back toward her, seeming not to know what to do next.

"Haven't we done this before?" Raisa stripped off her cloak, limp and heavy with water. "Remember? In Ragmarket. You abducted me from Southbridge Temple and dragged me through the rain."

"It seems to rain a lot wherever you are," he said.

"I was thinking it was you," she said loftily, handing him her cloak. He wrung the extra water out of it and steamed it dry with his hands. Then hung it next to his own.

It was easier, somehow, to spar with him than to let that loud silence between them build to a crescendo. It had occurred to her that if Cuffs Alister *wasn't* trustworthy, coming here had been a really boneheaded move.

Cuffs Alister was a wizard. A gang leader, a thief, a possible killer—and now a wizard. Had he shown any sign of it the last time they'd met?

The blood rushed to her face as she recalled every time he'd touched her. He'd wrapped an arm around her and pressed her up against him, his knife at her throat. He'd picked her up and carried her, searched her for weapons, gripped her hand and yanked her across South Bridge. Her skin prickled and burned at the memory, but she couldn't recall any sting of wizardry. Nothing like this.

What about the murdered street runners? They'd been burned and tortured—by demons, some said. But what if it had been done by a wizard, the head of a rival gang?

No. She refused to believe it.

Melancholy gripped her, as if Cuffs Alister had been stolen from her a second time. First he was dead. Now he was magical—and therefore untouchable. The ground had shifted again, and the door of possibilities between them had been shut.

What possibilities? You'd rather he was dead than a wizard?

"Rebecca."

Startled, Raisa looked up at Cuffs. He flipped her a coin, and she caught it reflexively. It was a five-penny piece.

"For your thoughts," he said. But he didn't smile.

"Where are we, exactly?" she asked. Shivering, she extended her hands toward the fire. This was a step up from Cuffs's lair in Ragmarket, at least.

"We're in the stacks, sixth floor, Bayar Library," Cuffs said.

"The *Bayar* library?" Raisa shivered, wrapping her hands around herself.

Cuffs tilted his head, surveying her through narrowed eyes. "It's all right. Nobody comes up here unless they're keen to read crop records from a thousand years before the Breaking."

"So," Raisa said, "this is your new hideout."

"Always got to have a crib," he said. He seemed ill at ease, almost shy. He stuffed his hands into his pockets and rocked on his heels, not meeting her eyes.

"I thought I saw you," Raisa said. "At the start of fall term. On horseback, near the stables on the Wien House side of the river."

"That was me," he admitted. "I thought that was you." He squinted at her. "Your hair is different," he said, fingering his own.

Raisa chose a book at random and pulled it from the bookcase. "I had no idea you were a wizard," she said, thumbing through it . . . something about oats and barley.

"I wasn't. Not before."

"People are born wizards," Raisa said. "I never heard of anyone turning into a wizard later on." She jammed the book back onto the shelf.

He just shrugged away the mystery. "Strange, huh? Please. Sit down." He gestured at the single chair. "Do you want tea? Might warm you up." He seemed to be working hard to be a gracious host, displaying his tattery manners.

"Tea sounds good," Raisa said. And then, unable to help herself, "How did you end up *here*?"

Color stained his cheeks. "I go to school here, like I said," he said, a little defensively.

"How can you afford it?" Raisa blurted. She was immediately sorry, thinking the question sounded arrogant and nosy.

He gazed at her for a long moment, as if debating how to answer. Then said, "I sold my wristplate. They went for a good price." He held his wrists out for inspection. The silver cuffs were gone, though the skin underneath still looked raw and unweathered.

This surprised her. The cuffs were his trademark. It seemed like he'd hang on to them.

He must be really hungry for an education, she thought.

He dug into a box in the corner and found a cup, spooned loose tea into it from a tin, heated a pitcher of water between his hands, and poured. He handed it to Raisa.

"You've learned a lot of wizardry already," Raisa said, sipping at her tea. It was a smoky, upland blend, and she felt a pang of homesickness. "I'm impressed. You must be a quick study."

Cuffs shrugged the compliment off. "I've been hard at it. It's all I got to do here. And I have a . . . a tutor. Who's helping me out." He stopped abruptly and wet his lips.

Raisa cast about for something else to say, eager to keep him talking about himself. "Listen, Cuffs. I was wondering if—"

"I don't go by that name down here," he interrupted. "Since—you know—the cuffs are gone. My actual name's Hanson Alister. Han."

A memory came back to Raisa—the scene in Father Jemson's study, Cuffs Alister with his arm tight around her waist, his knife pressed to her throat, his heart thudding wildly against her back.

393

Speaker Jemson saying, *Hanson! You're better than this! Let the girl go*.

Jemson had believed in Hanson Alister. Had his faith been misplaced?

Raisa looked up to find Cuffs/Han waiting expectantly for the question she'd begun. It had flown out of her mind as she careened between her private thoughts and public speech.

He must think I'm a real muddle head.

"D–Does the school provide your amulets, or did you have to find one on your own?" she asked.

"We bring our own," he said. "I bought mine used off a trader before I came south." It sounded like a well-rehearsed story. He made no move to display the amulet again.

Raisa knew something about magical artifacts from working with her father. They fascinated her, that marriage of magic and metal and stone crafted into a bewitching whole. Most of them were gorgeous art pieces in and of themselves.

"Could I see it again?" she asked.

"Well, if you want," he said, as if he didn't really want to show it to her but couldn't think of a reason not to. Fishing inside his neckline, he pulled it free and dangled it toward her. It spun before her eyes, glowing green and orange like a fire opal in sunlight.

It was a finely crafted gemstone serpent with ruby eyes, its coils layered over gold. The serpent's mouth was open, and it was so detailed that Raisa could see the drops of venom collected at the tips of its fangs.

"Oh!" Impulsively, she reached for it, and Han yanked it back.

"Better not touch it. It bites," he said, sheltering it with his other hand.

"What? Do you mean it . . . the snake . . . ?"

He shook his head. "It's unpredictable. It's charred a few curious fingers."

Raisa stared at the jinxpiece, teasing out a strand of memory. "I think I've seen it before. Is it a reproduction of an old piece? From before the Breaking?"

Han nodded. "So I'm told." He slid the amulet back under his shirt. Then, as if to change the subject, he said, "What are *you* doing here? If *I'm* allowed to ask a question."

That sounded more like his old self.

Raisa sneezed, swiping at her nose. The dusty room was getting to her. "Same as you. I'm going to school. I'm at Wien House."

"Wien House!" Han looked her up and down, skepticism and amusement softening his face. It made him look younger, more like the wild upstart boy she'd met at Southbridge Temple. "You going to be a bluejacket or Highlander or what?"

"Well, no. Not really." Raisa desperately tried to recall which stories she'd already told. She really needed to keep better track of her lies. "You see, my employer offered to send me here to school if I attended Wien House."

Han's face went flat and hard, his eyes like chips of sapphire. "Lord Bayar, you mean?"

Raisa practically choked on her tea. "What?"

"Why would they send their tutor to Wien House? The Temple School . . . I'd get that."

Raisa was momentarily lost. Then it came back to her. She'd

told Cuffs she worked for the Bayars that night in Ragmarket. Why did Han Cuffs Alister have to have such a damnably sharp memory?

She slid a glance at Han. He stared at her, lips tight together, and his right hand had crept to the blade at his waist. Unconsciously, she thought.

"Are you still working for the Bayars, Rebecca?" he asked, soft and even. Something in his voice made her shiver.

"Well, no, not exactly. I'm . . . ah . . . trying to better myself," Raisa said. "The commander of Lord Bayar's personal guard thought I had potential. He was the one who paid my tuition. He said if I did well, then I'd have a chance to . . ." She trailed off. Han seemed distracted, lost in memory. "Why?" she asked. "Do you know the Bayars?"

Han paused for a heartbeat, then said, "I'm in class with two of them. At Mystwerk. Micah and Fiona. Micah used to be in my dormitory."

Hanalea in chains, she thought. So they *are* here. All she needed was for Han to mention to the Bayars that he'd run into their old tutor Rebecca. Or suggest they all meet for a cider on Bridge Street.

That seemed unlikely, though. Knowing Micah and Fiona, they would treat a Ragmarket-bred wizard like dung.

"Listen," she said, leaning toward him and clasping her hands together. "Please, please don't tell them I'm here. It would be awkward, you know? They don't think of me as a peer, exactly."

He blinked at her, looking puzzled. "But you're a blueblood," he said. "You talk like them and you're—"

"I'm of mixed blood," she broke in. "My father was clan

and my mother a Vale-dweller. Perhaps you've noticed that the Bayars don't approve of clanfolk."

"Aye," he said, nodding, his confusion clearing a fraction. "I've noticed."

Hmm, Raisa thought. Maybe the key to lying well was telling the truth in a misleading way.

"Your turn," she said. "You said you followed me?"

"Well, yes. See, Cat told me she saw you. Outside of the Temple School." He cleared his throat. "She said that you might live in Grindell, because—ah—Corporal Byrne did."

"Did she, now?" Raisa pressed her lips tightly together, feeling the blood boil into her cheeks. What would Cat have told him, after seeing Raisa spying on Amon?

"So I . . . wanted to find out if it really was you. I watched outside your dormitory and saw everybody else go out."

You didn't have anything better to do on solstice eve? Raisa thought.

"Then I saw you leave alone. So I tagged after you."

"You stalked me, you mean. That was inappropriate, Alister. You're lucky I didn't break *your* finger."

He raised his eyebrows in a way that meant, *That would never happen.*

"See. I wanted to make contact with you," he said. "But I didn't know . . . if I would be welcomed. Or how things stood between you and Corporal Byrne."

"What does my friendship with Corporal Byrne have any-thing to do with you?" Raisa said icily.

"You want more tea?" Han asked, reaching for her cup as if eager to dispel the tension that crackled between them. Their

397

hands collided, and Raisa jerked her cup back, spilling what was left.

"I'm sorry," she said. "I'm clumsy tonight."

She was acutely aware that they were alone together, continually measuring the space between them. Her eyes kept straying to the snarl of blankets in the corner. What was it about Alister that got her thinking that way every time they met?

The bells in Mystwerk Tower bonged. Raisa counted. Eleven. An hour until fireworks.

Han seemed to take it as a signal to get to the meat of the matter. "Listen. Rebecca," he said. "The reason I followed you was, I got a favor to ask."

Raisa looked up in surprise to find Han looking down at his hands. Clearly, he wasn't used to asking favors of anybody. Or getting them when he did.

"Well," she said, mystified, "I'll certainly . . . What can I do for you?"

"I just wondered . . . would you be . . . Would you tutor me?"

"Tutor *you*?" She studied his face to see if he might be joking. He looked perfectly serious, but he wouldn't meet her eyes.

"I thought you already had a tutor," she said.

"Right. I do. But there's things I need to know that he doesn't cover."

"But . . . you know I don't know anything about charmcasting," she said. "I can't help you with that."

"That an't—that isn't what I want," he said, fingering his wrist where the cuff had been.

Raisa didn't know what else to say that wouldn't be insulting. Would a streetlord have much previous education? If not, he'd be struggling in his classes at Oden's Ford.

"Well . . . what do you need help with? History? Grammar or rhetoric? Languages? Arithmetic?" Raisa named off the subjects she was good at. She hoped he might want help with arithmetic. She was especially good at numbers, having spent so much time in the clan markets. "I've got some books that—"

Han waved his hand impatiently to stop her recitation. "No, I'm good on that lot. Father Jemson gave me a good start. And I get stuffed full of that in class every day."

"Then what could I possibly—"

"Rebecca." Han leaned forward. His eyes were clear and blue as deepwater ice. "I want you to teach me to pass as a blueblood."

"What?" Raisa stared at him.

"I'd pay you," he rushed on. "I have money. You could name your price. And I wouldn't take too much time away from your studies. We could meet a couple of times a week, and you could, you know, give me assignments to do on my own."

"Why would you want to pass as a blueblood?" Raisa asked. "I mean, want it enough to pay for tutoring?"

The gang lord stood and paced back and forth as if he were too agitated to stand still. "Look, I only have two friends here at the academy—one's clanborn and the other's street-raised. Dancer and me, we're misfits in Mystwerk House. The rest of the newlings—they're all cake-eaters. Bluebloods, born and raised. But that's who we'll have to deal with if we want to get anything done. They're the ones'll be running the Wizard Council once we go home. They'll be the ones calling the shots."

Han stopped pacing and leaned back against the hearth. "I

knew how to do business in Ragmarket—I made a living for my family and a dozen Raggers, too. I could outsmart any gang lord in the city. But this is different. Now I got to be able to face off with wizards. So I need to speak the language, dance the dances, pick up the right fork, and know what clothes to wear, or they'll never take me serious."

Raisa hadn't really thought about the former Cuffs Alister interacting with wizards. In Ragmarket his violent reputation had protected him. What must it be like for him, sharing a classroom with the magical nobility? They would despise him and make fun of him. They'd remind him every day of his slum origins. The faculty would condescend to him. He'd undermine himself every time he opened his mouth.

"Why do you want them to take you seriously?" she asked, thinking they'd never accept him anyway. "What is it you want to get done?"

Han gazed into the fire. "I'm tired of people dying because they were born in Ragmarket or Southbridge. I'm sick of people in power picking on the weak. I'm going to help them." He brushed at his eyes with the heels of his hands and cleared his throat.

Was he *crying*? Raisa took a step toward him, hands extended, but he turned his back to her and poked at the fire with a stick.

"You don't really need tutoring in those things, you know," Raisa said, touching Han's shoulder. "The language and manners, I mean. Here at school, you'll be mixing with all kinds of people. You're smart. You'll pick it up naturally in time."

Han shook his head. "That's too slow. Anyway, to tell the truth, bluebloods an't that eager to mix with me outside of class." He looked back at her and rolled his eyes. "I got to take advantage of being here because I don't know how long I can stay."

Why? Is it the money? she almost said. But thankfully didn't. One thing hadn't changed. Han Alister still unbalanced her, making her lose her usual nimble footing.

Is it because he's wicked? she wondered. Like Micah Bayar? Like Liam Tomlin and Reid Nightwalker? Like every other boy she'd ever found appealing?

Because he's forbidden? Like Micah? Are you like your ancestor Hanalea, whose lust for the wrong man brought down the Seven Realms?

No. She wouldn't spend her lifetime mimsy-toeing around, for fear she'd repeat the mistakes of a millennium ago. There were plenty of new mistakes to be made.

"All right," Raisa said. "If you think it would help, I'll tutor you."

He swung away from the fire and looked at her. "Really? You're serious?"

He thought I'd refuse, Raisa thought. She nodded.

Han smiled, then, a bright, charming smile that lit up the room, more dangerous than any blade.

All you ever needed was that smile, she thought. I'd have given in immediately.

Crossing the room to her, he fished eagerly into his breeches pocket, producing a purse. "How much will you—"

Raisa put up a hand. "I won't charge you for the tutoring," she said, remembering Dimitri and the concept of *gylden*. "But you'll owe me. One day I'll call in the debt."

Han stood staring at her for a long moment. "I'd rather just pay you," he said finally. "I don't know if I'll be in a way to repay favors."

"I'll take that chance," Raisa said. "What you *will* do is pay me a fivepenny every time you say 'an't' and 'I got to.' I'll be rich on that alone before the term is over."

"Hey, now," Han said, raising both hands in protest. "I an't going to—"

She stuck out her hand and wiggled her fingers. "A fivepenny, please. That's the deal. Take it or leave it."

Grumbling halfheartedly, he dug into his purse and produced another Fellsian fivepenny coin. He flipped it to her, and she stuck it in her purse.

The new fivepenny had Mellony's image graven on it. Raisa wouldn't dare ask for a crown, called a *girlie* on the street. They carried her own likeness, in profile.

"We'll need a place to meet," she said. "I don't want Micah or Fiona to see me here on the Mystwerk side."

"We can meet at your end of Bridge Street," Han suggested. He paused. "There's an upstairs room at The Turtle and Fish you can rent by the hour."

And how do you know that? Raisa wanted to ask.

"Maybe not Bridge Street," Raisa said. "The Bayars likely eat over there every night."

Han laughed. "Not at the Turtle. It's all Wien House. I'm risking my skin going in there." He paused, furrowing his brow. "You should know that. Don't you ever go out?"

"No," Raisa admitted. "I don't."

"How about Tuesdays and Thursdays?" Han said.

"Tuesdays and Thursdays, for now," Raisa agreed, wondering how she would fit that into her already taxing schedule. "In the meantime, there's a book I want you to find in the library. It's called *Fellsian Heraldry and Tradition* by Hauldron Faulk. Read as much of it as you can before Tuesday. And don't make that face. I had to read the whole thing and recite from it when I was a lot younger than you."

"Sounds riveting," Han said, scribbling the name down on a scrap of paper, just the same.

A boom rattled the windows. Light poured through the glass, turning the gloomy room bright as midday.

"The fireworks," Raisa said. "We'd better go down." She gestured at the window, too high to reach. "Do we go back the same way?"

"Let's go back up," he said. "I got—I have an idea for where we can watch the show." Han snatched up Raisa's cloak and held it while she slid into it, an awkward attempt at gallantry. Standing behind her, he gripped her around the waist and lifted her high so she could reach the window. Pulling herself up, she slithered through. He leaped, gripped the stone sill, and swung easily through the opening.

"This way," he said. He led her around the base of the bell tower to the far side, where the roof slanted down to a joining with one of the wings. He spread his cloak over the rough tiles. Bracing his feet against the flashing, Han leaned back onto the slanted roof so he was lying at a slight angle, looking up at the sky. He patted the spot next to him. "Here."

Raisa lay down beside him.

Boom! The shell exploded nearly over their heads, showering streamers of colored sparks over the greens.

"It's spectacular," Raisa said, turning her head to grin at Han.

"I thought this would work," Han said, looking pleased with himself.

The missiles rippled into the air, glittering red, purple, green, silver, and gold. Great chariots charged across the sky, pulling the sun behind them. Dragons roared overhead, breathing flame, drawing lusty cheers from the crowds down below. Fireworks were mostly clan made, and some said there was magic built in.

"Oooh," the crowd said in unison. "Aaah."

Raisa floated on a sea of homesickness. Queen Marianna presided over solstice fireworks in Fellsmarch, the shells exploding over Hanalea and Lissa and all the other mountains. They'd go to temple by candlelight, and thank the Lady for the sun's return.

May the sun come again, Mother, she thought, and meant it.

"What did you like best about solstice at home?" she asked, looking over at Han.

"The food," he said, without hesitation.

"What kind of food?" Raisa asked, recalling the groaning tables in the palace.

"Enough to fill you up," he said simply. Pillowing his head on one arm, he reached down and took her hand.

You're a bold one, she thought, but didn't pull away.

"Before the war got bad," he continued, "there was always plenty of food around at solstice. The temples had extra, and some of the rich houses gave out leftovers from their feast days. Since the war, there hasn't been plenty, but still more than usual, anyway.

"The markets had toys and candy, fried honey cakes and spun-glass stars you never saw any other time of year. My sister, Mari, loved those honey cakes and sugar suns. I could've snabbled a whole bakery cart, and she'd still want more. She'd get powdered sugar all over her face."

He sighed and fell silent, lost in his own thoughts.

"I miss the snow," Raisa said, wiping cold mist off her face with the sleeve of her cloak. "It made the city look like a fairyland." Her family would ride through the streets in a horse-drawn sleigh, wrapped snug in furs, bells jingling.

"And the river didn't stink as bad, once it was frozen over," Han said.

She laughed. "You're right." Even in their different lives, they'd shared the stinking river.

"We'd sneak out at night and slide down Quarry Street Hill on dustbin lids until the bluejackets chased us off," he went on. "Sometimes bluebloods came down the way in big sleighs. We'd catch a ride, standing on the runners in back until the footmen clubbed us off."

Raisa's breath caught. "They *clubbed* you?"

"Well." He looked sideways at her. "If you were any good, they'd miss."

A succession of quick explosions drew their attention skyward. It was the climax of the show, a symphony of sound and light. Then it was over, leaving brilliant images on the insides of Raisa's eyelids and a ringing in her ears.

She could feel Han shifting position on the roof beside her, moving closer. She just lay there, unwilling to move. Wishing she could just stay up there, avoiding the turmoil of her life below.

Finally she opened her eyes to find him propped up on his elbow again, looking down at her, indecision in his eyes. Looking at her lips, to be specific.

He wants to kiss me, she realized. But he's thinking about what happened earlier with Tourant, and he doesn't want to press it.

"Thank you," she said, pushing upright, and the moment passed. "My solstice eve turned out better than I hoped. But I'd better get back."

He stood and helped her up, steadying her on the slippery tiles. "I'll walk you back and make sure you get in all right."

Before tonight she would have refused the offer. Despite Micah's presence, Oden's Ford had seemed safe, sequestered from the real world. She'd been wrong.

They walked back across the still-crowded bridge, lost in their own thoughts. All the way back, she second-guessed her decision to tutor Han Alister. Was it frustration over Amon that had made her say yes? A desire to do something she knew he wouldn't approve of? First the letter to Queen Marianna. Now this.

Wouldn't it be better to keep her distance from anyone attached to the Fells? Wouldn't it be better to keep her distance from someone who made her heart race and her tongue tangle up? From someone who made her want to forget the rules?

Was there anyone in all of the Seven Realms who had more counts against him? Anyone who would be less acceptable to every faction in the Fells than Han Alister?

Well. It wasn't like she meant to marry him.

At the edge of the Wien House quad, she paused. "I'm all right now," she said, pointing. "My dormitory is right over there."

"Worried Corporal Byrne will see us?" Han said, tilting his head toward Grindell.

Which was exactly what she was worried about.

"Why would you think I'd be worried about that?" she snapped.

"Just a guess."

"You seem to think that there's some kind of—of thing between us," she said. "I don't know what Cat told you, but whatever it is, it's not true."

"Well," he said, rubbing his chin, "there's definitely a *thing*. I'm just not sure what kind of *thing* it is."

She huffed out a breath to show him what she thought of that. "Thank you, Newling Alister, for the tea and the fireworks," she said, inclining her head. "I had a wonderful time. Now, if you will excuse me." She strode across the quad toward Grindell, head held high. When she was nearly there, he called after her in a carrying voice, "See you tomorrow night, Newling Morley!"

She swung around. "What?"

"Tomorrow is Tuesday," he said, bowing at the waist. Then he turned and disappeared into the night.

Raisa stood looking after him, a dozen sarcastic responses crowding forward, then dying on her lips.

CHAPTER TWENTY-FOUR
NEWS FROM HOME

When Raisa splashed up the steps to Grindell Hall and opened the heavy front door, a single light burned in the common room, leaving the corners in shadow. Amon Byrne sat bolt upright at the library table, an unopened book in front of him. When he saw it was Raisa, he sagged a little, looking relieved.

"Finally," he said. "Where have you been? I sent Mick and Talia out looking for you. I was afraid something had happened."

"I was watching the fireworks," she said. "I came straight back."

"Fireworks? I thought you were staying in." Amon rubbed his forehead with the heel of his hand.

"I changed my mind," Raisa said. She shed her cloak and hung it by the fire.

Amon looked up at the clock on the mantel. "The fireworks ended an hour ago," he said. "It took you this long to get back?"

"Why are *you* home already?" Raisa said, annoyed. For the

shortest day of the year, this had been one of the longest nights of her life, and it wasn't over yet. "Did you and Annamaya have a fight or what?"

"Rai," Amon said. "Don't."

"Well, you're interrogating *me*." Guilt always made her short-tempered. Images of Amon and Han reverberated in her aching head.

He sighed. "We had dinner, but I decided not to stay for the fireworks. We were both tired." And he did look tired. And sad. Raisa felt immediate remorse.

"There's no curfew tonight, you know," she said more gently. "There were still lots of people on Bridge Street when I walked back."

"Bridge Street?" Amon's eyes narrowed. "Is that where you were?"

She was too tired to lie, or even give the long version. "I decided to go look for Hallie and Talia. Henri Tourant attacked me in an alley on the way. He thought I needed to be taught a lesson."

"What?" Amon erupted from his chair and took hold of her elbows, looking into her face. He had gone white to the lips, so his gray eyes looked nearly black. "I *knew* something had happened. That's why I left after dinner, to look for you. But then it seemed . . . Are you all right? What did he . . . Are you . . . ?"

"I'm fine," Raisa said quickly, to put a stop to the tumble of words. "Just a few bruises and a bump on the head is all. Thanks to you, for teaching me street fighting. I guess he never expected it from me."

Amon held her out at arm's length, looking her up and down

for damage. "Did you call the provosts? Is he in gaol? *Why didn't you send for me, Rai?*" His voice nearly broke on the last sentence. "I know it's been awkward lately, but you have to know I . . ."

Raisa shook her head. "I didn't want to draw the attention," she said. "Besides, I think he's learned his lesson."

Amon still looked stricken, as if all his worst fears had come to pass. "That's it. You can't walk around unescorted, not anymore."

"Listen to me," Raisa said, thrusting her chin forward. "This could have happened to any female who damaged Henri Tourant's pride. It's not about who I am. An escort is not the answer. How would we explain that to the Gray Wolves, let alone all the other students?"

They glared at each other for a long moment.

"I'll talk to Master Askell," Amon said finally. "He'll deal with Tourant. Askell won't put up with this." Gently, he ran his fingertips over the back of her head, locating the swelling where she'd hit the brick wall. "How do you feel?"

"All right. Good thing I have a hard head."

"So after all this happened, you just went on to the fireworks?" Amon raised an eyebrow.

"Then Cuffs Alister showed up."

Amon pressed his fingers into his temples again. "I'm dreaming, right? I fell asleep and this is a nightmare." He went back to the table and sat.

"Alister faked his own murder to get the Queen's Guard off his trail," Raisa said, dropping into the chair opposite Amon's. "Remember when I thought I saw him over by the stables? That *was* him." It gave her some satisfaction to say this, after

Amon had persuaded her she'd been mistaken. "He's a student at Mystwerk House."

Amon planted both hands on the table. "Mystwerk? But . . . what's he—"

"Cuffs Alister is a wizard," Raisa said. "And he's not Cuffs anymore. He sold his silver bracelets to pay for school, so now he goes by Han."

Amon sat thinking, his brow furrowed. "That can't be right. People don't just turn into wizards. He must have been one all along." He looked up at her. "Why would a wizard live in Ragmarket?"

Raisa shrugged. "I never saw any sign of wizardry before. And I never felt power leaking through his hands until tonight."

At this, Amon's head came up sharply. "He was . . . *touching* you?"

If you expect an explanation of that, you're going to be disappointed, Raisa thought. "We watched the fireworks together, and then he walked me back."

"Your Highness, forgive me, but are you *out of your mind*?" Amon's weariness fell away, replaced by agitation. He rose and paced back and forth. "That is the most boneheaded idea you've—"

"What did you expect me to do? Club him on the head and throw him in the river? He knows me as Rebecca Morley, the name I'm using here. What do you think would arouse the most suspicion? Running away or continuing to be who I'm already pretending to be?"

"You didn't have to go watch fireworks with him. Or—or let him *fondle* you."

411

"Fondle?" Raisa raised her eyebrows. "When did I mention fondling?"

Amon stopped pacing and swung around. "Are you doing this to get back at me because of Annamaya? Because, if so, you're—"

"You think this is all about you?" Raisa shook her head. "On the contrary, I hope you and Annamaya will be very . . . *happy*!" It would have been much more convincing had she been able to keep her voice from trembling.

Someone cleared her throat on the stairs, making them both jump. Raisa looked up. Hallie was standing at the top of the stairs in her nightclothes. "Sorry to intrude," she said, "but you two are terrible loud, and I'm trying to sleep because I have to leave in a couple of hours."

"Sorry," Raisa said, her face burning. "I'll be up to bed in a minute."

They both stood and watched until Hallie had disappeared again.

"You know Alister's up to something," Amon muttered, poking viciously at the fire. "He must be. Maybe he followed us here."

"Why would he follow us here and then hide out for four months?" Raisa asked irritably. "Anyway, why would he follow us here at all?"

He followed you tonight, an annoying voice said inside her head. *He came looking for you.*

"I don't know," Amon said. "All I'm saying is that things are getting more and more tangled, and somebody's going to pull a thread, and the whole thing will unravel." He sat down on the edge of the hearth and put his face in his hands.

All the anger whooshed out of Raisa as if somebody had pricked the bubble of her indignation, leaving only pain behind.

Raisa sat down next to him, put her hand on his knee, rested her head on his shoulder. "Amon, I'm sorry. I am so, so sorry. I'm trying to be gracious about all of this, I really am. I'm just not very good at it. It would be easier if we didn't have to be together all the time. And if we didn't have all this trouble hanging over our heads."

She shivered. The fire had died down and the room had gone chilly. She just wanted to crawl into a warm bed and sleep.

"You should get out of those wet clothes," Amon said abruptly, as if his mind had been chasing down its own path. "But . . . I wanted to tell you—there's news from the Fells."

"Oh!" Raisa said, jolted awake. That explained Amon's distraction. It was the first news they'd had since their arrival four months ago.

"I got a letter from my da," Amon said. "It's two months old, sent by ship from Chalk Cliffs, which I guess he thought was safer than sending it overland." He smiled faintly at her eager expression. Fishing under his uniform tunic, he withdrew a creased letter, stamped with a plain wax stamp, not the sword-and-wolf insignia of the Captain of the Queen's Guard. The seal had been broken.

"He was afraid it might fall into the wrong hands," Amon said.

Like his liege queen's hands, Raisa thought guiltily.

Amon extended the letter toward her. "Read it, and you'll see why I was worried. Then we'd both better get to bed."

Raisa took the letter from Amon's hand. She unfolded it, recognizing Captain Edon Byrne's small, precise script.

Son,

May this find you and your fellow cadets well and safe. I hope you've limited your time on Bridge Street and have applied yourself to your studies so as to reflect well on our family name.

I received your message about the Waterwalkers. I am doing everything in my power to resolve that situation. Lieutenant Gillen has been recalled to Fellsmarch. Corporal Sloat was killed in a skirmish near the West Wall. I have handpicked Gillen's replacement. The Briar Rose Ministry has allocated funds to buy foodstuffs for the Fens as well as Ragmarket and Southbridge. So relations with the Fens have improved, though, as you can imagine, they are still strained.

It has been a difficult season here in the capital. Her Majesty is under extreme pressure from the Wizard Council and others among the nobility, given the continuing absence of the Princess Raisa and speculation as to her whereabouts.

Relations between HM and the High Wizard have suffered. The High Wizard suggests that by departing the Fells against the queen's express wishes, the princess heir has forfeited her claim to the Gray Wolf throne. He also speculates that Princess Raisa may be dead or under control of a foreign power. Lord Bayar argues that confusion regarding the succession puts the Fells at risk. He favors naming the Princess Mellony as princess heir until and unless the Princess Raisa returns to the Fells to claim her birthright.

Raisa looked up at Amon, aghast. "Mellony as princess heir? Why would they . . . ?"

Amon tapped the letter with his forefinger, shifting so his hip pressed up against hers. "Keep reading," he said.

It may be that this is merely a threat intended to reach the true heir's ears and bring her back to court. Certainly, the High Wizard and other members of the Wizard Council aligned with him have made no secret of these opinions. The clans have been equally vocal in opposition to any change in the succession. Averill Demonai, the royal consort and father of both princesses, has made their position clear. The nobility are split on the issue of the succession. The tension at court is palpable.

This public debate has resulted in an unexpected effect. When word spread that Princess Raisa might be set aside as heir, riots erupted throughout Ragmarket and Southbridge. Because of the Briar Rose Ministry, the princess enjoys great support among the common people in the capital, who see her as their champion. The High Wizard, these days, is the object of widespread suspicion and disdain. He cannot go abroad in the streets without an armed escort.

Ha! Raisa thought. Serves him right. Still, she had no illusions that slumdwellers could prevail against Gavan Bayar.

Funds have continued to flow to the Briar Rose Ministry despite the princess's absence.

Raisa looked up again. "Who is sending money to Southbridge Temple, do you think?" Raisa asked.

Amon shrugged. "I don't know. Could be ordinary citizens, some among the nobility, and maybe your father."

That made sense. Averill was one of the few people besides Speaker Jemson who knew how her ministry had been funded in the past.

She turned back to the letter.

The clans have threatened to cut off trade to the other six realms if the princess is set aside. They may not be able to control trade by sea, but certainly the loss of trade routes to Arden, Tamron, and the other realms would significantly reduce the flow of taxes that support the royal treasury. They have also restricted the flow of amulets and other magical devices to wizards in the queendom. The Wizard Council complains bitterly about this, suggesting that these actions by the clans threaten the security of the realm. Relations between the Wizard Council and the clans are at a low ebb.

Thus far, HM the Queen has resisted making any changes in the succession. She is spending more time with the speakers in the temple, and this seems to be a source of strength for her. So you could say that matters are at an impasse and therefore as stable as they can be. However, it seems clear that there are persons in the queendom whose agendas might be advanced by the Princess Raisa's death or permanent disappearance. It seemed they view Princess Mellony as a more tractable heir.

Raisa looked up at Amon. He poked at the fire, a muscle working in his jaw. That explained the search party, his relief at her return, and his suspicions about Han Alister.

She read on.

I apologize for sharing such unsettling news in a letter. I know you will use your good judgment about how much of this to share with your fellow cadets. I would caution all of you against acting on impulse. If after reading this you are moved to return immediately to the Fells, I must strongly advise against it. Stay where you are, study hard, keep a watchful eye, and prepare yourself for the challenging tasks that lie ahead of you. I will send word if you are needed here at home.

And let us pray that the princess heir, wherever she is, remains under the Maker's care until she can safely rejoin the queen her mother.

Best, Your Father

It was unsigned beyond that.

Raisa stared down at the letter. Her eyes filled with tears, blurring the letters on the page. All of this had flowed from her decision to flee the Fells. It seemed rash and cowardly in retrospect. Now Queen Marianna was on her own, except for Captain Byrne and the help Averill could provide. Help Marianna might not be willing to accept.

Raisa had been bemoaning her love life, learning history and playing at war, relishing the independence of being anonymous Rebecca Morley. Meanwhile, her mother and her father and Edon Byrne had been struggling to hold the queendom together.

And now she might be at risk of losing her throne.

"This is all my fault," she said, taking a deep, shuddering breath.

"Raisa. Come on. It's not," Amon said, patting her back awkwardly.

"Yes it *is*," Raisa said, like a small child who won't be comforted. "I've made a mess of things. I should have stayed."

Shaking off his hand, she stood, staring down at him. "We *should* go home," she said. "I should never have left my mother alone."

"She is the queen, Rai," Amon said softly. "Not you. And we all agreed that you couldn't risk staying and being married off to Micah."

"I could have handled Micah," Raisa said. "Maybe it wouldn't have been so bad."

"He may be young, but he's powerful," Amon said. "And even if you managed Micah, could you have handled Lord Bayar and the rest of the Wizard Council?"

"I'll have to manage them sooner or later," Raisa said. "I may as well start now."

"When you're sixteen?" Amon raised an eyebrow.

"Some of the Gray Wolf queens were even younger when they were crowned."

"But you're not queen," Amon pointed out. "Your mother is queen, and she's made some bad decisions."

"She's still the queen," Raisa said sharply. And then, sighing, "I'm sorry. I just can't help defending her. She hasn't given in, don't you see? It's been five months since I left, and she's held firm. I should go back and relieve her."

"The letter is two months old," Amon pointed out. "Who knows what the situation is now? Da said stay away, that it's too dangerous to come home. I believe him."

"The letter is two months old," Raisa repeated. "Maybe things are different." Hah, Raisa thought. Rightly or wrongly, we just can't help defending our parents.

"What about the clans?" Amon persisted. "They'd never put up with your marrying a wizard. They'd go to war over it. The Demonai would kill Micah rather than let it stand."

There he was probably right. Raisa massaged her aching neck. How could she return home and protect her rights to the succession yet avoid a forced marriage?

Hopefully Hallie would bring an answer back from Marianna.

She looked up at Amon, who watched her as if to divine what she might do next.

"If you insist on going," Amon said, "we're all coming with you."

"I'll think about it," Raisa said, handing the letter back to Amon. He dropped it into the flames, where it shriveled and smoked into ash.

CHAPTER TWENTY-FIVE

BLUEBLOOD WAYS

"How do I look?" Han asked, turning around in his new clothes. The tailor had measured true—his jacket and breeches fit like a second skin. The hard part had been escaping the tailor.

Dancer looked up from his book. When they'd returned from supper he'd parked himself in a comfortable chair with one of Firesmith's nasty old books. "Stunning," he said. "What's the occasion?"

"I'm going to see a girlie."

"I've never seen you dress like that to walk out with a girl," Dancer said. He raised an eyebrow. "You're not getting married, are you?"

Han shook his head. "I'm taking blueblood lessons from that girlie I told you about. Rebecca Morley."

"Hmmm. Well, you have the look down. Only, tilt back your head and look down your nose." Han complied. "That's it. Perfect. You're a natural."

"Must be my Waterlow bloodline."

Dancer's blue eyes glinted with amusement. "Now say, 'Copperheads are little more than leeches on the body of society—a necessary evil.'"

Han laughed. "I don't think I can manage. Guess I'm not cut out for this."

Dancer shrugged. "How long will this class take? Cat's in another recital tonight, over at the Temple School. I'm going over. Want to come?"

Han shook his head. "Can't. I've been jammed with work." He held up his copy of Faulk's *Heraldry*—a doorstop of a book. How many masters did he have: Crow, Abelard, and now Rebecca? And the new term hadn't even begun.

Dancer marked his place with a finger and sighed. He watched Han for a few minutes, then said, "I'm worried about Cat."

"What? Why?" Han tried to recall the last time he'd seen her. It had been a while. It was almost like she was avoiding him. Or maybe it was just that he was never around.

"It seemed like she really liked it here, was getting on at the Temple School and all," Dancer said. "But all of a sudden she seems unhappy again. I wondered if she'd said anything to you."

"No," Han said. "Do you think her marks came in low?"

He and Dancer had just received their marks for fall term. Even Gryphon had given them both passing grades, though the master had scrawled a note on Han's report: *Newling Alister should make an effort to arrive to class promptly and prepared, and thereafter should endeavor to stay awake.*

Dancer shook his head. "I don't think that's it. I've only heard good things about Cat's classes, and she's a brilliant musician. That's why I hoped you could come along. She might be more likely to talk to you about whatever's bothering her."

"I wish I could. But I promise, I'll try to talk with her soon."

The Mystwerk Tower bells bonged once for the quarter hour. "Blood and bones, I got to go," Han said in a sudden panic. "I'm late. Tell Cat I'm sorry to miss her recital." As he charged down the stairs, he heard Blevins shout, "You keep that up, you're going to fall down them steps again!"

The taproom of The Turtle and Fish was lightly filled. The bartender was slumped over the bar, looking like he'd over-sampled his own wares. He raised his head when Han walked in, eyeing his finery with yellowed eyes. "The girlie's up there waiting for you," he said, trying to wink but blinking both eyes instead. "She din't want to stay down here."

Heads turned all over the room. Han loped up the stairs, his book under his arm.

Rebecca looked up when he entered, and her green eyes flicked over his attire without comment. She wore a long dark wool skirt and a long-sleeved white blouse, like one of Jemson's strictest schoolteachers.

"You're late, Alister," she said without preamble. She looked cranky.

"Sorry," he said. "I got caught up in a—"

"Some of the most important rules of etiquette relate to punctuality," Rebecca said, bulling right over his excuses. "For business appointments, you are to be on time or a few minutes early. For social engagements, you should never arrive early. You

421

should err on the side of being a few minutes late. The more important you are, the later you arrive." She paused. "This is a business appointment."

Han blinked at her. To be honest, being on time had never been a priority before. He'd set his own schedule in Ragmarket. Being streetlord meant people and events waited on him. Rough judgment based on the angle of sun and shadow was good enough. Even Jemson wasn't strict about class times. He was just happy when you showed up.

"I understand," he said, picking his way carefully. "I apologize. I'll try to be on time in the future."

"You *will* be on time in the future," Rebecca said, sticking her nose in the air and flinging her mop of hair back, "or this will be our last tutoring session."

Where's the girlie from the roof? Han wanted to ask. *The one that laid on her back beside me to watch fireworks. The one I almost kissed.*

Seeking to change the subject, he looked around. A small table was set for two, with plates, bowls, cups, napkins, and a fistful of forks, spoons, and knives at each place.

"Did you order supper?" he asked. "I thought we said we'd eat before we came."

"We are not actually eating," Rebecca said. "I thought about the best way to teach you, and decided we'd try some playacting. Today we're going to talk about arriving and departing, and table manners."

Arriving and departing? Han thought. How complicated could that be?

Very complicated, it turned out. Bluebloods seemed to give more thought to coming and going than whatever came in between. There were all kinds of rules for who arrived in what order, and who bowed and curtsied to whom, and when; who said what to whom; who got to leave the room first, and how you left the room. For instance, if you left before someone more important than you, you backed away, bowing, until you hit the door.

The only time Han backed out of a room was when the person he left behind was likely to stick him in the back.

There were also rules for figuring out who was more important than you, which was just about everybody.

Rebecca slid from role to role, sometimes playing the downstairs maid, sometimes the hostess, sometimes a lord, sometimes a lady, first a person more important than him, then someone less important.

"You're a good actor," Han said. "You're as good as any of the players I've seen at the Palisade." That was an open-air theater in Southbridge, where you could get standing room for a fivepenny piece. Or sneak in for free.

"Well," Rebecca said, "that's one thing bluebloods are good at—acting."

Finally they moved on to table manners. There was a lot on getting up and sitting down, how big a portion to take, how much to leave behind, what foods to eat in what order, what utensils to use, where to put your napkin, and about blotting— not wiping—your face. The whole time, you were supposed to make conversation. And every time Han slipped up and said "an't" or "got to," Rebecca stuck her hand out.

By the end of it, Han was considerably poorer and his head was spinning.

"Do you ever just freeze up because you can't think of what you're supposed to do?" he asked. "Do you ever get so hungry and frustrated you just grab with your hands? Or get in a spot where you can't think of another blessed thing to say that you're allowed to say?"

"Well," Rebecca said gravely, "some ladies resort to fainting. Men are on their own."

Han laughed. "I thought it was tough on the streets," he said. "I had no idea."

Outside, the bells bonged ten times. Two hours had flown by.

"We'll meet Thursday, then, and I'll expect you to be on time," Rebecca said. "Read chapters four to six. On Thursday we'll discuss rules of inheritance and classes of nobility, and I'll quiz you on table manners."

"Could I ask a question?" Han said, though he knew he should get on to Bayar Library and Crow.

"Well, we're just about out of time. . . . What is it?"

"What are the rules for walking out?" he asked, riffling the pages of his book. "Is there a chapter on that?"

"What do you mean?" Rebecca asked, even though Han suspected she understood.

"Walking out. You know, courtship. Marriage. Like that. There have to be rules on that. Who goes out with who. Who can marry who. Who you can kiss, and how often, and who starts." He looked straight at her, and her cheeks pinked up.

"Of course there are rules," she said. "There are always rules." She rose abruptly and curtsied deep, meaning she wasn't about to tell him what they were.

He rose too, and got off a fair bow. "Thank you, Rebecca, for taking the time to tutor me," he said. "I've learned a lot already."

She preceded him down the stairs, her head up, her back very straight. They were nearly at the bottom when someone called over, "Hey! Rebecca!"

Rebecca stopped so abruptly that Han ran into her. He grabbed hold of her arms to keep her from toppling.

Two Wien House cadets occupied a nearby table. Both girlies, with big grins on their faces. One wore faculty bars on her uniform.

"Hello, Talia," Rebecca said, practically choking on it. "Hello, Pearlie."

They raised their mugs. "Who's your friend?" Talia asked, winking.

"My friend?" Rebecca said, pretending she didn't know who they meant. "Oh." She looked over her shoulder at Han, as if surprised to find him right behind her. "This is—ah—Han. Alister. I know him from home."

"Good to meet you," Han said, nodding at Pearlie and Talia.

"Didn't you used to be called Cuffs?" Talia asked.

Han nodded. "Used to be."

"Whoa, Rebecca," Talia said, smiling even wider. "Walking on the wild side, are we?"

Rebecca seemed to think the situation needed more explaining. "He—uh—I'm tutoring him."

"She is," Han said solemnly. "She's very good. I'm learning a lot."

Pearlie snickered. "What's she teaching you?"

"Well," Han said, "we're jumping around a lot."

The two cadets howled with laughter, but Rebecca didn't

425

look amused. She walked straight to the door and out, ignoring her friends.

Crow displayed a certain arrogant interest in Han's sessions with Rebecca. "Who is this young woman?" he asked. "Where did you find her?"

"Her name is Rebecca Morley," Han said. "She worked as a tutor in a noble household. I met her back at home, before I came here."

"A *tutor*," Crow said, wrinkling his nose. "Do you know anything about her family?"

"She is not as well connected as I'd like," Han said sarcastically. "But Queen Marianna was busy."

"Queen Marianna?" Crow looked puzzled. Then his face cleared. "Oh, yes. Of course."

Brilliant as he was, Crow sometimes seemed to be a step behind, particularly when it came to understanding Han's jokes. Maybe blueblood humor was different. Crow *was* funny, in a bitter-edged way.

Crow persisted. "Are you certain that this Rebecca really—"

"She was a tutor for the Bayars," Han said. "Apparently she was good enough for *them*."

"The Bayars?" Crow asked, stiffening. "She works for Aerie House?"

"She used to," Han said. "Now she's in school here."

"How do you know she's not a spy?" Crow asked. "Or an assassin?"

"I don't know," Han said. "But it's not like I had a flock of applicants. I had to practically get down on my knees to get her to do it. We've been meeting for a month now, and I'm not dead."

"Well," Crow conceded, "we'll see. I hope you are being careful, at least." He eyed Han critically. "Your choice of clothing is improving. Your speech as well."

Han just rolled his eyes. At first he hadn't really cared about becoming a blueblood—it was Crow's price for the ongoing lessons. Now he was realizing how much there was to learn. How it could open doors for him.

For whatever reason, he was getting on better with Crow. These days his teacher's barbs had less sting to them. He'd also broadened their curriculum to include other, more intricate aspects of magic beyond hex charms. Han could tell that Crow loved this stuff, and loved having someone to share it with. When Han mastered a difficult bit of spellwork, Crow would lift his face to the heavens and say, "The boy is brilliant! Truly he is!" A touch sarcastic, but a compliment all the same.

Han compared Crow to Rebecca—his other private tutor. He admired her backbone, even when it got in his way. He tried not to dwell on her green eyes, brilliant against her coppery skin, the flashes of ankle beneath her long skirts. He noticed everything—the way she drew her dark brows together and bit her lower lip when she was thinking; the way she waved her hands around when she talked; her shape under that dirtback uniform.

He'd let her know he was interested. Usually that was all it took, but she'd ignored his signals for weeks. Maybe bluebloods went about it a different way.

Or maybe she had no interest in walking out with a street rat turned wizard.

"Let's discuss power management," Crow said, wrenching Han away from his thoughts and signaling it was time to get down to business. "There are ways to leverage the power you have so that you don't squander it all doing relatively minor tasks."

"Leverage," Han repeated dutifully.

"For instance, it takes less power to persuade someone else to do a task for you than to use magic to do it yourself. You can explode a boulder, or you can magically influence someone to smash it with a pickax. The second option requires less power, especially if that person is weak-willed."

"Less power for you," Han pointed out. "But not for the person with the pickax."

"Of course," Crow said, brushing the point aside as if that were obvious. "Here's another example. You could set young Bayar aflame, which would require considerable power, especially if he resists, as is likely. It would be less taxing although more hit-or-miss to burn down his dormitory while he sleeps."

It was still there, that constant incitement to action against the Bayars before they came after him again. Han tried to take what he could get from his sessions with Crow without allowing himself to be goaded. He'd be getting in the way of the Bayars soon enough, and his primary target was back in the Fells. It was easier to ignore them now that they'd moved out of his dormitory.

Anyway, Han had his own questions to ask. "Sometimes, after I return from Aediion, I can't seem to wake up," he said. "When I finally do, I'm still exhausted. Is that normal, that it should take that much out of me?"

Crow studied him, eyes narrowed. "How often does that happen?"

Han shrugged. "Nearly every time."

Crow rubbed his chin. "It's possible that the Bayars loaded some kind of hex magic into your amulet before it came to you."

"But it only happens after Aediion," Han persisted.

"The other possibility is that it's happening because the magic we're practicing is much more demanding than anything you are doing in class," Crow said. "Either way, the answer is to build up as much magic as you can before you come. That will not only counteract anything the Bayars have done, it will enable you to do the work without draining yourself completely."

That was always Crow's answer—build up more power. Easy for him to say.

"There are ways to drain magic from others," Crow went on, "without their being aware of it. I can show you how." He looked Han in the eyes, as if to divine his reaction.

"I don't need to be stealing power from others," Han said. "I'm not a thief anymore."

Crow shrugged. "We are all thieves of one kind or another."

Han's upcoming lesson with Abelard's army had been weighing on his mind, too. "Remember I mentioned before that Dean Abelard is mentoring a small group of students?" he said.

Crow nodded. "I do remember that, yes," he said. "The Bayar twins are in it, you said."

Han nodded. "Now Abelard wants me to teach them how to travel to Aediion. She thinks it would be useful if they go to war against the Spirit clans."

"She is right, of course," Crow said. "But it's unlikely any of them will be successful, with the amulets they have. Which is a good thing. We don't want them stumbling in on us in session."

"I don't really want to get into it," Han said. "Especially with the Bayars. Their flash may be more powerful than we think. But I have to. Abelard has threatened to expel me if I don't."

"Hmmm," Crow said, frowning, "there is a way for you to bring them with you, rather than letting them come on their own. We'll go over that next time."

Han opened his eyes to a dusty gray light. He blinked, confused and disoriented. Had he slept overnight in the library again? He sat up, swaying, propping his hands against the floor to stay upright. He knew without checking that his amulet was completely drained, though power was trickling back into him.

Scrubbing his hands across his eyes, he looked around, puzzled. He was in the library—surrounded by floor-to-ceiling shelves of books—but the room was unfamiliar. The air was stale, as if it hadn't been breathed in a long, long time.

Scrambling to his feet, he went to the window and swiped the dust from the grimy pane. It was light out, and he was high in Bayar Library, higher than he had ever been before, looking across the Mystwerk quad to the north. How had he gotten here?

Wiping the dust on his breeches, he took a closer look at the books on the shelves. Old books. Very old books. They made Firesmith's books look fresh and new. Han pulled one down from the shelf and turned the fragile pages carefully. They were handwritten, in flowing ink, in an archaic language Han could not decipher. The illustrations fizzed on the page. It was a magical text—pages of spellwork and gestures.

The last he remembered, he'd been in Aeidiion with Crow. He'd entered the dreamworld from the usual place, several floors below where he was now.

He scanned the other shelves. Most of the books were charms and spells. One shelf held a collection of journals: each entry carried a date from the Breaking time. Many of those books were clean of dust, and the dust on the floor in front of the shelves had been scuffed up. Someone had been poking through them recently. They all carried the same emblem—Han traced it with his forefinger. A twined serpent and staff poked through an elaborate crown. Must be one of the wizard houses, Han thought. Maybe they donated the books to the library.

Whoever had been there seemed to be gone now.

Han touched his amulet, allowing what power he had on board to trickle in as he debated the possibilities. Was he sleepwalking? Crazy? Several times before, he'd slept over in Bayar Library—but he'd always awakened in the same place.

A battered wooden hatch stood open in the floor. Peering down, he saw a metal ladder extending to the level below. Carefully, he descended the ladder, his hand on his amulet. The next floor was more of the same, rows of shelves loaded with ancient books. Another hatch, another metal ladder, and he'd reached familiar ground—the sixth floor of Bayar, where his hiding place was.

But how had he ended up on the eighth floor—when he hadn't even known how to get up there until now?

Just then, he heard footsteps coming up the stairs from the fifth floor.

Han dodged back into the stacks, positioning himself so he could see the stairwell between the shelves. Moments later, someone emerged from the lower floor.

It was Fiona Bayar, a carry bag slung over her shoulder. She looked around, her gaze sliding over Han's hidey-hole, then crossed to the pull-down ladder to the seventh level.

Han swore silently. He hadn't slid it back into place yet.

Fiona paused at the foot of the ladder, looking around again, her head cocked, listening.

Han kept shut and still.

Fiona shrugged, took hold of the ladder, and began to climb.

Han knew that what he should do was take this opportunity to pike off before he was noticed. But his curiosity was piqued. What was Fiona Bayar doing so high in the library, skulking around like she didn't want to be seen? Han waited a few moments, then ghosted up the ladder after her.

When he cautiously poked his head through the opening on the seventh floor, Fiona was nowhere to be seen. Easing himself through the hatch, he slipped between two rows of shelves, heading for the rear of the library.

"What are *you* doing here?"

Han whirled around, his hand on his useless amulet.

Fiona stood between Han and the open hatchway. Her usually pristine clothes were streaked with dust, and she wore a black smudge, like a gang sign, on her right cheek.

"Studying," he said. "Reading. What else would I do in a library?"

"Without notes? Without papers?"

Han looked at his empty hands as if he'd never seen them

before. "I left all that downstairs. Too heavy to carry." It was not his finest hour as a liar.

She put her hands on her hips. "Were you following me?"

"Not on purpose," Han said. "I heard a noise, so I came to see what it was." That was better. "What are *you* doing here?" He waved his hand at the shelves of moldering books.

"Studying," she mocked. "Reading. What else?"

Han wasn't going back to his crib, not with her there. So he turned to the shelf behind him and pretended to scan the titles. He watched her from the corner of his eye in case she made a move on him.

Not that he'd be able to defend himself, depleted as he was. He hoped she couldn't tell.

She stepped in close. "*Tithe Records for the Cathedral Church*?" Fiona was reading over his shoulder. He could feel her breath on the back of his neck.

"Do you mind?" Han said. "You're bothering me."

"Alister," Fiona said softly. "Why is Dean Abelard protecting you?"

Han turned around and ended up nearly nose to nose with her, his back against the shelf. "What makes you think she's protecting me?"

"Micah said she told him to leave you alone," Fiona said.

"Maybe she's just doing her job," Han said. "You know. Keeping students from killing each other."

"Micah and I don't agree on everything," Fiona said, fingering her amulet. "Our interests don't always coincide." She paused as if considering whether to go on. "Have you ever thought that it might make sense for *us* to work together?"

"Us?" Han repeated. "You mean, you and me?"

Fiona nodded.

"No," Han said, too astonished to lie. "I've never thought that would make sense."

"You're different than when we first met," Fiona said, bringing her pale brows together. "Your speech, your clothing—it's like your rough edges have been polished away." She reached toward Han and brushed her fingertips along his jawline. Her touch stung his cold skin. "Though we come from very different backgrounds, we may be more alike than you think. You don't play by the rules. Neither do I."

Han stood his ground, refusing to flinch away. "By that logic, the Raggers and Southies ought to get on because they don't abide by the queen's law," he said.

"Hear me out," Fiona persisted. "Some in the Wizard Council claim they want to make changes. Maybe they don't go far enough."

Han was lost, but he knew better than to let on. "What do you suggest?"

"My father wants to marry Micah into the Gray Wolf line," Fiona said.

"I've heard that," Han said, shrugging like he didn't care either way. "So?"

"He wants to establish a new line of wizard kings married to Gray Wolf queens," Fiona went on.

"The clans will never stand by and watch that happen," Han said.

"Exactly," Fiona said, nodding. "If we're going to do this, why not go all the way? Why should we cling to the Gray Wolf line at all? What does it gain us? The clans will go to war regardless."

"What's your plan?" Han said, curious in spite of himself.

"Why not a wizard queen?" Fiona said.

Han finally got it. Lord Bayar's current scheme left poor Fiona out in the cold. Being a rich blueblood wizard wasn't enough. Apparently.

"I'm guessing you have somebody in mind." Han raised his eyebrows.

Fiona gripped Han's forearms, looking intently into his face. "Why shouldn't it be me instead of Micah? I've always been the better student. I've always been more focused. Micah's always distracted by his latest conquest. I think with my head, not with my—"

"Why are you telling me this?" Han interrupted. "I'd think you'd keep shut about it. We're not exactly friends."

"We could be," Fiona whispered. "We could be very good friends." She pulled him toward her and kissed him, her lips sizzling against his, her hands tangling themselves in his hair. "We could help each other, you and I," she murmured, pressing into him.

Han gripped her shoulders and pushed back from her. "You still didn't answer my question," he said. "Why me? Why not lovelorn . . . Why not Wil?"

"I don't know." Fiona cleared her throat, her eyes still fixed south of his nose. "There's just something about you. Something so . . . irresistibly dangerous . . ." She tried to move in again, but Han planted both hands on her shoulders, keeping her at arm's length.

"Something about me?" Han said. "Something irresistibly dangerous?" Letting go of Fiona's shoulder, he closed his hand on his amulet and dangled it in front of her eyes. "This, maybe?"

She stared at it for a long moment. "Well," she admitted grudgingly, "that's part of it. But not all of it."

"Who do you think I am?" Han said, sliding the serpent pendant under his shirt. "Some country-bred nick-ninny on a city weekend? You'll have to do better than that."

"I have information about the amulet," Fiona said in a rush. "Information you need. The amulet is the key. It's more important than you know—but it's also dangerous. That's why my father wants it back so badly. I can help you take full advantage of it."

"I don't need your help."

"Really?" Fiona said skeptically. "You're saying that amulet has never given you a moment's trouble? You've not had any . . . unusual experiences?" She tilted her head.

"My life is full of unusual experiences," Han said. "But I'm getting along on my own."

"The amulet's not the only risk," Fiona said. "If you ever come back to the Fells, my father will crush you like a cockroach."

"And you think you can stop him?"

"You would be surprised what I can do," Fiona whispered, looking into his eyes.

"And where am I at the end of it?" Han said. "Buried with the Gray Wolf queens?"

"Of course not," Fiona said, drawing back a little, looking huffy. "There would be a role for you, of course. A position in my court. You would be well compensated."

"As errand boy? Magical enforcer? A petticoat pensioner at best?" Han shook his head. "I got—I have my own plans. I won't play servant or bravo to you." He pushed past her, leaving her standing amid the ancient stacks.

Han left Bayar Library by his usual route, avoiding the proficient reshelving books on the second floor.

All the way back, he chewed over what had happened. Fiona's offer was just part of it. Did she really know something useful about the amulet? Was it possible the Bayars *had* put a curse on it? Did she have anything to do with his ending up on the eighth floor? Or was he losing his mind?

CHAPTER TWENTY-SIX

DANGEROUS DANCING

The spring term was well under way, and Hallie still hadn't returned from the Fells. It's a long way to Fellsmarch, Raisa told herself. Even longer in these unsettled times.

Maybe Hallie had decided not to come back to school. Maybe, after seeing her daughter, she couldn't bring herself to leave again.

"Why isn't there any place for children here?" she asked Amon one day as they worked out with their staffs.

"What?" He parried her quick jab to his middle and swung his staff at her head. She ducked, and it whistled past her ear. While he was off balance, she penetrated his defenses and gave him a good smack on the rump.

Raisa was glad they still had this time together. It was a relatively safe way to work off the tension between them. She just had to be careful not to hit too hard.

"You mean classes?" he panted, spinning around and bringing

up his staff to block her next blow. She slammed her staff across his and felt the vibration clear up her arms.

"Well, yes, and a place for students to live with their children."

"Don't you think that would be a distraction?" Amon asked. He swept his staff low, nearly knocking her off her feet.

"Don't you think it's even more distracting to be missing your child?"

"Cadets are supposed to bond with each other," Amon said. "Would that happen if they were caring for a family?"

"I don't think we can ignore the fact that some students have families," Raisa said. "If Hallie's daughter were here, she wouldn't have traveled home on her own." Mopping sweat from her face, she held up her hand to signal the end of the bout. "The Temple School could offer classes for them, like Southbridge does. But there's no housing for them in the city."

"Hmmm," Amon said. "Well, if you want to pursue it, start with Master Askell. He's on the governance council for the academy."

The spring term was easier academically than the one before. Raisa didn't have Proficient Tourant to deal with, for one thing. Tourant had left the academy entirely, and nobody seemed sorry to see him go.

Infantry drilling had been replaced with horsemanship, in which Raisa excelled. She enjoyed riding Switcher, who'd grown fat and lazy last term. She liked getting out into the countryside again, even if it was flat.

Askell was a rare visitor to her classes these days. And so she had to make an appointment to speak with him about her idea regarding family housing.

"Sit down, Newling Morley," Askell said, when his orderly ushered her into his office. "Be at ease. Would you like tea?" He gestured at the teapot on its little burner.

"No, sir," she said. "Thank you. It won't take long."

She felt different, more confident than she'd been the last time. Both times she'd come as a supplicant. But now she felt like she had some footing, like she didn't need to apologize for her presence. She'd achieved high marks in all her classes, save Tourant's. That class she'd failed.

As if he'd read her mind, Askell said, "If you are here about your marks in History of Warfare, that record has been amended."

"Oh!" Raisa said, surprised. "I'm not here for that reason, but thank you, sir."

"Why are you here, then?"

Raisa explained her idea and the reasons for it.

Askell frowned. "It has never been done before, and yet we've managed to scrape along for more than a thousand years."

"Applications to Wien House are dramatically down," Raisa said.

Askell raised an eyebrow. "Who told you that?"

"Arden has always sent more cadets to Oden's Ford than the rest of the Seven Realms," Raisa said. "But they've been at war for a decade, so the young people who *would* have come here are already fighting. To get enough quality students, you've been accepting older, less traditional ones. And many of those have families."

Askell sat back. "I can't imagine this affects many of our students," he said.

"One in five," Raisa said. "One in three proficients and masters students."

"How do you know this?" Askell asked. "That sounds like more than a guess."

"I surveyed all six classes of cadets," Raisa said. "Of course, I couldn't survey those who never came here because they couldn't risk leaving their families behind." She leaned forward. "The Wien House dormitories are half empty. There would be room for some families, at least. We could start with Wien House and expand to the other schools if it's successful."

"You have been busy, Morley," Askell said. "Clearly your workload is too light this term." Dipping his pen into a bottle of ink, he scratched a few notes. "I cannot promise anything," he said. "The military is the most conservative of organizations, particularly my countrymen within it. But you make a solid case for investigating this."

"That is all I can ask," Raisa said, but couldn't resist adding, "I would hope that this investigation does not take too long."

"I have a question," Askell said, looking at her over the rim of his teacup. "Proficient Tourant's behavior was abysmal all term, and yet you never complained," he said. "Why not?"

Raisa shrugged. "If I can't manage the Tourants of the world, I'm unlikely to succeed as queen of the Fells. Some days it seems like I'm surrounded by Tourants."

"I thought you might return to the Fells at solstice," Askell said.

"I'm waiting for word from home," Raisa said. "I'll likely leave as soon as I receive assurances that it's safe to do so." If that ever happens, she thought.

"Is there any chance you'll return next year?" Askell asked, tapping his pen on his blotter.

Raisa shook her head. "I can't imagine that I would. I've learned so much, but I've been away too long as it is."

"I see," Askell said. He cleared his throat. "I wanted you to know that if you returned next year, I planned to offer you command over a triple of newlings. Your performance this year has been impressive." A smile ghosted across his face. "And not just because my expectations were so low."

"Thank you, sir," Raisa said, a little flustered. "I am honored. And it would be an honor to serve, if I were returning."

"I realize that the role of corporal is a step down from princess," Askell said, "but I wanted you to know my mind."

"Thank you," Raisa said. "I want *you* to know that I will never forget my time here at Oden's Ford. It's been an incredible gift to step out of the role of princess and into the role of student."

Askell stood, signaling that it was time for her to go. "If you are still here, I hope that I will see you at the Cadets' Ball."

"Oh. Yes. Well. I hadn't really thought that far ahead." Raisa had heard of little else for weeks—the Wien House end-of-term party. It was kind of a target to aim at, an excuse to leap over the work remaining to be done.

"It's not that far off," Askell said, smiling. "I hope that if you do leave before then, you will come and say good-bye."

"Thank you, sir, I will." She saluted Askell, her fist over her heart, and left.

The bloody Cadets' Ball, Raisa thought as she descended the steps. I'm not going.

Amon had continued his proper courtship of Annamaya. Every weekend that he was off duty he put on his dress uniform and crossed the river to visit her at the Temple School. Raisa could picture them sitting all straight-backed in the garden. At least she didn't have to see it for real. But she wouldn't be able to avoid it at the dance.

Talia and Pearlie were going together. Since Hallie hadn't returned, Raisa would be a loose thread dangling. A princess without a dance card at the ball. That would never happen at home.

She didn't have friends at home, either—not real friends to pester her to death.

"I don't know why you don't ask Han," Talia said, as if she and Han were old friends. These days, she and Pearlie often showed up at The Turtle and Fish on Tuesday and Thursday nights. Sometimes Mick and Garret came, too. When Han's tutoring session was finished, he would buy a round, and Raisa would end up staying late.

"He's so good-looking and charming, and the way he looks at you—it sends shivers right through me," Talia sighed. "Girlies used to knife fight over Cuffs Alister back in Ragmarket, you know. He's not my type, but if he was . . ."

"He's not my type either," Raisa said, then rushed to add, "I mean, I like him, and all that, but . . . I know it won't work out in the long run."

Talia raised her eyebrow in an "Oh, really?" kind of way. "I know you're a blueblood, but it's not like you have to marry him."

Speaking of. It was nearly six. Time to meet the amazing Han Alister for tutoring.

"I have to go," Raisa said.

"Say hello for me!" Talia winked at Raisa.

He was waiting for her in the upstairs room at The Turtle and Fish. He was always early, ever since that first class when he'd been late and she'd laid into him. (He was definitely teachable.) He'd taken to ordering dinner (he said as payment), so they'd gotten into the habit of eating together before or after their sessions. He claimed he needed to practice his table manners with actual food.

"What if I used the right fork, but used it to stuff sausage in my mouth, or guzzled down my ale like a soaker in his cups?" he said. "All your hard work would have gone to waste."

Han worked hard himself. He did the assigned reading and participated without complaint in Raisa's role-playing. His speech had improved dramatically over the past two months, though he still used thieves' slang now and then because that didn't result in fivepenny payments. His table manners were nearly flawless, when he paid attention.

There were times, though, that he seemed desperate for sleep, yawning after dinner and twice actually dozing off.

"Should you be spending time on this right now?" Raisa asked one evening when she could tell he was exhausted. "Like I said, you can learn manners on your own."

"I apologize," he said. "It's not the company. If there's anybody I want to be awake for, it's you. I was up late last night is all."

It seemed he was up late every night. Is he seeing someone? she wondered.

It's not my business if he is.

It was clear he was used to having his way with girls, and in a dozen ways he let her know that he was interested in her. She'd feel the pressure of his eyes, and turn around to find him gazing at her as one might a complicated, layered painting. The intensity of his attention was seductive.

Sometimes he'd pull his chair around so they could share his book. He'd sit about an inch away, always maintaining that tiny distance, as if he knew exactly where she was at all times.

As he bent his head over Faulk, she'd find herself staring at the curve of his jaw with its pale bristle of beard, the jagged scar that narrowly missed his right eye, his muscular forearms corded with veins.

She noticed everything—the way he yawned and stretched, arching his back like a cat, belatedly covering his mouth with his hand. The many colors in his hair—pale butter and cream, reddish gold and platinum. How he often repeated a question, as if to buy time to conjure up the answer. The way he always sat facing the door, perhaps a leftover from Ragmarket, and groped for his knife when startled. How he constantly slid his hand into his shirt, releasing power into his amulet.

He wasn't proud or arrogant, but there was a self-confidence about him that said he knew what he wanted and he was going to get it, and you'd better not get in his way. It had probably served him well as streetlord of the Raggers.

How could she be noticing Han Alister when she was still brokenhearted over Amon Byrne? Did the destruction of one dream leave a vacuum that required filling with another?

Is a broken heart more vulnerable? she wondered. Am I fickle or self-destructive?

I am not going through this again.

But she'd come to look forward to their twice-weekly meetings more than she cared to admit.

Often they continued beyond the agreed-upon two hours. Raisa had tried to enforce the deadline at first, but gave up. Han Alister could always charm her into staying longer.

This evening, when she arrived, sandwiches and cider were set out on the table. Along with a beautifully enameled and jeweled music box.

"This is lovely," she said, opening the lid and examining the intricate mechanism with her trader eye. It was clanwork, probably an antique. She looked up at him, puzzled. "What's it for?"

"It's for you," he said, gesturing awkwardly. "A gift."

"I can't accept this," she said, feeling the blood rush to her face. She tried to give it back to him, but he put his hands behind him, so she set it down on the table.

"I brought it for selfish reasons," he said. "I want you to teach me to dance."

Raisa looked up at him, startled. "What? Why?"

"There's always the chance I'll be invited to a party," he said. "I want to be ready just in case." The blue eyes were wide and innocent.

"There are so many other topics we haven't covered yet," Raisa protested. "Officers of the court, appropriate dress for social situations, protocols of the hunt, correspondence guidelines . . ."

"I hear lots of business is done at parties," Han said, sticking out his chin. "I know some clan dances, but I need to know how to dance city-style."

"What kind of dances do you want to learn?" Raisa asked, rolling her eyes.

"The kind where you hold your partner," he said, winding up the music box. "What's that one called?"

We call that trouble, Raisa thought as the music began.

It was a northern song, "Flower of the Mountains." A rush of homesickness overwhelmed her. "Oh!" she said. "I love that song. Where did you get this?"

"There's a music store on the Mystwerk side, close to the Temple School," Han said. He stood in front of her, holding out his hands, waist high.

Raisa pulled her hands back. "First, let me show you the footwork. This one's called High Country Step." She demonstrated. "Now you try." She watched as he attempted it. "That's almost it, but it's step-step-back-step-slide." He tried again. "And then forward."

After a few more practice steps, Raisa held out her own hands. "Let's try it together now. Follow me." She placed his right hand on her left hip, keeping hold of his left hand with her right. The magic in his hands was well controlled, subtle, and potent. It went to her head like Bruinswallow wine.

"Now, step-step-back, good, good, forward . . ." They practiced over and over, recranking the music box when needed, snatching gulps of cider and bites of sandwich in between.

It's a good thing I like this song, Raisa thought.

When Han had mastered the High Country Step, they moved on to Square Round, If My True Love Would Just Be True, and Rose Among the Thorns. The last one was complicated, and even though Han seemed to be a natural dancer, they repeatedly got their feet tangled up.

"Wait! Wait!" Raisa said, when they seemed in danger of toppling over. "Stop, stop, stop!"

They ended up holding on to each other to keep from toppling, flushed and laughing, panting from the exertion.

"I think I need more practice," Han said, shaking his head.

"Nobody ever gets that one right," Raisa replied. "Never mind. I think you're ready for dancing."

"Good," he said, grinning. "Now ask me to the Cadets' Ball."

"Cadets' Ball! Who told you about the . . . ?" Raisa said, baffled, and then it came to her. "Talia told you! I know it was her." She shook her head. "I'm not going."

"Please, Rebecca," he coaxed. "There's more to a dance than dancing. It would give me a chance to practice everything—table manners, blueblood talk, the whole lot. And it's not just that. I want to go with you." He put his hands on her shoulders. "Unless you're already walking out with someone."

Raisa thought about lying, but knew Talia would have spilled the truth already. "No." She shook her head, avoiding his eyes. "I'm not walking out with anyone."

Don't you dare, she thought. Don't you dare tell me you'll make me forget Amon Byrne.

But he didn't. Instead, he put his fingers under her chin and lifted her head so she was looking up at him. "Lucky me," he murmured, and kissed her. Slowly and thoroughly, like someone who knew what he was doing.

Raisa had loved kissing Amon Byrne, but it seemed they'd never had an uninterrupted kiss.

With Micah, every kiss had been a skirmish in their ongoing war. Exciting but brutal.

Reid Demonai was talented enough, and certainly experienced . . .

But she'd never been kissed like this.

And, like a fool, she kissed him back. Kissed him in a way that would leave no doubt how she felt about him. Kissed him because she knew that chances were slim she'd have very many kisses like that in her lifetime.

Which is a sad thing when you're only sixteen.

He backed up until he came up against the chair, and he sat, pulling her onto his lap. And there were more kisses—hungry kisses that seemed to have been stacking up during the weeks they'd been meeting. She gave in to them completely, winding her fingers into his pale hair, pulling his head down for more.

There was wizardry in his kisses, but it was subtle, like the after notes of something rich and intoxicating on its own.

She ended up with her arms wrapped around him, shivering, her cheek pressed against his chest, breathing hard, not wanting to let go. But knowing she had to.

"We can't do this," Raisa whispered, almost to herself. "It's just going to make matters worse."

Han stroked her hair, shifting his body under her. "Why? What are you afraid of? Thieves or wizards?"

"Both," she said.

"Is it because I'm not a blueblood?" He asked this matter-of-factly, as if he really wanted to know.

"That's the least of it," Raisa said, taking a shuddering breath. "This is just going to lead to heartbreak, and I refuse to have my heart broken again." She looked up at him. "I thought I could play at love. I thought I had the right, same as . . . as any courtier or a . . . a streetlord."

He shook his head. "Rebecca, listen, I—"

"But I've found out I'm not made that way," she interrupted. "I can't play this game if my heart's not in it. That's me personally. I'm not judging anyone else."

"I see," he said. He tightened his arms around her, brushing his fingers along her collarbone, setting her nerves tingling. "What's your heart saying now?"

She wanted to be honest with him, even though she'd probably pay for it. "I'm in trouble," she whispered.

Han didn't say anything for a long time. "I can't guarantee I won't hurt you," he said finally, "because there's a lot I can't control. What I can tell you is that hurting you is the last thing I want to do."

"You won't be able to help it," Raisa said, swiping at her eyes. "And it's not just a matter of you hurting me. I will hurt you too, even if I don't mean to. I'm not the girl you think I am. And you will remember this conversation, and wish that you'd listened to me." She burrowed her hands into his. "How can you want this if you know from the beginning that it will end badly?" *Tell him the truth*, said a voice in her head. But she just couldn't. She didn't dare.

He searched her face with his eyes, as if trying to surface the story behind the words. Then he kissed her eyelids and the tip of her nose, and once again, her lips. With each kiss, her resistance dwindled.

"I live in the present," Han said, "because the future is always chancy. When it comes to being with you, I'm willing to take the risk. Are you?"

"Now I'll feel like a coward if I don't." Raisa leaned back against him. Looked up at his face and traced the scar above his eye with her forefinger. "How did you get this?" she asked.

"Took a risk," he said, his blue eyes fixed on her face.

"Was it worth it?"

He thought about it. "Yes."

"All right," Raisa said, giving in. "Let's take a risk. But we'll go slow."

His arms tightened around her again. She felt the thud of his heart against her back. "I don't want to go slow," he whispered in her ear. "Like I said, I live for the present. Every time I try to set something aside for the future, it gets taken away."

"I know," Raisa said. "But we *will* take it slow, just the same."

CHAPTER TWENTY-SEVEN

WHEN DREAMS TURN TO NIGHTMARES

Han opened his eyes and found himself staring at the ceiling in his library hideout room.

He was on the hardwood floor, and knew immediately from the stiffness in his joints that he'd been lying there for hours. He rubbed his hand over his face. It was stubbly. How long had he been there? As usual, it seemed there were great chunks of time he couldn't account for.

Massaging his temples, he tried to remember what had happened in his session with Crow. Crow had shown him how to bring other wizards with him to Aediion. He'd demonstrated the technique and made him memorize the charm.

Han sat up, waited for his head to stop spinning, then levered himself to his feet. Something crinkled under his coat. Sliding his hand inside, he found several pages folded together. Carefully, he unfolded them. Yellowed and fragile, they looked like pages torn from one of the ancient books on the floors above.

One was a map, the ink faded and water-spotted. A wavery title arched over the drawing. "Gray Lady." He sat back on his heels. Gray Lady was the mountain at the edge of the Vale where the Wizard Council House was located, along with homes of the most prominent wizards in the Vale. He scanned the drawing. On the map, the mountain appeared to be honeycombed by tunnels, with several entrances marked prominently.

A note was scrawled on the back, in his own handwriting. *Keep hidden; keep safe. —H. Alister.*

It was totally unfamiliar. Where had it come from? What did it mean?

Was Aediion bleeding over into real life?

He sorted through the other pages. They were charms, written in a language so archaic he could scarcely make them out. At the bottom, initialed with a series of large elaborate letters, was *HRMAW.* And an insignia—the serpent, staff, and crown he'd seen before.

HRMAW?

Crossing to the window, Han looked out. The lamplighters were kindling the lanterns that hung from the academy buildings. Which meant he'd missed dinner. He felt weak, starving, and completely depleted of power.

But that didn't make any sense. He'd met with Crow after dinner. The lamps would have been lit a long time ago. Was the amulet so packed with evil power that it was making him sick?

Swearing, he gathered up his books and papers, cramming them into his carry bag, putting the ancient pages in on top. He skipped the longer route across the rooftops, and took a chance with the back staircase to the main floor of the library. The proficient at the main desk looked up, blinking, from his textbook. "The library's closed, Alister. I thought everybody had already gone."

"Sorry," Han said. "I fell asleep." He paused by the desk. "What day is it?"

The proficient grinned. "You need to quit working so much. It's Sunday."

Sunday. He'd met with Crow Saturday evening. So he'd lost an entire day. And gained a map of Gray Lady. And some charms.

And suddenly it came to him—what was going on. He'd been a fool for sure.

Han sped past the proficient and shouldered open the large double doors.

Crossing the Mystwerk quad, he loped up the steps of Hampton Hall two at a time, hoping Dancer was there. But the entire dormitory seemed deserted. Was everyone at dinner?

Stopping in front of his door, Han bent and retrieved the matchstick that had fallen from the latch. Someone had opened the door to his room since he'd last been there.

Han slid his hand inside his cloak and rested it on the hilt of the knife he still carried everywhere. His drained amulet would do him little good now. Gently easing the door open, Han scanned the room. Nothing out of place. No one there.

Slipping inside, he shut the door, latched it, and took a closer look around. At first, everything seemed undisturbed. Then he noticed that some objects had been shifted. The papers spread over his desk were slightly off from where they had been. He pulled open the drawer in his wardrobe. The lentils he'd carefully arranged on the lip of the slide had been dumped into the drawer. The bit of powder he'd puffed onto the latch of his trunk was smeared.

Over the last few weeks, Han had left off placing his magical barriers so he could save all his power for his sessions with Crow. He'd set up his little gambits two days before, after he'd returned to his room and found a window open that should have been closed.

He rubbed his chin. Would Micah chance it, after what had happened to his cousins? Not unless he'd found some kind of countercharm or talisman.

It was possible Dancer had come in looking for something.

Someone banged on his door, nearly stopping his heart. "Hunts Alone!" Dancer called through the door.

Han swung it open to find Dancer in the doorway, dressed in his formal Mystwerk robes. "Where have you been?" he said. "It was the Dean's Dinner tonight. Abelard wasn't happy when you didn't show. She said to remind you to come to her office next Wednesday at seven, or else. She said you would know what it was about."

That would be the "class" on Aediion.

Han swore and dropped onto his bed, putting his face in his hands, feeling besieged.

Dancer put his hand on Han's shoulder. "Are you all right? Are you sick?"

Han shook his head. "My problem is I don't know where I've been all day." He explained what had happened.

Dancer shook his head, an "I told you so" expression on his face. "I think you're a fool if you go back there. I don't care if

Crow's taught you how to turn dung into gold, it's not worth losing your mind. I don't trust him. I think he's up to something."

"I have to go back to Aediion next Wednesday, remember? Abelard insists I teach her protégés how to do it, or I'll be expelled."

Dancer raked back his hair. "I'm glad I'm just a copperhead, beneath notice."

"Crow doesn't think they can do it with the amulets they have. He showed me how to bring them along." Han sat in glum silence for a long moment. "Do you want to hear my theory?"

Dancer sat down in Han's desk chair, resting his hands on the arms. "Please."

"A couple of times Crow has kind of slid into my head to demonstrate a charm or technique. I don't know how else to describe it."

"Slid into your head?" Dancer raised his eyebrows. "He *possessed* you?"

It sounded even worse, hearing it spoken aloud.

Han nodded, staring down at his hands. "Now I think he's doing it just as I close the portal and cross back. I think he crosses with me. Then he takes over." He looked up at Dancer. "One time I found myself on the eighth floor of Bayar Library, with no idea how I got there. Tonight, I had documents stuffed inside my shirt that I'd never seen."

"What kind of documents?"

"Old papers and maps. From the library, apparently." Han pulled the strange documents from his carry bag and spread them out on the bed.

Dancer looked them over and shook his head. "Don't go back," he said. "There's your solution."

"I'm going back," Han said. "I won't let Crow keep me out of Aediion. It an't—isn't his turf. But I need to find a way to keep him out of my head."

"What you need is a talisman," Dancer said, stretching out his legs. He wore leggings and clan boots under his wizard robes. "One that protects against mind magic."

Han recalled what Mordra had said—that the clans had developed talismans against possession, making it less useful as a tactic.

"You know where I can get one?" Han said, feeling somewhat more hopeful.

Dancer shook his head. "Back home, maybe. Here, I'd have to research and then make it. I'll talk to Firesmith."

Han's hopes faded a little. "Can you really do that?"

Dancer shrugged. "I've never done it before. And there's no good way to test it ahead of time." He tilted his head back. "That's why you should stay away."

"Like I said, I don't have much choice."

"You go back day after tomorrow?"

Han nodded.

Dancer rocked to his feet. "I'll get to work, then."

Han held up his hand. "Dancer. One more thing. Were you in my room today?"

His friend shook his head. "No. Not until now. Why?"

"Someone's been in here. I thought maybe you'd come in to get something."

Dancer shook his head. "Maybe you were here and didn't know it," he said, rolling his eyes.

"Did you see anyone else hanging around? The Bayars?"

Dancer shook his head. "They were at the Dean's Dinner. First I saw them all day. I was with Cat until I had to get ready to go."

"You were with Cat?" Han asked, surprised. Since when did they spend time together willingly?

Dancer nodded. "She says she might leave the academy." He slid a glance at Han. Not accusing, exactly, but close.

Han stared at him. "Why?"

"Why don't you ask her?" Dancer said pointedly.

"Let's go see her now," Han said, stung by guilt.

"You go," Dancer suggested. "I have to research your talisman."

But when Han walked over to the Temple School, Cat wasn't there.

CHAPTER TWENTY-EIGHT

WORD FROM HOME

After a tenuous, three-month visit to Oden's Ford, winter went north again, leaving behind bursting bulbs, like farewell fireworks in her wake.

It was already warm enough that three hours' strenuous riding left Raisa damp and flushed, and Switcher sweating and blowing. Raisa rubbed the mare down, murmuring silly endearments to her and singing snatches of "Flower of the Mountains."

You're not usually a giddy kind of person, Raisa said to herself. Is this what being in love does to you?

She would see Han Alister tonight. Her heart beat a little faster at the thought.

As she led Switcher into the stall, Raisa noticed that the stall next to her was now occupied by a shaggy gray mountain pony with a white blaze on his face.

Hallie's gelding.

Raisa forced herself to finish up, shoveling grain with shaking hands and replenishing Switcher's water. Hallie could be bringing any kind of news, she told herself. Good or bad. Or none at all.

Raisa ran across the stable yard, threading between the buildings to the grassy quad. She bolted up the steps to Grindell Hall. Mick sat by the open window in the common room, scowling over his mathematics. He looked up when Raisa burst into the room.

"She's upstairs in your room, putting her things away." He paused for a heartbeat, then said, "She brought honey cakes."

Raisa ran up the stairs, around and around and around until she reached the third floor. Hallie was kneeling by her trunk, folding clothes into it. She stood when Raisa entered and opened her arms.

Embracing Hallie was rather like embracing a sturdy oak tree.

"I'm so glad you're back!" Raisa said. "I've missed you so much, and I was beginning to worry. How's Asha?"

"I've missed you too," Hallie said, her cheeks pinking up. "Asha is good. She's huge, bigger 'n all the other two-year-olds." She let go of Raisa and dug into her carry bag on her bed. "Here. Lydia, Corporal Byrne's sister, she made me another picture." She extended a framed pencil sketch of a solemn-looking little girl with a stubborn chin and a ribbon in her hair.

"She's beautiful," Raisa said, passing back the drawing. "She looks like you."

"Well, she wouldn't be beautiful if she looked like me," Hallie said, grinning. "But she is rum clever. She learned to say Mama while I was there." Hallie paused. "I already spoke with Commander Byrne about being late coming back. I nearly missed the whole term. It shouldn't have happened, but it was hard to leave her when it came down to it. I cut my time too close and run into bad weather on my way back."

Master Askell had better listen to me about providing for children, Raisa thought.

"I brung you some honey cakes," Hallie said, pointing to a cloth sack on Raisa's bed. She looked up at the ceiling. "Let me see, there was something else. . . ."

"Hallie! Don't tease," Raisa said.

"I brung a letter to you. From your mama." Hallie groped in her duffel and brought out a military dispatch bag. She extended it toward Raisa. "Lord Averill, he said to give this into your hands directly."

Raisa stood frozen, hugging the leather bag to her chest.

"I'm going down and talk to Mick," Hallie said. "Read it over and come down when you're ready."

Raisa sat down on her bed, still cradling the bag. With trembling fingers she undid the buckles and lifted the flap.

Inside was another envelope, a large one, with *Lightfoot, Lord Demonai* scrawled on it. It was sealed. She pulled it open.

And inside was an envelope with *Lady Rebecca Morley* written on the front. Inside that was another envelope, sealed with the Gray Wolf.

Using her belt dagger, Raisa slit it open and shook out the page inside. The pages bore her mother's elegant script.

Daughter,

It is not easy for those of royal blood to say we are sorry. The stars realign and the world remakes itself so that our mistakes seem prescient in hindsight.

I never meant to drive you away. I meant to save your life, and perhaps I succeeded, for now. There are many on the Wizard Council who do not want to see you on the Gray Wolf throne. Even at your young age, you are viewed as difficult, headstrong, and too close to the clans.

Governance of the Fells has always been a balancing act, with each strategic move precipitating unintended consequences. My marriage to Averill quieted the clans but prompted the Wizard Council to build an alliance with the army. General Klemath is in league with the council. He has filled the army with mercenaries loyal only to him.

Your father sent you to Demonai Camp so you could learn to be a warrior. He and the other Demonai see you as one of them, because of your Demonai blood. Elena Cennestre in particular believes that the Demonai blood is strong in you. A faction of warriors favors setting me aside and crowning you as a queen more to their liking.

When the Wizard Council learned of this, they hatched a plot to murder you. It was to happen when you returned from Demonai Camp.

I feared they would succeed. To forestall that, I proposed a marriage between you and Micah Bayar, knowing that Lord Bayar would see this as an opportunity to expand his power and perhaps eventually put his son on the throne. The conspirators conveniently disappeared.

This bought us time, at least until your name day. Captain Byrne has been working to grow the guard and to undo the damage Klemath has done to the army, but it is a slow process and difficult to undertake unnoticed. I had hoped to delay your nuptials until that happened, but as your name day approached, Lord Bayar pressed me to keep our bargain.

So I decided to allow the marriage to proceed. I mistakenly believed that you would accept Micah because you were already seeing him on the sly. I was wrong. We are so very different. It is difficult for me to predict what you will do.

Your absence has defanged the opposition for now. The Demonai have no candidate to rally around. Lord Bayar is unwilling to make a move without knowing where you are. As long as you live, I live, because a Marianna is preferable to a Raisa.

Do not write to me again—there is too much risk that our correspondence may be traced. As you will have seen by the contents of this letter, it is dangerous here. I will contact you when it is safe for you to return. In the meantime, trust no one. Know that we are surrounded by enemies.

—*Love, Mother*

The letter slid from Raisa's nerveless fingers. She slumped back against the wall, her eyes burning with hot tears.

Couldn't you have told me, Mother? Couldn't you have trusted me a little? We could have worked together instead of at cross-purposes.

That was just it. It might have been Lord Bayar's influence, but Marianna didn't trust her daughter. She might have even suspected Raisa of plotting with the Demonai to take her throne. Imagine if she knew that Amon Byrne was already bound to her.

Maybe that was the real purpose of the marriage to Micah. It would have put a stop to Demonai schemes. A Queen Marianna was preferable to a Raisa married to Micah.

And the Demonai—had they really planned to set her mother aside and put Raisa on the throne? Did they think she would go along with that? Were her father and grandmother in on it?

A memory trickled back—Reid Nightwalker urging her to come with him to Demonai Camp instead of fleeing the country. *No one will touch you at Demonai,* he'd said. *No one should force you from your birthright.*

Was her life just a series of lies? Was this what she had to look forward to—a lifetime of manipulating others to serve her own purposes?

It's not just the real, but the perception of real that counts, Mother, she thought. If people perceive you as weak, then you are weak, even if it's a survival strategy.

Interesting that her mother hadn't mentioned Mellony, or the pressure from the Wizard Council to name her princess heir. Did she not want to worry her? Did she not want her to rush back into danger?

Or did Marianna mean to keep Raisa in the south until a change in succession could be accomplished?

Trust no one. Never had her mother spoken truer words.

Raisa felt more trust in her friendship with Talia and Hallie than with anyone at court, save Amon.

Had Raisa done anything to encourage the intrigue swirling around her? Why was the council so convinced that she would be troublesome?

And now what? The term was nearly over. Should she wait here meekly until her mother called her home? If she returned home, would it knock down the fragile house of cards that was her queendom?

Could she possibly be more alone?

Raisa flopped onto her back, tears leaking from her eyes and running into her hair.

CHAPTER TWENTY-NINE

A Babe in the Woods

Han cut across the greening lawns, heading for Bridge Street. It was Tuesday—the day before his class with Dean Abelard. He'd stayed up half the night for the second night in a row. He and Dancer had spent the afternoon experimenting with a talisman Dancer had crafted from a flying rowan. It was challenging to create a talisman that wouldn't interfere with Han's own magic while protecting him from someone else's.

And now he was late for his meeting with Rebecca.

The flower vendors lined the street leading to the bridge. That was one thing they had more of in Oden's Ford than at home—flowers. They grew pansies all winter long, the deep red blooms called Blood of Hanalea, white solstice stars, flowering cactus of all kinds from We'enhaven, magnolias with big saucer flowers you could serve dinner on, orchids of all colors and sizes. And now tulips and daffodils and bulb irises.

Rebecca loved flowers. She said she missed her garden at home.

On impulse, Han stopped long enough to buy a fistful from a vendor.

When he entered The Turtle and Fish, the common room was half filled with cadets, but Talia and Pearlie weren't there. Han nodded to Linc, the bartender, walked straight past the bar, and climbed the stairs to the second floor.

Just as he put his hand on the latch of their meeting room, the door flew open and Rebecca stood in front of him, her carry bag slung over her shoulder, her cheeks flushed with anger—obviously on her way out.

"Well!" she said, looking him up and down. "If it isn't Hanson Alister." She paused ominously. "The *late* Hanson Alister."

There was a raw, ragged edge to her voice, an emotional vibration he'd never heard before. Blueblood or not, she could rough him up better than any girlie he'd ever known.

He groped for the right thing to say. "Rebecca, listen. I know I'm late. I'm sorry. I was . . . working on a project . . . and I lost track of time."

"I warned you," she snapped. "You think the rules changed because we kissed?"

"I'm meeting with the dean tomorrow," he said. "I was getting ready for that." He paused, and when she said nothing, added, "Please forgive me. It won't happen again."

"That's what you said last time." She glared up at him. "*You're* the one who wanted tutoring. Do you think I have nothing better to do? You can squander your own time, but when it comes to *my* time . . ."

"It is valuable. I understand that." Usually he could charm and cajole her out of any foul mood, but today she was all clouds and rain—tense, snappish, and downhearted.

Belatedly remembering the flowers, he produced them from under his coat and extended them toward her. Irises and Blood of Hanalea, tied with a ribbon.

"Here. You said you liked flowers."

She stared at the flowers as if astonished, then looked up into his face as if he'd been swapped out for somebody else. "*Another* present?"

Well, admittedly, he wasn't the present-giving, flower-buying kind. He'd never had need of that. Nor the money. "Making up for lost time," he said. "And, to be honest, that last present was for me as much as you."

She took the flowers grudgingly and sniffed them. "Thank you."

"Is something wrong?" he asked, taking advantage of the lull in hostilities to shoulder open the door.

She allowed herself to be ushered back inside. "What's wrong is that you're late," she said.

"I'll buy you dinner after we're done," he suggested. "Anywhere you want."

She dumped her carry bag on a chair, then sat down at their usual worktable. "We'll see. First, I want to see evidence that you've read chapter twelve."

Fortunately, he *had* read chapter twelve, which dealt with Fellsian court protocol, and was about as interesting as reading crop reports. But somehow, when Rebecca talked about it, it came alive. He was amazed at how much she knew about the history and inner workings of the court in Fellsmarch. She quizzed him on the role of the Council of Nobles, the Wizard Council, and the Office of the Royal Steward.

Some parts she had to fill in—parts that weren't in Han's books. Faulk tended to focus too much on the royal family.

"What's the difference between the Wizard Assembly and the Wizard Council?" Han asked. "For instance, how do they choose the council members?"

Rebecca sat back, narrow-eyed, as if wondering what he meant to do with that information. "The assembly is made up of all gifted citizens in the registry on Gray Lady. The council really holds all the power. The major wizard houses have vested seats on the Wizard Council, dating back to before the Breaking," she said. "The eldest gifted child of the council member replaces his or her parent, unless the child steps aside. Also, there's one seat voted in by the assembly, and one member chosen by the queen. The council elects the High Wizard from among those on the council."

"If the queen dies, does the High Wizard stay on?" Han asked.

"No," Rebecca said. "Each High Wizard is bound to an individual queen, so when the princess heir is crowned queen, a new High Wizard is named."

"But it isn't an inherited post," Han said. "Any wizard can serve, right?"

"Well, theoretically," Rebecca said. "But most, if not all, of the High Wizards have come from the vested wizard houses."

"Which are . . . ?" It seemed that every day Han became more aware of how little he knew, and how much he needed to know.

"The Bayars, the Mathises, the Abelards, the Gryphons," Rebecca said vaguely. "Some others."

"What keeps the High Wizard from overpowering the queen?" Han said. "Magically, I mean?"

Rebecca's head jerked up and she stared at him. "Why do you ask that?"

Han shrugged. "Well, it stands to reason that it could be a problem. Wasn't that what happened after the invasion?"

She licked her lips. "The Binding is supposed to prevent that."

"What do you mean, is *supposed* to?" Han said, catching an odd inflection.

Rebecca shifted her gaze away. "The Binding *does* control the High Wizard," she said, nodding as if to reassure herself. "The speakers conduct a ceremony that binds the High Wizard both to the queen's will and to the good of the queendom."

Han tapped the cover of his book. "It says in here the High Wizard serves as a counselor to the queen on magical matters, represents her to the Wizard Council, and uses magic to support and protect the army, the realm, and the throne."

Rebecca nodded, her shoulders slumping a little, the curtain of her hair obscuring her face. "That's right."

"But he's not in charge," Han said. "The queen's in charge, right?"

She nodded. "The queen rules alone. Queens of the Fells are forbidden to marry wizards, and even the man she marries takes the title of consort only."

"But there used to be wizard kings," Han persisted. "Right?"

"Right," she said. "But not since the Breaking. After the

kings nearly destroyed the world, they decided it was a bad idea." She reached for Han's book, seeming eager to change the subject. "I had no idea you were so interested in politics. Now, let's review the rules surrounding royal succession and accomplishments of some specific queens."

"How can you remember all those names?" Han said.

"My family's been at court for generations, you know," Rebecca said. "Some of it had to soak in. You've heard those songs, haven't you, that name off the Gray Wolf queens in order?"

Actually, he knew some drinking songs that named off the queens, but they didn't bear repeating to a blueblood. "I don't have to memorize them, do I?" he asked. "I'd just as soon skip over that. To tell the truth, I don't give a rat's arse about the queens."

She flinched, as if he'd slapped her. "All right, but I just thought—"

"The queens, the nobility, that whole lot—they're just bloodsuckers feeding off the people. They don't care at all what happens in the streets."

"You don't know that," Rebecca said, color staining her pale cheeks. "You don't know anything about Queen Marianna and what she—"

"You're the one that doesn't know anything," Han said. "Forgive me for being a cynic, but I know how people are treated outside of the castle close."

"What makes you think I don't?" Rebecca said, her voice rising. "I was in Southbridge Guardhouse, remember? I saw how you'd been beaten. I saw what happened to your friends. But you can't think the queen had any—"

Han plowed right over her words. "The queen has had everything to do with every bad thing that's happened to me in the past year."

Raisa sat frozen, her green eyes fixed on his face, speechless for once.

Why are you telling her this, Alister? Han thought. Just shut it. Not the way to follow up on flowers. But he opened his mouth and the story came pouring out.

"Me and my mam and little sister lived over a stable in Ragmarket," he said. "My mam did washing for the queen until she was dismissed for ruining one of her dresses. I'd given up thieving, so we had no money at all. That was the start of it."

Rebecca leaned forward, lacing her fingers together. "I never realized that your mother worked for the queen," she said. "Perhaps . . . perhaps there's a way to get her reinstated. I . . . know some people and . . ."

Han shook his head. "Don't try and fix this. It's not fixable. Just listen. The queen's responsible for public works, right? For the water supply and like that. Well, the wells went bad in Ragmarket, and my sister, Mari, caught the fever. While I was out trying to get the money to buy some medicine for her, the bluejackets came looking for me, thinking I was the one hushed the Southies that died. When they didn't find me, they set fire to the stable with Mam and Mari inside."

"What?" Rebecca whispered, her face now gone ashen.

"They burnt to death, Rebecca," Han said, his voice low and fierce. "And the bluejackets did it, on the queen's orders. Mari was seven years old."

She stared at him, shaking her head. "Oh, no," she whispered.

"No. That can't be true." Her mouth formed the word *no* even when no sound came out.

"You *said* the queen's in charge." Han knew he should stop, but he'd had this stuffed up in his heart so long that it was like the floodgates had opened. "After that, somebody came back and murdered the Raggers and the Southies. Some of them were *lytlings*, too. The ones you saved from Southbridge Guardhouse—they're all dead."

Tears pooled in Rebecca's eyes. "So . . . Sarie and Velvet and Flinn are . . ."

"All dead, far as I know," Han said. "Cat's the only one that escaped."

"It was all just a waste?" Rebecca's voice wavered. "Why didn't you tell me? About your family and . . . and everything?"

"You never asked," Han said. "People die in Ragmarket and Southbridge every day. They don't count in the blueblood world. It's just one more sad story."

"But . . . we're not all like that," she said, her lower lip trembling.

"'Course not." He snorted. "Her bloody Highness the princess heir tosses her pin money our way and we're supposed to get down on our knees and thank her."

"That's not what she wants," Rebecca whispered, looking stricken. "She's not looking for gratitude. She just—"

"Of course you'd stick up for her," Han said. "Bluebloods always stick together."

This time, Rebecca didn't try to respond. She sat, twisting a gold ring on her forefinger, staring straight ahead, her face as pale as scribes' paper.

As silence grew between them, guilt crept over Han. Of course she'd defend them. She'd grown up in the court, and her friends were bluebloods. She wasn't the enemy.

"Look, I'm sorry," Han said. "I didn't mean to jump all over you. You may be a blueblood, but you're not to blame for what happened." He closed his hand over hers.

None of what he said seemed to make her feel any better.

It wasn't her fault that his life was a disaster. He was trying to figure out a way to say that when she slammed her chair back, nearly toppling it, and stood.

"I have to go." She snatched up her bag. "Please accept my . . . sincere . . . condolences at the loss of your family," she said, voice hitching. "I am . . . so very sorry."

She flung herself out the door as if she were being chased by demons, leaving her flowers behind. He heard her banging down the steps. Then nothing.

Han sat frozen with surprise for a moment. "Rebecca," he shouted. "Wait!"

He scraped together his books and papers and stuffed them into his carry bag, then launched himself down the stairs.

By the time he reached the common room, Rebecca was gone. The patrons stared at Han with greedy interest. He ran out onto Bridge Street, looking both directions, and saw her, head down, striding back toward Wien House and her dormitory.

He raced after her, dodging students and faculty who strolled the streets, enjoying the spring weather.

His long legs proved an advantage—that and the fact that Rebecca was crying flat out and probably couldn't see where she was going. Han caught up with her and took hold of her arm.

"Rebecca, please, please, don't run off," he said. "I'm sorry. I shouldn't have said the things I did."

She just shook her head, her eyes squeezed tightly shut as if she could make him disappear. Tears leaked out of the corners of her eyes and rolled down her cheeks. "Leave me alone. I'm going back to my room."

But she made no move to do so, just stood in the middle of the street, fists clenched, while the crowds parted on either side of her, staring and nudging each other.

"Come on," he said, sliding an arm around her shoulder and guiding her back toward the bridge. He looked up at the sign that swung over the doorway. The Scholar and Hound. "Let's go in here."

She didn't say yes, but she didn't say no, either, so he herded her through the door and into the warmly lit interior. It was crowded, but he spotted two bleary-eyed students leaving a table in the corner. He shouldered his way through the standees and claimed it, staring down a hulking cadet in a beer-stained tunic lurching toward it.

"The girlie needs to sit down," Han said. "Back off."

The cadet backed off, peppering him with black looks. Han settled Rebecca into a chair facing the corner, to make her tear-stained face less apparent. He sat facing the room, his usual position, and motioned to the server. He held up two fingers and tapped his midsection, and she nodded, moving off toward the kitchen.

Han looked back at Rebecca; she'd undergone a transformation. She'd wiped the tears from her face, and the ragged quality was gone from her breathing. Even her hair was in better order.

Her cheeks and the tip of her nose were still pink, or Han would have never known she'd been crying. She'd tapped into that steel core of hers, pulled herself together, and put on a street face to hide the misery within.

The girlie's tough, for a blueblood, Han thought. Maybe tough enough to be with me. But something's eating at her. Should it worry me that she's so good at keeping secrets?

"I'm sorry," she said. "I didn't mean to fall apart like that. I just . . . I have a lot on my mind already and . . . it's just . . . when I heard about your family and—and the Raggers—I just felt like everything I'd done—or tried to do—was a waste of time."

"It ambushes me too," Han said. "It's like getting run over by an oxcart."

"How do you even stand it?" She studied his face like she really wanted to know.

"I don't have much choice, do I?" He shrugged, thinking that, in a way, it helped to share the secret eating at him. It was like lancing a boil—it relieved the pain and pressure. "But I'm not lying down for it. That's why I'm here. For next time."

She frowned, biting her lip. "What do you . . . ?" She jumped and looked up as the server set mugs of cider in front of them, along with steaming bowls of stew.

"I hope stew is all right," Han said. "I haven't had anything to eat all day."

"Stew's good. I haven't eaten, either." She stared down at her dinner, but made no move to take a bite.

Meaning to teach by example, Han spooned up some stew. "It's good," he said, with his mouth full. "Sorry," he said, wiping his mouth with a napkin. Sometimes, when he was tired, he just couldn't play the blueblood role. "I can't make you, Rebecca, but you'll probably feel better if you eat."

She nodded mechanically and took a bite, and then another. Once she got started, she finished it off, washing it down with cider until that too was gone.

"You said you had things on your mind," Han said, once she'd dropped her spoon into her bowl. "What's going on?"

She rubbed her temples with the tips of her fingers. "I just don't know what to do. I feel like I should go back home. I . . . my mother needs me."

"Why? Is she sick?" Han asked, ordering another cider.

"Well," Rebecca said, "not exactly. But she's not herself. And even when she is herself, she's . . ." Her voice trailed off, as if she suddenly realized she'd said too much.

"So she's asked you to come home?"

"No," Rebecca said. "She told me to stay away. But she may not be thinking clearly. And it may not be in my best interest to stay away."

"Well," Han said. "Mind, I don't know anything about your family. But being here at Oden's Ford—this is a real opportunity for you, isn't it?"

She nodded, pushing her empty mug away and pulling Han's full one toward her.

Better go easy on that, Han thought. *Cider isn't strong drink, but you're a small person.*

"Isn't there anyone else you can talk to and find out what's going on?" Han asked. "What about your father?"

"Well, he and my mother don't always get on," she said. "And he's away a lot on business.

"Brothers and sisters?"

"I have a sister," Rebecca said. "But I think she might be part of the problem." She paused. "I'm afraid I'll lose everything if I don't go back now."

Han frowned, confused. Then it came to him. Families like Rebecca's—they had legacies. "You mean they might cut you off? Disinherit you?"

She nodded. "Maybe. It's a possibility."

Han's instincts said she wasn't telling him everything. It was like peering through a keyhole into a room you wanted to break into. You could see some of what was going on, but there might be a nasty surprise waiting in the part of the room you couldn't see.

"I don't know that I can give you advice," he said. "And I don't know what you stand to lose." He reached out and fingered a tendril of her hair. "If you don't know what your mother wants, you should think about what *you* want, and the best way to go after it, whether it's staying here or going back and getting things straight with your mother."

Rebecca's face went all cloudy again. "It's not about what I want," she said. "I have a lot of other people depending on me."

"Why *can't* it be about what you want—sometimes, anyway?" Han said, closing his hand over hers. "You just got to . . . you just have to claim it. I've learned that nobody's going to hand you anything. You don't get what you don't go after."

She looked down at their joined hands. "I don't know whom to trust," she whispered.

"Trust me," he said, leaning across the table and kissing her.

The fact was, he wanted Rebecca to stay in Oden's Ford, and

it wasn't just that he was learning things from her he wouldn't learn anywhere else.

She was prickly and proud, used to ordering people around and getting her own way. She was smart and opinionated—she could talk the tail off a dog. But she was fiercely kindhearted—she'd cross the street to give a coin to a beggar, and always backed the underdog in any fight. She'd shed tears over Mam and Mari—though she'd never even met them.

She demanded a lot—but demanded even more from herself.

He still held her hand within his, rubbing his thumb over her palm. Her hands were remarkably small, but calloused. Hands that weren't afraid of hard work. She wore a heavy gold ring on her forefinger, engraved with circling wolves.

Han wanted to see one of those smiles that lit up her eyes. He wanted to see her happy again. He wanted to be the one who made her happy.

He wanted Rebecca Morley in every way. He'd been living like a dedicate for months.

In the end, he walked Rebecca all the way back to Grindell Hall. She was stumble-step sleepy more than anything else, and this time he'd make sure she got home all right.

It wasn't quite curfew when they arrived at her dormitory. Han meant to deliver Rebecca and take his leave at the door, but the common room was empty.

"Where's your dorm master?" he asked. If he'd showed up at Hampton with a girlie on his arm, Blevins would've been all over them already.

"Don't have one," Rebecca mumbled, yawning. "Just Amon. I mean Commander Byrne."

"Where's he?"

Rebecca rubbed her temples with the heel of her hand. "Probably already in bed. Or over at the Temple School, visiting Annamaya." She said this without emotion.

The dormitory had a definite military look about it. For one thing, it was much more orderly than Hampton Hall. "Who else stays here?" Han asked.

"The rest of my triple," Rebecca said. She took his hand and tugged him toward the stairs. "Come up with me?"

Han hesitated, his heart hammering out a yes. "Are you sure? I don't want to get you into trouble."

"It's all right," she said, her face pinking up a bit. "I room with Hallie and Talia. Talia will be glad to see you—she's been playing matchmaker, you know. Hallie just got back from the Fells. If she's still awake, she can tell us the news from home."

Well, Han thought, I do want to hear the news.

They climbed the narrow stairs, still holding hands, up and up, past the snores emanating from the second-floor sleeping quarters, to the third-floor landing.

Here, there was a small sitting room with a cluster of chairs around a fireplace. An arched doorway led into an adjacent room. It was the kind of place the commander should have. Or the dorm master.

"This puts Hampton to shame," Han said, looking around.

Rebecca laughed. "It's supposed to be for the dorm master. There are three female cadets in Grindell, so we share it."

She pushed open the door to the bedroom, calling, "Hallie? Talia?" Han hoped they weren't already asleep in there. He hoped they weren't there at all.

She motioned him forward. "They're not here."

Han hesitated in the doorway, looking around. Three single beds were lined up against the wall, each made up with military precision, each with a large trunk at the foot of the bed. Three study desks had been jammed in under the window, for the best light.

Rebecca's familiar book bag lay on one desk, with her writing implements laid out next to it and the music box centered in a position of honor on the blotter.

"This is posh," Han said. So much for the rough life in the military.

Rebecca's purple scarf dangled from a hook by the door. She hung her bag next to it and held out her hand for Han's.

"You sure I shouldn't get going?" he said, handing it over. "It's nearly curfew."

What was the matter with him? He was never this well behaved.

Rebecca sat down on her bed, practically bouncing on the taut coverlet. She patted the bedclothes beside her. He sat down next to her, sliding his arms around her. He kissed her, and she drew back in surprise, pressing her fingers to her lips, eyes wide. "Your lips seem to be—quite potent tonight."

"Sorry," Han said. He took hold of his amulet and allowed power to flow into it. "Let's try again." Gingerly, he pressed his lips against hers, eyes open for her reaction.

"That's better," she said, winding her arms around his neck. She lay back, pulling him down beside her, pressing against him. He kissed her again, then began working at the buttons of her uniform jacket. He was glad he hadn't joined the army after all.

The military was entirely too fond of buttons.

"You know, I've never had a girlie say that to me before," Han murmured, sliding her jacket from her shoulders and tossing it aside. "That my lips were potent."

"I say that to all the wizards I kiss," she said. "I think you should know."

"I see," he said, trying hard not to wonder what wizards she'd been kissing. Not Micah Bayar, he thought. Don't let it be Bayar.

"What's it like?" he asked.

"What do you mean, what's it like?" She squinted at him suspiciously.

"Being kissed by a wizard."

"Why? Haven't you been?" she asked, looking surprised.

There was Fiona. Han pushed that out of his mind. "Being kissed by a wizard when you're not one, I mean."

"Hmmm." Rebecca scrunched up her face, thinking. "It's kind of a sizzling sting that goes all the way into your throat, like brandy going down."

Han pressed his fingers against his own mouth. "Like brandy? Really?"

"And sometimes it goes to your head and . . ." Her voice trailed off and her eyes narrowed. "Blood of the demon," she growled, readjusting her shirt. "Don't make fun of me."

"No, no," Han said, snorting with laughter. "I want to know. This is fascinating."

Picking up her pillow, she smacked him with it. There ensued a wrestling match that destroyed the well-made bed and was nearly Han's undoing several times. They ended up flushed and laughing, entwined with each other.

Putting one hand on the back of her neck and the other at her waist, he kissed her again, long and slow, since he'd been a long time between kisses and he didn't know when he'd get back to it again.

He planted quick kisses along Rebecca's jawline, slid her shirt from her shoulders and kissed her bare skin, raising goose-flesh. She wore a silk camisole under the shirt. He couldn't help noticing the small rose tattooed above her left breast.

He sat back for a moment, trying to slow his breathing, to control the pounding cadence of his heart. *Easy, Alister. Just because you're eager doesn't mean she is.*

"Rebecca," he said, resting his forehead against hers, "can we lock the door? Like I said, when I put things aside for the future, they disappear on me."

"I know," she said. "But I just . . . things are already complicated enough. I'm not taking maidenweed and I don't know where to get any around here. And Hallie and Talia could be back any time." As if to put the lie to the words, she reached out and untied the neck of his shirt, fumbling with the buttons, sliding her hands inside, caressing his skin. Before he knew it, she was fingering his amulet.

"This is so beautiful," she whispered, as the piece kindled in her hand. It burned with a greenish light, seeming to make her skin translucent. "I never realized . . ."

"Rebecca!" Han said, pushing her hand away. "Don't . . ."

Light and power exploded between them with a loud *crack*, leaving Han's ears ringing and Rebecca sucking on her fingers.

"Are you all right?" Han said anxiously, taking her hand. "Did it burn you or . . . ?"

Rebecca shook her head. "It didn't even hurt. I . . ."

Feet pounded up the stairs. The door slammed open and Corporal Amon Byrne stood in the doorway, shirtless, breathing hard, sword drawn.

"Blood of the demon!" Han swore, rolling to his feet.

"Get away from her!" Byrne shouted, advancing with the sword.

Han backed away. Byrne stood between him and the door, but the window was behind him.

"R—Rebecca, are you all right?" Byrne asked, continuing to advance until he was between Han and Rebecca.

"I'm *fine*, Amon," Rebecca said, looking from one to the other. "Listen, this is all just a—"

"What's up, sir?" Three more disheveled cadets peered in at the doorway. When they saw Byrne with his sword drawn, holding Han at bay, they crammed through the doorway like pigs through a gate.

"Take Morley downstairs and stow her someplace safe," Byrne said, never taking his eyes off Han. "And find her a shirt."

"Commander Byrne!" Rebecca shouted, standing in her camisole as if she were the general of all the armies. "Stop it at once! Han Alister is my *guest*."

Han knew next to nothing about military matters, but he had to think that cadets weren't allowed to shout at their commanders. Let alone order them around.

Byrne looked from Han to Rebecca and back again. He looked lost for a moment, then his resolve seemed to harden.

"Cadet Morley, you know that guests are not allowed in Grindell Hall after curfew. I order you to go immediately to the common room and await disciplinary action while I deal with your *guest*."

Han didn't like his chances with Corporal Byrne. "That's all right, Corporal Commander," he said. "No need to deal with me. Good to see you again. I was just going."

"Han," Rebecca said. "Wait! You don't have to go."

"I always say yes to the man with the sword," Han said.

By now, his backside was pressed against the window frame. Turning, he pushed open the shutters. Gripping the top of the window frame, he swung his legs up and through the opening, praying there was a gable below. Looking down, he saw a peaked roof a story beneath him, and let go.

He landed gracelessly, twisting his ankle and skinning his palms. At least he didn't punch clean through the roof.

"I'll see you Thursday!" Rebecca shouted out the window. His cloak landed next to him on the tiles.

Shrugging into it, Han took off, limping, across the roof to the connecting gallery. Above him he heard the shutters slam shut.

His mind raced faster than he could travel on foot.

There was something more there than a commander's concern for curfew or the virtue of one of his cadets. Did Byrne want it all—both Annamaya and Rebecca?

He didn't seem the type to be so greedy. But Han didn't know him all that well.

Could Rebecca have used Han to make Byrne jealous? If so, she was willing to go pretty far to make a point. Cynical and streetwise as he was, he couldn't believe that.

Han laughed, shaking his head. Poor Alister. You may be a thief and a streetlord and a rogue. You may be a legend of sorts in Ragmarket, but you're a babe in the woods among these bluebloods.

When it came down to it, even if he'd been played, he had no cause to complain. It wasn't like Rebecca had made him any promises. It wasn't like she'd made any claims on him, either. They'd kissed. Danced a few dances. Had a pillow fight.

He'd really enjoyed that kissing, though. Wanted more, in fact. He carried the memory of her touch on his skin. She stirred him up more than any girlie in memory.

Corporal Byrne had ruined Han's evening, but he had a feeling he'd returned the favor. The thought cheered him.

See you Thursday! she'd said.

You don't get what you don't go after, he'd said.

Somewhere nearby, temple bells bonged out midnight.

He'd hoped his ankle would loosen up, but instead it seemed to stiffen as he hobbled along. That would make it difficult to outrun the provost guards if they spotted him. So he kept to the side streets and shadows as best he could.

He crossed the bridge, avoiding the guards searching out stragglers. As he wound his way toward Hampton, the back of his neck prickled, as though someone were watching him. Once, he spun around, hearing a footstep behind him. But he saw nothing and no one.

Surely Byrne wouldn't send anyone after him to exact revenge, Han thought. Nah. Byrne was an honorable sort, full of scruples. Besides, maybe he and Rebecca were busy kissing and making up. Jealousy twanged through him.

When Han reached Mystwerk Hall, he chose not to cross the open quad, where he might be spotted, but kept close to the building, using it as cover as he threaded his way closer to Hampton. Maybe he'd go up over the roof again. He'd been through enough drama. He didn't want to deal with any more.

Han turned down the cobbled pathway that led to the back gardens. There was a hidden corner between the buildings that offered good handholds for climbing.

Han wedged one boot into a crevice and reached high, gripping the rough stones on either side. He hoped his ankle wouldn't give him trouble on the high road.

At that moment, someone behind him said, "Keep your hands where they are. I got a blade, and I'll use it."

The voice was low and rough. Whoever it was, he was smart enough not to touch Han, and so give away his position.

"What do you want?" Han asked, thinking that if idiocy were a capital crime, he might soon pay the price.

"You got a purse on you?"

Han did have a purse on him, but he didn't want to give it up.

"Nuh-uh," Han said. "It's nearly end of term. I'm flat broke."

"Liar." A whisper of air, his ear stung, and then blood trickled down his neck. The thief had sliced his earlobe, with a blade so sharp he'd scarcely felt it.

"Your purse," the thief repeated. "Or next I cut off your hand." His voice shook a little, like he was nervous. He sounded young, too. That wasn't reassuring. A nervous larcener with a sharp blade was dangersome. And Han wouldn't be quick on his feet, with his ankle unreliable as it was.

"All right. I got a purse," Han admitted. "You want me to fetch it out?" He didn't plan on making any sudden moves.

"Tell me where it is," the thief said.

"It's in a pouch, slid onto my belt, tucked into my breeches in front," Han said. It was a thief's carry, where a slide-hander or pickpocket was least likely to dive unnoticed. If the thief went fishing for it, it might provide an opening, at least.

But the larcener didn't go for it. Han felt the whisper of steel sliding close, and his cloak slid to the ground, sliced through down the back and across the shoulders.

That was smart—getting all that fabric out of the way first. He hoped this street lifter didn't plan on slicing his breeches off, too.

"What's that around your neck?" the thief asked.

Han's amulet glowed faintly, illuminating the dark corner in front of him.

"Nothing," Han said, tilting his head down to cover it. "Just something I bought on the streets, for the festival. It lights up."

"Looks pricy to me," the larcener said. "Like it might be worth real money."

"I'll sell it to you," Han said. "Paid a fivepenny for it, I'll sell it for a girlie."

You have a death wish, he thought, wishing he could suck the words back down. The clans' great wizard champion would die sliced up by a street larcener. Abelard's assassin would fall to a common rusher.

"Take it off and toss it back toward me," the larcener said. "Move slow."

"Look," Han said. "How about I toss you my purse instead?

My girlie give me this neckpiece, and she'll skin me alive if I lose it." If he reached into his breeches he could fetch out his own knife.

"*I'll* skin you alive if you don't give it here," the thief said.

"All right. I'm unfastening it now. Here I go." Han slowly lowered his arms from the wall and reached to the back of his neck, fumbling with the clasp on the chain.

He wondered how much power was left in the flashpiece; if it would distract his attacker enough so Han could chance a move on him. It had reacted to Rebecca, anyway.

"Lift the chain over your head," the thief said. "You don't got to unfasten it."

How does he know that? Han thought. Unless the whole point of this shoulder-tap was to get hold of the jinxpiece. Fear snaked down between his shoulder blades.

Han lifted the chain over his head. He palmed the amulet, feeling it vibrate faintly at his touch. Not much to work with. He started to turn.

"Don't turn 'round," the larcener said sharply. "Just give it a toss over your shoulder." Yes. There was something familiar about the voice.

Han tossed the amulet over his left shoulder with his right hand. As the piece flew past his ear, he kept turning, yanking his knife from his waist. As he'd expected, the larcener was momentarily distracted, his gaze following the falling star of the amulet.

Han launched himself toward the rusher, slamming his shoulder into him with all his weight behind it. The thief fell, striking his head on the stone wall. He fell flat on his face on the cobblestones, his arms stretched out in front of him, knocked out cold.

Han looked down at him. He was dressed all in black, with narrow black trowsers, black boots, and a hooded jacket that fit close to his slender body. Dressed like an assassin. So why hadn't he just cut Han's throat and robbed his body at his leisure?

The whole thing had gone down almost silently. Han grabbed up his amulet and dropped the chain over his head, keeping it in his hand. He stood in a half-crouch, with his knife in his other hand, expecting to see the thief's accomplices running at him.

But a single figure detached itself from the shadows at the side of the building and came toward him.

"Keep back," Han said, waving the knife. "Or I'll stick you and your friend."

"Don't kill her," Dancer said, stepping into the light that leaked onto the path from the street. "We need to find out why she did it and who she's working for."

Her? Han slumped back against the wall, his knife dangling loosely, his head spinning. This is a dream, he thought.

Dancer knelt next to the prone larcener and relieved her of her knife. He gently turned the body over.

It was Cat Tyburn.

CHAPTER THIRTY

THIS ROUGH
MAGIC

Mick and Garret took hold of Raisa's arms, trying to tug her out of her room while Han backed toward the window. Amon advanced on him, sword extended.

"That's all right, Corporal," Han said. "No need to deal with me. Good to see you again. I was just going." His gaze met Raisa's for a long moment, his blue eyes hard and brilliant as sapphires. He turned, jerked open the shutters, and slid feetfirst through the window like an eel. Dropping his sword, Amon leaped forward, grabbing at him, but missed.

Pulling free from Mick and Garret, Raisa ran to the window and pushed in next to Amon. He seized her arm, like he thought she might jump out after Han.

She leaned out of the window in time to see Han limping across the gallery roof, away from them.

"I'll see you Thursday!" Raisa shouted after him. She grabbed his cloak from the hook and tossed it through the window. Han scooped it up and walked on, not looking back when Amon slammed the shutters closed.

"All right," Amon said. "He's gone. The rest of you, out. I want to speak with Morley in private. If Abbott and Talbot come back, keep 'em downstairs."

Mick and Garret gave Raisa sympathetic looks before they trooped out of the room. Raisa heard their boots on the stairs. Then silence.

Raisa leaned her hip on the window ledge and glared daggers at Amon Byrne. He glared thunderclouds back. Each waited for the other to begin.

Finally, Amon gave in. "Did you really ask Cuffs Alister up to your room?"

"Han," she said.

"What?"

"He goes by Han Alister now."

Amon rolled his eyes. "Han Alister, then."

"What of it?" Raisa said, furious and embarrassed and frustrated, all at once.

"You know what the rules are," Amon said. "Just because we don't have a dorm master doesn't mean they're not enforced. No guests are allowed on the second and third floors. No guests at all after curfew. I promised Taim Askell that—"

"Taim Askell has nothing to do with this and you know it!" Raisa said. "If you'd found a girl hiding in Mick's room, you'd not have driven her off with a sword."

"If he was snuggling with a known thief and gang leader, maybe I would," Amon said. "Especially if that thief had already abducted him at knifepoint and held him captive overnight.

Especially if that thief had suddenly turned into a wizard." He thrust his head forward like a turtle from its shell. "As a matter of fact, I'd be seriously wondering if Mick had lost his wits."

"I know what I'm doing," Raisa said, pulling her shirt on. "It's not like I've tried to keep it a secret or anything. I told you he was here at Oden's Ford."

Just stop talking, Raisa thought. There's no reason you should feel guilty.

"You said you wouldn't pretend not to know him," Amon said. "You didn't tell me you were going to ... to ..." He waved his hand, taking in the rumpled bed. "Rai, you hardly know him. And what you do know is no recommendation."

"I know more about him than you think," Raisa said. "I've been tutoring him for months."

"*Tutoring* him?" Amon raised his eyebrows. "Is *that* what you were doing?" He snatched up his sword and rammed it home in his scabbard like he was skewering an enemy, muttering something about *tutoring*.

"What was that?" Raisa said. "What did you say?"

"I *said*, If you were tutoring him, what was the bloody *subject*?"

"None of your business," she said. "Anyway, every other night you're crossing the river to be with Annamaya."

"That's different. We're not ..." Again he waved a hand at Raisa's bed.

Raisa put her hands on her hips. "Do you even *want* to? You shouldn't be marrying someone you aren't in love with."

"Well, I don't have much choice, do I?" He sat down on the edge of the hearth and put his head in his hands.

Raisa stared at him for a long moment, then went and sat next to him on the hearth. She put her hand on his knee. "I know," she said. "I'm sorry."

"Neither of us can quit being what we are," Amon said through his fingers. "You're supposed to pretend that I'm your commander, but as soon as I give you an order, you turn into the princess heir. Meanwhile, the rest of the Wolves are watching. Should I blame them if they begin to think that the orders I give are optional?"

"I'm sorry," Raisa said again, "but it doesn't help when you evict my guests at swordpoint."

Amon dropped his hands into his lap, fingering his wolf ring. He looked over at her, his gray eyes dark with pain. "I have no right to ask this, but—what's between you and Alister? Is it—is it just a fling or . . ."

"It's not to get back at you, if that's what you're asking," Raisa snapped.

Amon's cheeks flushed red. "I wasn't suggesting . . ."

"It was tempting, but no," Raisa said. She thought for a long moment. "I don't know what to say. He's brilliant, and he doesn't let me get away with anything. I've learned so much from him. . . . I think he makes me a better person."

Amon rolled his eyes. "It sounds like he's your priest, not your lover."

"He's not my lover!" Raisa retorted. "Well, not exactly."

"Not exactly? Or not yet?"

"Amon."

Amon rubbed his eyes wearily. "By the Lady, Raisa. I'm doing the best I can."

"I know." Raisa bit her lip. What could she tell him? *I notice everything about him, from his flawed nose to his battle scars to his eyes as blue as an upland lake at midsummer. Sometimes I see the boy he would have been had it not been for his life in Ragmarket. He wears his pain on his face in unguarded moments; at other times, I can see just how dangerous he is.* No, she couldn't say any of that.

"I'm going to the Cadets' Ball with him," Raisa said. "Just so you know."

"Rai," Amon said, taking her hands in his. "Whatever you do, don't fall in love with him."

Raisa nodded, knowing it was already too late.

CHAPTER THIRTY-ONE
BETRAYAL

Sitting back on his heels on the cobblestones, Han stared down at Cat. A purple bruise bloomed over her right eye where it had struck the wall. Her brow bone puffed out, making her face lopsided. A little different angle, and she might have put her eye out.

He looked up at Dancer. "Did you know she was stalking me?" he demanded.

"Shhh." Dancer put a finger to his lips, looking up and down the pathway. "I knew she was up to something, so I followed her," Dancer said. "I wouldn't have let her cut your throat or anything."

"That's reassuring." Han stood and scooped up his ruined cloak. "When did you plan to step in?"

"Let's get her inside before the provost guard shows," Dancer said.

"Why should we? Let them take her to gaol," Han said. "I'm done." Han had been blindsided by someone he'd considered to be a friend. He'd never have expected her to try a stab and grab on him. After all that had happened, he was at his limit.

Dancer didn't honor that with an answer. "Come on," he said. "We can't drag her over the roof and through the window. I'll carry her; you go in front and distract Blevins if he's awake." Dancer stowed Cat's blade away and slid his hands under her, lifting her. She groaned but did not open her eyes.

Han walked into the dormitory ahead of them, scouting the common room for Blevins. The dorm master was sound asleep in his chair next to the fire. Waiting up for them. He'd be peeved not to catch them sneaking in after curfew.

Han motioned Dancer forward, and they soft-footed past Blevins and climbed the stairs, keeping to the outsides of the treads so they didn't squeak.

Fortunately, they reached the fourth floor without meeting anyone. Han pushed his door open, and Dancer followed him in, depositing Cat on Han's bed.

"I'll get some cold water for her head," Dancer said. He picked up the basin and left, heading for the third-floor washroom.

He's awfully considerate of someone who cut up my good cloak and threatened me with a knife a few minutes ago, Han thought.

Han lit two candles to drive off the shadows. The dawn was still hours away.

Cat groaned, pressing her hands to her forehead. Han patted her down thoroughly, removing three more knives. Dancer returned with the basin, wet a rag, and laid it over the lump on Cat's head. She reached up and yanked it off, and he replaced it again. She batted his hand away and opened her eyes.

"Get away from me, you dung-eating copp . . ." She stopped abruptly, as memory seemed to flood back in. "Blood and bones," she whispered. Focusing on Han's face, she flinched and closed her eyes again.

"Why didn't you kill me?" she whispered, licking her lips.

"I might still," Han said. "But Dancer thought you'd have something to say first."

"I got nothing to say," Cat whispered. "Just cut my throat and be done with it." She tilted her head back, exposing her throat, a wolf submitting to the alpha of the pack.

Dancer sat down on the bed next to her. "No. You saved our lives in Arden. You deserve a hearing. I want to know what's wrong with you. These past few weeks you've seemed different. Kind of desperate."

"What are you talking about?" Han said irritably. "You hardly know her, so I don't know how you could—"

"You're never around," Dancer said. "You have no idea what's going on with your friends."

Han waved a hand at Cat. "This is a friend?" He rolled his eyes. "Friends don't hush friends in back alleys."

"Cuffs is right," Cat said, opening her eyes and looking at Dancer. "You *don't* know me very well. I'm a thief. I betray my friends. I deserve to die." Tears gathered at the corners of her eyes and trickled into her hair on either side. "I should've just left, but I needed money to get home," she said. "There's nothing for me here. I'm not cut out to be in school."

"What did you want with the amulet?" Han asked, a terrible suspicion growing in his mind. "If you needed money, you should've taken my purse."

"I wasn't going to go poking in your breeches for it," Cat said. "For all I knew you had a stash of weapons in there."

"You were after the amulet all along," Han said. "Weren't you?"

After a long pause, she nodded. "I . . . thought I could sell it," Cat said. "You acted like it was valuable. And you always kept it with you, so I had to take it off you."

Han blinked as the puzzle piece fell into place. "You were the one who tossed my room," he said. "You were looking for it."

"I didn't never toss your room," Cat flared. When Han raised an eyebrow, she mumbled, "How'd you know? I put everything back where it was."

"It was the night of the Dean's Dinner, so you knew neither of us would be here," Dancer said. He was looking at Cat, and she was looking at him, and Han suddenly felt like he was an outsider, just a bystander in the room.

"I . . . I came here because I thought I could help," she said, keeping her eyes locked on Dancer's face as if she were witchfixed. "I felt bad. I thought I could . . . make up for what happened in Fellsmarch." She swallowed hard. "I should've stayed away."

"What do you mean, what happened in Fellsmarch?" Dancer asked, his voice low and soothing, like a witch-talker.

"To Cuffs. To his mam and sister. To . . . to the Raggers," Cat whispered.

Dancer removed the rag, resoaked it, wrung it out, and replaced it. "Why did you feel that *you* had to make up for it?" he asked.

Cat jerked the rag off her forehead and flung it away. "Because it was my fault."

Han stared at her. Cat had a lot to answer for, but he wasn't going to let her take the blame for that. "No," he said. "That one is mine. My fault." He remembered how distraught Cat had been the night of the fire, how she and the other Raggers had kept him from going into the stable after Mam and Mari. She had saved his life that night, too.

"There's no way you could've saved them, if that's what you're thinking," he said, softening a bit. "You can't blame yourself."

She just shook her head. "You don't know nothing." She sat up, then, swaying, looking like she might topple back over. Dancer put an arm around her to steady her, and for once she didn't jerk away.

"Who did you think you could sell it to?" Han asked. "The amulet, I mean."

Cat rolled her eyes as if Han were an idiot. "The Bayar jinxflinger came to see me a few weeks ago. He threatened me. He said he'd tell on me if I didn't steal the jinxpiece back for him. He said it was his to start with, that you'd taken it from him."

That would have been after Bayar and his cousins had been evicted from Hampton. After the dean had told Bayar to back off.

Something was missing, something Cat was talking around but not saying. "What was Bayar going to tell me?" Han asked. "What didn't you want me to know?"

Cat took a deep breath, and the words came out in a rush, like she'd been waiting forever to confess. "It was me," she said. "I was the one told the young Bayar where you lived, when they were hunting you in Ragmarket. They'd took Velvet; they said they'd kill him if I didn't tell. So I did. I figured it was him or you, and I loved Velvet, and I didn't love you. I figured they'd toss the place, find whatever it was you'd stole from them, and that would be that. I never thought . . . I never expected they'd . . ." Her voice broke, and tears streamed down her cheeks.

"You never thought they'd burn up Mam and Mari," Han said.

He backed away from Cat until he came up against the wall. He flattened himself against it, wishing he could disappear, that he could just blink out like a cinder so he wouldn't have to hear any more.

Tears pricked at his eyes. "You didn't know who you were dealing with."

"I found out," she said, her voice bitter as chicory. "They killed Velvet anyway. Then they come and killed everyone else. It was a slaughter. They were looking for you, trying to make somebody tell where you were. I'd be dead myself if I was there." She took a shuddering breath. "I wish I had been."

Han should have known all along. He'd thought it was Taz Mackney, but no. It made sense that he'd been betrayed by someone close to him, someone who could direct the Queen's Guard through the maze of streets in Ragmarket, who could point out the stable in a place with no numbers and no names written down.

"After, I wanted to kill them," Cat said. "I wanted to kill everyone." She smiled sourly. "I always thought I was good with a blade. But I'm smart enough to know that as a killer, I'm nothing next to them. It'd be like throwing myself into the fire. I still would've done it if I thought I could take a few of them with me.

"So I took Jemson's offer to go to Oden's Ford. I never wanted to see Ragmarket again. I got as far as Delphi, then I just got stuck. I was too scared to go on, and I couldn't go back. When I ran into you, when I found out you was still alive, I got this idea that maybe it wouldn't be so bad being in the south if you was there. I knew you'd get on, wherever you went. You were the best streetlord I ever knew. But I knew if you ever found out I was the one that cackled on you, you'd cut my heart out."

She looked at Han, rather hopefully. "So. Kill me. You got rights. That way, I wouldn't have to keep thinking about things I should've done different."

Han slid down the wall until his backside hit the floor. He pulled his knees up and wrapped his arms around them. He felt numb. He'd been nursing his guilt for so long, he wasn't about to hand any piece of it to Cat.

"I'm not going to kill you, Cat," he said. "I'm sorry about that, but I'm not. You just got in the way when the Bayars came after me, that's all. You and everybody else. That's what I'll be carrying for the rest of my life."

They all sat in silence for a while.

"What now?" Dancer said to no one in particular. He took Cat's hand and cradled it in his. Again, she didn't resist.

"I'll go away, if that's what you want," Cat said. "You'd be a fool to trust me ever again. And you never been a fool." She looked up at him. "But I want to stay and help you. I know who you're up against, and I promise—I'll do whatever you say."

"No," Dancer said. "This is our fight—we can't avoid it. But you're not in it."

"I am too in it," Cat snarled. "For Velvet and Jonas and

Sweets and Sarie and . . . everybody else. Mari was just a baby. And they burned up . . ."

"Stop it," Han said, putting up his hand. "I just . . . stop it." He waited until he thought he could control his voice. "I'm going to be in a war pretty soon, likely against the Bayars and a lot of other charmcasters," he said. "It'll be something different than what you're used to. It's not just a street fight, though there might be some of that. It'll be politics and spying and putting a word in where it'll do the most good. And it'll be all over the realm—in the mountains, in Ragmarket and Southbridge, in the castle close, too."

"You'll need help," Cat said. "You can't do it all on your own."

"You should stay here," Han said. "It's amazing, what you've done in a short time. Jemson was right. You could become a ladies' maid or governess. You could teach music. It's your chance to get out of Ragmarket for good."

"You think I'd rest easy between the sheets in some mansion house knowing you're in a war?" Cat said. "I want to swear to you again. I want to help you. I couldn't go up against the Bayars on my own, but maybe I could with you."

Han studied Cat, debating. Hope crowded into her face.

"You'd be putting Cat at risk," Dancer argued. "She'd be going up against wizards. She'd be defenseless."

"I an't defenseless!" Cat snapped, producing a blade from some unknown hiding place and waving it at Dancer. He jerked his head back to save his nose.

Han rubbed his chin. "I need people who'll do what I say, whether it's going to school, or doing slide-hand on the street, or keeping an eye on people that need watching. I won't have time to argue with you. You can't just pick and choose the jobs you like."

Cat nodded, her eyes fixed on his face. "I promise I'll do what you say."

"You need to keep up on your schooling," he said. "Music, art, language, all that. You need to be able to mix in with bluebloods. If it's good enough for me, it's good enough for you."

"You sound like a blueblood already," Cat muttered.

"There won't be gang shares, not like before," Han went on. "I have some money, but that might dry up, depending on which way I jump. And you can't be doing side work if you work for me. You can leave any time, but if you decide to go with somebody else, you need to tell me and split clean."

"I got it," Cat said. "No side work."

"Least you know what the risks are," Han said, half to himself. "I don't feel as bad asking you, because you'd be going into it with open eyes."

"Hunts Alone," Dancer said. "Don't let her throw her life away."

Cat gave Dancer a look to shut him up. Then she slid off the edge of the bed and onto her knees. "I, Cat Tyburn, swear to you, Cuffs Alister," she said. "I pledge my loyalty, my blades and weapons to your use, and place myself under your protection. I'll do what you say. Your enemies are my enemies. I won't do no side work. I promise to bring all takings to you and to accept my gang share from your hands as you see fit." And she smiled her radiant, dangerous smile.

CHAPTER THIRTY-TWO

SHIFTING ALLIANCES

Abelard's crew trickled into the dean's meeting room, clustering on the other side of the table from Han, eying him with mistrust. Micah sighed and rolled his eyes, as if expecting little out of this session, but underneath the boredom, Han could smell a visceral fear. Nobody seemed eager to go anywhere with Han Alister at this particular time.

Except Abelard and Gryphon. And maybe Fiona. Her expression of cool appraisal told him that she hadn't given up winning him to her cause.

The Demon King amulet hung around Han's neck. Alongside it hung a Demonai talisman carved from rowan and oak. This bit of bagged flash was supposed to protect him from possession. He and Dancer hadn't been able to test it, of course, because, despite Mordra's seminar, neither of them knew how to go about possessing someone.

Han's amulet was packed with power. Crow had mentioned

stealing power from someone else, but Dancer had uncovered a charm that allowed him to donate power to Han by linking their amulets together.

"It's all right," Dancer had said, grinning. "I didn't have any big magical plans anyway."

As soon as Han had entered the room, Micah's eyes fixed on the serpent amulet. He stared at it, then looked up and met Han's eyes. Probably wondering if Cat had made a try for it yet. Micah had probably hoped Han would have to come before the dean without it.

"Now that we're all here, we'll begin," Dean Abelard said. "When Alister joined our study group, I told you that he had been successful in traveling to Aediion. This afternoon he will share his expertise with us. Hopefully you have arrived with fully charged amulets." She nodded to Han. "The floor is yours."

"All right, then," Han said. He wasn't sure whether he should get up or stay in his seat. He elected to stand. "You probably know that it's not easy getting to Aediion. Some wizards think it doesn't even exist. But it does. The first time I went was in Master Gryphon's class. But I've been there several times since."

"And always came back, it seems," Micah drawled, as if he'd rather he hadn't.

"Well, that's important, isn't it," Han said, tilting his head back and looking down his nose at Micah. "You wouldn't want to get stranded there. That'd be bad." He kept looking at Micah until Micah looked away.

"Some people think the key to getting to Aediion is in the amulet you use," Han went on. "Others think that once you get there, it's easier the next time. Kind of like you're breaking a trail you can use over and over." He looked around the table. "How many of you have tried to go to Aediion?"

Everybody raised a hand.

"How many of you have succeeded?"

"Be honest, now," Abelard put in.

The hands went down.

"How do we know *you've* been there?" Mordra asked, fingering her amulet.

Han looked at Abelard, who said, "I am convinced of it, and that's all you need to know."

Mordra shrugged, and Han continued.

"Today I'll help you get there, using my amulet and the trail I've made," he said. "I can't guarantee you'll be able to go back on your own, but it may make it easier for you the next time."

This was complete rubbish—a story that he and Crow had worked out together—but Han was a rum liar, and they all nodded, even Gryphon, though he looked a little puzzled.

"Now, we have to be touching," Han said. "Let's lie down in a circle."

He'd asked Abelard to lay out seven straw mattresses in a circle by the window. They all laid down, with their heads nearly meeting in the middle. Han heard some muttering and snorting as they assumed their positions. He helped Gryphon to get down, then lay down on the remaining mattress.

Han knew they felt ridiculous, but he didn't want vacated bodies toppling over and crashing to the floor.

"See?" he said. "Just like a séance at the Temple School."

Nervous laughter rippled around the circle.

"All right, everyone touching?" Han felt the buzz of power

from Gryphon on one side and Abelard on the other. He guessed they'd wanted to be next to him to make extra sure they wouldn't be left behind.

"Now, here are some things to remember," Han said, staring up at the ceiling. "You probably know all this already, but it bears repeating. You can change your appearance in Aediion—your clothing, your physical characteristics. So try that out. You can create illusions at will—it's the dream world, remember. Magic works—so be careful with it. And don't use up all your stored power experimenting. You'll need it to get back.

"We're all going to the same place so we can find each other. We will stay about ten minutes. You'll need my help to return, so we will all meet and come back together. If anyone's amulet is running low, tell me right away." He paused. "Any questions?"

"Where are we going?" Gryphon asked.

"Bridge Street," Han said. "Is there anyone who hasn't been there?"

This was met by more nervous laughter.

"We'll meet under the clock in front of The Crown and Castle," Han said. "Don't stray too far from there. Ten minutes goes by quick in Aediion. Ready? Hands off your amulets. Here's the charm you'll be using."

Han told it to them and had them repeat it. It was the same charm Gryphon had taught them back in the fall. Han would be using something different—the potent charm that would actually carry them all across.

"All right, ready?" Han said. "Open your portals."

Han gripped his amulet and spoke Crow's charm. The break between worlds was longer and deeper this time—long enough to worry about being stuck between. When the darkness finally faded, he stood alone under the clock on Bridge Street. Gryphon immediately materialized in front of him, eyes closed, holding tight to his amulet.

"Gryphon!" Han said softly.

Gryphon opened his eyes. He was a Gryphon made whole, without leg braces and crutches. He looked down at himself, and a pleased smile broke across his face. He took a few tentative steps, then reshaped himself, growing taller, more muscular, better matching his handsome features.

Abelard appeared, then Hadron, deVilliers, and the Bayars last. When Micah and Fiona arrived, Gryphon's clothing became just a little finer and better-fitting.

"All right," Han said, "everyone's here. Now try changing the scene a bit." Han gestured, and large purple flowers burst from the pavement, waist high. "Go easy, though; we don't want to end up in a tangle."

The others conjured flowers and fireworks, fields and waterfalls, though Micah didn't really join in the fun. He stood back, hand on his amulet, his eyes fixed on Han as if expecting him to make a move on him.

"You can also change your clothes if you want, or the clothes of those around you."

A battle of dueling apparel erupted as they manipulated each other's attire. Even Abelard joined in. Soon everyone was laughing.

"From what I know," Han said, "what's real in Aediion is wizards, amulets, and magic. Everything else is illusion. We all came from the same room," he went on, "but we could be spread all over the Seven Realms and still come together in a common place, if you planned ahead of time. Otherwise, you'd never find each other."

"Is bad weather coming in?" Mordra said, shivering and peering up at the sky. "It sure looks real."

A cold wind ripped between the buildings, raising gooseflesh on Han's exposed skin. Dark, mottled clouds rolled in, turning midday into a peculiar twilight. Han conjured a deerskin jacket lined with fleece. The others followed suit, donning warmer clothes in the face of the drop in temperature.

"Did you do that?" Gryphon asked Han, eying the sky. "Change the weather, I mean?"

Han shook his head, at a loss to explain it. Could one of the others have done it? Micah or Fiona? They still clutched their amulets, but they both gazed skyward apprehensively, so it seemed unlikely. Han had never visited Aediion in a crowd before. It was hard to say who was really in control.

Lightning brindled the sky, turning it garish shades of green and purple. A clamor of thunder made everyone cover their ears.

"That's enough, Alister," Mordra said, pulling her head in like a turtle. "You've made your point."

Han gripped his amulet and tried to conjure better weather, but with no success. Illusion or not, the oncoming storm was hard to ignore.

"Who is that?" Dean Abelard asked, shading her eyes and squinting past Han.

Han turned, then stood gaping in surprise.

It was Crow, dressed more finely than Han had ever seen him, in brilliant cloth of gold that set off his midnight hair, a jewel-encrusted sword in his hand. By now the sky was as black as darkman's hour, but it didn't matter. Crow lit up the whole street.

He strode purposefully toward them, his sword extended, a bone-chilling smile on his face, flame rippling around him like a halo around a saint.

Han stepped in between Crow and Abelard's crew. "What are you doing here?" he demanded. He hadn't said anything to Crow about the time of their visit or the place of their meeting. How had he found them?

"Alister!" Abelard said. "Explain this at once! Is this person your creation or someone you know?"

Crow twitched in irritation. Turning, he flicked his hand, and a mammoth wall of flame erupted from the street, separating Han and the Bayars from the others. With a gesture he set it rolling, driving the others down the street. Beyond the blaze, Han could hear screaming and shouting.

Han swung around to face Crow again. "What are you doing?"

"My business is with you and the Bayars," Crow said. "We don't need interference from them." He stood before the Bayar twins, growing in size and brilliance until he dwarfed the pair. "Ah," he said, gloating, "finally. I've been waiting for this for a long time."

"What are you talking about?" Micah demanded, shading his eyes with his forearm. "I don't know you."

"But I know you," Crow said. "I know who and what you are." Lazily, he flicked flame from the tip of his sword. It rocketed toward Micah, and Micah dodged aside.

Fiona's eyes shifted from Han to Crow and back again. "Why are you doing this?" she said.

Han shook his head. "Go on," he said to Crow. "Get out of here. You're not invited."

"I'm making good on a promise," Crow said. "I promised to destroy Aerie House. I'm going to start with these two."

"Alister, if this is your idea of a joke, I am not amused," Micah said. "I should have known better than to go along with this scheme."

"Arrogant. True to your breed," Crow said. He sent another gout of flame jetting toward Micah and Fiona. They leaped to either side, rolling as they hit the ground. Fiona answered with a flaming attack of her own, but Crow let it sizzle through him with no apparent ill effects.

Micah put up a shimmering wall, like solidified light, between him and Fiona and Crow and Han. Crow sent flame roaring right through it, and once again, Micah and Fiona dodged out of the way. Crow seemed to be toying with them, every attack a near miss.

Han stepped between Crow and the Bayars, skin prickling with anticipation of the flame, knowing he'd likely get fried from front and back. He felt betrayed—played like a loaded mark.

"Stop this, Alister," Fiona said, "or I will stop you." She took hold of her amulet and extended her hand toward Han.

"Crow!" Han said. "Forget it. I'm not going to let you kill them."

"Why not?" Crow demanded. He shifted from side to side, trying to get a clear shot. "They tried to kill you several times. And it's not like they'd shed a tear over you."

"I have a plan," Han said. "And this isn't it."

"Perhaps you want the pleasure of killing them yourself?" Crow got off a little bow. "Fair enough. Be my guest." He disappeared.

Han felt a kind of pressure, then a rough mental push, as if his mind were being straight-armed. Then another and another, as if someone were beating on his skull. It was Crow trying to get in, and getting bounced. Han fingered the rowan talisman and breathed a silent thank-you to Dancer.

"Give it up," Han said, just managing to sidestep the balls of flame Fiona lobbed at him. "It's not going to work this time."

Crow slammed into his mind again. And again and again.

"Come on, I can't fight three on one like this," Han said. "Do you want to get me killed?" He screamed as one of Micah's fiery blasts grazed him, setting his clothes aflame. Frantically, Han beat at his clothing, then with a gesture, turned the street under Micah and Fiona into a mudpot. They sank to their waists.

"Kill them, Alister," Crow whispered in his ear. "Or they'll kill you."

"Kill them yourself, you sponging goat-swiving huff," Han said, putting up a shield to hold off a series of small tornados embedded with shards of glass. "I'm not going to fight your battles for you."

Why *didn't* Crow kill them himself? He knew more magic than the three of them combined. Surely he could come up with a death charm the Bayars couldn't counter. His flaming attacks seemed to go right through Micah's defenses, but every blow had missed or been deflected or somehow not connected. Han,

Micah, and Fiona were doing more damage to each other than Crow had done to anyone.

A suspicion kindled in Han's mind.

Crow changed strategy. As Micah and Fiona struggled their way out of the ooze, Micah staggered backward as if struck, his eyes widening in surprise. He stood stock-still for a long moment. Then, gripping his amulet, he turned and extended his hand toward Fiona.

"Micah?" Fiona blinked at him. "What are you . . . ?"

"Fiona! Look out!" Han shouted, pushing Fiona to the ground as Micah launched his charm and flame roared over their heads.

"Micah!" Fiona screamed, rolling to her feet. "What are you doing?"

Micah's next shot blistered Fiona's arm before she could leap aside.

While Micah focused on burning his sister to a cinder, Han tackled him around the waist, sending them both flying face-first into the mud. "Run, Fiona!" Han shouted, spitting out mud. "Get out of here or he'll kill you."

"I'm not leaving my brother!" she screamed at him. "You'll kill him!"

"This an't your brother!" Han shouted back. "Can't you tell? He's possessed." Han ripped Micah's hands away from his amulet for the third time.

Fiona hesitated, her hand on her amulet, hand extended, unable to get a clear shot at Han without striking her brother.

"Kill me, and you'll never get out of here," Han shouted, exasperated.

Micah struggled and kicked, doing his best to rid himself of Han so he could hush his sister. But Micah had a lot to learn as a street fighter.

Han wasn't sure how to evict Crow without killing Micah. But he had a theory.

Keeping a tight grip on Micah, he yanked off Micah's amulet.

Crow materialized again as himself, mad as a cat in a downpour. Moments later his consciousness slammed into Han again. And failed again to penetrate.

While Han was distracted, Micah smashed his fist into the side of Han's head, making him see stars. "Give me back my amulet, you gutter-spawned pretender!"

Han smacked him with an immobilization charm, and Micah finally went down and lay still, staring up at the sky. It worked so well, Han did the same for Fiona.

"Now kill them, Alister," Crow said, standing over the Bayar twins like the Breaker, eager to snatch up some souls. "Kill them now."

"Nuh-uh," Han said, swiping blood from the side of his face. He nodded toward Micah and Fiona. "If you want them killed, then you do it."

"Hurry," Crow said. "You're running low on power. You'll have to go back before long."

Han broadened his stance, folding his arms in defiance. "You can't do magic on your own, can you? You've been using mine all along."

Crow flinched, and Han knew he'd guessed right.

"How can you say I can't do magic?" Crow said. "How

could I be here otherwise? How could I do this?" And he sent flame spiraling down the street.

"You can do illusions," Han said. "You showed me that the first day. But you can't do magic in the real world. You can't do magic that would kill them"—he pointed at the Bayars—"without me."

"I'm not going to honor that with a response," Crow said haughtily. "I've forgotten more magic than you'll ever know."

"You know it," Han said. "But you can't perform it."

"You are out of your mind," Crow said. "Are you going to kill the Bayar vermin or not?"

Micah's eyes shifted from Crow to Han, watching this exchange with interest and not a little alarm.

"Show me how it's done," Han said, pointing.

Crow made one more halfhearted attempt to slide into Han's head. "How are you shielding yourself?" he demanded.

"You're the one should be explaining what your game is," Han said. "Not me. You going to hush them or not? If not, we'll be off. As you said, we've been here too long already."

Crow gazed at Han for a long moment, as if trying to look through his skin. "I've underestimated you," he said finally, shaking his head.

"It's a common problem," Han replied. "Especially with bluebloods."

Crow blinked out like a dying ember.

Han waited a few moments to see if Crow would reappear. Then squatted next to Micah and Fiona.

"You two listen to me. I'm going to release you. We'll go find the others and then go back. You have a dispute with me, it can wait till we're out of here. You spill anything to Abelard, I'll leave you behind. You kill or disable me, none of us gets back, and that's the truth. *Do you understand*?" Han waited, and of course they didn't do or say anything in their immobilized condition, but he knew they weren't idiots, so he gave them the benefit of the doubt and disabled the charm.

They levered to their feet, slapped their hands on their amulets, and eyed him like he was a wild beast.

"Come on." Without looking back, Han strode down the street toward Crow's wall of flame, which had died to nothing in his absence.

"Alister!" A tall, angular figure walked toward him, carefully stepping over the scorched site of the wall. "You'd better have an explanation for this."

It was Dean Abelard, her hand wrapped around her amulet. The others trailed behind, all except for Gryphon, who rushed ahead to take Fiona's hands and peer anxiously into her face.

"Are you all right?" he said. Fiona nodded wordlessly. Gryphon slid an arm around her when she seemed in danger of falling.

"Alister!" Abelard repeated, her voice flinty. "What happened?"

Han shook his head. "I don't know," he said. "I wish I did. This never happened before, not any of the times I crossed over. I never saw anyone I didn't plan to meet or bring with me."

"You're injured," the dean said, looking at each of them in turn, her dark brows drawn together.

"That cove tried to kill us," Han said. "Just laid into us like a mad tom, sending flames flying and spouting one charm after another. We held him off, but it was touch and go, even three on one." He shuddered. "Then finally he just blinked out. Disappeared. He must've run out of power."

Abelard frowned. "You don't know this man? You never saw him before in the real world, either?"

"I never did," Han said. He shot Micah and Fiona a warning look. "You ever?"

They just shook their heads, eyes wide, their faces pale as plaster.

"We didn't know where you were, or if you were—if you were still alive," Hadron said, looking up at the Bridge Street clock. "It's been a lot more than ten minutes—thirty, at least."

"Proficients deVilliers and Hadron attempted to go back on their own when we knew it was past time for us to return," Abelard said. "They were unsuccessful."

They were all white-lipped and scared to death, except for Gryphon and Abelard.

The dean's face was creased with puzzlement and suspicion. Gryphon looked happier than Han had ever seen him, the layers of pain and frustration and bitterness fallen away. He looked like a dedicate who'd seen the face of the Maker.

Peculiar.

"I'd love to chat further about this," Han said, tearing his eyes away from Gryphon, "but we've been here too long, and I don't want to risk another ambush."

"Let's *go*," Mordra said, gazing around uneasily.

"Everyone reach in and take hold of me." The other six stood in a circle around Han, jockeying for position until they all had a grip. "Now, you'll speak the charm to open the portal, while I speak mine."

The world went dark in a jumble of competing voices. Han opened his eyes to Abelard's meeting room and felt the weight of someone on top of him. It was Fiona. They were in a kind of tangle on the mattresses. Han quickly extracted himself and stood.

He counted. All had returned. He let go a sigh of relief.

Abelard took her own head count. "Well," she said briskly, "at least we didn't lose anyone, even if there were a few injuries." Her tone suggested there was no making omelets without breaking eggs. "Congratulations on traveling to Aediion, something not many can say they've done. I will let you know whether there will be any follow-up on this. In the meantime, I shouldn't have to remind you to say nothing about this to anyone."

"Excuse me, Dean Abelard," Han said. "You all can do what you want, but I'm not going back. It's not worth the risk."

Several of the others nodded in agreement.

Abelard tightened her lips but said nothing more as they filed out silently.

Micah and Fiona waited for Han at the bottom of the stairs. "I want to talk to you," Fiona said, gripping his arm, her fingers digging into his flesh.

"Hands off," Han said, his knife pressing into Fiona's throat. "I'll give you to the count of three. One."

She jerked back her hands. Han's knife disappeared.

"Just because I didn't hush you in Aediion doesn't mean we can all be friends," Han said. "I want to get a few things straight with you. Now, let's walk out onto the quad, where it's nice and public. I'm not meeting in back alleys with a pair of connivers like you."

He walked out into the center of the quad and sat down on a bench on the pavilion surrounding Bayar Fountain.

The Bayars followed him. Han gestured to a nearby bench. They sat.

"What were you thinking, Micah, sending a street rusher up against a wizard?" Han said, idly tossing his knife and catching it. "That was a mismatch. She's talented, I'll admit—there aren't many Temple students who can cut your heart out through your clothes. But she's never been a steady hand as a draw-latch."

"I don't know what you're talking about," Micah said at the same time that Fiona said, "Who?"

"Cat Tyburn doesn't crew for you anymore," Han said. "Sorry."

"Who is Cat Tyburn?" Fiona asked, looking from Han to Micah with narrowed eyes.

Micah eyed him, his curiosity clearly battling with his desire to keep denying what Han already knew. "What happened? Where is she?" he said finally.

"Where do you think?" Han flipped his knife, caught it.

"You killed her?" Micah's expression was all horrified fascination.

Han shrugged. "I don't want to talk about Cat."

"Well, I do," Fiona snapped, glaring at her brother. "What have you been up to?"

"Later," Micah said. "Let's talk about what happened in Aediion. Who is Crow? Or was he just a bit of conjury you put on for our benefit?"

Han tried the edge of his blade against his thumb. "To tell you the truth, I have no idea who Crow is, or what his game is. I was as surprised as you when he showed up."

"But you know him," Fiona pressed. "That was obvious."

"I've met him," Han said, putting his knife away. "Can't say I know him. Let's just say that your visit to Aediion was a case of getting in over your head. Magically, I mean." He closed his hand on the Demon King's amulet. "Now. We need to get something settled. I've had enough of always watching my back, waiting for somebody to pick my pocket or jinx me or slide a blade between my ribs." He waggled the amulet. "You want this, come and get it."

Micah shook his head. "We're not stupid. You'll attack us. Or we'll get expelled for attacking you."

"I promise. Cross my heart. I won't attack you. If you can take it, you can have it." Han smiled, all toothy and slantwise. "Either one. Come on. Who's first?"

"Toss it over here," Fiona said.

"Now that would be stupid, wouldn't it?" Han said. "You with three amulets between the two of you, me without any." He held the amulet up by its chain. "Nah. You come take it from me."

Micah shook his head again. "No. I don't trust you."

Han sighed. "Guess you're way too smart for me. See, this thing is choosy about who uses it. Touch it, and you're nothing more than a smudge of ash and a lingering stench on the breeze."

"You're forgetting that I've used it before," Micah said.

"Then come get it," Han said, grinning, caressing the serpent's head. "Now or never."

Fiona pursed her lips. "You're saying you can handle it and

we can't? When we are the rightful owners?"

"You Bayars keep saying this jinxpiece belongs to you," Han said. "It doesn't. You stole it from Alger Waterlow a thousand years ago. It was supposed to be destroyed, but your family's got a whole stash of illegal magical weapons, don't you?"

The two Bayars sat perfectly still, not blinking, their hands cradling their own probably stolen jinxpieces.

"You can't prove any of that," Fiona said finally.

"Sure I can. All I have to do is hand this amulet over to the clans and tell them where I got it. They'll believe me. I'd say my word with them is better than yours. Besides, Hayden Fire Dancer was there that day on Hanalea, and he's well connected with the Spirit clans."

"You won't hand it over," Micah said. "The clans will destroy it."

"Maybe," Han said. "Maybe not. But I promise you this—you won't get it back. Your father murdered my mother and my sister. The Queen's Guard locked them in a stable and set it on fire. They burned to death. Lord Bayar didn't light the fire, but he might as well have. My sister was seven years old."

Micah's gaze shifted away. "You were wanted for murder. The queen—"

Han raised his hand to stop the spray of words. "Murders I didn't commit. Oh, there's plenty of blame to go around. The queen's on the list too. But I'm not stupid. Don't ever make the mistake of thinking that."

Fiona shook her head, eyes fixed on Han's face. "No. I won't."

"After that, somebody—your people or the queen's—

somebody murdered my friends in Ragmarket, trying to get them to tell where I was. Some of them were *lytlings*, too. They didn't pick the street life, you know. It was that or starve." Han tilted his head. "You going to tell me the queen was hunting me because of some Southies that died?"

"You stabbed our father when he tried to negotiate the return of the amulet," Fiona said. "You nearly killed the High Wizard of the realm. I would say that's reason enough for the guard to go looking for you."

"Negotiate?" Han stared at her. "*Negotiate*? You bluebloods got your own patter flash. On the street we call it *having tea with the pigs*. He told me straight out he was going to take me back to your place and torture me to death."

Micah shifted impatiently. "So what's your point?"

"The point is, I paid a really high price for this amulet," Han said. "There's no way either of you can use it. And I'd rather it was melted down and destroyed than back in your hands. Do you believe me?"

"I believe you," Fiona whispered, her face even paler than usual. "But you're a fool if *you* continue to use it. You don't know how dangerous it is."

"I'll take my chances," Han said. "You know, Micah, that first night, when I saw you on Bridge Street, I wanted to kill you. I wanted to cut your throat and watch your blood soak into the dirt. I wanted to wrap a strangle cord around your neck and throttle you while you kicked and messed yourself."

"I'm shaking in my boots," Micah said, looking Han dead in the eyes.

Han stood and took a step toward him. "I'm what's hiding in

the side street when you walk home from The Four Horses," he said. "I'm the shadow in Greystoke Alley when you go out to take a piss. I'm the footpad in the corridor when you visit the girlie at Grievous Hall."

Micah's eyes narrowed, his self-assurance wilting a bit. Han could tell he was going back over a hundred suspicious sights and sounds. "You've been following me?"

"I can come and go from your room, any time I want," Han said. "I can tell you what you say when you talk in your sleep. I know what your down-low girlie whispers in your ear." He laughed. "You can't keep me out of any place I want to be in. I would've known about Cat sooner, but you always met with her when I was in class."

Micah licked his lips. "Perhaps you take some kind of perverse pleasure in stalking me, but—"

"What I'm saying is, if I wanted you dead, you would already be dead a dozen ways. I let you live because now I got a different plan. You Bayars need to learn that you can't have everything you want. I'm going to teach you. This is just the beginning."

Micah's eyes narrowed. "Is that a threat?"

"Absolutely." Han smiled. "Any time you start a fight, you'd better know who you're coming up against." He stood. "Be seeing you."

CHAPTER THIRTY-THREE
MATRIMONY OR MURDER

It was a gray and gloomy Thursday—though warmer and more humid than any April day had a right to be. Raisa was done with classes for the day, but she didn't want to go back to Grindell Hall and watch Amon watch her. He'd been edgy for days, even before the episode with Han.

"What is the matter with you?" she'd demanded the night before in the practice yard. "I've never seen you so jumpy."

"I have a feeling you're in danger," he said. "I can't shake it."

"Is this about Han Alister?" she'd asked, pausing with her staff across her body.

He shook his head. "No. Not entirely, anyway. I've felt like this since Hallie came home. Like something bad is about to happen." He adjusted his grip on his staff, carefully placing his hands. "I've learned not to ignore those instincts. Please be careful, Rai."

She'd debated whether to show Queen Marianna's letter to

Amon, and had decided against it. Could Amon's worries have anything to do with that? Could he sense how unsettled she was, how tempted she was to travel back home?

In the midst of all this, Raisa had exams to study for, and a decision to make about what to wear to the Cadets' Ball. Female cadets had the option of wearing either their dress uniform or a gown. The uniform would be easier, but Raisa was afraid she'd be taken for somebody's boyish young squire who'd been allowed to stay up late.

Sometimes she actually missed dressing up.

Still, it was probably too late to hire a seamstress, and unlikely she'd find something to fit her in the secondhand shops along Bridge Street.

Tonight she'd meet with Han. Her heart accelerated. She'd sent a message to Hampton Hall.

Han, I apologize that our evening ended so abruptly. It was wonderful up until then. AB apologizes also. Well, that's not strictly true, but I apologize for him. Looking forward to Thursday, and to the dance.
—Rebecca

There'd been no reply.

Maybe I should see if he shows for tutoring tonight before I look for a dress, Raisa thought glumly. She was tempted to cross the bridge and find Han at his dormitory, but that could end badly in a number of ways.

Amon's edginess was catching. Raisa found herself constantly looking over her shoulder, feeling the itch on the back of her neck that said someone was watching her. Gray wolves clustered on the quad, their ears pressed back against their heads, and she heard their plaintive howls late at night.

Finally, she hid out in an upstairs reading room at the Wien House library and tried to study. But Han Alister kept intruding into her thoughts. And Amon Byrne. And Marianna, her mother. One moment she decided to return home to the Fells as soon as exams were over, the next she worried that her return might precipitate a crisis. She read the same paragraph over and over until she fell asleep, her face pillowed on her arms.

"Newling Morley?"

Raisa looked up to see a nervous-looking cadet standing in the doorway. She blinked at him hazily. "Oh! I must have fallen asleep! What time is it?"

"It's after nine o'clock," he said. "The library's closed." He scanned the room as if to make sure, then added, "Everyone else is gone."

Then it struck her. Nine o'clock! She was supposed to meet Han at eight. On Bridge Street. Madly, she scraped her papers and books together, stuffing them into her carry bag. Would he have waited? Would he have come at all?

The click of the door latch made her look up. The cadet had stepped inside and shut and locked the door.

On second glance, he didn't look so cadetlike. Maybe it was his ill-fitting uniform and the fact that he was older than most of Raisa's classmates. Perhaps it was his flat black eyes and the way his nervousness dropped away like a cloak he wore against the weather.

Maybe it was the way he moved toward her, like a predator.

"Thank you for waking me, Corporal," Raisa said, her heart thudding under her jacket. "What's your name?"

"My name's Rivers," he said. "Corporal Rivers." He circled

around the table toward her, seeming unaware of the fact that he was wearing a cadet scarf. Not a corporal's.

Wolves slunk along the walls, whining uneasily.

When Rivers got within range, Raisa snatched up her jar of blotting sand and flung it into his face.

He was quick. He nearly managed to dodge out of the way, but some of it went into his eyes. He scrubbed at them with the heels of his hands, and that's when she saw the garrotte dangling from one fist. Grabbing up the study lamp from the desk, Raisa smashed it into the side of his head and ran for the door.

Somehow, he was on top of her before she could get it open. Grabbing a fistful of her hair, he yanked her head back, looping the strangle cord around her neck. As he pulled back to tighten it, Raisa slid her hand between the garrotte and her windpipe— another trick from Amon Byrne—braced her feet against the door, and launched herself backward, smashing her head into the assassin's chin with an audible crack.

The assassin's head struck the edge of the table, and they both went down on their backs, Raisa on top. Raisa ripped away the strangle cord, rolling to her feet and groping for her dagger.

But Rivers lay still, his head at an impossible angle.

Raisa turned and fumbled at the latch, her hands shaking so hard she could scarcely manage it. Finally, she yanked the door open and ran straight into Micah Bayar.

He closed his arms tight around her, pinning her arms to her sides. Lifting her, he carried her back into the room, turning her so she was pressed up against him, her back to his front.

She fought for her life, screaming and kicking and squirming and flinging out her elbows, employing all the street-fighting skills Amon had taught her. Micah held her in such a way that it was difficult to gain leverage enough to do any real damage. She smashed her heel into his kneecap, and his breath hissed out in pain, but he didn't loosen his hold. Instead he smacked her knife hand against the wall until she dropped the blade. He kicked it away, and it pinged as it hit the wall. She tried to memorize its location, in case she had the chance to get it back.

Power trickled into her, a current that ran down her arm and into Elena's talisman ring. A fraction of Micah's usual output.

"Is that the best you can do?" Raisa said, still struggling to free her arms. "Magically impotent today, are we?"

Unexpectedly, Micah laughed. "I am a bit drained at the moment, I will admit," he said. "I have missed you," he murmured, pressing her close, his lips against her hair. "Truly. And to think you were right here, all along. What a wasted opportunity for clandestine trysts away from that wretched nurse of yours."

"I haven't missed *you*," she retorted. "Go away, and I'll let you know when I do. If I don't cut my throat instead."

"We need to talk," Micah said. "I could stand here holding you, which I am thoroughly enjoying, but it is difficult to talk to the back of your head. I would prefer to look at your face. If I let go of you, can we have a civil conversation without my risking the fate of the unfortunate on the floor?"

Well. If they were going to talk, Raisa wanted to be able to read Micah's face, too, and try to discern what lay behind the words.

"All right," she said. "I promise to hear you out."

Micah loosened his hold and took a step back. When she turned to face him, he looked her up and down, taking in her soldier's tunic, her shaggy cap of hair, the Wien House emblem embroidered on the front. "You are transformed, Your Highness," he said. "Are you really at Wien House?"

"I'm in a special program for royalty in exile," Raisa said. "For princesses who refuse to marry at swordpoint. We're learning to fight off unwanted suitors."

"There were no swords in evidence, as I recall," Micah said. He paused for a heartbeat. "My father was most displeased with me when I let you slip away on what was to be our wedding night. I wish you could have been there to share it."

"Your father's displeasure, or our wedding night?" Raisa said.

Micah laughed again. "Both. It has been a less interesting world without you."

Micah looked different from the last time she'd seen him. His hair was shorter, cropped into a student cut. His face seemed thinner, as if he'd lost weight, though it was hard to tell under the cloak. But he was as breathtakingly handsome as ever, his dark eyes shaded by his black brows, shadows layering the fine bone structure of his face.

He also looked scuffed up and bruised, as if he'd recently been in a fight.

Micah glanced down at the man on the floor. "Brava, Your Highness," he said. "He's really very good." He drew off his leather gloves and slapped them thoughtfully against his palm. He was trying to radiate confidence, but his hands shook a little.

"Well, he can't be that good," Raisa said, trying to sound off-hand. Trying to control her own shakes.

"On the contrary, he is. He just underestimated you. We all did. We've been looking for you for months. I should have known you'd be down here with Corporal Byrne. And that your copperhead father was in on the conspiracy."

"I don't know what you're talking about," Raisa said. Damn, damn, damn, she thought. The Bayars would welcome an opportunity to be rid of the Byrnes and Lord Averill, to remove those voices from the queen's ear.

"We thought it peculiar when a cadet from Oden's Ford visited Lord Demonai, and Demonai went to the queen," Micah said. "So when the girl left, we thought it worthwhile to have her followed. She came straight back here, to Grindell Hall. With a focus that narrow, it didn't take long to pick you out."

"And so you sent an assassin after me," Raisa said.

"Four, actually," Micah said. "The other three were waiting downstairs while Rivers came in to find you. They were puzzled that you didn't come out when the library closed."

"Why kill me?" Raisa asked, figuring she might as well know before she died. "Was it because I jilted you at the altar, or . . ."

"Well," Micah said, "we Bayars *are* very sensitive about being jilted, after that episode with Queen Hanalea. But my father also worries about your rebellious nature and your close connection to the clans. You even look like a mixed-blood."

"I *am* a mixed-blood," Raisa said, lifting her chin.

"Mellony is also, but she doesn't look like a copperhead. She looks like her mother. So my father has set his sights on her. He would like to see a more malleable queen on the throne. He has been unsuccessful in persuading the queen to disinherit you, and needs to get you out of the way so his plans to marry me to Mellony can proceed." Micah said all of this matter-of-factly, his black eyes fixed on her face.

Raisa stared at Micah, her stomach clenching into a miserable ball. It was a good thing she'd missed supper, because she would have lost it right then.

She felt impotent, utterly frustrated—and frightened. As the Montaignes had amply proven, nobody was more at risk than someone who competes for a throne—and loses. The Bayars would cut her throat or strangle her and leave her in some back alley—the apparent victim of a street thief. Too bad rebellious Raisa had left the protection of Fellsmarch and got herself killed.

"Mellony is thirteen," Raisa said. "I hope you have experience babysitting, Micah, because you're going to need it. Assuming the Demonai don't assassinate you first. Married at thirteen, widowed at fourteen. Poor Mellony."

Angry tears stung her eyes. "Even if you survive, you'll be ruling over a country torn apart by civil war. The Fells will become the Arden of the north. You'll never win against the clans in the mountains, I'll tell you that right now."

She extended her hand toward Micah and spat out a curse worthy of any of her clan ancestors. "By Hanalea's blood and bones, if you marry Mellony *ana*'Marianna and mount the Gray Wolf throne, may you be fighting for the rest of your short and miserable life. And may Mellony's babies be copperheads, every one."

Micah blinked at her, stunned to silence. His gaze dropped to her extended hand, and his eyes widened. Seizing hold of her hand, he dragged her into the pool of light spilling from the sconce on the wall. He nudged Elena's wolf ring with his forefinger, turning her hand so it caught the light.

"Where did you get this?" he asked.

Raisa shrugged, pretending indifference, though her heart was pounding. "I think it was a suitor gift. For my name day."

"It looks like clanwork," he said, frowning.

"Most of my jewelry is clan made," Raisa said, trying unsuccessfully to pull her hand free. "That's no surprise. They are the best metalsmiths in the Seven Realms."

Micah tugged at the wolf ring experimentally, then with more force. It did not budge.

"Take it off," he said, thrusting her hand back toward her.

"Have you turned robber as well as murderer?" Raisa asked. "The Bayars aren't rich enough as it is?"

"That ring looks like a talisman," Micah said. "It might account for your resistance to wizardry."

"It's just a ring," Raisa said, tugging at it herself. Even if she'd been trying hard, which she wasn't, it wasn't going anywhere. "And it seems to be stuck. So unless you want to chop my finger off, you'll have to let it be."

"All right," Micah said, raising both hands. "We'll let it be. For now."

"Why are you here, anyway?" Raisa asked. "Did you want to dip your hands in my blood and curse me for the crime of refusing to marry you? Did you want to see if your assassin did the job right, or join in?"

Micah nudged the dead man on the floor with his foot. "To be precise, he's my father's assassin," he said. "Not mine."

Raisa stared at him, speechless.

"I came to offer you a choice," Micah said, turning the ring on his own finger. "I can take you downstairs and deliver you to the assassins waiting outside," he said. "Or you can return to the Fells and marry me."

Raisa collapsed into an armchair. *"What?"*

Micah smiled thinly. "I think you are exactly right. The copperheads will have no doubt who is responsible for your murder. Even if you are dead, naming Mellony princess heir and marrying her to me will cause a firestorm of protest. The clans will rise in rebellion. It would cast a pall over our reign and any children we would have."

Our reign, Raisa thought. Our *children*? Micah and Mellony? The notion made Raisa's skin crawl.

"You are close to the copperheads," Micah went on. "You fostered with them, and you carry their blood. My father sees that as a negative; I see it as an advantage. You're the blooded heir, and you're persuasive. If you came out in favor of our marriage, it might go a long way toward convincing the clans to go along with it."

No, Raisa thought. They'll never accept a wizard consort, let alone a king. Never ever. But, given the circumstances, she saw no reason to say it aloud.

Micah kept his eyes fixed on Raisa, as if trying to read through her skin. "The whole matter of the wedding was badly handled. I begged my father for time to convince you to marry me willingly. He was in a hurry. He never saw your consent as being important. He doesn't know you the way I do."

No doubt Micah was recalling their back-corridor romance in the months leading up to her name day. No doubt he had been counting on his considerable charm to prevail.

We could be good together, he'd said.

You don't know me as well as you think you do, Raisa thought. The queendom always comes first, before matters of the heart.

Raisa licked her lips and chose her words carefully while her mind raced. "Well, I must admit, I felt betrayed. The queen had never mentioned a match between us before that night. I hadn't planned to marry so young. I couldn't understand why I was expected to marry on my name day."

Why are you doing this, Micah? Raisa thought. Why aren't you just letting matters proceed as planned? Crossing your father is as dangerous as crossing the clans. Why take this kind of risk?

This goes beyond politics. Micah wants to marry me. *Not Mellony.*

That was amazing. Mellony was the beauty of the family—blond, tall, and willowy, she mirrored their mother. Raisa's younger sister was a child now, but she wouldn't always be. In the meantime, Micah would no doubt continue his back corridor prowling.

If Micah married Mellony, he couldn't leave Raisa alive. Even if he had no stomach for her murder, there would be no way he'd want to leave a living, breathing competitor for the Gray Wolf throne—someone an opposition could rally around.

One thing Raisa knew—she was no Queen Regina, ready to throw herself over a cliff to avoid marrying a wizard. She'd return to the Fells and marry a butcher or a ragpicker or a cleaner of privies if that's what it took to stay alive and hang on to the Gray Wolf throne.

If she could stay alive, she'd find a way to win.

"Death or marriage," Raisa said, rolling her eyes. "You

Bayars really know how to charm a girl."

Micah shrugged. "Not the proposal I would have preferred, but it's not up to me."

"Do you think your father will accept this?" Raisa asked. "Or will he simply wait for a new opportunity to murder me?"

Micah's face went hard, his lips whitening. "My father knows as well as I do that a marriage between us is the politically savvy thing to do. He *will* accept it."

Are you trying to convince me or yourself? Raisa thought.

"All right," she said. "You win. I will marry you if it assures that the succession remains unchanged."

Micah stood looking at her for a long moment, as if to uncover the girl behind the mask. "Perhaps," Micah said finally, with a crooked smile, "we should seal our bargain with a kiss."

He put his hands on her shoulders and drew her in, sliding his arms around her and bending his neck to press his lips to hers.

This is a test, Raisa thought, and she did her best to pass it. Micah put a lot into the kiss as well. It left her flushed and breathless and Micah looking reassured.

"We will leave in a few hours, then," Micah said. "I need to pack my belongings and notify the stableman. Do you still ride that piebald mare?"

Raisa nodded, hope kindling. Was it possible that Micah was so confident, he would allow her to go collect her things?

"I'll fetch your horse," he said, as if he'd read her thoughts. "The clothes on your back will have to do. You can borrow anything else you need from Fiona. We'll travel light and fast."

As if Fiona's clothes would fit me.

Micah fished under his cloak and brought out a small stoppered bottle filled with a purple liquid. A tiny copper cup was attached with a chain. He swirled the bottle to mix the contents, then pulled the stopper and poured.

"Here," he said, handing the little cup to Raisa. "Drink up."

She sniffed the brew unhappily. It had a sharp, sweet scent, like dessert wine. "What is this?"

"Something to keep you quiet until we leave, since my wizardly charms no longer seem to work on you." When she scowled at him, he shrugged. "I'm not so foolish as to trust you, Raisa."

"Why should I trust *you*? I don't know what's in that. Maybe you mean to poison me yourself."

Micah rolled his eyes. "You're not really in a position to dictate terms," he said.

"What about the assassins downstairs?" she asked. "If this knocks me out, you'll have your hands full, and I'll be helpless."

"I'll handle them," Micah said. "Now drink it before they come up looking for us."

Seeing no way around it, Raisa drank the purple potion. It *tasted* like dessert wine too, with a bit of a bitter aftertaste. "Turtleweed?" she guessed.

Micah nodded. "Sorry. It does cause that nasty headache after."

"Do you always carry turtleweed around with you?"

He shook his head. "I haven't really needed it up till now."

Turtleweed was fast-acting, and Raisa was a small person. It wasn't long before her head began to swim. Wolves crowded in around her, as if trying to prop her up. She dug her fingers into their thick coats, trying to cling to consciousness.

Was Han waiting for her? Would he have gone to find her at the dorm?

No one knew where she was.

Would Amon be able to tell where she'd gone, and come after her?

"Don't get any ideas while I'm asleep, Bayar," she mumbled.

He sighed. "I can't control what ideas I have," he said. "But don't worry, we'll have a lifetime to carry them out." He slid his arms under her, lifting her, covering her with his cloak. She felt woozy, loose-limbed, and floppy, and waves of sleepiness rolled over her. Micah's heart thudded under her ear as they descended the stairs and pushed through the front doors.

Raisa tried to lift her head and look around, but couldn't seem to find the strength. "Where are they? The assassins?"

"They're already dead," Micah whispered in her ear. "I killed them on my way up. Else I would have been there sooner."

CHAPTER THIRTY-FOUR

SHOULDER
TAPS

Han waited at The Turtle and Fish an hour past their usual meeting time. Maybe she's having trouble getting away, he thought. Maybe Corporal Byrne is keeping her to quarters.

Or maybe Rebecca and her corporal had kissed and made up, and Han was on the outs again.

Han wasn't a fool, but he would have said the kisses he and Rebecca shared had been honest. And Rebecca didn't seem like the type to ditch him without an explanation.

And what about the Cadets' Ball? Should he assume it was on until he heard otherwise?

Finally, he left a note on the table and clumped back down the stairs. Linc looked up sympathetically. "Trouble?"

Han shrugged. "I don't know."

He thought about walking over to Grindell but didn't want to cause more trouble for Rebecca. Or show up where he wasn't wanted.

So he walked back to Hampton, nodding to Blevins in the

common room and mounting the stairs. He hoped Dancer was home. He'd stayed out all night the night before, which wasn't unusual. Sometimes he slept at Firesmith's forge when he was trying to finish a project. Han hadn't even told him what had happened in Aediion.

When Han arrived on the fourth floor, precious stones and metal findings littered the tabletop, and the cup of tea next to them was still warm, but Dancer was nowhere in sight. Clearly he'd been there, working, not long ago.

In fact, there were two cups.

Dancer's door was closed. "Hey! Dancer?" Han tried his door, and it was latched from the inside.

"Don't come in," Dancer said. Han heard shuffling and rustling on the other side of the door.

"Well, I can't very well, since it's latched," Han said. "Are you in bed this early?"

He heard muffled whispering inside, and yanked his hand back from the door. "Sorry!" he said, backing away. "Ah . . . sorry."

He hadn't even known Dancer was walking out with anyone, but then he pretty much kept such matters to himself.

Han sat down at his work desk and halfheartedly leafed through his Faulk. He supposed he could study on his own, but it wouldn't be the same. He put the book aside and pulled out his notes from Gryphon's class. He had an exam the next day, but his thoughts kept turning to Rebecca.

After a few minutes, Dancer's door opened and he poked his head out. "I thought this was your tutoring night," he said. "You're back early."

"Rebecca didn't show," Han said, shrugging. "Maybe because

of that incident at her dormitory on Tuesday with Commander Byrne."

Dancer leaned on the door frame. "Hmmm."

"You going to introduce me?" Han said, nodding toward the doorway.

Dancer looked over his shoulder into his room. "Do you want to be introduced?" he asked.

A moment later, the girlie poked her head out.

It was Cat.

"Oh," Han said. "So. When were you going to tell me?"

"It's pretty new," Dancer said. "We wanted to wait and see if it was working out."

Han struggled to keep from grinning. "And?"

"You shut up, Cuffs Alister," Cat said. She stalked past him, nose in the air, fluffing out her curls.

"Hey, now, I want to know," Han persisted. "I mean, last I heard, you hated him. And being as you're both friends of mine, seems like . . ."

"If you must know, it's *fine*," Cat said, floppng into a chair, stretching out her legs, and curling her bare toes. Tilting her head back, she looked over at Dancer through slitted eyes. "He'll do."

"Glad to hear that's settled," Han said. Dancer was right: Han did need to pay more attention to his friends.

"What happened with Abelard and the Bayars?" Dancer asked.

"That's what I wanted to talk to you about. I had the chance to try out the rowan talisman yesterday," Han said, poking at an enameled bird with his forefinger.

Dancer tilted his head. "And?"

Han told him about what had happened in Aediion.

"So you don't think Crow has any power of his own?" Dancer said.

Han shook his head. "He just parasites off me. Or any other charmcaster in range. He *told* me he knew how to drain magic from others. I should have known."

Dancer drew his brows together. "What *is* he, then? How did he get there?"

"Well, he's not just a ghostie out of my imagination, because he scared the devil out of everyone else." Han chewed his lower lip. "I wonder if there'd be anything helpful in the Bayar Library."

"I say leave it alone," Dancer said, sitting sat back down at his worktable. "Tell me you're never going back there."

"I'm never going back there," Han said.

Choosing a bar of silver, Dancer squeezed it in his fist until liquid silver ran out of his hand and into a mold.

"Better not let Blevins catch you doing that up here," Han said. "If there's not a rule against it, he'll make one up."

"You say that now, but wait until you see what I made for you." Dancer unfolded a square of chamois. Inside was a cunning replica of the Lone Hunter amulet Elena *Cennestre* had made for Han—the one he'd loaned to Dancer.

Dancer laid the two amulets side by side on the chamois. They were almost impossible to tell apart.

"That's amazing," Han said. "I had no idea you could do work like this. Or that you had the right materials."

"It doesn't work that well," Dancer said, shrugging away the praise. "I'm good on the stonecutting and metalsmithing, but I haven't mastered the flash part. I wanted to return your amulet, but I guess I need to keep it a while longer."

"No rush. Keep it." Han ran his finger over the replica jinxpiece. It flared up a little, but nothing like the original. But it would likely fool any wizard who didn't touch it.

"Why didn't you make a fire dancer?" Han asked. "Like the one you lost?"

Dancer shrugged. "I didn't have it to copy. I thought maybe the design fueled the function. I'm hoping to get some answers from Master Firesmith this summer."

Han and Dancer both planned to spend the summer working with faculty mentors—Dancer with Firesmith and Han with Abelard. He'd also planned to increase his time with Crow. Not anymore.

"You do beautiful work, Dancer," Han said. He weighed the intricate carving on his palm, turning it to catch the light. Magic aside, the workmanship and materials made it valuable. He went to give it back, and Dancer shook his head.

"Keep it," he said. "I made it for you. I thought there might be times you'd want to hide the Waterlow amulet."

The next morning, Han awoke to the slow stomp-stomp-stomp that meant Blevins was toiling up the stairs to the fourth floor. Han rolled off his bed and yanked on his breeches. Cat had stayed over with Dancer, and Han wanted to make sure there were no telltale signs in their makeshift common room. He dropped a cloth over Dancer's metalsmithing tools just as Blevins's head appeared above the threshold.

"Don't know why they put fourth floors on buildings, indeed I don't," he gasped. "They should build more buildings, if you ask me, which nobody does."

"Is there something you need?" Han asked, as Dancer joined them, closing his door behind him.

"You're not using an open flame up here, are you?" Blevins demanded, eyeing Dancer's worktable. "That's not allowed."

"No flames," Dancer said.

"Hmmph." Blevins eyed him balefully. "Well, there's someone here to see you, Alister. Won't give a name. A copperhead." He slid a look at Dancer, like he might be to blame.

Dancer and Han looked at each other. Not many clan found their way to Oden's Ford. "Well, why didn't you send him up?" Han asked.

"It's a girlie is why," Blevins said. "Scary-looking, if you ask me."

"But nobody does," Dancer said.

"And she asked for me by name?" Han said.

"She called you by a different name at first. Then switched to Alister when I said there wasn't no Hunts Alone here. You need to meet up with her down in the common room." Blevins leaned closer. "I'd watch yourself, if I was you. If you've done her wrong, I'd go out the back door and keep running. I've heard that if you cross one of 'em, they'll cut off your—"

"I'll watch myself," Han said. "Thank you."

"I'll come with you," Dancer said.

They pushed past Blevins and clattered downstairs, leaving the dorm master to toil along behind them.

Han was a little ahead of Dancer on the stairs, so he saw her first. He froze midway down the last staircase, gripping the banister for support, looking down into the common room.

It was Bird.

CHAPTER THIRTY-FIVE
OLD
FRIENDS

Bird stalked restlessly around the common room, hands clasped behind her back. She sorted through the books on the table and peered up at the paintings on the walls, mostly aged banners of wizard houses and portraits of Mystwerk masters from years past.

Han could tell from the way she carried herself that she was nervous but trying not to show it.

Dancer came up behind Han, looking over his shoulder. "Bird?" he whispered.

She turned and saw them. Her copper skin was bronzed a bit more by the sun, and her curls were cropped shorter than Han remembered. She was clad in Demonai traveling garb—deerskin leggings and tunic, and soft, well-worn boots, her bow and quiver of arrows slung over her shoulder. She was leaner and more muscular than before.

Han's gaze was drawn to the glittering Demonai amulet around her neck.

"Hello, Digging Bird," Han said. "This is a surprise." He made no move to descend the rest of the way. He liked having the high ground.

Bird inclined her head stiffly. "Hunts Alone," she said. "And Fire Dancer. My name is Night Bird now."

Her Demonai name. Had she chosen it to match Reid Nightwalker? Han wondered, with a twinge of jealousy. Or had Reid chosen it for her?

"Cousin," Dancer said, brushing past Han, "it's good to see you. Please share our fire and all that we have." The ritual greeting to the visitor.

Walking toward Bird, Dancer opened his arms, smiling. She looked torn between rushing forward and hanging back.

"It's all right," Dancer said. "The amulet drinks it in. You won't even feel it."

They embraced. Bird rested her head on Dancer's shoulder, closing her eyes.

Well, guess Dancer's forgiven her for the way she treated him, Han thought. And if I'm waiting for an apology, I'll likely wait forever.

"You have had hard traveling to get here, cousin," Dancer said. "I'll put the kettle on for mountain tea. Are you hungry? Have you had breakfast?" This rush of words, so uncharacteristic of Dancer, said that he was nervous too.

"I would like tea," Bird said, her eyes flicking to Han, still on the stairs.

Dancer pumped water from the cistern and filled the kettle, setting it on the hearth to heat and spooning tea into the ceramic pot. The flurry of hospitality suggested that Dancer knew that Han wouldn't step in as host.

"There's cheese in the pantry, and some biscuits I brought back from the dining hall, if you are hungry from the road," Dancer said. He gestured to a grouping of chairs by the hearth. "Here, come sit by the fire."

Bird made no move to sit, but stood shifting her weight from foot to foot. "I need to speak with Hunts Alone in private."

Han wasn't sure he wanted to visit one-on-one with Bird. "Dancer can hear whatever it is you came to say," he said. "I don't mind." He knew he sounded petulant, but he felt wounded and wanted to wound her back.

Bird looked from Han to Dancer. "No," she said. "He can't."

"Hey, now," Han said. "You've only just come, and Dancer is glad to see you." He put the emphasis on *Dancer*.

"It's all right," Dancer said. "I'll visit with Bird later. I was assembling a complicated piece anyway. I'll get back to it."

Dancer loped up the stairs, ignoring Han's pointed look.

"So," Han said, when Dancer had gone, "we're alone." He didn't know what to think, what to hope for.

Bird folded her arms across her chest, gripping her elbows to either side—a familiar gesture. "I'm not going to shout. Are you coming down or should I come up there?"

Feeling a little foolish, Han walked down the stairs and crossed to the hearth, where the kettle was already steaming. Using a rag, he lifted the kettle and poured water over the leaves.

"Sit down," he said, waving her to a chair by the fire. She finally sat, and he sat also, resting his hands on the arms of his chair.

Han felt the loss of her friendship like a huge aching hollow in his middle. He and Dancer and Bird had been inseparable every summer of his childhood. This past summer his relationship with Bird had evolved into something more. Memories churned forward, despite his efforts to tamp them down—slow kisses and the warmth of her summertime skin, her drowsy voice as they lay on the riverbank. He'd thought he'd seen his future in her eyes.

Now there were secrets between them, mistrust and betrayal creating a chasm so wide he doubted it could ever be bridged. She was a Demonai warrior, committed to a thousand-year-old fight against wizards. She'd chosen that vocation despite the fact that Han was a wizard. She'd chosen it instead of him.

"So you're a full-fledged Demonai warrior now?" he said, fingering the worn damask on the arm of the chair.

She nodded. "Since November." Silence grew between them again, until she said, "You're looking well. Are you taller than before?"

He shrugged. "Maybe." Once, they'd measured their heights against each other. "It seems like being a warrior agrees with you."

"Oh, it does," Bird said, her eyes lighting with enthusiasm. "I thought I knew about tracking and traveling light on the land, but I've learned so much about weaponry and battle strategy. Nightwalker is a wonderful teacher, so patient and . . ." Her voice trailed off when she focused on Han's face.

He tried to reorganize whatever it displayed into an expression of polite interest, to cover up his thoughts, which were, *They call him Nightwalker because he visits all his girlfriends whenever he's in camp.*

Bird changed topics. "So. How have you been? You are taking classes in jinx . . . in wizardry, then?"

Han nodded. "We just took our end-of-terms. Our examinations. That's one year down, out of three or four."

"Have you learned very much, or is it mostly . . . preliminary?" Bird asked. There was something in her face that told Han she wasn't just making small talk. Apprehension prickled between his shoulder blades.

"I've learned a lot," Han said, thinking of Crow. "I still have plenty to learn."

We sound like enemies meeting in the market, jousting for position, Han thought.

He tried to think of something else to say. "Didn't Nightwalker come with you?"

She shook her head. "I came alone. He is busy organizing strategy for summer. We were already spread thin because of the problems along the border with Arden. And now there's a new crisis. That's why I came here to see you."

No apology, then, Han thought. Let alone a rekindled romance. "Reid needs some advice?" he asked. "Or is there trouble between the two of you?"

Bird frowned. "You're different," she said. "I don't know if I like you as well."

"What do you want, Bird?" Han said. "I have things to do."

Bird leaned forward, hands on her knees, her expression grave. "We've received word that Queen Marianna has given way to pressure from the High Wizard and plans to name Princess Mellony as her heir." She sat back, dropping her hands into her lap and looking at Han as if she expected him to leap up and cry, "Not while I live and breathe!"

"Who's Princess Mellony again?" Han asked, pretending ignorance.

Bird drew her brows together in a frown. "She's Princess Raisa's younger sister."

"Ah. Hmmm. Well, what does Princess Raisa say about it?"

"She's in hiding. She ran away back in midsummer, on her name day."

That seemed familiar. "Oh. Right. I heard she had a fight with the queen."

"They tried to marry her off to Micah Bayar, the son of the High Wizard." Again, she looked at him expectantly, as if anticipating some violent reaction.

Huh, Han thought. That's interesting. So poor Micah got left at the altar. Wish I'd known that yesterday.

"Why do the Demonai care which princess is heir?" Han said. "Long as the princesses aren't fighting about it."

"Princess Raisa is the true heir. She's Hanalea's line. We can't allow the Wizard Council to put a usurper on the throne."

Han shrugged. "They're all the same bloodline, right? Doesn't seem like it would make much difference."

Bird rolled her eyes. "Once they name Mellony princess heir, they'll marry *her* off to Micah Bayar. The Wizard Council will get what they couldn't get before—a wizard married to the queen of the Fells. That's been forbidden since the Breaking."

This was interesting. He recalled what Rebecca had said, feeling grateful for her tutelage. "Even if that happens, aren't there magical tethers the speakers use to control the High Wizard? Couldn't they use those on Micah?"

Bird snorted. "They're not working very well on the current High Wizard. The Bayars must have found a way around them."

Maybe they're using something from their stash of illegal magical tools, Han thought. He could mention that to Bird. Or not.

"We expect that the young Bayar will declare himself king," Bird said.

King Micah. Han didn't like that much. "He's here, you know. Micah Bayar."

"Here?" Bird looked around the room, her hand straying to her blade.

"Well, he's not here right *now*," Han said. "He used to live in this dormitory, though."

Bird chewed on her lower lip. "He can't marry Mellony if he's *dead*," she said.

Han stared at her. "You'd kill him just because you suspect that's what the Bayars are planning?"

"Why are you taking his part?" Bird demanded. "Have you become friends down here in the flatlands? Have you forgotten what—"

"I don't forget *anything*," Han said, figuring she could take her pick from a range of meanings. "But the world is full of wizards, if they want to marry one off to the princess. Killing Micah Bayar won't solve your problem. If it comes down to killing, I think you should aim higher." He looked straight into her eyes, a challenge.

Bird tightened her lips but didn't respond.

"Do you have proof?" Han went on, "or is it just Reid Demonai's theory?"

"Nightwalker has a network of informants in the Vale. They tell him that there is to be an announcement very soon. Lord Demonai and Elena *Cennestre* are concerned too," Bird said, a little defensively. "They believe it is time to bring the princess heir home, if a way can be found to do it safely."

Han felt oddly removed now. He was a fly on the wall looking down at himself and Bird, a sharper with no money left on the table.

"Well, good luck with all of that," he said.

Bird looked down at her hands, then pulled back her sleeve and picked at a scab on her forearm. She's nervous, Han realized. She doesn't know how to say what she's come to say.

"So," Han said, "did you come here just to give the news?"

"The Demonai are requiring you to honor your agreement," Bird said, looking straight ahead. "They are calling you home to the Fells to protect the princess heir and to join them in their fight against the Wizard Council."

For a long moment Han couldn't speak. His face felt frozen, his lips numb. "What?" he whispered. "Now? I've only just started."

"You're needed now," Bird said. "We cannot allow the Wizard Council to put a puppet on the Gray Wolf throne. We will go to war to prevent it. We need your help."

Han shook his head. "Nuh-uh. Our agreement was that the clans would sponsor my schooling at Oden's Ford in exchange for my help."

"We did," Bird said, though she still wouldn't meet his eyes. "We have kept our part of the bargain. We would have preferred that you'd had more training, but we have no control over the Wizard Council and what they do."

It's my own fault, Han thought. I should never have made a bargain with a trader.

It took him a moment to get his tongue unstuck. "So let me make sure I understand: you mean to send me against Lord Bayar and the Wizard Council—mostly master-level wizards—with two semesters of training?"

"You won't be alone," Bird said. "The Demonai will work with you, to—"

"Wait a minute," Han said. "You said you came for *me*. Not Dancer."

Bird nodded, still not looking at him. "Not Dancer."

"Not that I want to bring him into this, but why just one of us?"

Bird toyed with the hilt of her knife. The Demonai unlidded eye was engraved into the bone handle. "Because the Demonai would like Fire Dancer to stay at school to continue with his studies. We know that your lack of training puts you at a disadvantage. So we hope that eventually Fire Dancer can better assist you in the future."

"If I'm still alive," Han growled.

"It's natural to be afraid, Hunts Alone," Bird said. "Nightwalker says—"

"Blood of the Demon!" Han growled. "Don't quote Reid Demonai to me. I have my own reasons for going after the High Wizard. When I do, I'd like better odds. I wouldn't start a gang war like this, against a ruthless opponent, when I don't know the game, I'm outnumbered, and I have very few weapons. I'd like to win, and I'd like to survive. I don't think that's asking a lot."

"I'm sorry, Hunts Alone," Bird said, braiding and unbraiding the fringe on her carry bag. "That is the message I was ordered to bring you. Is there a reply?"

Han remembered the night he'd agreed to the clans' sponsorship. He'd asked what would happen if he refused to carry out the terms of the agreement. Averill Lightfoot Demonai had told him that the clans would hunt him down and kill him.

Would Bird be given that assignment, he wondered, glancing at her. Maybe she already had. Her face was a stony mask, but her lower lip quivered just a bit. She'd been sent to do this job on her own. If he refused, would one of them end up dead?

Was that all Bird was to Nightwalker: an expendable tool?

Just like Han was to the clan leadership.

The clans were hedging their bets. If Han didn't survive this fight with the Wizard Council, they'd have Dancer in reserve, hopefully better trained by then.

Han's fingers found his amulet and closed around it. He sighed, feeling the welcome release of the magic building up within him. "Dancer's my friend," Han said. "What makes you think he'll agree to stay and let me go on my own?"

"We won't tell him," Bird said. "That is why I wanted to speak with you alone. If Dancer knows you are returning to the Fells to fight wizards, he'll insist on coming too."

"He's not stupid," Han said. "Don't you think he'll figure it out? He knows about the deal I made with the clans. You show up out of the blue, we talk, and leave together?"

"Well . . ." Bird cast about for a solution. "We can make up a story. We can tell Dancer we're back together and you're returning with me to Demonai Camp."

"Dancer knows how I feel about the Demonai," Han said, not bothering to soften his speech. "And how the Demonai would react to that. He'll never believe that story."

His mind churned furiously. He really didn't want Dancer— or Cat—coming with him, maybe throwing their lives away in a lost cause. Secondly, he didn't intend to be dragged back to the Fells like a runaway child. He'd go on his own, on his own terms.

"I'll go alone," Han said. "I'll make up a story, say I have to go somewhere for one of the faculty. You'll stay here for at least a week to throw Dancer off the scent. By the time he realizes that I'm not coming back, it will be too late for him to track me."

Too late for you to track me, either, he thought.

Bird shook her head. "I'm supposed to escort you to Marisa Pines Camp," she said. "Nightwalker said—"

"Why is that?" Han said softly, looking her in the eyes. "Do you think I don't know the way? Or do you think I'll bolt? What did Nightwalker tell you to do if I refuse to come? If I try to cut and run, are you expected to hunt me down?"

Bird licked her lips, speechless for once.

"I'll keep my word," Han said. "I'm asking you to believe me."

They sat looking at each other for a long moment. Then Bird nodded. "All right. We'll do it your way, Hunts Alone. Just know that the Demonai are . . . unforgiving. And I . . . I'm risking a lot."

"So am I," Han said.

Bird chewed her lower lip. "Does anyone know you're working for us?"

Han shrugged. "*I* didn't tell anyone." He paused, and when she said nothing else, he stood up. "All right. I'm going out. I have some things to take care of. Tell Dancer I went to see Dean Abelard about a project. I'm going to spend the next couple of days in the library. Day after tomorrow, we'll have a nice evening together, just like old times. Then I'll go."

Bird shifted in her seat, clasping her hands together. "There's not much time. It will take a while to travel to—"

Han struggled to control his temper. "I *get* that. Look, I'd like to have a fighting chance. I want to research the Wizard Council and speak with some of the masters here before I go. Surely you can spare me that much. Assuming I'm not just a throwaway."

Bird stood also. "Hunts Alone," she said, her face troubled, her eyes focused on his face. "I'm sorry about . . . the way things turned out. For us."

It wasn't much of an apology, but it was more than he'd expected.

"I'm sorry, too." Han put a hand on her shoulder, and she flinched away. "I'll be back," he said, swiveling away from her. Snatching his cloak from the peg next to the door, he walked out.

He strode down the street, headed for the river. He'd cross to the Wien House side and speak with the stableman about his horse. Then go back to his place in Mystwerk Tower and gather up some books and other items he wanted to take with him.

He was distracted, making mental lists, thinking about all he needed to accomplish, and so his guard was down as he crossed Bridge Street into Wien House territory. As he passed a side street, someone grabbed his arm and yanked him into the space between two buildings. He struggled and kicked, trying to reach his amulet, but his attackers knew what they were doing. Two of them pinned his arms to his sides, holding him immobile.

There was no sting of wizardry through the grip on his arms, though, and when he looked up, he found himself facing Corporal Byrne. The corporal's face was hard, intent, focused. Turning his head to either side, Han saw that he was being held fast by Hallie and Talia, their faces set and grim.

Blood of the Demon, he thought. Just what I need, along with everything else—being beaten up by Rebecca's jealous . . . um . . . commander?

Han remembered what he'd said to Rebecca at solstice about Byrne. *There is a thing between you. I just don't know what kind of thing it is.*

Why would Hallie and Talia be in on it? If anything, they'd encouraged him to walk out with Rebecca.

"Hey, now," he said, trying to pull free. "What's this all about?"

"Have you seen her?" Byrne demanded. "Have you seen Rebecca?" He looked scruffy and haggard, as if he'd neither shaved nor slept in days.

"Rebecca?" Han shook his head. "I've not seen her since we—ah—since the last time I saw you," he said. "Up in . . . up in her room."

Byrne stuck his hand under Han's chin, shoving his head back against the wall and practically cutting off his air supply. "Are you sure? Are you sure you haven't seen her?" His eyes narrowed. "What happened to your face? Have you been in a fight?"

This wasn't like Byrne, to manhandle a prisoner.

"Let go of me," Han said evenly, "and we'll talk. I'm not guilty of anything, all right?"

Byrne stared into Han's eyes for a long moment, then let go, nodding to Talia and Hallie. They let go also, but stood close in case he tried to make a break for it.

"We were supposed to meet for tutoring last night," Han said. "She didn't show. I thought maybe you had restricted her to quarters, or whatever you sword danglers call it."

"But you didn't come looking for her," Byrne pointed out.

Han shook his head. "After last time, I wasn't sure what kind of welcome I'd get at Grindell." He rubbed his arms where Talia and Hallie had gripped them. "And I got this face during a— ah—magical practicum. Why? Rebecca's missing? Since when?"

"Nobody's seen her since yesterday afternoon," Byrne said. "Her things are still at the dormitory, but her horse is gone."

"Since yesterday?" Han rubbed his chin, wondering if Byrne kept such a tight leash on all of his cadets. "When she missed our meeting, I assumed she wasn't allowed to come, she didn't want to come, or she's mad at me."

Byrne shook his head as if Han were a hopeless idiot. "She's in *danger*," he said, his gray eyes glittering like agates. "I need to find her." He fingered the hilt of his sword. "Where have you been last night and today?"

Han thought back. Well, he'd fought in a pitched battle in Aediion, had it out with the Bayars, found out his ex-girlie and his best friend were walking out together, and been given a suicide assignment by another former girlfriend.

"I was at my dormitory," Han said. "I've been there pretty much the whole time except for that practicum with Dean

Abelard. I have people who can vouch for me."

Byrne glared into his face a moment more, then shook his head. "I'm sorry," he said, rubbing his forehead wearily. "Any idea where she might have gone? Is there anyone else you've seen her with? Could she have gone riding with someone?"

Han shook his head. "We met for tutoring twice a week, but the other night was the first time I—ah—saw where she stayed."

"Do you know Micah Bayar?" Byrne asked abruptly.

The hair stood up on the back of Han's neck. "I know him," Han said. "Why?"

"He's gone too," Byrne said. "He and his sister and cousins have cleared out and left Oden's Ford, even though exams aren't over yet. Any idea where they've gone?"

Han shook his head. "We aren't close," he said, his stomach knotting up. "But why is that important? I mean, Rebecca used to work for him, but not anymore."

Byrne just looked at him as if he didn't have an answer for that. Not an answer he wanted to give, anyway.

Han seized hold of Byrne's lapels with both hands and jerked him closer. "I *said*, why is that important? What about Bayar? What do you know?"

"Hey," Hallie said, putting her hand on Han's arm. "You don't touch the commander." She didn't raise her voice, but she meant business.

Han reluctantly let go. "Why would Micah Bayar have something to do with Rebecca's disappearance?" he persisted, looking from Byrne to Talia to Hallie.

Memories trickled back, how Rebecca had begged him not to tell the Bayars she was in Oden's Ford. How she didn't want to cross to the Mystwerk side for fear of running into them. How Han asked her if she ever went out, and she'd said no.

A terrible possibility occurred to him.

"Did Bayar hurt her when she worked for him?" Han said, his heart thudding against his rib cage. "Was that why she was so afraid of him?"

Byrne's face might have been a stone slab. "Ask all you want, I'm not going to tell you any more than this—if she's disappeared, he might have something to do with it."

Rivulets of flame ran along Han's hands and arms, and he gripped his amulet to discharge it. He recalled his words to Bayar when they'd parted.

You Bayars need to learn that you can't have everything you want. I'm going to teach you.

Maybe he was wrong. Maybe the Bayars would always get everything they wanted. Everything Han cared about. Including Rebecca. Had Micah found out they were walking out together? Would he go that far to get revenge on Han?

It seemed like destiny, a bad dream repeated relentlessly.

"Where would he take her?" Han demanded. "Bayar, I mean."

"That's what I'm trying to find out," Byrne said. He squinted at Han. "There's something different about you," he whispered, almost to himself. "Something that reminds me of . . ." He caught himself. "If you see Rebecca, if you hear anything that might be useful, find me. No matter what time it is." He motioned to Hallie and Talia.

Han watched the trio of cadets walk away.

All the way to the stables, Han chewed over Rebecca's

disappearance like a tough piece of meat. She'd seemed stressed and unhappy the last time he'd seen her, worried about her mother, talking about going home. Maybe she'd up and left.

But would she leave her belongings behind? No.

Was it possible that Byrne himself was responsible for Rebecca's disappearance, and was trying to deflect blame? After all, he was the one who'd driven Han off at swordpoint.

No. Han hadn't lived as long as he had by misjudging people. Byrne was a hopeless liar, and he'd seemed genuinely distraught.

How could Han leave Oden's Ford with Rebecca missing?

Han paid his bill at the stable and made arrangements to have Ragger and Simon, his spare horse, reshod and ready to travel later in the week. "Don't give up the stalls. I'll be back," he said, to cover his tracks in case anybody asked. "I'm going to Tamron Court to do some research."

The stableman grunted, making it obvious he didn't care, and probably wouldn't remember if anyone did ask.

As he walked back toward the bridge, Han saw a crowd of cadets in their dirtback uniforms outside the Wien Hall library, studded here and there with the colors of faculty robes—Wien House and Mystwerk. He saw Dean Abelard with a group of Mystwerk masters and proficients, apparently directing an investigation of the grounds.

The crowd hummed with excitement, like a mob on Chatt's Hill on execution day.

As Han looked on, two healers carried a body wrapped in a blanket down the steps of the library, followed by a clutch of provost guards.

No, he thought, his heart stalling in his chest. Oh, no.

Han pushed and shoved his way through the onlookers, drawing scowls and curses along the way, until he stood next to the walkway as the healers passed by. He grabbed the sleeve of one of the provosts.

"Ma'am? Who is it? Who's dead?"

The provost ripped her arm free. "Leave go, boy. We'll issue a statement."

"But my friend—she's missing," Han said. "Since yesterday."

The provost stopped so suddenly, the person behind her practically ran into her. She turned off the path, pulling Han by the arm. "What's your friend's name?" she asked.

"Rebecca Morley."

"Come with me." The guard pushed Han back toward the library. As he passed Abelard, she looked up and fixed him with a piercing gaze.

They walked through the heavy double doors and up the steps. Around and around they climbed, while Han's heart sank lower and lower.

Finally they reached the top of the staircase and threaded their way through a warren of small reading rooms. The door to one room stood ajar.

"In there," the guard said.

Han halted just inside the door, half sick with dread. The room was small, with a desk under a window on one wall, a fireplace on the other, a worktable facing the door. Books and papers lay scattered over the surface of the table. A lamp lay smashed on the floor, and bits of glass glittered in the sunlight from the window. Blood splattered the wooden floor between the door and the table.

A stocky man in Wien House master's robes stood looking out the window.

"Master Askell," the provost said. "This boy says he's friends with Rebecca Morley."

Master Askell turned toward Han, his broad face etched by years of sun, and completely impassive. He took in Han's attire, the amulet at his neck. "Who are you?" he asked, without preamble.

"Han Alister. Newling at Mystwerk House," Han said.

"How do you know Rebecca?" Askell asked.

"She was tutoring me," Han said. "We met back home."

Askell pointed at the worktable. "See if you recognize the materials on the table as Rebecca's."

Sand and glass gritted under Han's boots. Blotting sand was also scattered across the tabletop, the jar overturned. Here were pages of notes in Rebecca's familiar, angular handwriting. Here was her ornate pen and enameled ink bottle.

Han shut his eyes and swallowed hard. Blood and bones, he thought. Bloody, bloody bones. Would the carnage in his life never stop?

"These are hers," Han said, looking at Askell, his voice thick with despair.

The master held up a dagger by its tip. "We found this lying next to the wall," he said.

"That's hers too," Han said. He crossed the room to take a closer look. There was no blood on the blade. So Rebecca hadn't gotten any back.

I should've hushed Bayar when I'd had the chance, he thought. I should've stuck with what I know—street rules.

"You better send someone for Commander Byrne," Han said hollowly.

"He's on his way." Askell set Rebecca's blade on the table.

"How did she die?" Han asked, leaning his hands on the stone sill and staring out the window. "What killed her?" Would Bayar have been so arrogant as to use wizardry?

When Askell didn't answer, Han turned to face him, leaning his backside against the window frame. The master looked perplexed. "Are you talking about Rebecca?" he asked.

"Well, yes," Han said. "I saw them carrying out the body."

Askell shook his head. "We found four bodies, in fact, two men, two women, none of them students, though they all wore cadet uniforms. One was in here. He seems to have smashed his head against the table during a struggle. The other three were outside, and they appear to have been killed with wizardry."

"What?" Han stared at Askell. "That doesn't make sense."

Askell shrugged. "There are many things in this world that don't make sense," he said. "Rebecca may be dead, but we did not find her body."

CHAPTER THIRTY-SIX
DETOURS

Raisa opened her eyes to darkness and motion and the stench of damp wool. She felt dizzy and confused. Her head pounded, and her mouth tasted like the dregs of a bad barrel of cider. She tried to raise her arms, but they were wrapped tight in fabric, confined close to her body, and a hood was pulled up over her head so she couldn't see.

She was on horseback, riding double. She could feel the heat of another body against her back. She struggled to free her arms so she could yank off the hood, and Micah Bayar slid an arm around her waist, pulling her tightly against him.

"You're finally awake," he said, his lips close to her ear. "Careful you don't fall off. We're aboard Raider, and it's a long way to the ground."

As the rest of her senses awakened, she became aware of the sound of horses in motion around her—hooves on a hard-packed road, the squeak of saddle leather, the murmur of voices.

Raisa shook her head from side to side, trying to dislodge the hood. That set her head to pounding with the headache typical of a turtleweed hangover. For an awful moment she thought she might spew over the both of them.

"Where are we?" she asked, when the danger had passed.

"We're north of Oden's Ford, on the road to Fetters Ford," Micah said. He tugged the hood back so she could see, and the fresh air helped. They rode through dense forest, the canopy of trees nearly meeting overhead.

Raisa looked around. Switcher followed behind on a lead line, loaded with supplies. Ahead she could see the rest of the party, four other riders who must be the Mander brothers, Fiona, and one other wizard.

"Who's that?" she asked. "With Fiona and the Manders?"

"Wil Mathis," Micah said. "He asked to come north with us."

Raisa knew Wil from court. He was sloppy and good-natured, unusual for a wizard. Two years older than the Bayar twins, he'd been in love with Fiona for as long as Raisa could remember.

They each led a spare horse, carrying baggage and supplies. Off to the right, through the trees, Raisa caught glimpses of water. That would be the east branch of the Tamron River.

"What day is it?" she asked.

Micah laughed softly. "You haven't been sleeping that long, Your Highness. It's the day after we met in the Wien Hall library. We left in the middle of the night. I expect we'll be four days to Fetters."

"Will you . . . Will we head up through Demonai Vale, then?"

she asked. That would provide another opportunity, if she could somehow get away.

"No," Micah said. "We'll go east, skirting the mountains, and up through Delphi. I have no desire to meet up with any of the Demonai." He snapped his reins and their horse picked up the pace to catch up with the others. Even though Raisa was small, Raider was feeling the burden of carrying two riders.

Was there any chance Amon would come after her? It seemed unlikely. Until now, she'd managed to avoid Micah Bayar and the other wizards from Fellsmarch. Amon would have no reason to suspect them. Maybe he'd even think she'd decided to go home on her own. No doubt he'd be searching for her, but he'd have no idea where to look.

Would his magical connection tell him she was in trouble? Might it lead him to her? She prayed it would, but worried what would happen if it did.

They stopped for lunch in a small clearing between the road and the river. They did not build a fire. Raisa, Micah, and Fiona stood among the trees, eating cold meat, bread, and cheese, and washing it down with cider while Wil and the Mander brothers grained the horses and led them down to the river to water them.

"Now that I'm awake, maybe I should ride Switcher, so Raider doesn't tire," Raisa said.

"Oh no, Your Highness, I'm enjoying our time together, and hope you are too," Micah said, brushing his lips across her cheek. "I think Raider understands."

Micah might be arrogant, but he'd never been stupid.

It was a cloudy, cool spring day, the air so laden with moisture it was like breathing underwater. Raisa shivered, her skin pebbled with goose bumps, though it wasn't that cold. She swiped wet tendrils of hair off her face, feeling unsettled.

Fiona did her best to ignore Raisa's presence, but her disapproval was palpable. Clearly, she believed the assassins should have been allowed to do their job.

Raisa stared out into the surrounding forest, trying to ignore Fiona. The dry bread and cheese were hard to choke down. Shadows moved under the trees. She blinked, and they were still there, gray shapes sliding through the mist. Gray wolves.

It seemed she was seeing them more and more—but maybe that was a reflection of the way her life was going. Were they there because of her present predicament? Or did they signify some new threat?

The wolves surrounded her, tongues lolling, ears flat, bumping their great heads against her middle, nearly knocking her over.

"Great lot of good you do me," she grumbled. "Why can't I teach you to attack wizards on command?"

"Excuse me, Raisa?" Micah said. He touched her arm, looking a little concerned. "Were you speaking to me?"

"Nothing. It was nothing."

She swiveled, scanning the woods around them. Even in spring, with some trees not yet leafed out, Tamron Forest seemed thick and oppressive, crowding in on all sides. Too close.

"Is something wrong, Your Highness?" Micah asked. "You're not eating."

"Do you hear anything?" Raisa asked. The forest around

them was silent, even the birds had gone eerily quiet. The hair stood up on her arms.

"Micah," she said, putting her hand on his arm. "Let's go. Something's wrong. I think we'd better . . ."

Her voice failed as soldiers stepped out of the forest on all sides, crossbows cocked and ready.

"Put your hands in the air. Now!" shouted a young man with dark hair and mud-brown eyes. A red officer's scarf was knotted around his neck, and a red hawk was emblazoned on his tunic.

Micah and Fiona glanced at each other, then slowly raised their hands. The others, including Raisa, followed suit.

The soldiers were clad in wool uniforms that had seen hard use. Some wore mismatched armor pieces, others had none. Some bore the red hawk, others were unmarked. From their haggard appearances, they'd been on the road for months. Could this be one of the roving bands of mercenaries Amon had warned her about?

"Don't even think of touching those jinxpieces," the officer went on.

Micah leaned toward Fiona. "He's gifted," he said out of the corner of his mouth.

"I noticed," she snapped. "What is the meaning of this?" Fiona demanded, glaring at the officer. "Who are you?"

"Collect their jinxpieces and any other weapons you find," the officer said to his men, ignoring Fiona. "Don't touch the pendants directly. Hold 'em by their chains."

The soldiers went from person to person and collected the wizards' amulets, daggers, and swords. When he came to Raisa, she shook her head.

"I don't have an amulet," she said. "Nor any weapons. Sorry."

The soldier glanced at his officer, who said, "She won't have one. She's not gifted."

The soldier patted her down anyway, coming up empty-handed, of course, because she'd lost her belt dagger in the library.

When they were all disarmed, the officer motioned to his men to put down their crossbows, though they kept their hands on their swords. "Let me introduce myself. I'm Marin Karn, Commander of the Army of the King of Arden."

Which king? Raisa wanted to ask, but didn't.

"Arden!" Micah tilted his head. "But we're in Tamron. Arden is across the river."

"Damn!" Commander Karn said, grinning. "Guess we went astray again, boys."

The other soldiers snorted with laughter.

"That doesn't make sense," Fiona said. "You're a wizard. But wizardry is forbidden in Arden. You burn wizards in . . ."

"Aye," Karn said, nodding. "That's so. The church has strict rules against it."

Fiona frowned. "Then how can there be gifted soldiers in the king of Arden's army?" she persisted.

Karn shook his head. "Oh no, we'd never admit to that. Most who come up against us don't survive to tell tales. Those that survive don't remember. And only wizards can recognize others with the gift."

"So you're using wizardry in the Ardenine Wars," Raisa whispered.

"We are just getting started," Karn said. "We've more than a dozen jinxflingers. Many are young, recruited on their way to Oden's Ford. Most haven't had any training. Some don't have amulets. That's where you come in."

"What do you mean?" Micah said.

"I'm guessing you're students from Oden's Ford. You've been getting top-notch training at the academy there. We want you to teach our recruits spellcasting."

"I'm afraid that won't be possible," Micah said, glancing at Raisa. "We have pressing business in the Fells, and we can't risk getting involved in your civil war."

Karn seemed unfazed. "Think hard before you say no," he said. "We've hundreds of soldiers camped this side of the river, and an army several thousand strong on the other side." He looked toward the river and came to attention. "Here comes the king now."

A small group of men walked toward them from the river-bank. Four burly men, armored up and carrying weapons, surrounded a slender man in a tunic emblazoned with the red hawk signia, silver gauntlets, and breastplate, a sword belted at his waist. He wore a circlet of gold on his light brown hair, and his blue eyes were pale blue and cold as the ice in Invader's Bay.

It was Prince Gerard Montaigne, the youngest of the warring Montaigne brothers, Raisa's unsuccessful suitor at her name day party.

"Hanalea in chains," Raisa muttered. Could things get any worse? She yanked her hood over her head and stared at the ground, hoping he wouldn't recognize her. Surely he wouldn't, not here, so out of context.

Why was Gerard Montaigne in Tamron? And why did he have his army collected just across the border? He should be back in Ardenscourt, facing off with his brothers.

Karn bowed to his king. "Your Majesty. We have five jinxflingers from Mystwerk."

"Good," Montaigne said, his eyes flicking over Micah and the others. "Have you explained to them the services we require?"

"The answer is no," Fiona said, straightening to her full height. "Now release us immediately."

Montaigne moved, quicker than light, smashing his gauntleted arm into Fiona's face and knocking her to the ground.

Micah leaped forward, but Wil Mathis was closer. With a cry of rage, he sprang at the prince of Arden, who drew his sword and calmly ran him through.

Wil and Montaigne ended face-to-face, a foot separating them, Wil's eyes bulging wide in amazement. Then Montaigne shoved him away with his booted foot, freeing his sword. Wil teetered, then fell backward, hit the ground, and lay still, blood pooling around him.

"Wil!" Fiona cried, trying to scramble to her feet, but Micah knelt next to her, gripping her shoulders and holding her in place.

"No," he said fiercely. "You can't help him."

"Does anyone else wish to have a conversation about this?" Montaigne asked.

No one moved and no one spoke. Raisa had to bite her lip to keep her acid tongue in check. Wizard or not, Wil had always been among the best of the breed. More than that, he was a citizen of the Fells, and so, her responsibility.

Montaigne paced back and forth in front of them, his sword in his hand. "Now that we understand each other, perhaps we can do business. Captain Karn has convinced me that jinxflingers will be useful in bringing this long war to a conclusion. If he is right, it may be that we will only require your services for a limited time."

He'll never let them go, Raisa thought. Gerard Montaigne will always have use for an army.

"Like I said, think hard before you say no." Karn ran his eyes over the captives. "So, what'll it be?"

"All right," Micah said abruptly, standing. "We will teach your charmcasters what we know, and aid you in any way we can. The sooner you achieve victory, the sooner we can be on our way. Bear in mind that we are just first-years, so our knowledge is limited."

He walked forward and put a hot hand on Raisa's shoulder. "I would, however, ask you to release our servant. She is not gifted, and so would be of no help to you."

Raisa froze, scarcely breathing. Was Micah really trying to engineer her release? She turned her head slightly so she could see his face. His expression didn't change, but she felt the pressure of his fingers as he squeezed her shoulder.

"Your . . . servant, is she?" Montaigne said. He looked at Karn, and he nodded.

"She is not gifted, Your Majesty. I wondered why she was traveling with them."

Montaigne restored his sword to its scabbard, not bothering to wipe off the blood. Raisa kept her head down, peering up through her lashes at the prince of Arden. He toyed with the hilt of his sword, his lower lip caught behind his teeth.

"Well," he said finally, "let's have a look at you." He reached toward Raisa and tugged back her hood.

Raisa lifted her head, and their eyes met. They stood staring at each other, and then Gerard Montaigne smiled in his bone-chilling way. Raisa's heart plummeted.

"Ah, Karn," he said softly. "You have overlooked the greatest prize of all."

Karn looked from Raisa to Montaigne. "What do you mean, Your Grace? Who is she?"

Montaigne kept his eyes fixed on Raisa's face. Taking hold of her hand, he raised it to his lips. "Princess Raisa *ana*'Marianna," he murmured. "Welcome to the new kingdom of Arden."

Karn looked from Raisa to Montaigne. "She's a princess?"

Montaigne nodded. "We met at her debut party nearly a year ago. She is heir to the throne of the Fells." His eyes raked over her. "She was dressed quite differently last time I saw her, but there's no mistaking her." His grip tightened about her wrist. "But why would the princess heir of the Fells ride through Tamron with wizardlings?"

Raisa knew there was no point in continuing to deny her identity. "I've been attending the academy at Oden's Ford," she said. "I'm traveling home for the summer."

Montaigne shook his head incredulously. "The Fells would send a gently bred woman through Tamron with no more guard than *this*?" He gestured toward the Bayars and the Manders.

"Tamron is not at war, Your Highness," Raisa said, looking him in the eye with a confidence she did not feel. "I would not expect to be waylaid by brigands along the way." She nodded toward Wil's prone body. "You've already murdered one member of my guard. Now that you know who I am, I expect you will allow us to continue on our journey unmolested."

Montaigne smiled, his face lighting with triumph. "Ah, no, Your Highness," he said. "That's much too risky, as you've seen." He jerked her toward him, cupping her chin in his hand. "I think it's time we continued our conversation about an alliance between Arden and the Fells—an alliance cemented by our marriage." He smiled. "I'll have Tamron, Arden, and the Fells. All the riches of the mountain mines and access to an unlimited supply of jinxflingers and magical objects. Eventually we'll rule the Seven Realms."

"That will never happen," Raisa said, lifting her chin.

"Watch me." Montaigne handed Raisa off to Karn. "Take these wizardlings and the princess back across the river, and keep a close watch on them. Bring their horses. We'll talk more tonight." The prince of Arden straightened his silver gauntlets. "Ah, Karn, this changes everything."

Karn gripped Raisa's arm and dragged her toward the river's edge. The other Ardenine soldiers herded Micah and the others after her.

Snick. A soldier fell just behind her, both hands clutching at an arrow sticking out of the middle of his chest.

Snick. Snick. Snick. The sound of crossbows. More soldiers fell.

"Your Highness! Take cover!" Karn let go his hold on Raisa and thrust his bulk in front of Montaigne, who pawed at his sword.

The Ardenine soldiers scrambled for cover as a troop of horse soldiers exploded from the forest, threatening to overrun them. Riderless horses ran in all directions. Raisa sprinted for the trees, toward the road and away from the river. Out of the corner of her eye she saw Micah grab Fiona's hand and drag her behind a fallen tree.

The cavalry wore a signia of a purple-and-gray heron, wings spread, landing on water. The emblem of the king of Tamron.

"To me!" Montaigne shouted. More Ardenine soldiers appeared at the run, coming from the direction of the river. A pitched battle erupted—the Red Hawk of Arden against the Heron of Tamron.

Raisa raced blindly through the forest, leaping over fallen trees and other obstacles, meaning to gain as much distance from the fight as she could. Montaigne was preparing to invade Tamron, that much was clear. If Arden's thousands of soldiers crossed the river, there could be no doubt as to the outcome of this skirmish. Weaponless as she was, she had few illusions about the contribution she could make.

Looking back over her shoulder for signs of pursuit, she nearly ran headlong into the side of a horse.

"Hanalea in chains!" she said, skidding to a halt.

It was Fiona's horse, Ghost, a tall, spirited, gray stallion with four white stockings. Raisa leaped forward and caught hold of his reins. The horse laid back his ears and shied away from her hand, but Raisa still managed to swarm up and into the saddle. The stirrups were set far too long, but Raisa clung to his back like a thistle and drove her heels into his sides. Ghost extended his long neck, accelerating into a gallop, twisting and turning through the trees.

He probably doesn't even know I'm up here, after Fiona, Raisa thought.

Pressing herself flat against the stallion's neck to avoid being unhorsed by low branches, she gave him his head and let him run.

She needed to put as much distance as possible between herself and those who might soon be chasing after her. That meant riding straight west as far as the road. The traffic on the road would hide evidence of her passing, and she'd make good time, whichever direction she chose.

Which way?

She had Fiona's saddlebags, but no idea what was in them. She had a little money in the purse still tucked inside her coat.

If Micah and Fiona got free of the battle, they would guess she'd return south, to Oden's Ford, and rejoin Amon and the others. They would not expect her to travel north on her own, especially after what had just happened.

Montaigne, on the other hand, might expect her to continue north, making for home, or west to Tamron Seat, for sanctuary. Hopefully the Tamron army would keep them occupied for a time. Surely Montaigne wouldn't chase after her, with an invasion under way. No doubt he'd continue on to the capital.

So north it was. If she could make it as far as Fetters Ford, perhaps she could get word to Captain Byrne to send an escort. They'd either go north through Demonai Vale or east via Marisa Pines, depending on the news at that time.

Ghost needed no encouragement to leave the clamor of battle behind. Raisa gave him direction with her knees and hands while her mind picked over events of the past and prospects for the future.

She longed for the simple safety of childhood, the ability to give over responsibility to the Captain Byrnes of the world, sheltering under their protection.

But adulthood slipped up on you, she thought. It was forced on you whether you liked it or not. She had changed. She was not the same person who had run away with Amon Byrne ten short months ago.

She was more able, but less confident. She was better equipped to judge people, and less convinced of her ability to do so. When she'd left the Fells, she thought of people as being sorted into lots—good and bad, brave and cowardly. Now she realized that there were bits of both in most people—and which elements prevailed often depended on circumstance.

Micah Bayar, for all his faults, was a mixture of good and bad. She might be dead at an assassin's hand, if not for him. He'd tried to free her when they were captured by Gerard Montaigne. But he presented different faces to different people, and his efforts to keep her alive were likely selfish at their root.

Raised on romance, Raisa would have said that it was impossible to love two men at once. That there was one true love for every person, if you could only find it.

But it wasn't true. She still loved Amon Byrne. Her feelings about him were too raw for close examination. And she loved Han Alister, if she understood love at all.

Would she ever see him again, and if so, could they build from a relationship based on a lie?

And what did she expect to build on that shaky foundation? *By the way, Alister, I've been lying to you for more than a year; I'm actually a member of the royal family you despise. There's no future for us, but I'd still like to be friends.*

Would Raisa herself be satisfied with friendship, when the memory of Han's kisses and caresses haunted her?

Would Amon and Han be able to set aside their antipathy and put the pieces of her disappearance together?

Her mother was a weak queen—but she'd been mired down by circumstance. Maybe when Raisa returned, there would be a way to connect with her, to join with her, to help her, and become a better queen herself someday.

Ahead she saw the break in the trees that meant they were coming up on the road. Reining Ghost in with some difficulty, Raisa slowed their pace to a walk. Pausing in the last fringe of trees, she looked up and down the road and saw no one.

"Let's go," she said, applying her heels. "We need to go a lot farther before we rest." They turned north, setting a more sustainable pace.

After nearly a year, she was going home. The decision had been forced on her. But more and more, she believed it was the right one.

CHAPTER THIRTY-SEVEN

A PARTING
OF THE WAYS

Han had meant to spend his last days at Oden's Ford preparing for his mission in the north. Instead he spent it desperately searching for clues about Rebecca's disappearance.

The dead at the Wien Hall library had been strangers to Oden's Ford. None were wizards. They'd been seen around the academy for several days, asking questions. Either they carried nothing in their pockets, or whoever had killed them had stripped them of identification.

Han slipped into Micah's dormitory, familiar from his many visits, and tossed their rooms. They had departed in a hurry— leaving many of their belongings behind.

It couldn't be a coincidence. Had they left because they'd murdered her? Or had they taken her with them? No matter how Han put it together, it didn't make sense. Three of the dead had been killed with wizardry. Had Rebecca been witness to the killings, and been killed or carried off for that reason?

Han walked over to Grindell Hall the morning before he planned to leave. The dormitory was a hive of activity—cadets running up and down stairs, packing their belongings.

Byrne met with him in the common room. The bluejacket had lost some of his military edge—his eyes were ringed with dark circles, and he hadn't shaved in several days.

"Looks like you're leaving," Han said.

"Rebecca is no longer in the area," Byrne said. "I believe she's gone north. We received a report from Tamron Seat that someone resembling Rebecca was caught in a skirmish with Ardenine forces along the border between Tamron and Arden. We're riding to Tamron Seat to investigate. It's possible she's there, in the capital."

Han hesitated, then went ahead and said it. "You think she's alive, then," he said.

"She's alive," Byrne said, as if he hadn't a doubt. He ran his hands through his hair. "But I need to find her. If she's in Tamron, she's in grave danger. Gerard Montaigne has invaded from the east. He's got the capital encircled, demanding their surrender."

"And you're going into that?" Han shook his head. "You're a mettlesome one, Corporal." He paused. "If Bayar carried Rebecca off, and she's still alive, I'd guess he'd take her back to the Fells, wouldn't you? And if she left on her own, she'd head home, too."

Byrne nodded. "If we don't find her in Tamron, I'll keep heading north, looking for signs she went that way. If I find her trail, I'll follow it. Otherwise, I'll cross into the Fens and enter the Fells at Westgate. If you hear anything, send a message there."

"I will," Han said. "But I came to let you know that I'm going back to the Fells, too. I didn't want you to think I'd kicked town on you."

"Which way will you go?" Byrne asked.

"I'll go north to Fetters Ford, then east to Delphi," Han said. "I'll search for Rebecca that way, ending up at Marisa Pines Camp. If you find anything, or hear anything from the capital, send word to me there."

After a moment's hesitation, Byrne extended his hand. "Be careful," he said.

Han gripped the offered hand. "You too," he said. "See you at home."

Abelard sent a runner for Han in the afternoon. When he entered her office, she stood staring out the window. "Did you know that the Bayars have left school?" she asked without preamble.

"I heard," Han said. "They left in a hurry. With their cousins. And Wil Mathis." He told her what he'd found at their dormitory.

Abelard turned around and looked at him, her expression unreadable. "Sit." She motioned to a chair.

He sat. "That incident at the Wien Hall library, those people that were killed," Han said. "I think the Bayars had something to do with it."

"Do you?" Abelard toyed with a small jewel-encrusted dagger. Sunlight reflected off it, sending sparkles racing over the walls. "Why would you think that?"

"They disappeared the same night. Along with a friend of mine."

"Friend?" Abelard tilted her head. "Who?"

"A Wien House cadet. Rebecca Morley. She used to work for the Bayars. She disappeared the same time they did."

"I don't know her," Abelard said, dismissing Rebecca. "But it *is* likely the Bayars had to do with the killings at the library, in an indirect way." She paused, those gray-green eyes assessing him. "The four dead are all assassins in the employ of Aerie House."

"Assassins?" Han rubbed his head as if he could reshuffle his thoughts and be dealt a better hand. "Why would they come here? And who would've killed them?"

"I thought perhaps *you* could tell *me*," Abelard said, running her thumb over the honed edge of the blade.

"Me?" Han shook his head. "I'm not following."

Abelard gave him a *don't try to fool me* kind of look. "They worked for the *Bayars*," she said. "They were killed with *wizardry*."

It finally clanked into place. "You think *I* did it?"

"Who in Oden's Ford would the Bayars want to kill?" Abelard said. "An attack on the High Wizard can't go unanswered forever." She shrugged. "And who might be most likely to survive such an attack?"

Han leaned forward, hands on his knees, willing her to believe him. "Look, I don't know why they were here, or who hushed them, but I had nothing to do with it."

"It speaks for your reputation that Lord Bayar sent a team of four to do the job. I think that when Micah and Fiona found out what happened to their father's assassins, they decided to leave before you came after them."

Han shook his head. "It wasn't me. Like I told you, my friend

Rebecca disappeared from the library where the one assassin was found."

"Perhaps she saw something she shouldn't have?" Abelard said.

Han stood. "This is a waste of time," he said, fighting back fury. "If you think I would have had anything to do with—"

"Sit down, Alister!" Abelard said. "It's in your best interest to hear me out."

Reluctantly, he sat, arms folded, glaring at her.

She rolled her eyes. "Oh, don't look so distraught. There was nothing at the scene to tie it to you. And, I must say, I am more impressed than ever with your abilities."

Han gave up. There was no way he'd persuade the dean that he hadn't done the four, not when it all fit together so well and he had no other story to tell.

"Well, I think the Bayars left town for another reason," he said. "And that's what we should be looking into."

Abelard nodded, tapping the desk with her blade. "You may be right. I would prefer to keep young Micah Bayar under my eye since he is central to his father's ambitions."

"I'm going back, too," Han announced. "Tomorrow. I won't be here for the summer after all." He tipped his chin up and looked her in the eyes.

Propping her elbows on the desk, Abelard laced her fingers, resting her chin on her hands. "If you are thinking of taking revenge on the Bayars, I would advise you not to do anything rash," she said.

"Never worry," Han said. "If I take revenge, I'll do it with great forethought and deliberation."

The dean laughed. "You are amazing, Alister. Your clothing,

your speech—you've gone from street rat to courtier in less than a year." She paused. "I'd advise you to stay. If you go back now, you'll be on your own. I can't offer much protection from here."

"I'm going anyway," Han said.

Abelard shrugged. "I do have allies, however, and I will tell them to watch out for you. I intend to come back home in the summer or fall for an extended stay. Matters are accelerating such that I believe they require my close personal attention."

Abelard reached into her desk drawer and pulled out a heavy purse. She plunked it on the desk in front of Han. "This will tide you over in the meantime." The dean went on to give Han a list of jobs to do and people to meet after he arrived.

"The important thing is to keep the Bayars from further consolidating their influence with the queen," she said. "I'm told that in the absence of the Princess Raisa, they hope to see Mellony named heir and married off to Micah. It may be why he's returned home so suddenly. You must do everything you can to prevent this."

"Everything?" Han raised an eyebrow.

Abelard smiled. "Good-bye, Alister. Stay alive until I get there."

Han's head spun as he descended the stairs. Was it possible that Micah Bayar was headed home for a wedding? And if he was, what could he, Han, do about it? Assassinate the bride and groom? Plan a massacre at the marriage feast?

Han had too many gang lords.

Cat and Dancer helped Han carry his saddlebags and panniers down so he could load his horses. "I still don't understand why

Abelard is sending you to Tamron Seat," Dancer said. "Even if they have a large library, they can't have much of a magical collection."

"It's more about politics," Han said. "I need to keep her happy if I want to come back to school in the fall."

Han scratched Ragger between the ears, and the pony laid back his ears and showed his teeth, ill-tempered as usual. "You like being lazy, sucking up hay in a warm barn, don't you?" Han murmured. "Well now you have to get to work again. Both of us do."

There had been little time for riding over the past few months. Now they'd get reacquainted.

"Can't you at least stay until Dig—Night Bird leaves?" Dancer said. "She'll be gone by the time you come back."

"Night Bird and I haven't got much to say to each other these days," Han said. Their evening together had been awkward at best. Too many secrets divided them.

"She came all this way to see us," Dancer said. "I think she's getting used to the idea that we're wizards. I mean, I think she's sorry for the way she reacted when we—"

"The Demonai are just like everyone else: they ditch their high-minded principles whenever it's convenient," Han said.

Dancer frowned, his eyes searching Han's face. "This is *Bird* we're talking about," he said. "You should give her a chance."

Han didn't really want to have a heart-to-heart about Digging Bird. Night Bird. Whoever she wanted to be these days. "Anyway, you've been working on amulets since exams were over, too," Han said.

"I have to work on flash in the summer," Dancer said. "It's

not part of the curriculum at Mystwerk House."

Cat had been all twitchy during this long exchange, flinging back her hair, pacing back and forth, signaling that she had something to say.

"You should let me come with you," she said. "I can't watch your back if your back is in Tamron and I'm here."

"I want you to keep looking for Rebecca," Han said, strapping down his bedroll. "Keep asking questions. See if anyone knows anything. There's a chance somebody saw something. And watch Dancer's back. That's what you should do while I'm gone."

When everything was in readiness, Han leaned back against his pony, strangely reluctant to leave. There needed to be places like this—places to read and write and study and argue and debate with all different kinds of people and not have to look over your shoulder all the time. Places where the desire for knowledge overwhelmed boundaries and differences.

It was part of the reason he'd resisted hushing Micah during those first few weeks when his anger had threatened to spill over into violence.

His first task was to make it to Marisa Pines Camp without getting killed or recruited into somebody's army. He'd look for Rebecca along the way. Corporal Byrne had seemed convinced she was alive, but Han couldn't conjure up much hope.

Once back home, he'd find the Bayars and make them talk.

Han embraced Dancer, then Cat, and mounted Ragger.

"Travel safely," Dancer said, in Clan. "Return to our hearth."

Han nodded, wondering if he would ever return to Oden's Ford.